THE
ROUND
DOZEN

THE ROUND DOZEN

ELIZABETH CADELL

WILLIAM MORROW AND COMPANY, INC.

NEW YORK   1978

Library of Congress Cataloging in Publication Data

Cadell, Elizabeth.
    The round dozen.

    I. Title.
PZ3.C11427Rm 1978 [PR9499.3.C37] 823'.9'12 77-27363
ISBN 0-688-03284-2

BOOK DESIGN   CARL WEISS

Printed in the United States of America.

First Edition

1   2   3   4   5   6   7   8   9   10

THE
ROUND
DOZEN

1

THE INTERCOM BUZZED, AND WILLIAM HELDER SPOKE INTO
it.

"Yes?"

"Mrs. Helder has arrived, Mr. Helder. Shall I ask her to
wait?"

He glanced at his watch: four fifteen. But this was Friday,
a day on which he usually left the office early.

"No. Show her in, will you?"

He was tidying away the papers on his desk when his stepmother was ushered in. She hesitated on the threshold.

"If you're not through yet," she said, "I'll come back later."

"I'm almost ready, Stella. Come in."

He kissed the proffered cheek, installed her in one of the
deep armchairs, put her coat on another and brought her the
footstool kept in the office for her exclusive use. She leaned
back and gave a sigh of contentment.

"Thank God for a comfortable chair," she said. "In fact,
thank God for a chair of any kind; I've been on my feet on a
platform for the past two hours. Old women like me should be
allowed to sit down at these functions."

He raised his eyebrows.

"Old?"

"Feeling as I do at this moment, yes. Decrepit. Spent. Washed out."

She did not look it. Relaxing in the chair, handbag on her lap, neat ankles crossed, she was the picture of a rich, elderly woman, perfectly groomed, discreetly made up. Her figure was slim and shapely. Her face was broad, her features too blunt for beauty, but her eyes were alert and intelligent, and she carried herself with distinction.

William had always liked her. Below her dry, sometimes sardonic manner lay a good deal of humour, and he found her company stimulating. He had met her only occasionally during the twelve years in which she had been married to his father, but since his death, fourteen months ago, he had put himself at her disposal for those occasions on which she needed an escort. As she had a great many friends, most of them male, he was not often called upon to act in this capacity, but she was, like himself, a music lover and they enjoyed going to concerts together. For the rest, they led separate lives and had few friends in common.

She was giving the room a leisurely survey.

"Those curtains," she commented. "Too dark. I warned you. They're much too somber."

"Yes. I should have let you choose them."

"You should. You wouldn't have made a good interior decorator. You always— For heaven's *sake*, William. You've got— how many?—five, six hundred employees, most of them in this building, so do you have to tidy your own desk?"

"Habit."

"Wrong. Heredity. You're growing fussy, as your father was doing before he married me. You take after him—in your ways, I mean. You don't look like him. Your looks, such as they are, come from your mother's side of the family."

He glanced up at the portrait of his father hanging above the fireplace.

"His chin," he claimed.

The portrait—the sole one displayed on the walls of the room—was always that of the last head of the firm. While William Helder the late hung on the wall, William Helder, his son and successor, sat at the outsize desk to conduct the firm's affairs until the time came for the portrait of his father to be removed and his own put in its place. One day, he reflected, his own likeness would look down on . . . on whom?

His stepmother, who had what he sometimes thought an uncanny ability to read his thoughts, spoke.

"That's something else you've inherited from your father," she said. "Dilatoriness. He was nearly forty when he married your mother." She made an impatient movement. "Are you ready to go, or do you have to polish that desk as well as tidy it?"

"I'm ready."

She rose and put her coat over her arm.

"You're going to give me tea, aren't you?" she asked.

"And dinner too, if you've changed your mind. I bought two theater tickets, just in case."

"No. I'm sorry. I'm going out with one of my aged admirers. Thanks all the same."

"Did you come in your car?"

"Yes, but I sent it away. Jordan will have to be up late tonight. You can send me home in the office car after tea."

He opened the door and she preceded him into his secretary's office. This was a small room which opened into a far larger one in which were about twenty desks occupied by junior members of the staff. Mrs. Helder walked through the central aisle; William followed her, and at their appearance there was a concerted movement as his employees pushed back their chairs and rose. William paused to speak to one or two of the staff as he went. The door at the end of the room was held open and he and his stepmother passed through it to a hall from which three lifts could be seen operating. He ushered her into his small private elevator and pressed the button marked *Residence.*

"When are you going to stop that ridiculous royal progress through the outer office?" she asked irritably. "Can't you arrange some other way of getting to this lift?"

"You're lucky the progress is so swift. My father—"

"I know, I know, I know. Your father used to stop and shake hands with all the bearded old clerks. Outdated employer-employee relationship. Paternalism. Now that they're all bearded young clerks, you should cut down on the traditional ceremonies."

The elevator doors opened. They stepped out into a square, spacious hall and Mrs. Helder paused, as she always did on getting out of the lift on her visits to William, and spoke with a kind of grudging approval.

"It's really lovely, William."

They were on the top floor of the five-storey, Thames-side building which for nearly three hundred years had housed the firm of Helder & Son. The firm's sign, a towering, two-way one which could be clearly seen from ships going up or down the river, had once jutted from the roof, but now hung outside the floor below. For William, on his father's remarriage, had put into execution a plan he had nursed throughout his boyhood: to turn the almost disused top floor into a home for himself. The view had always fascinated him; he loved ships of all kinds—pleasure craft, liners, fishing boats, tugs, barges, lighters, dredgers—and from here he could look down on a never-ceasing procession.

The rooms he had converted had once been the home of the heads of the firm, but when the family mansion was built in Hertfordshire, the office rooms had ceased to be used.

William had created a hall opening onto a narrow balcony; on one side of the hall was a comfortable servants' suite. On the other side, visible through glass doors, was a drawing room with ceiling-to-floor windows overlooking the river. Behind this room were two bedrooms and bathrooms; beyond it was a dining room and beyond that, a roof garden.

Mrs. Helder moved out to the balcony and William followed her. It was late June, but it had been an unsatisfactory spring and was proving a wet summer. There was a mist over the city, and low clouds that threatened rain. The view, on clear days far-reaching, now comprised no more than storage sheds and warehouses and dispirited-looking cranes. They stood looking down at the river up which, for over three centuries, had sailed ships bringing goods from the Dutch branches of the firm—Leyden, Amsterdam, The Hague. The Helder fortunes had followed those of their patrons, the princes of the House of Orange. When Prince William III of Orange became King William III of England, the Helders established themselves in London and entered a period of prosperity which had sometimes dimmed but which had never been extinguished. Today, William ruled not over a firm but over an empire.

"But lovely or not," his stepmother continued, "you shouldn't be living here. You should have gone back to Hertfordshire when your father died."

He made no comment. He knew that after his father's death, she had hoped that he would move out of this riverside apartment and return to the family home, leaving the apartment free for her occupation. She had lived for most of her life in London, and had left it reluctantly on her marriage to William's father. On his death, she had waited until it became clear that William did not intend to move, and then bought a share of a house in Berkeley Square and settled down to a life divided among dressmakers, hairdressers, theaters, concerts and bridge. The house in Hertfordshire was left unoccupied except for the occasional visits paid by William.

"It's chilly," she remarked after a time. "Let's go in."

In the drawing room, a middle-aged manservant was wheeling a tea trolley towards one of the windows.

"Good afternoon, Dirk." Mrs. Helder sank onto the sofa and gave her coat into his keeping. "Is your wife better?"

"Yes, thank you, madam." Dirk, short and stolid, nodded a bald head in satisfaction. "I made her go to the osteopath. When I say made her, it was Mr. Helder made her go. He sent her in the car."

"A good cook, that Elise," commented William, "but a mulish woman. She wouldn't agree to attend the massage sessions either, so the masseuse came here. Dirk, I said there were to be no cream cakes for Mrs. Helder."

"But there are, and I shall eat them all," she said. "Put them on this little table beside me, Dirk. When I've had tea, I'll go along and have a chat with Elise."

Dirk withdrew. William came to take the cup of tea his stepmother poured out, and took a low chair beside her.

She studied him in silence for a time. He roused in her much of the affection that his father had done, but in William's case it was tempered by irritation. She was by nature impatient, impetuous, a thruster, disposed to attack and overcome problems. William, deliberate of speech, calm in temperament, believed, as his father had done, that most problems, if left to cool, resolved themselves. The fact that this was often the case only increased her irritation.

"Been shopping?" he asked.

"No. Hairdresser, and then the Bridge Club luncheon for the presentation of the competition trophies."

"Were you one of the winners?"

"I was the trophy giver. Which was why I rang you up and asked you to give me tea."

He waited for an explanation of these unconnected remarks, but she went on to speak of something else.

"How long is it since you went down to the house?" she enquired.

"I was there last week. I spent a night there. The gardens were looking very nice."

"I hear you've refused two offers to rent the place."

"Three."

"Why? Why leave a lovely house like that empty?"

"It's never had strangers in it. I know I moved out, but when I'm down there, I still have a strong feeling that it's a family home. All those children's rooms with toys and books still in them. My father's study, my—"

"You needn't go on; you'll only make me angry. Why can't you look for a wife and get married, for God's sake, and fill all those children's rooms?"

"Time enough."

"You're thirty-four. Your father was forty-two when you were born. Do you want to be forty-two years older than your son? It was something he always regretted, that he hadn't been younger when he became a parent. He said that he never felt he could close that forty-two-year gap. And that's how you're going to feel one day. When I married your father, you were twenty-two and I could have had you married before you knew what was happening—but your father detested matchmaking, and so I did nothing. And now I'm sorry. A lovely home in the country, all that money, to say nothing of your sound health and your splendid education and your on the whole harmless disposition—all thrown away. You ought to marry, even if it's only to keep the Helder line going. You could have had children at school by now. You could have been attending Speech Days and Founders' Days . . . Why did I get onto this topic? I'm wasting my breath. Do you want another cup of tea?"

"You just gave me one. In the middle of that bit about having me married before I knew what was happening."

"Why do I care? Why do I still care, after all these years? Why don't I just sit back and watch you growing into a nice, comfortable old woman? I do, most of the time—and then something comes over me out of the past and upsets me. Like that trophy awarding today. If you've finished your tea, I'd like a cigarette."

He gave her one, held a light, rang the bell and waited until Dirk had removed the trolley. Then he looked at his stepmother.

"There's something on your mind," he said.

"Yes, there is." Her eyes were on a glass-fronted cabinet standing against the wall at one end of the room. She gestured with her cigarette. "I came to talk about those."

"My new acquisitions?"

"No. I'm not interested in your new acquisitions. I'm talking about the flagons."

"Well?"

"I haven't heard you mention them since your father died and you brought them to this apartment. I don't suppose you ever glance at them. Do you?"

"My friends do. Most of them object to the label."

"What label?"

"They think they shouldn't be called flagons. The purists argue that a flagon's a glass bottle for holding liquid. The Bible students quote the Song of Solomon. The uninformed consult the dictionary. When the tumult dies down, I explain that they were called flagons when they were given to the Helders, which is why we call them flagons today."

"Whatever you label them, they're lovely."

He agreed. Eleven in number, they stood on the top shelf of the cabinet, each about five inches high, silver, with two charming decorative handles. He waited for his stepmother to ask the inevitable question.

"Are you ever going to do anything about that last one?"
He hesitated.

"I haven't given the matter much thought," he said at last.

"You haven't given the matter any thought at all. You're going to be yet another Helder who goes to the end of his life sitting and gazing at eleven of a set of twelve, without putting out a finger, that's to say putting out a foot, to find number twelve. Haven't you the smallest interest in trying to make it a round dozen?"

"Well, I—"

"The answer's no. You don't give a damn." She ground out her cigarette with angry force. "I don't understand how generation after generation of you Helders have sat back and yawned and said 'Yes, there should be twelve, but we never located the last one.' Why didn't they locate it? Because they never looked for it, that's why."

"My father—"

"Ah! Your father. Yes, he looked. And who was it who prodded him, argued with him, bulldozed him into looking at last?"

"You did."

"Correct. I did. And I hoped you might have gone on where he left off, but it's over a year—to be exact, it's fourteen months since he died, and what have you done? Nothing."

He did not deny it. The set of twelve had been given in 1689 by King William and Queen Mary to a head of the Helder firm for notable services during the Coronation. When the Helder house in Hertfordshire was built in 1702 and the family moved into it, it was discovered that five flagons were missing. Not many of the succeeding generations of the family had shown any marked interest in recovering them. From time to time, at very long intervals, an enthusiast had done some detective work; by the end of the nineteenth century, four of the missing five had been recovered. There the search ended. William's father, like the majority of his forebears, had shown very little interest in continuing it, but his second wife, unlike her serene and placid predecessor, had found the incomplete set not only an irritation but a challenge, and had driven her husband into making some effort to locate the twelfth. He had begun halfheartedly; after a time he had caught some of his wife's enthusiasm, but nothing had come of his efforts, and at his death the set was still incomplete.

"It isn't as though you hadn't had time to make enquiries," Mrs. Helder was proceeding. "But you never exert yourself. All you do with your leisure is play golf or ski or fish or—"

"Isn't that exerting myself?"

"No. It's amusing yourself. You're getting to be as self-centered, as selfish as I am. It's different for me. I'm old. I've retired. I've done what I considered my duty towards others, and now I feel I'm entitled to spend the rest of my life doing my duty towards myself. But you're young, and you've got to pull yourself out of that rut you're falling into. And you ought to be willing to take up the search for that last flagon where your father left it."

She rose and walked to the cabinet, and he followed her.

"Look at them—they're beautiful," she said.

"Yes," he agreed. "They're beautiful. So why wouldn't anybody who had number twelve want to hang on to it?"

"If someone knew that it was the last of a set of twelve, and that the owner of the other eleven would pay a lot to get his hands on it—"

"There isn't a big dealer, or for that matter a small dealer in this country," William reminded her, "who hasn't got a note of that flagon on his books. You can ask dealers to keep a lookout, just as you can ask booksellers to keep a lookout, and that's what we did. And while I admit that I haven't done anything practical, I do go through catalogues and I do sometimes drop in at sales. But if the flagon turned up, it would probably be put into a group with other miscellaneous objects, so searching isn't as easy as you think." He turned to look at her. "Why this renewed interest?" he asked. "Have you picked up the scent?"

"No, I haven't." She returned to the sofa. "But something happened today that—well, it brought the matter to my mind."

He held open a cigarette box. She shook her head and he went to lean against the mantelpiece.

"What happened?" he asked.

"I told you. I gave away the Bridge Club trophies. The names of the winners were announced, but I happened to glance at the prize list and I saw the addresses: the winning pair came from Steeplewood."

She paused, her eyes on him. William merely waited.

"Doesn't the name mean anything to you?" she asked.

He searched his memory, then shook his head.

"No. Should it?"

"It should. Steeplewood was the town in which that man Horn was living."

"Horn?"

"You don't remember?"

"No."

She raised her shoulders in a gesture of exasperation.

"Then I wish I hadn't wasted an entire afternoon in an attempt to raise a spark of interest in you. Your father—"

"Wait." He held up a hand. "Horn."

"Ah. You do remember?"

"I remember that my father mentioned the name. But not the place."

"The place was Steeplewood. It's a name that stuck in my mind, I don't know why. He—"

"One minute." Memory was still stirring. "Horn wrote a letter saying he had some Dutch pieces, and my father went to see him."

"No, he didn't. I think—though I'm not sure—that he answered the letter and told this man Horn that he'd be interested in going to look at his collection—but he couldn't go at once, because he and I were on the point of leaving for a holiday in Greece." She paused, staring unseeingly at the wide expanse of window. "When I look back, I wish to God I'd called off the Greek trip and made your father go to Steeplewood. If he had—but wishing's no use. At the time, there didn't seem any hurry about going to look at Dutch *objets d'art*, especially as no details had been given in the letter. So we went on our trip. And when we came back—but you know what happened when we came back."

William knew. On their return, she had parted from his father in London and had driven down to Kent to spend the weekend with her sister. His father had gone to stay with an old friend in Cambridge, a visit that coincided with the annual reunion of the survivors of his old regiment. He had returned to his office on Monday morning. It was his last working day. That evening, he had suffered a heart attack while walking home from the station. He had died within sight of the house.

William heard his stepmother's voice.

"Get the flagon file, will you?"

He went to the writing desk, opened a drawer and drew out a green leather folder. He took it to the sofa and sat beside her. Together they looked at the papers neatly filed inside.

The first entries were in ink, in fine, faded handwriting. The date on the first notes was 1730—the beginning of the attempt to locate the five flagons that had been lost, or stolen, during the family move from London to Hertfordshire. There were forty, sometimes fifty years between the entries, but each entry gave briefly and clearly the steps taken towards recovery, and the result of the search. The last accounts were typewritten and ended with an admission of failure.

"Here it is," Mrs. Helder said. "The Horn letter."

It was a few lines written with a tremulous hand on thick paper. The writer, Jasper Horn, of the Manor, Steeplewood, Bedfordshire, said that he was a collector and owned some interesting objects of Dutch origin. He had been in conversation with a dealer in Salisbury who had mentioned Mr. Helder's name, and he was now writing to ask if Mr. Helder would care to call and see his collection.

"If he'd been talking to a dealer," William said slowly, "then—"

"Yes. That's what your father thought when he read the letter. The dealer might have, *must* have mentioned flagons. Why else would he have given this man your father's name?" She gave a sigh. "It's ironic, isn't it? I was the one who pushed your father to the point at which he'd really worked up some interest in finding that last flagon, and yet when a lead like this turned up, I decided that investigation could wait until we'd had our holiday. Your father would have been happy to go to Steeplewood straight away."

William nodded in agreement. He knew that his father would have considered the visit to Mr. Horn of more urgency than the visit to Greece; Greece would still be there if they postponed the holiday, but the flagon—if Mr. Horn had it— might not. And finding the flagon had become a matter of importance to his father, not so much from a desire to complete the set as from the pleasure he would have got from gratifying the wishes of his wife. He had been a quiet man, a man who seldom disclosed and never discussed his feelings, but he was also a man who delighted in going to great trouble in order to obtain something which a member of his family wanted. He would say nothing, express little interest—but one day, the gift would appear and he would watch with a smile the surprise and excitement of the recipient. Yes, he would have liked to go and see Mr. Horn.

Mrs. Helder echoed the thought.

"He would have liked to go," she said regretfully. "Especially as he discovered that Mr. Horn—like the Helders—was of Dutch extraction."

"How did he find that out?"

"Someone at the office happened to know the name, and said he thought that the family was once called Hoorn. Which means, your father said, that if Mr. Horn had seen the flagon, he would have recognized the Orange coat of arms. But he only found out the day before we were leaving for the Greek trip."

A long silence fell. Mrs. Helder broke it at last.

"When your father died," she said, "I didn't expect you to think about flagons. Not at once. But it's over a year now, and you've not shown the smallest interest in picking up the threads. This afternoon, when I saw the name Steeplewood, I wondered whether—well, if you went there, there might be something to learn."

William closed the folder and replaced it in the drawer.

"You'd like me to go down there?" he asked.

"Yes. No. I'd like you to want to go. I pushed your father; I don't want to push you. I'm not going through all that again. It's up to you. If you found that last flagon, you could at least leave a full set to your son, when you have one. And that's all I've got to say. If you don't want to do anything, then don't."

She rose. He followed her across the hall and left her to have a talk with Dirk and his wife. Then he took her down to the office car and directed the chauffeur to drive her home.

When she had gone, he returned thoughtfully to the top floor and sat for a time listening to the latest additions to his collection of cassettes. His recordings had at first comprised the available classics, but he had lately been taping, with the cooperation of musical friends, unrecorded or little-known string quartets and quintets. But even listening to the latest of these failed to drive his stepmother from his mind.

After a time, he remembered that he had two tickets for the theater. He went to the telephone and for a few moments leafed absently through his indexed list. Then he selected a name and in a few minutes had arranged to take a woman friend out to dinner and the show.

He put down the receiver with a strong sense of dissatisfaction. Look for a wife, his stepmother had advised. You didn't have to look far. All you needed was a phone and, however short the notice, you could always find a woman to say yes—to anything. It would be interesting, he thought, going to his room to have a bath and change, to come across one of that extinct species, a girl with a dragon of a mother. Or a fierce father. Or—big joke—a girl with old-fashioned scruples.

Dinner was not a success. He would have liked to talk, but his companion was bent on filling in every detail of every moment of every day that had passed since they last met. The play was an Oscar Wilde revival; while Lady Windermere talked of fans, he found flagons coming and going in his mind.

Leaving the theater, he fell in with a party of friends going on to a night club. He skillfully grafted his companion onto the group, and went home to bed.

Dirk was waiting up. Dirk had been working for him since his father's death, but he had never been able to persuade him not to wait up. Why he waited, he could not discover; he had never come home drunk, he never wanted anything to eat and if he wanted a drink, it was there to his hand.

"There's sandwiches, sir, if you'd like some."

"No, thanks, Dirk."

"Two phone calls, sir. Not urgent. I put the messages on your bedside table."

"Thanks. Good night."

"Nothing else?"

"No."

Dirk was at the door before William spoke again.

"Yes, there's one thing."

Dirk turned.

"I'll be using the office car tomorrow. About ten thirty."

"Very good, sir."

"Tell Anton to bring it round. He needn't wait. I'll be driving myself."

"Yes, sir. Good night."

"Good night."

So he was going. In that case, he'd better look at a map. He went to his desk to get one.

2

NEXT MORNING, SEATED IN HIS CAR WITH A MAP OPEN BESIDE him, William wondered why he was making the journey, especially on a Saturday morning, when it seemed to him that ten million of his fellow Londoners were, like himself, on their way out of town. His stepmother had stated that she would not push him, but some kind of pressure seemed to have been applied, or why was he on his way to Steeplewood, on an errand that should have been performed over a year ago?

She had probably been right, he mused, about his tendency to selfishness. A man living alone, a man with no financial worries, with no responsibilities outside his work, tended to grow selfish. Self-centered. He had endeavoured, at intervals throughout his adult life, to share with those less fortunate the advantages which Providence had bestowed on him. His attempts at do-gooding, he recalled, had not come to much. Three evenings a week at the local Youth Club, until its members broke it up. Teaching football on the local inadequate playing fields, resigning after hopeless attempts to persuade the players to adopt the recognized rules and abandon their tooth-for-a-tooth technique. Personal service had given way to what he admitted was mere checkbook generosity.

His mind went to his stepmother's irritation at his single state. He had not avoided matrimony. He had imagined, when he was younger, that by the time he reached the age of thirty he would be the father of sturdy sons. But their mother had in some way failed to materialize.

He found himself driving into rain and closed his windows. The sun came out again as he neared Cambridge. He would have to skirt the county in order to get to Steeplewood, and this was a pity, as it would have been pleasant to drive through countryside familiar to him from his university days. It might be a good idea to go through Cambridge on his way home; stop there for lunch, perhaps, and look up old friends. Yes, a good idea.

In the meantime he had to keep his eyes open for a Steeplewood sign. There were plenty of woods ahead, but so far no steeple.

He was still on the London road. Presently he found himself on rising ground, and after some miles came to a turning signposted Steeplewood. After he had driven for a short distance on a bad surface, the road forked. The left fork led to Steeplewood and the right continued up the hill. On an impulse, he took the steeper road, and at the top of the hill stopped to look at the town spread below him.

Spread was the word, he thought. Apart from some congestion in the center, the residents seemed to have been anxious to locate themselves as far away from one another as possible. It was an old town; a picturesque town. The streets on the outskirts were broad and some were tree-lined. He could see a busy open-air market, and cattle in pens. There were two churches with steeples and one with a Norman tower. Many of the older houses were large and rambling, surrounded by trees or by wide lawns. Here and there were cottages which had been given a modernized London Mews look which he thought out of place in this setting. There were some outlying farms, with a sluggish river making a loop round them. In the distance, beyond the level stretch of the town, rose another hill, and on it he could see a half-ruined castle. The scene had a peace, a serenity that recalled an earlier and more leisurely epoch.

He was about to return to the lower road when he saw through the trees a wide wrought-iron gateway. He got out of the car to make a reconnaissance, and to his astonishment and delight found himself looking at a beautiful old building which could only be the manor he was looking for. He had not known what to expect—the term was nowadays applied to a variety of modern structures—but this was a veritable, a true manor. Even more beautiful than the building was its setting—a background of trees whose wide variation of size, shape and colour turned them into a medieval tapestry.

From town level, he judged, the Manor, hidden by trees, would be invisible, but he had no doubt that the view he was now enjoying would be on sale, highly coloured and postcard-size, in the tourist shops in the town.

He saw that this gate was not in use; the padlock and chain hanging from it looked as though they had not been touched for years. He would have to go down the hill and look for another entrance—and before entering, he must do what he had omitted to do before leaving London: telephone to find out if Mr. Horn was at home and, if so, would consent to see him.

The road followed the encircling walls of the Manor, and as he drove down the hill, he tried to estimate what a present-day builder would charge for putting up a wall so extensive, in brickwork of such beauty. The grounds seemed to embrace the entire hill; Mr. Horn must be in a position to pay for a very handsome collection.

He rounded a curve and saw on his right a gateway over

which was an arch in brickwork that matched the wall. He slowed down to study it in passing.

But he did not pass. He brought the car to a stop and sat gazing at the sign that hung from the center of the arch.

THE MANOR SCHOOL FOR GIRLS
PRINCIPAL: MISS VALERIE HORN

He considered the situation. He did not think that Mr. Horn had written from a girls' school; the address on the letter had been simply The Manor. But that was—how long ago? A year and two months. A lot could happen in fourteen months. Was Mr. Horn dead? Was he alive and living here, perhaps in the lodge which could be seen through the arch? It was certainly occupied, for there was a car on the gravel drive, and four bicycles were propped against the wall under the diamond-paned windows.

There could be no harm in making enquiries. He drove in and stopped in front of the neat front door. Beside it, let into the wall, was a small plaque:

MISS VALERIE HORN
RESIDENCE

He parked the car behind the other and walked to the door. It was half open, and he could see a hall with a floor of black and white marble squares. A door on the left was open; one on the right was closed and a murmur of voices could be heard. At the end of the hall was a carpeted corridor, and from a door at its end came an occasional sound of crockery. Everything he saw—furniture, carpets, curtains—showed that Miss Valerie Horn had excellent taste, and money enough to indulge it.

"Anybody there?" he called.

There was no response. He knocked on the panel of the door, and from the room at the end of the corridor a girl appeared and came unhurriedly towards him.

"Did someone leave the door open?" she asked in surprise, and without waiting for an answer opened it wider. "Come in, won't you?"

It would have been difficult to keep him out. She was about twenty-five, slender, dressed in pale green. Her hair was fair and, left to fall into its own style, had chosen to curl inwards and frame a face whose chief beauty was a pair of large, wide, clear grey eyes. The only thing that marred the pleasure he felt in the encounter was the realization that she was giving him only a fraction of her attention. Her manner was polite, but impersonal to the point of vagueness.

"Come this way, will you?"

He followed her into the open-doored room, which he saw was an office with windows overlooking the drive. There were a large desk on which papers rested in some disorder, a swivel chair and a filing cabinet. In the corner were two armchairs and a low table spread with newspapers and magazines.

"Please sit down."

He remained standing. She was looking for something among the papers.

"I had a list of names," she told him. "Yes . . . here—no, that's not it. It's odd how things get lost. It must be in this drawer."

She searched in the drawer, and he noted without surprise that she was wearing an engagement ring; the only wonder, he felt, was that she had not been swept into matrimony long ago.

"Yes, here it is. You're Mr. Trenchard. But you're—"

"No. I—"

"—much too early."

"No, I'm not."

She frowned—not, he thought, in annoyance, but in an attempt to bring more of her mind to bear on the matter.

"I've got a copy of my letter to you somewhere," she said. He watched as she made another unavailing search. "It doesn't seem to be here, but I remember what was in it. I offered you eleven fifteen and you phoned to say—I made a note of the call on the letter, only I can't find it—that the time would suit you and your wife very well. Couldn't she come?"

"No. You see—"

"I hope she isn't ill?"

"No. I—"

"Then it would have been much better if she had come with you. Miss Horn always prefers to see both parents. Still . . . please sit down. I'm afraid you're going to have rather a long wait."

"There's a mistake," William told her.

She had withdrawn her attention; she had gone to tidy the pile of magazines on the low table, and something in one of them had caught her eye. She looked at him enquiringly.

"You said?"

"I said there was a mistake. I'm not Mr.—whoever it was. My name's Helder. William Helder."

She put down the magazine.

"I don't remember a Mr. Helder," she said. "I'm Hazel Paget; you probably made your appointment with the senior secretary, Mavis Field. If you wait a moment, I'll look in the book . . . It doesn't seem to be here, but—"

"I didn't make an appointment. I just, as it were, turned up."

"You made no appointment?"

"No."

"Did you write for a school brochure?"

"No."

"Are you a parent?"

"No."

"A prospective parent?"

"No."

"A guardian?"

"No. In fact, I didn't know this was a school."

"Then you don't want to see Miss Horn?"

"Well, it depends. You see, I—"

"I'm afraid it will be absolutely impossible for you to see her this morning. This is Saturday, and she reserves Saturday mornings for interviews with parents. The entire morning is given up to them." She waved a hand in the direction of the room across the hall. "There are parents with her now. When they go, it'll be time for her to have her morning coffee. She always has it at this time."

"Five o'clock," he commented mildly, "is tea time."

She looked at the clock.

"It's stopped again. It does that," she explained. "When it goes, if it goes, it gains. When Miss Horn has had her coffee, she'll see Mr. and Mrs. Trenchard, and after that—"

"I didn't come to see Miss Horn. I came to see Mr. Horn."

"To see . . ." She stopped, staring at him in astonishment. But before she could speak, the door on the opposite side of the hall opened and a middle-aged woman came out, followed by a middle-aged man who could be seen making a polite bow before closing the door. A bell sounded in the office.

"Excuse me. I've got to see those people out," she said.

She accompanied the visitors to the front door. At the same moment, William saw coming down the corridor a girl carrying a tray. Irish, he told himself without hesitation: black hair smoothed into a knot low on her neck; bluest of blue eyes, and a round, red-cheeked face with a short blunt nose. He placed her at about twenty-two, and noted regretfully that a pleasantly curved figure was spreading into billows; she would be matronly before she was thirty, and massive at forty.

She knocked lightly at the principal's door, entered and a few moments later came out without the tray, closed the door and walked across to the office. She waited for Hazel Paget and the two entered the room together. Then the newcomer spoke, and William learned that his guess at her nationality had been incorrect: her accent was Welsh.

"I'm sorry I've come so late, Haze. Those catering people kept me. Such stupids they are, they can't understand even the simplest things you tell them. I'll take over now—you go home." She turned to William. "Good morning. You're Mr. Trenchard. I'm Mavis Field. You've come a little bit early, so . . . Haze, did you forget to wind the clock?"

"I must have done. What's the time?"

"Eleven three. Will you sit down, please," she asked William. "I think you were for eleven fifteen. Did you check the appointment, Haze?"

"I couldn't find the book. But in any case, he's—"

"It's in the drawer." Miss Field drew it out. "Miss Horn doesn't— You've put it at twelve three, Haze."

She made the correction herself. Since her entry, she had been putting papers in order, tidying the room, adjusting the calendar. A competent young woman, William noted with approval; composed, efficient. The other one would not have lasted a week in his office.

He was still standing. Miss Field indicated an armchair.

"Please sit down, Mr. Trenchard."

"He's not Mr. Trenchard," Hazel Paget hold her, "and he isn't a parent, present or prospective, and he isn't a guardian. And he's not too early, he's too late, because he came to see Mr. Horn."

"Then you told him—"

"I haven't had a chance to tell him anything yet. He— *You* explain," she asked William.

He addressed himself to Miss Field.

"I came to see Mr. Horn. I should have telephoned before leaving London; I was on my way to find a phone in Steeplewood when I passed the Manor and saw the notice at the entrance. Miss Horn's name was on it, and I came in to ask if Mr. Horn was still living here. Is he?"

There was a pause. Miss Paget was making preparations for

departure. Miss Field was regarding him with a somber glance.

"Are you related in any way to Mr. Horn?" she asked.

"No."

"I asked, see, because if you'd been related I would have broken the news gently. Mr. Horn is dead. He died last year, on April thirtieth."

"I'm sorry. Is Miss Horn his daughter?"

"No. She's his niece. Mr. Horn left her the Manor House in his will, and as well, he left her everything inside it. This school was started in June of last year. Is that all you want to know?"

"Not quite. Mr. Horn was a collector. Did Miss Horn keep—"

"Oh no!" Miss Field shook her head. "No, no. She didn't keep anything at all, except some pictures. All she wanted was the house—to have the school in, see?"

"What happened to the contents of the Manor?"

"They were sold after Mr. Horn died."

"Everything?"

"Yes, everything. Miss Horn was in Scotland and she didn't come down until the sale was finished. There were two sales, one after the other on two days, because of so much stuff." She turned to her colleague. "Haze, you haven't gone, and you're so late. I'll see you at one o'clock. Perhaps sooner, because the last appointment is cancelled."

Miss Paget turned at the door to nod casually to William. Looking out of the window, he saw her emerge onto the drive and get into the car he had seen parked outside. It was a very old model, and looked battered. It was some time before she could get it to start, and he wondered if he would be required to go outside and push.

"It always gives trouble," Miss Field said calmly from her desk. "In a little while, it'll go."

As she spoke, he heard the engine. The car moved, gained speed and went out of sight.

He turned his attention to the view. Somewhere in the distance, hidden by trees, was the Manor, but he could see two wide terraces and below them, at the foot of the hill, a large, level expanse of playing fields. A series of games seemed to be in progress.

"Those aren't our girls." Miss Field had come to stand beside him. "Every weekend, Miss Horn lets out the school playing fields to the other schools in town. It helps them, because they haven't got enough room for games, and it helps us because they pay for the upkeep of the grounds, so it's what you call mutual benefit."

"How many girls in the school?"

"A hundred and eighty-four. All day. No boarders. In her other school in Scotland, Miss Horn didn't have boarders either, only day. They go home to eat in the middle of the day, or they bring their lunch and eat it in the school. For the staff —we're eighteen altogether—Miss Horn hires a caterer. I give them the numbers, and they bring the food all ready and they serve it and then they take away the leftover things and the dirty plates. Miss Horn eats with the staff in the daytime, but she lives in this lodge and she's got her own domestic staff. I do most of her cooking, and there's a cleaner who comes every day, and there's a housekeeper who lives here."

"The school must have grown very fast," William commented.

"Fast?" Her eyes widened, her hands spread in an expressive gesture. "Fast? You can say truthfully that it exploded. When Miss Horn came to start it up, she expected to have just a few, and then afterwards more. I worked for her in Scotland before we came here. As soon as she put that notice up in the entrance—and she put in adverts, too, notices in the papers—parents began to register their children. Before we knew what was happening, there was a waiting list that long."

"Why? Was Steeplewood short of schools?"

"There was no school like this one. How it was, this Manor was always as you might say the showpiece of Steeplewood. When Mr. Horn lived here, nobody got in unless they were his friends or if they came to see his collection. To have a school here, in such a beautiful place, with such beautiful grounds, that was something new. There wasn't a school shortage the way you meant it, but there wasn't a school where people who had a lot of money could send their children—some parents like a smart school, you know. So that's how we started so well. There was a sort of slowing down when people found out that Miss Horn was taking black children as well as white children, but only a few dropped out; the rest kept coming. Even when the children knew that there was a uniform they'd have to wear—navy blue skirts or trousers, white blouses, red cloaks for going between the school and the playing fields—even then they still wanted to come. The waiting list gets bigger and bigger." She turned to face him. "Look, Mr.— Haze didn't tell me what your name was."

"Helder. William Helder."

"And you aren't related to Miss Horn?"

"No. But I'd very much like to see her. If you could go in there and snatch away the coffee tray before she helps herself to a third cup, could you induce her to spare me ten minutes?"

She studied him for a few moments.

"All I can do is try," she said.

She left him and went into the room opposite. When she came out she was carrying the tray. She put it on the desk and addressed him in a conspiratorial whisper.

"Ten minutes—that's all I could get for you. Come. There's a car coming—that'll be Mr. and Mrs. Trenchard, but I'll try to keep them happy."

He followed her across the hall. She opened the principal's

door, announced William and stood aside for him to enter. The door closed behind her and his first impression was that the room had grown very dark. He then saw the reason: Miss Horn had risen, and was so tall and so wide that she blotted out the light from the window. She gave a slight bow, resumed her seat and waved William to an armchair opposite. He saw that this was not an office but a drawing room—small, but perfectly furnished. The view from the window, now that he could see it, was of a green lawn and well-tended flowerbeds.

"I understand," said Miss Horn, "that you came in the hope of seeing my uncle."

Her voice was firm, so firm as to add to the impression he had already received of a woman who knew what she wanted and also knew how to get it. She was about fifty, handsome in a heavy way, with short, greying hair arranged in neat waves. Her manner was dignified, verging on pompous, and below it he sensed a hardness that made him feel he would not care to cross her.

"I should have telephoned before leaving London," he said, "but I'm afraid I didn't. I only learned just now that Mr. Horn is dead."

"What did you wish to see him about?"

"Just over a year ago, he wrote a letter to my father, asking if he would care to come and see Mr. Horn's collection, which he said contained some Dutch pieces. My father was particularly interested because Mr. Horn had heard of him through an antique dealer in Salisbury, and it seemed possible that the dealer might have mentioned an object my father very much wanted to find—a small silver flagon missing from a set of twelve. The set had been a gift from William of Orange to the Helder family. My father knew that Mr. Horn was of Dutch extraction, and so would have recognized the arms engraved on the flagon."

"I see. Your father didn't come to see the collection?"

"No. He and my stepmother were on the point of leaving for a holiday, and he thought that he could put off his visit until his return. But he died a few days after returning to England. I don't even know whether he answered Mr. Horn's letter, but I feel sure he must have done."

"If he did, it will perhaps be among my uncle's papers. They are still in the hands of the lawyers. There hasn't been time, since I came to England, to go through any of them. You came here, of course, in the hope of seeing the collection, so now you will want to know what became of it. Perhaps I had better explain what happened after my uncle died. Or perhaps I had better go further back and give you a fuller picture."

He waited, taking in more impressions. Everything about Miss Horn spoke of good organization, efficiency—and success. She spoke without haste, her enunciation clear.

"Since you didn't know my uncle," she said, "there are certain things you should know about him. He called himself a collector, but he was in fact a dealer. He bought objects for what he called his collection, and then wrote to people he thought would be interested in buying certain selected items. The fact that there was no specific mention of a flagon in his letter to your father wouldn't mean he didn't have it. He would, of course, have found out your family's origins; hence his mention of Dutch objects. If he had the flagon, he would have preferred to let your father find it when he came to look at the collection."

"To put the price up?"

"Precisely. I said he was a dealer. I should have added that he was a very shrewd one. For objects of relatively low value —that's to say, five hundred pounds or so—he always demanded payment in cash. He gave no receipts. It was illegal, of course, but as dealers go, he was honest; he never sold anything he couldn't guarantee as genuine. I tell you this because I dislike pretense of any kind. My uncle was not of Dutch origin. He liked people to think so. He said that the name was originally Hoorn—which it wasn't. He had a touch of what my mother—she was his sister—called *folie de grandeur*; as she had none whatsoever, they didn't get on. I was very much surprised when I heard that he had left me the Manor and its contents. I was part owner of a school in Edinburgh, and planned, with the money I inherited, to become the sole owner —but I met unexpected obstacles, and so I changed my mind about selling the Manor, and decided to open a school here. I didn't want any items from the collection; I had seen most of them when I paid an Easter visit to my uncle some years ago, and I realized that his taste and mine did not agree. All I wanted to keep—and did keep—was his pictures."

His eyes were on the one hanging above the fireplace.

"Van de Velde?"

"Yes. The Elder. Do you recognize the other?"

"Cuyp. I have two at home."

"You would naturally be interested in the Dutch school. But to return to your problem, you will see that I can be of no assistance in telling you what became of the things in my uncle's collection. The sale—the sales—took place before I arrived. I can ask my lawyers to give you any details they have. You can ask my secretary, Miss Paget, if she could get you a list from the auctioneers. They were a London firm, and she gave them some secretarial assistance while they were here. She could . . ." Her hand went to a bell push on the wall, and then she paused. "I'm afraid she will have left. She only works part time here, and goes home at eleven. But I will ask my other secretary, Miss Field, to give you her address, and she will also tell you how to get there. I am sure Miss Paget will be of assistance."

She rose, and they shook hands.

"Will you ask Miss Field to see me for a moment before she

shows anybody else in? After that, she will give you directions as to how to get to the Pagets' house."

He sent in Miss Field and waited for her in the hall, the office being occupied by a man and a woman whose expressions indicated that she had kept them, but had not kept them happy. When she had shown them into the principal's room, she turned her attention to William, and they walked together to his car.

"You're going to see the Pagets?" she asked.

"Yes."

"It's an easy place to find," she told him. "It looks like a farm, but it isn't really; just a few animals. It's the first thing you'll see when you get out of town. The only thing is, don't go through the town, because it's market day and you'll get delayed. You don't have to turn left, only right whenever you see a turning, and when you get out of town, you'll see the Pagets' place, straight across the fields."

"I drive across the fields?"

She laughed. "Oh my goodness, no! You go along the road and it's on your left. It's called Grazings, but there's no notice, so you wouldn't know. It used to be a farm once, but now it's just what's left of what they didn't sell off. They— Is this your car?"

"It's the office car. I use it occasionally."

"Such a lovely one! If I didn't have to work until one o'clock, I'd ask you to give me a lift home, just for a ride, you know? I live on the Pagets' place."

"How do you get home?"

She waved a hand towards the bicycles propped against the wall.

"That way. If you're going to see the Pagets, would you like me to tell you about them?"

"Please."

"Well, there's three of them. Haze used to keep house for her brother until he got married. His name's Hugo, and he's the organist at the church. Choirmaster, too, but as well as that, he used to teach music in a school in London—he went by train every day. He met Dilys there. She's his wife now— she was teaching history in the same school as him, but she gave it up when they got married and she came to live at Grazings, and she ran the house, and Haze went away to London to get a job. She wasn't here when I came. Hugo and Dilys had a little tiny cottage they didn't use, and I asked if I could live in it, and they said I could. So I started to be their paying guest. I didn't need anything during the week, because I did my own breakfast and I had lunch here at the school, but on Saturdays and Sundays Dilys cooked for me. And it went fine until about eight months ago, and then Hugo gave up his teaching job in London. You see, he composed things, and he wrote a piano concerto and it was played last year and the soloist was called Dessin; did you ever hear of him?"

"Yes."

"Well, they say he's very famous and he told Hugo that he must give up teaching and compose all the time, so that's what he's doing. But then Dilys had to earn money, so she went back to teaching—not in London, but here at this school. She's the history teacher. As well as that, she does extra coaching, and what with teaching and coaching and looking after Hugo and the house, it was too much, so she asked Haze if she'd come home. So Haze came. That was four months ago. Then she got engaged. Now she looks after the house and cooks for me. They've only got two people working for them: there's a cowman called Bernie; he looks after the animals and grows the vegetables. He lives with his mother in the rooms over the stables, and his mother does the rough work in the house. That's all. Does that help you to know them?"

"Yes. Thanks."

"You didn't leave an address—or did you give it to Miss Horn?"

"No." He took out a card, wrote a number on it and handed it to her. "That's the business address; the number I wrote is my house phone."

"Will you be coming back to see Miss Horn?"

"She said she has to go through her uncle's papers. I'd like to come back and see if she comes across anything that would help me to find what I'm looking for."

"Then I'll get the papers from the lawyers and give them to her."

"Thank you. Goodbye."

She smiled.

"For now."

He drove away. As he approached the town, he saw that the streets were crowded with shoppers, and was glad that he was to avoid the town center. Each turning to the right took him into a road which looked exactly like the one before it—wide, with good surfaces, and with rows of uninteresting houses on either side.

When he approached the outskirts, uniformity ended; the pavements disappeared and the road surface became stony. He turned into a lane flanked by artistically converted cottages. The predominant colour was pale pink, with shutters in a contrasting shade. Every cottage had a long front garden. There was no traffic, and there were no pedestrians; he thought that the tenants of the houses must be out shopping, or indoors preparing lunch.

He was nearing the end of the lane when from the last wooden gate sprang a young dog. In pursuit of it, without a glance to right or left before crossing the lane, came an elderly woman. Both stopped a bare ten yards ahead of William's car.

He was fortunately travelling slowly, but he was too close for the brakes to be effective. He had only a few seconds in

42

which to decide on a course of action: he could avoid the woman and run over the dog—or he could avoid both and go for the wooden fence.

The impact was not great, but the fence was fragile and not built to withstand assault. A large section of it fell backwards and lay flat on the flowerbeds. A loud wail came from the woman.

"My roses! Oh, my beautiful roses! Rupert, Rupert, come here and look. Someone's ruined my flowers!"

A man came out of the house—a man of about forty, in tan linen trousers, a silk shirt and a brown pullover. William, after one glance, had no difficulty in recognizing him. Nobody who ever opened a glossy magazine could fail to recognize him: a well-kept figure, a handsome face with an expression of calm superiority, photographed against elegant backgrounds, wearing his own creations: Caradon clothes. Rupert Caradon. Caradon suits for men. For gentlemen. Delegates stepping from their cars into the United Nations building, diplomats boarding aircraft on their way to summit conferences, Cabinet Ministers pausing to utter a few platitudes to the press—all wore Caradon suits.

But it was not the formal wear that had brought him his greatest success. The Caradon leisure wear had bridged the gap between the slacks and sports shirt wearers and the figure-hugging-jeans, lurid-sweater and soiled-sneaker section of society. He had made smart sportswear unfashionable, and had substituted clothes as comfortable as they were picturesque, using fabrics and colours that had previously been considered suitable only for women's wear. His designs were revolutionary but found an instant market among the youth of the country; his puma-patterned trousers had graced royal legs. He had also made the most of the current craze for young couples to dress alike; his "Identa-kits" were shirts made to match the partners' trousers, trousers made to match the partners' shirts.

William owned Caradon clothes, in spite of his stepmother's comment that everyone who put on a Caradon suit put on a Caradon sneer.

Mr. Caradon was not sneering now. He was shouting.

"What the hell do you think you're doing?" he asked William. "Not a bloody thing on the road, and you knock down someone's fence. This is my mother's cottage, and that fence was only put up a couple of weeks ago and you've ruined it. To say nothing of the flowerbeds. Can't you drive?"

William was standing by the car.

"I swerved," he explained, "to avoid the lady and the dog."

"Rot! I saw the whole thing from that window. In the first place, you were going much too fast."

"Much too fast," corroborated his mother. "When I came out of the gate, there was nothing in sight. He must have—"

"Leave this to me, Mother."

William took a card from his wallet and handed it to Mr. Caradon.

"You needn't suppose that paying for that fence is going to settle this," Mrs. Caradon said belligerently. "It took time and money to make this garden."

"You'll be hearing from me," her son said coldly to William.

William got into his car.

"And not a word of apology, you notice," snarled Mrs. Caradon.

William addressed her through the window.

"No apology is necessary," he assured her kindly. "I'm sure you usually look before leaping in pursuit of your dog." His eyes went to her son. "I was driving slowly, but nobody can avoid something a few feet away from their mudguards. I had a choice: hit the lady, kill the dog or flatten the fence. If I made the wrong choice, I'm sorry."

He drove away. That hadn't been witty, but it had been the last word.

He was out of the lane, driving between fields. About a mile ahead was a huddle of buildings which he thought must be the Pagets' farm. As he drove nearer, he saw that there was no direct approach to the house. The property had a wire fence. A wide, three-barred gate gave entrance to a muddy yard; on three sides of this were dilapidated farm buildings: an open barn, a granary, a feed store, stables, cowshed. The fourth side was open to fields, with a wide flagged path from the yard to the door of the house, and continuing round it. A narrow tributary flowed from this to a small cottage built close by. The buildings—farm, house, cottage—looked to him as though nothing in the way of upkeep had been done since they were put up.

At the end of one of the fields he could see a spreading and well-kept vegetable patch, but there was no sign of a garden. He thought that it would have been difficult to cultivate one, since all the animals seemed to range freely. A mare and her foal, two cows and a heifer grazed close to the house; hens and baby chicks, ducks and a lone goose wandered at will.

He left the car and walked across the yard. Three dogs came barking from the back of the house, scattering the cats and kittens sunning themselves on the front doorstep. He paused to reassure the barkers and then approached the house. Before he reached the door, it opened and Hazel Paget appeared in the doorway. She was wearing rubber boots, and over her dress was a paint-smeared smock. She was carrying two small food troughs. She gave a loud hail.

"Bernie. Oh, Bernie."

From the direction of the yard came a man dressed in gaiters, patched breeches and a jacket with leather inserts at the elbows. He looked about forty—short, thickset and muscular. Hazel gave him the troughs and he walked away, the cats and dogs following, growling, spitting and squabbling as they went.

"That's two lots fed." She spoke with relief. "Come in. Miss

Horn told Mavis to phone and say you were on your way."

He followed her through a large, square, unfurnished, stone-floored hall from which rose a staircase with beautiful oak treads. Three of the rails of the banisters, he saw, were missing. Then he found himself in a room which appeared to be a combined kitchen, living room and laundry. There was a large, old-fashioned cooking range on which were saucepans and a pressure cooker. In the center of the room was a plastic-topped table on which were the preparations for a meal. Four wooden chairs were ranged round it. Across the ceiling was slung a clothesline on which garments were airing. In a corner was an ironing board. A window, wide open, gave a pleasant view of the cottage and the surrounding fields.

"We interview distinguished visitors in the sitting room." She nodded towards an open hatch on which there was a television set on a revolving stand. "But I'm getting lunch ready, so do you mind if we talk in here?" She indicated a chair. "Sit down. I'll work; you can talk. You want to know what happened to the things in Mr. Horn's house?"

"Yes. Miss Horn said you were working for the firm of auctioneers who—"

"I wasn't working for them. They brought their own staff from London. All I did was make a few lists, and I acted as a sort of liaison between them and the lawyers."

There had been time to look around. He saw nothing that was not more or less in need of replacement, nothing that was modern in design. The saucepans looked like those he had sometimes glimpsed on rubbish dumps; the dresser against the wall opposite was hung with an assortment of plates and cups, none of which matched. A row of widemouthed glass jars contained stores that bore no relation to the labels gummed onto them—the one marked sugar held coffee, the one for coffee held rice. Eyeing the out-of-date implements and equipment, he wondered whether this girl was a better cook than secretary; she seemed to have the same difficulty in finding anything she was looking for.

There were no wall cupboards, but on the doors of two large ones standing in corners he saw paintings of fruit and flowers and vegetables in what he thought odd juxtaposition: carrots with camellias, turnips with tulips, roses with radishes.

"Like them?" she asked. "Or don't you like lilac teamed with lettuces?"

"It's—they're original. You did them?"

"When I was twelve. What do you think of them?"

"They show great promise."

"They do. They did. Unfortunately, the promise wasn't fulfilled. Why do you want those lists?"

"Lists?"

With an effort, he brought his mind back to his own business. He raised his voice to make himself heard over the hissing of the pressure cooker.

"Did you see the list of things that were sold?" he asked.

"No. The ones I made were handed over to the auctioneers. I didn't see any lists after that. What exactly are you after?"

"A small silver flagon. Do you remember putting that on a list?"

She took a moment or two to consider, and then shook her head.

"No. Did Mr. Horn have one?"

"I don't know. He wrote to my father and offered to show him his collection. My father meant to come, but didn't want to put off the trip that he and my stepmother were about to make. He died shortly after returning to England."

"When did Mr. Horn write to him?"

"At the end of March. The twenty-eighth. My father left England on the thirtieth and got back on the tenth of April. He died three days later."

"About three weeks before Mr. Horn." She moved the pressure cooker to one side to reduce the hissing. "Why have you waited fourteen months before coming to find out if Mr. Horn had it in his collection?"

"I shouldn't have waited. I should have gone on where my father left off. I wouldn't have started on this search if my stepmother hadn't pointed out that this might be a last chance to complete the set of twelve flagons."

"Was this one stolen?"

"Nobody knows. It disappeared during a move. Five disappeared. Four were subsequently found."

"When did they disappear?"

He hesitated.

"In the year seventeen hundred and two."

Her eyes, widening in astonishment, left the salad she was mixing and rested on him. They were not grey, he saw; they were greeny-grey.

"*What* did you say?" she asked slowly.

"You asked me when the flagons disappeared. I told you."

"You said—you said seventeen hundred and—"

"—and two."

"But that's—that's over two hundred years ago!"

"Correct."

"After two hundred years, you've begun to look for this flagon?"

"Well, I've not—"

He stopped. A smile had appeared on her face, had widened and had become a gurgle. Sinking onto a chair, she gave way to unrestrained laughter; when she tried to stop, she only became more helpless. It was an infectious sound, and there was an answering smile on his lips.

At last she sobered.

"I'm sorry about that. I don't know why it struck me as being so funny. But—"

She was off again. When she could speak, she put a question.

"What started you off, after two hundred years?" she asked.

"It isn't exactly a start. It's been a kind of intermittent search. Every fifty years or so, one of my forebears stirred in his sleep and spread the word that there was a large reward waiting for anyone with any information—that kind of thing. My father was the last one who tried to pick up the scent."

"Did Mr. Horn know about it?"

"He wrote to my father after he'd talked to a dealer in Salisbury. The dealer, like the majority of reputable dealers in this country, had been asked to keep an eye open. He must have mentioned that the flagon had a Dutch connection. The Helders were originally Dutch. I thought the Horns were too, but Miss Horn said they weren't. If Mr. Horn by any chance had the flagon in his collection, he would have known that he might have a good customer in my father. So he wrote to him—not mentioning the flagon. I don't say there's much hope that he had it, but if he had it, it must have been sold in one of those sales at the Manor. So I'm trying to find out who bought it."

She studied him for some moments—the first look of real interest she had accorded him. He saw no reason why he should not study her while she was studying him. Nice little nose. Almost dead straight eyebrows, not fair like her hair, but dark, like her eyelashes.

In the silence, there came from a room above the sound of chords constantly repeated, played on a piano.

"Your brother, composing?" he asked.

"Yes. Who told you he was a composer?"

"Miss Field."

"I wish things fitted better in this life," she said. "Look at you, trying to connect Mr. Horn and a flagon. Hugo's trying to connect his music with a publisher and a conductor and a first-class orchestra. You're not in the music business, I suppose?"

"I'm afraid not."

"Pity. He'll find his conductor in time. I hope you find your flagon. I'll do what I can to get something out of the auctioneers, but I don't think you'll find it by waiting to get hold of lists. There are quicker ways."

"For example?"

"Well, *think*. Mr. Horn lived at the Manor all his life, and it was a big place and he needed servants. There was a large staff up there once, but that was before my time. What he had all the years I knew him was what he called the loyal remnants —cook, housemaid, housekeeper. The three of them were with him for as long as I can remember, and they were with him when he died. So why don't you ask them if he had your flagon?"

"Are they in Steeplewood?"

"Yes. The cook's living in a caravan. The other two are sisters and live in a small house they bought. Mr. Horn left all of them quite large legacies. If you want to see them, I'll give you their names and addresses. Seeing them seems to me a better bet than trying to get hold of lists."

"Did you know Mr. Horn well?"

"I knew him all my life, but I can't say I knew him well. I didn't often see him. I used to go up when invited, if I couldn't get out of it. I don't know anything about antiques and I thought he was rather a silly old man. I only saw part of his collection. It was always changing—he'd sell some things, buy others." She paused, glanced at the clock and found that it had stopped. "I'm sorry—I forgot all about asking you if you'd like some coffee. It's too late now, isn't it?"

"I wouldn't say so."

"You want some?"

"Yes, please."

"Wouldn't you rather have beer?"

"No."

"Well, there's coffee in that jar, and water in the tap, and a mug on the dresser and milk in the fridge. Help yourself."

It was instant coffee, which he disliked. The mugs—he took down two from their hooks—were of the plain, thick white type he had rejected for the firm's canteen. Getting out the milk, he saw her engagement ring resting on the edge of the refrigerator.

"Who's the second mug for?" she asked.

"You. I never drink alone."

"You won't have to." She was looking out of the window. "Here's Dilys."

"Your sister-in-law?"

"Yes. She teaches history at the school during the week, and on Saturdays she coaches pupils in the town." She waited until her sister-in-law came in. "Dilys, this is Mr. Helder, who's here asking about Mr. Horn's collection."

Dilys looked about twenty-eight. She was tall and thin, with a long face, long, tapering fingers and long, storklike legs. Her hair was dark and smooth and short, her eyes brown. Her manner was quiet but authoritative, and he could imagine the history classes springing to attention. She nodded to William and then her glance went to the ceiling and she stood listening to the sound of the piano.

"Any idea how it's going?" she asked Hazel.

"No. But it's going. He was working when I came in, and he hasn't stopped since."

"You didn't go up with any coffee or anything?"

"Of course not."

"Good. What time did you say you were meeting Rupert?"

"About one."

"You needn't hurry. When I passed, he and his mother were outside her house telling the neighbours how the fence got flattened. Some idiot ran into it."

"I ran into it," said William. "That is, if you're referring to Mr. Caradon."

"That's right. Hazel's intended."

He was not unprepared; there had been time to guess what was coming. There had also been time enough to wonder how she could possibly have become involved with, not to say engaged to, a man of that kind.

"You knocked down the fence?" Hazel asked.

"The dog ran out. Mrs. Caradon ran after it. Neither looked to see if anything was coming. I had a choice of spilling blood or crashing the fence. Caradon came out to investigate."

"He informed the bystanders that you'd been drinking," said Dilys. "I shall testify that I found you sober. Why are you making your own coffee?"

"Because I'm too busy to make it for him," Hazel said. "He could have had beer and saved himself the trouble." She unhooked a third mug, removed the chopping board and several jars from the table and pulled out another chair. "Mr. Helder came to Steeplewood to look for a flagon his family mislaid about two hundred years ago."

"Two hundred years?"

"That's right."

"Helder . . . Dutch?" Dilys asked William.

"Originally. The flagon was one of a set of twelve presented to the family by William of Orange."

"Five went missing," Hazel explained, "four turned up again, and he's hunting for the last one. He thinks it might have been in Mr. Horn's collection—but I made a list of the things, and there was no flagon."

"You're an expert at leaving things out of lists," Dilys said.

"Those lists were checked."

"I see. What made you think that Mr. Horn had it, Mr. Helder?"

"It was because—"

He stopped. A face had appeared at the window. There was silence for some moments; William looked expectant; the expression on the faces of Hazel and Dilys was one of complete bewilderment.

It was a handsome face; a cheerful, youthful face, flanked by luxurious black side whiskers and topped by a mass of tight black curls. A confident voice addressed them—a well-pronounced French greeting followed by English that had a strong Cockney flavour.

"Mesdames, monsieur. Bonjour. Sorry to disturb the coffee break. I'm looking for my fiancée, name of Mavis Field. This is where she lives, no? I asked at the station for Miss Mavis Field and then I asked at a couple of shops, and between them they got me here. Is she around?"

Hazel's expression was now one of consternation. As she seemed to have been struck dumb, Dilys answered the question.

"She lives in that cottage over there. She'll be back in about an hour."

"In that case, I'll join the party."

The face vanished. A few moments later the visitor, of medium height, well made, entered the kitchen. He was wearing a tight-waisted jacket, jeans, a turtle-neck sweater, and was carrying a canvas suitcase. He put the case on the floor and looked hopefully at the steaming coffee.

"Don't want to rob the natives," he said, "but how about squeezing out another mugful? The name's Purley, in case Mavis didn't mention it. Nathaniel Purley, spelt with a *u*. Joby for short."

"Sit down, won't you?" Dilys brought a fourth mug. "Does Mavis know you're coming?"

"No. Thought I'd give her a surprise." He took the mug of coffee and sipped it with noisy enjoyment. "I know the two ladies present: Mrs. Paget, Miss Paget. I don't know the gent."

"Mr. Helder," said Dilys.

"An honour. And the piano player upstairs, that's Mr.

Paget, the composer. You see, Mavis told me all about you. Did she tell you all about me?"

Hazel seemed to have recovered.

"All she told us, when she came back from her Easter holiday at Bournemouth," she said, "was that she'd met somebody there and was thinking of marrying him."

"No details?"

"None."

"I'm not surprised. Cagey, she is. It's the head of that school that's the trouble. Mavis has this cockeyed idea that she had to ask her permission. Why? She's well over the age of consent. And I can support her. My mum's got a flourishing hairdressing business in Bournemouth. She's given up doing hair, but she's still in charge—money, supplies, things like that. I'm head of what's called the salon. I've got a big clientele of ladies who won't let anybody but me attend to them. So I can't stay here long—they can't do without me. We'll have to go back tomorrow, or the day after that at the latest."

"We?" Hazel repeated.

"Well, of course. You don't think I came all the way from Bournemouth just to see where she lived, do you? Be reasonable. When I put her on the train after Easter to come back here, her last words were that the minute she got back to the school, she'd give in her notice. But did she? She did not. So I told Mum I'd come up and get her. 'Quite right, Joby,' Mum said. 'You do that.' "

"Couldn't you have told her you were coming?" Hazel asked.

"What was the use? I could tell from her letters that she'd fallen under the old witch's curse. Who's this Horn, for Pete's sake? Listen to me, Miss Paget, or let's make it Hazel. It's more than two months since she left Bournemouth, and still no notice, no goodbye to Steeplewood, no nothing. She can skate round what I say in my letters, but when I talk to her, she'll listen. And I'm going to have it out with the Horn, too, while I'm here."

Hazel rose.

"Look, I think the best thing you can do is wait for Mavis at the cottage. She won't be long. She leaves the door unlocked, so you'll be able to get in."

"Good idea. À bientôt."

He rose, picked up his bag and went out. In silence, they watched him walking across the short intervening space to the cottage.

"Didn't you have any idea he was coming?" Dilys asked Hazel.

"Good heavens, no!"

"Are you sure she didn't guess he'd come? She must know he's not the kind that sits and waits patiently."

"If she'd had any idea, she would have said something to me. She wouldn't have risked letting him come here and set the town talking. The station and two shops—you heard him. It'll get back to Miss Horn before the day's over."

William spoke for the first time.

"Does it matter if it does?" he asked.

She brought her glance to him; he had the feeling that she had forgotten who he was or why he was there.

"What did you say?"

"I asked—it's not my business—if it mattered that Miss Horn found out."

"Yes, it matters. It shouldn't. Mavis has a sort of . . . fixation about what she owes Miss Horn. In my opinion, she's paid back in work whatever Miss Horn did for her, but she won't see it that way. She's attractive; men like her and she goes out with them, and then after a time, Miss Horn finds a way of putting a stop to it. Not openly—just subtly. I've done what I could to argue Mavis into sense, but all she says is that she owes Miss Horn too much to let her down. The truth is that Miss Horn has got herself a combined cook, secretary, accountant, lady's maid and general runaround, and she's not likely to enthuse about losing her. As far as I can see, all Miss Horn did for her was pay for her secretarial training; but this is the one subject on which Mavis won't talk rationally."

"Here she is," Dilys said.

"Is she going straight to the cottage?"

"Yes. No. She's coming here."

Mavis entered a few moments later. She put a small package on the table.

"Honey," she told them. "A present from Miss Horn. She knows you've got your own, but—" She sensed tension, and stopped. "Has something bad happened?"

"Someone's waiting for you at the cottage," Hazel said.

Nobody could mistake the effect of this announcement; it was panic.

"Oh, my goodness! Who's waiting?"

"Nathaniel Purley. Joby for short."

"You're—you're making it up."

"Go and see."

"He's—he came here?"

"Yes. To take you back. He plans to leave tomorrow or the next day. He got tired of waiting."

"Oh, my Lord!" She sank onto a chair. "If Miss Horn knew about it, then—"

"What does it matter if she does?" Hazel asked reasonably. "Aren't you ever going to get away from her? Remember all that fuss in January, and last Christmas too, when she thought you might be getting serious about somebody—what business is it of hers?"

"She feels she's my—my guardian, in a way. You don't know what she's done for me."

"Well, exactly what?" Dilys asked. "Tell us, and we'll be in a better position to take sides. What exactly is this load of gratitude you're carrying?"

"She's done everything. You don't know about my mother and my brothers and sisters—eight of us altogether, and no money and living in a terrible broken-down house in Cardiff with three other families. My father went away and didn't come back, and my mother worked at whatever jobs she could get, and it was lucky that some of us were clever and got on well at school. When I was fifteen, I went to work in a shop in Abergavenny. That's only thirty miles from Cardiff, so I could go home every Sunday, and it was a nice place, and historic, too: it was burnt by Owen Glendower in 1404, and—"

"Never mind about Owen Glendower. Go on about Miss Horn," requested Dilys.

"Well, the shop was just a little one, but it had a lot of customers. I was one of the cash girls because I was good at figures. Miss Horn was on holiday and she came into the shop and saw me, and we talked a little and she came back three or four times and then asked if I would take her to see my mother. So I did, and she said she would like to give me a job as secretary in her school, but I would have to have a training first, and she would pay my mother what I had been paying her from my salary, until I was earning money again. I went back to Scotland with her and she sent me to a secretarial school and paid my fees, and she paid for my clothes. She even paid for my holidays."

"If she paid for the Bournemouth one, she may live to regret it," Dilys said drily. "What it adds up to is that she had you trained, and since then you've been paying her back. Are you going to stay with her forever?"

"No. Oh, no. Just for a little while more. If I go, she must find someone else, and—"

"Until you go," Hazel said, "she won't bother. How often

have I begged you, since you came back from Bournemouth, to go into her room and tell her definitely that you were going to get married?"

"I went. You know I went. You saw me go."

"I saw you come out again leaving everything the way it was. The first time, she put you off by saying she was busy with the exams. The second time, she pretended she hadn't been well and the doctor had advised her to avoid worry."

"It was true. She just said to wait a little while and we'd talk about it."

"Where exactly did you meet Nathaniel Purley?" Dilys enquired. "At his mother's salon?"

There was a pause. The answer came at last in a dreamy, reminiscent tone.

"Yes, there. But I didn't go to have my hair done. The prices were high, terribly high, much too high for me, because he's such a wonderful hairdresser. He went to Paris for his training. I only went to the hairdresser's to wait for a girl I made friends with in the train from London the day before. While I was waiting for her, he came over and talked to me, and he said he would like to do my hair and he wouldn't charge me anything, and he'd come and do it at the hotel where I was staying. I liked him, see? So he came. And that's how it started."

"How did it go on?"

"Well, we liked each other, and then he took a room at the hotel so we could see a lot of each other, and we fell in love and I promised to marry him but I said I had to come back here to make it all right with Miss Horn and give her proper notice."

"Did you tell her he was a hairdresser?"

"Yes. I think I hinted that he owned the business—because he will, one day. He took me to see his mother, and we got on very well together. She liked me."

"So now what?" Dilys asked. "Are you going to take him to see Miss Horn?"

"No. Oh, no! I couldn't do that. I'll have to break it to her little bit by little bit, sort of gently. He'll have to keep out of her way. I don't think she'd—well, she wouldn't understand anybody like him."

"Anything we can do?" Hazel asked.

"Please, couldn't you let him stay here on the farm for only a little while, two, three days? He isn't only good at hairdressing; he can do lots of things. And he isn't lazy. He'll do anything you ask him. He'll help Bernie; he likes animals. Couldn't he stay in the room above the stables that Bernie and his mother don't use?"

"According to him, he'll only need it for two days."

"He's got to go back soon. He's *got* to. Then I'll give in my notice and—"

"He's heard that before," Dilys remarked. "What happens if he tackles Miss Horn?"

"It would finish everything. You know it would—you know her. She wouldn't understand why I fell in love with him. I suppose you don't understand either, but he's—he's—I can't explain. He seems a bit spoilt, but if you saw the fuss they all make of him down there, you wouldn't be surprised. Long queues of ladies all waiting to make appointments, and they won't have any of the assistants; it has to be him. The place is making good money. The only thing Miss Horn could object to—she thinks I ought to put off marrying until I—"

"Until you pick out someone she's picked out for you," Hazel ended. "You'd better go over to the cottage. You'll have to share your lunch with him. Tell him if he's staying, he'll have to earn his keep, or be a paying guest, like you."

She was gone. They saw her walk at a sober pace towards the cottage. The door opened, and Nathaniel Purley stepped outside. With the greatest ease, he swung her plump form into his arms, carried her inside and closed the door with his foot.

"So there," said Dilys. "End of Act One."

"But not a comedy," Hazel said. "Miss Horn has got her claws in. I've heard her talking Mavis out of marriage. All said in a nice, cosy, motherly way. Mavis is no fool, but to deal with Miss Horn you need cunning, and she hasn't got any."

William had been on his feet for some time. With great reluctance, he said that it was time he went. Nobody contradicted him. Hazel walked with him to the car.

"I hope you find your flagon," she said.

"Flagon? Oh—thank you. You haven't given me the addresses of Mr. Horn's cook and housekeeper."

She hesitated for a moment.

"I'll do better than that," she said. "I'll take you to see them."

His drooping spirits soared.

"Thank you. When?"

"It would have to be a Saturday or a Sunday. Has Mavis got your phone number?"

"Yes."

"I'll get it from her and fix a day. I wouldn't expect too much if I were you; they didn't have much to do with Mr. Horn's collection. I'm sorry there wasn't time to hear more about the history of the flagon."

"I'd like to hear more of the history of Nathaniel Purley. One day."

"I can read his future for you. Miss Horn will get to know he's here; she'll send for him, make mincemeat of him and pack him back to his salon."

"You think so?"

"Don't you?"

"No. If you're taking bets, put my money on Nathaniel."

He drove back to London with his mind in considerable

confusion. He had planned to tell his stepmother about this exploratory visit, but flagons seemed to have been pushed aside to give place to personalities. He did not think she would be interested in a tangled tale of secretaries, hairdressers, cowmen, headmistresses or history teachers. She would perhaps be interested in hearing about Hazel Paget; but when he attempted to give his mind to this angle of the morning's adventures, it seemed to slip out of control. If he said anything at all about the visit, he decided, he would say as little as possible about the Pagets and nothing about Hazel.

It was only when he stopped the car at the Helder building that he remembered his intention of driving back through Cambridge.

3

THERE WAS NO TELEPHONE CALL. A SATURDAY CAME AND went, and another, and another, and all he could do was speculate: Caradon had been told of his visit and had ruled against her seeing any more of him. Or she had come to the conclusion that looking for a flagon that had been missing for two hundred years was not a matter of much interest to her. Or—the thought was painful—she had forgotten him.

He would have liked to know how much time Rupert Caradon spent at Steeplewood. His weekday activities were much publicized, showing that he had a full schedule; perhaps it was only at weekends that he could see his fiancée.

Speculating brought no solace. And music, which had once made his free evenings so pleasant, seemed to have lost its magic. He played his newest recordings and sat, he thought, listening, but he did not know when they came to an end. The view from his windows for the first time seemed to lack something; there was not enough woodland. His kitchen, when he went into it, seemed to have a bare, clinical look. He lunched, dined, went to the theater, but without any of his former enjoyment.

He had said nothing to his stepmother about his visit to Steeplewood. He would have to mention it when they met, but he shrank from giving her details. There was not much to report, and nothing to conceal, but he found himself increasingly reluctant to discuss the visit with her. He had not yet sorted out his own impressions; he did not want to listen to hers. If Hazel Paget did not telephone, if he heard nothing further from Miss Horn, he would drive down to the school and see if either of the secretaries remembered his previous visit. Perhaps there would no longer be two of them; Mavis Field might have followed her hairdresser back to his salon. It would have been interesting to know what had happened, but nobody was likely to tell him. Apart from knocking down a fence, he did not think he had created any stir in the town.

He was glad to go over to Holland on business; he spent two days in Delft and three at The Hague. He had always been glad to go; he had never been so glad to get back. There had been no telephone calls of interest during his absence. He had seen to it, before leaving, that every telephone was manned during every waking hour; but she had not kept her promise, if it was a promise.

He refused his stepmother's invitation to a concert, but agreed to dine with her. As she preferred dining out, he took her to a restaurant. She chose the food and he chose the wine, an arrangement they had come to in his father's lifetime. Over coffee, he brought up the subject of Steeplewood.

"I've been meaning to tell you," he said. He paused while the waiter held a light for her cigarette. "I went down to Steeplewood."

The hand that was lifting the cigarette to her lips stopped. Her eyes widened.

"You *went*! When?"

"Shortly after we'd been talking about it."

"Shortly— But that was *weeks* ago! And you've said nothing about it until this minute!"

"I'm sorry. Remember that I've been away. And there really was nothing to tell. Mr. Horn's dead."

"Dead? When?"

"Shortly after Father died. A niece of his, who lived in Scotland, inherited the Manor and everything in it. She didn't want the contents, but she kept the house. She's turned it into a girls' school."

"But the collection?"

"It was sold. There were two sales. She's going to see if she can get me the list of what was auctioned. She kept the pictures—Dutch school. But that story about the Horns being of Dutch origin has no basis in fact."

"Nothing else? No other leads?"

"A suggestion that I might talk to the servants who worked for Mr. Horn?"

"Do you know who they are?"

"I'm waiting to hear."

She said nothing for a time. Her expression was one of deep dejection.

"It's my fault," she said at last. "It was a chance, and we let it go. I let it go. One word from me, and your father would have been happy to put off the trip."

"You're being wise after the event, Stella."

"No, I'm not. We both had a *feeling*. I know I'm prone to them, but your father wasn't. We both felt that there was a strong possibility that Mr. Horn had that flagon. But we didn't talk about it on the trip. Thank God, we enjoyed ourselves; it didn't weigh on our minds. But I told my sister, when I went down to see her when your father and I got back to England, that as soon as I got back home to your father, I was going to make him go down to Steeplewood."

"Horn wasn't really a collector. He was a dealer."

"That makes the possibility even stronger. He wrote because he had something to sell. He wrote to your father because he knew your father would buy it."

"Perhaps. But if there was a flagon, it'll be listed, and we'll know who bought it, and we can go after it."

"You think so? I don't. I've never found that things worked out like that. A lost chance in my life was always a lost chance; there was never a second one. When are you going down again?"

"Possibly at the weekend."

"You wouldn't like me to go with you?"

"At this stage, no. I'll keep you in touch with anything that happens. If anything does."

He took her home and drove away with a feeling of frustration. Up to now, matters throughout his life had run smoothly. People were given orders, and as they had been chosen for their expertise, they carried out the orders promptly and efficiently. Any business, once begun, proceeded step by step to its conclusion. But he was now in a situation in which there was no continuity. He had made a beginning and it had proved to be the end. He had put in a coin, but the machine wasn't working. Nobody in Steeplewood had ever heard of the Helders, and nobody was interested in the number of flagons they possessed.

He sent Dirk to bed on his return, and poured himself a drink. He sat on the sofa and picked up the evening paper. There was nothing of interest. He tossed it aside, and it lay beside him; and he was about to rouse himself and get ready for bed when a name caught his eye.

Dessin.

Dessin was to play a Beethoven concerto. Dessin was the pianist who last year had played the piano concerto composed by Hugo Paget. Surely one of the three members of the family would show some interest in hearing him again? Dessin didn't often come to England; this was a rare chance for those who wanted to hear him.

If only she hadn't had a fiancé, it would have been so easy: "Look, I've got two tickets for next Sunday's concert, would you . . . ?" But that was out. And even if Dilys and Hugo Paget attended the concert, the hall would be full and he would not know whether they were present or not.

He went alone. The concert was at the Albert Hall, and every seat was sold. The cheaper seats, where he thought that people with as little to spend as the Pagets would probably be seated, seemed miles away, a sea of faces. He went to his own place resignedly. The music, at any rate, would be magnificent.

When the lights went up after the first part of the program, he did not go, as he usually did, to the bar. He twisted in his seat to allow passage to those thirstier than himself, and then settled down to gaze absently at the empty seats of the orchestra. Round him now was a mere scattering of the audience, and his eyes went without interest from face to face. Suddenly they rested on the face of Dilys Paget.

He was beside her before he knew he had left his seat. He heard himself speaking.

"Hello, Mrs. Paget."

"Oh, Mr. Helder. Nice to see you."

He longed for flowers to toss into her lap, to lay at her feet. He felt a deep affection for her for being here. She was a Paget. She was a link. She turned to the man seated beside her.

"Hugo, this is—"

"—the chap who knocked down Mrs. Caradon's fence. Happy to know you," Hugo said.

He was tall, thin, bearded, bespectacled. The eyes behind the glasses were like his sister's, and he had her way of speaking—a combination of vagueness and directness.

They moved to make room for William between them, and Hugo looked at him with frank interest.

"You weren't in Steeplewood for long," he said, "but you

seem to have left your mark. You ruined Mrs. Caradon's roses and you had the temerity to make a date with her son's fiancée. There was a scene in our kitchen. I had to break off and come downstairs to act as a referee. Caradon called you some very nasty names. Haze tried to give him back his ring, but she couldn't find it. The paying guests' pudding was forgotten, and burnt to a frazzle."

"It was sordid, but stimulating," Dilys supplemented. "So stimulating that Hugo went back upstairs and finished a passage he'd been stuck at for days. When are you coming back?"

"Your sister-in-law said she'd ring and fix a day for taking me to see Mr. Horn's old staff. So far, no word."

"I'm not surprised. She probably decided to let the dust settle after your last visit."

"I see."

"I don't think you do. It's all rather complicated and snarled up and even Hugo and I can't really see through the Caradon situation. But he didn't win the fight."

"It sounds rather as though he did."

"I thought of ringing and asking you to come down again, but this time to see Hugo and myself, and I'd take you on your flagon hunt, but Hugo said I was to keep out of it."

"What I said," Hugo amended, "was that if the matter seemed urgent and important to Mr. Helder, he would—"

"—get in touch. Well, you were wrong. He didn't. Do you often come to concerts?" she asked William.

"Yes."

"Music lover?"

"More. I'm a music producer."

"How's that?" Hugo asked.

William was about to explain when the signal sounded for the return of the audience. He rose and spoke impulsively.

"Look, will you join me for sandwiches after the show?" he asked. "I like going along to a little place not far from here for a bite after concerts. How about it?"

"If Hugo won't, I will," Dilys said decisively. "See you in the entrance. Hugo won't be with me; we'll have to wait for him. He's got to see Dessin."

They waited on the pavement. William was using the office car and it was parked not far away, but it was easier to walk to Bernstein's, a deceptively moderate-looking restaurant in a basement, with sandwiches on sale in the bar.

When Hugo joined them, his manner had changed. He had not withdrawn, but he had what William thought of as a music-soaked look. He often felt music-soaked himself on leaving a concert; he sometimes had the feeling, on getting outside, that he had drunk too much.

They walked slowly in the direction of the restaurant.

"He's a fantastic pianist, don't you agree?" Hugo came out of his absorption. "He seems to ignore his technical limitations. You heard the speed of that last movement? The critics say he attacks too fiercely, especially when he's playing Brahms, but I don't think so. Whenever I hear him play, I have the feeling that I'm listening to the work for the first time."

"That concerto of yours that he played—was it your first work?" William asked him.

"No. I played it myself at a charity concert up in Leeds, and he heard it and liked it. He asked me just now if I'd compose some two-piano works for him; he's getting married to a concert pianist, Polish, and they're going to form a professional team. I'll enjoy working on two-piano stuff again. I used to do it to amuse myself; I got an extra piano put into the church hall, and Haze and I used to play my compositions for fun."

"She plays the piano?"

"She used to, before I carted the piano upstairs. She's only an average performer, but she's useful at playing things I want to hear, and she copies out music for me, and so on."

"The symphony he was working on when you came to Steeplewood is finished," Dilys said. "Months of agony."

"Not all agony," Hugo said.

"Don't you think he ought to change his name?" Dilys asked. "Who's ever heard of a world-famous composer called Paget?"

"What do you think he ought to call himself?" William asked.

"Well, how about Pacini? There was a Giovanni Pacini who died in 1867—an Italian composer. Hugo could skip the Giovanni, but don't you think that Hugo Pacini would open more musical doors than Hugo Paget?"

"Maybe," Hugo said. "But I'll stay as I am."

They sat on stools in the bar and ordered cold beef sandwiches. To Hugo's offer of sharing the bill, William answered firmly.

"This is on me," he said. "I barged into your house and got your sister involved in a fight, and this is by way of apology."

It was a handsome apology. The men ate sparingly and drank beer, but Dilys followed the beef sandwiches with cold tongue and salad, biscuits and cheese and a large piece of chocolate cake. Her enjoyment was evident, and freely expressed.

"This is quite an evening," she said. "It's the first time I've ever sat in the most expensive seats at a concert—in fact, at any show. We would have been in the cheap seats if Dessin hadn't given Hugo two tickets."

"Did Nathaniel Purley go home alone?" William asked. "Or did Mavis go with him?"

"He's still around," Hugo answered.

"And likely to be for some time," added Dilys. "Miss Horn's reaction, when she heard of his arrival, was to invent a lot of extra work that keeps Mavis at the school until about eight every evening. She used to get home at six. So Joby's alone all day."

"He keeps busy," Hugo said. "He's a good worker, and he's

versatile, as Mavis said he was. He's done a lot of work round the farm. The only trouble is that he whistles while he works, and what he whistles doesn't go well with the anthem I'm trying to compose. Another disadvantage is that he doesn't get on with Bernie."

"Nobody gets on with Bernie," Dilys pointed out.

"True. But I would have said Bernie might have welcomed a bit of help."

"Perhaps not from Nathaniel Purley," suggested William. "He wouldn't appeal to everyone. Is Bernie a local man?"

"His parents worked on a farm about three miles away, in a place called Twinhills," Hugo told him. "His father was German, and when the war started, he and his wife and the baby —Bernie—disappeared. Nobody knew where they'd gone. After the war, the wife reappeared with Bernie, and asked my father for a job. He was only too glad to employ her. She said they'd spent the war in a prison camp, but she was pretty vague about where. I think they must have been in some kind of prison, because Bernie grew up with the feeling that it's wrong for any creature, man or beast, to be cooped up. Which means that he won't have any of the stock fenced in, which means that he wastes a lot of time fetching the cows back from the neighboring properties and looking for eggs all over the fields." He shook his head in response to William's offer of more beer. "About this flagon: what exactly are you going to ask Mr. Horn's old servants?"

"If they ever saw it in his collection."

"Is it an unusual piece that they'd be likely to remember?"

"I think so. Every flagon has the Orange coat of arms, and on the foot of each flagon the initials W.H."

"What set you off searching for it?"

"My stepmother. She presented a bridge prize to someone who came from Steeplewood, and came to see me to remind me that my father had only just missed the chance of seeing that Horn collection before he died. So I drove down to Steeplewood."

"Straight into Mrs. Caradon's fence." Dilys rose to leave. "Thank you for the lovely food."

"Would you ever have time to come and listen to my recordings?" William asked them. "They might interest you. I've got some musical friends. Three or four of them are professionals, and I can scrape a cello. We've recorded some quartets and quintets for our own amusement—Sammartini, Dittersdorf, Max Reger, among others. I can't assemble an orchestra and ask Dessin to play a concerto, but—"

"Max Reger?" Hugo said. "I'd like to hear something of his."

"When you've got some spare time, will you come and listen to them?"

"We'd like to. Thanks."

He walked with them to the car and drove them to the station. Dilys, getting out, paused to say something to William.

"I'm sorry Haze didn't call you. But she's had a lot on her mind lately. Things haven't been easy for her one way or another. But I'll be happy to go flagon-hunting with you. If you'll ring in a day or two, I'll let you know when I'm free."

"Thank you."

He drove away, happier than he had been for weeks. Matters would now move. In a day or so, he would telephone. He would drive down to the farm and Dilys would take him to see the Horn servants. A nice girl, Dilys. He wondered how she felt about having to give up housekeeping and going back to teaching while her husband shut himself away with a piano.

He did not have to telephone. The following evening, when he returned from dining with friends, Dirk told him that there was a message on his bedside table. It was not from Dilys: it was from Hazel. It was brief:

Miss Paget will be free on Saturday at ten thirty.

* * *

He reached the farm at ten fifteen. As he drew up at the gate, the cowman Bernie was detaching an empty trailer from behind a bicycle. William said good morning and was about to walk on when he spoke.

"Morning, sir. You wouldn't like some nice strawberries, would you? I took a grand lot to the market today, and I didn't see any finer. Big juicy ones. I'll pick some for you and you'll find them in your car when you come out."

"Well—"

"You'd best settle now. I mightn't be around later. Busy day for me, Saturday."

"Oh, well . . . how much?"

Bernie named his price.

"Cheaper than you'd pay if you bought 'em in the market. They were selling 'em at twice that."

"I've only got notes, I'm afraid."

"That's all right; I've got change." He leaned over to take a small canvas bag from the basket fixed to the handlebars of the bicycle. William saw that it was full of money.

"Here y'are, sir. Sixty-five, eighty . . . hundred."

William kept his palm outstretched.

"That's only eighty-five," he pointed out.

"You sure?"

"I'm quite sure."

"Oh, well, if you're sure . . ."

"You can count it."

"Oh, no need, sir. I can trust you not to do a poor man down. Eighty-five, ninety, hundred. Thank you, sir."

William walked on. A man to watch, he decided.

He saw Joby outside the cottage, in jeans and nothing more, painting the frame of one of the windows. He crossed over to speak to him.

"How's everything?" he enquired.

"So-so. I'm still here, you see. You'll have to pull me up by the roots when we leave."

"Any progress?"

"Not in the direction of Bournemouth. When you're dealing with women, you have to be—wait till I find that word— flexible. I saw that if I rushed her, she'd panic, so I changed the time schedule. Beside that, the old Horn showed her claws, and she's kept her working overtime. That's helped to prove to Mavis that she isn't the old duck she thought she was, but she's still yapping about what she owes her, and that." He suspended work for a moment, brush in air. "I don't wonder the old witch wants to grapple with hoops of steel. That's Shakespeare, did you know? I dunno which one, must be *Hamlet*, they're all *Hamlet*, aren't they? Did I see you giving some dough to that old swindler Bernie?"

"He sold me some strawberries."

"And shortchanged you, I bet. I lived in the room next to his over the stables for four whole days, so I know all about him. Biggest chiseller this side of Crook's Corner. You watch him, that's all."

"Have you fixed a day for going back?"

"Not yet. I'm biding my time. Then I'm going to make her give the old Horn a month's salary and skip the notice. And then we're off. Pity, in a way; I could make a good living in this town. I've been making a packet doing a bit of hairdressing. These chaps here wouldn't last long in a decent salon —amateurs, the lot of 'em. As well as hairdressing, I've done a bit of gardening here and there, and as well as that, a waiter chap lent me his clothes and I took his place at a couple of fiestas at the hotel, handing round drinks. Yes, I could do well if I stayed up here, but I couldn't leave Mum in the lurch."

"Well, good luck," said William.

"And the same to you. You'll need it. But I've been watching her and I reckon she's worth suffering for. Mavis says it's a pity you haven't come down here more often; you can't do much if you only stick to weekends, can you? Propinquity, that's the thing. I know that the Caradon clothes horse used to hang around, but you don't call him an obstacle, do you? If you do, which he isn't, aren't you the chap that knocks down fences? You owe it to yourself; you should have heard what he called you. I listened in to the fight they had in the kitchen. I look through keyholes, too. It's all education. Well, don't stand talking—go in and see her."

Hazel let him in and led him to the kitchen. She was not, he noted, wearing her engagement ring.

"I asked for the morning off," she told him. "Dilys took another coaching job and we thought it would be weeks before either of us found the time to help you. So I asked Mavis to take over for me at the school."

"Why should you help me at all?"

She was at the stove, making coffee.

"I haven't worked that out," she answered. "I told Dilys that if you could wait two hundred years, a few more wouldn't make much difference. But she said we ought to do what we could. She's a kind girl."

"Aren't you?"

"I do a good deed now and then, but I haven't got a kind disposition. Not like Dilys's." Her glance went to the ceiling, and she listened for a moment to the sound of the piano. "Like that, for instance. I don't think I could have gone back to work, as she did, and waited for my husband to become a successful composer. I would have done it, but not as cheerfully as she did." She took a saucepan of milk off the stove. "Black, or with milk?"

"Half and half, please."

They sat at the plastic-topped table. The sun slanted in, warming a sleeping cat. The dogs dozed at their feet. A hen clucked in the distance. They sat in silence, but he felt that it was a comfortable, friendly silence.

"Dilys loves this house, battered as it is," she said musingly after a time. "She used to like getting up early and making Hugo's breakfast and seeing him off, and he came home to dinner by candlelight, fire lit on cold evenings, drinks at hand, friends dropping in. They were on the point of starting a family. Now she's back at a job she likes far less than running a house."

"You gave up something too, didn't you?"

"No." Her tone told him that she was not going to discuss her own affairs. "I saw you talking to Joby."

"He says he's changed his tactics."

"He has. But he's left his options open. He's a pretty talented liar."

"Won't he be too much for her to handle?"

"No. I've learned a lot about him since he came—and a lot more about Mavis. She doesn't let him have things all his own way. Did he tell you he'd moved into the cottage?"

"No, he didn't. But now I come to think of it, he used the past tense when he said he'd lived in the room above the stables."

"He soon moved out of it. Just as well he did; he and Bernie were on the point of reaching for weapons."

"How did Miss Horn react to the move?"

"She didn't say anything about it to Mavis. But she knows. Bernie's a talker. He talks when he goes to the market on Saturday mornings, and he's at the Foresters' Arms every Saturday evening."

"He sold me some strawberries. Does he sell all the produce?"

"He sells the surplus. He keeps us in fruit and vegetables; the money he gets from the rest goes into his pocket because it's the way we pay him. We couldn't afford to keep him otherwise. Have you got a garden in London?"

"No. Unless you count a roof garden."

"Potatoes and cabbages?"

"No. Azaleas, and tubs with tangerine trees."

"We presumed you weren't married. Were you ever?"

"No."

"Didn't you want to be?"

"In a general sense, yes. I didn't think I'd still be single at thirty-four."

"Brothers and sisters—?"

"—have I none. And no mother. And a father who died before he had a chance to see Mr. Horn."

"Which brings us back to business. Before we set out to ask his old servants if they ever saw a flagon in Mr. Horn's collection, could you tell me what it looked like? I'm not too clear about the difference between a flagon and a goblet."

"A goblet's a large drinking cup without a handle. A flagon's got a narrow neck and can be large or small. Ours are miniature—not much larger than a wineglass—with two handles that look like little ears. I've never seen any others like them."

"Are they worth an awful lot?"

He hesitated.

"Mr. Horn—if he had the last one—would have thought so."

"Did he know it was the last of a set?"

"He must have done. The dealers certainly know, and the Salisbury dealer would have told him."

"Was your father searching on his own, or were you helping him?"

"He was searching on his own. My stepmother thought he ought to do something to get it back. Like you, she thought two hundred years a long time—too long."

She was getting up to clear away the mugs and to lay the table in the adjoining room. He rose to help her. He would have liked to go on sitting close to her, listening, looking. She had a quiet charm; her manner was unemphatic, almost casual, and she made no effort to entertain, but he found himself increasingly under a kind of spell. He felt dejectedly that she had little interest in him. He had not expected her to have any; she had her own life to lead, and it appeared to be a full one; but it was difficult for him to accept the situation without a feeling of frustration. He wished he could say something, do something, that would bring some curiosity to her eyes. Grey-green, beautiful—cool, impersonal.

"I haven't heard any more about the fence," he told her as they walked out to his car.

"You will. It was a new one, very expensive."

"Has Mrs. Caradon lived there long?"

"No."

Once more, there was the monosyllable, and nothing added to it. They could talk about him, it seemed, but not about her.

Seated beside him in the car, she made him pause before starting the engine.

"A brief briefing," she said. "All these three you're going to see are pretty old. Mr. Horn was eighty when he died, and these servants weren't much younger. I don't know whether they were fond of him or not; probably not, because he wasn't what you could call a likable man. But he paid them well, paid them far more than any other servants got in Steeplewood, and he made them very comfortable. Miss Horn keeps quoting him: 'Make your servants as comfortable as you make yourself, and they'll stay with you.' "

He started the car and followed her directions.

"You don't like Miss Horn, do you?" he asked.

"I suppose it shows—does it?"

"It sounds, when you talk about her."

"The part of her I hate is her attitude towards Mavis— patronizing, proprietary. Mavis thinks it's kindness, but it isn't. I've been close to it for too long; I suppose it gets on my nerves. But there are things about her—about Miss Horn

—you have to give her credit for. She takes an interest in the town; she's on several committees and she makes herself felt. Nobody's heard her air any views on racial prejudice, but the first time there was trouble inside the school over a black pupil, she threw out the white offenders. No argument, no fuss; she just told them they weren't to come back any more. Of course, the parents arrived in force to protest, but she simply told them that she was going to run her school in her way, and not in their way. So for that, I like her. What did you think of her?"

"I was only in the presence a few minutes. She was very grand, and very hard underneath, I thought. She accused her uncle of suffering from *folie de grandeur*, but I think she's got more than a touch of it."

"It was that manner that made such an impression when she first came to Steeplewood. See that castle up on that hill?"

The hill was some distance away, but the half-ruined building he had glimpsed on his first visit stood out clearly.

"It looks derelict," he observed.

"It is, more or less. Part of it is still habitable."

"Who owns it?"

"My godmother, Lady Storring. Ever heard of her?"

"There was a Lord Storring who used to campaign for the abolition of zoos. That one?"

"Yes. He was like Bernie: he couldn't bear to see anything in cages. His point was that zoos were originally meant to educate, but now that everybody can watch nature close-ups on colour television, the zoos ought to go."

"I think so too. Why did he stop campaigning?"

"He died two years ago. He left the castle to my godmother. He was her third husband."

"Did they live in the castle?"

"In what remained of it. His family had lived there for hundreds of years. She loathed it. She's a comfort lover. When she married him, she thought she'd be able to persuade him to move, but he wouldn't."

"Does she live in Steeplewood?"

"No. She came here when she married the first time; her first husband was a relation of a retired canon who lives here —Canon Cranshaw. That was when she became my godmother. Then her husband died and she went away and didn't come back until she married Lord Storring. When he died, she went to live down in Cornwall, but she appears in Steeplewood at intervals to try and get money out of her trustees. She spent all the money her first and second husbands left her, but Lord Storring tied his up. There were two trustees here in Steeplewood, but one of them died, and now there's just old Canon Cranshaw left to deal with her."

"What does she spend the money on?"

"Travel, mostly. And clothes. She's sorry she didn't buy jewels, because she could be selling them now. She was rather friendly with Mr. Horn; she went to see him every time she came to Steeplewood. They used to sit and look at the things in his collection. She hadn't enough money to buy anything, and he never reduced his prices. I think she always hoped she could charm him into making her a present of something or other, but he was charm-proof. And I supposed he knew that if he gave her anything, she'd sell it as soon as she got outside his door."

"But wasn't Storring—"

"—rich? Not very. He was much poorer after being married to my godmother for a few years. Now she's in Penzance, in a warm suite in a warm hotel. I see her whenever she comes up, either to try and get some money out of the Canon, or to interview anybody who looks like making a bid for the castle. It's been on the market for forty-two years."

"Didn't Storring have any heirs?"

"No. It's a pity when old families die out. He was a Studhart.

A lot of the places round here have the family name—Stud-hart Arms, Studhart Inn, Studhart Almshouses—now the town library—Studhart Woods. There aren't any more Studharts—not of that branch."

"Can people go over the castle?"

"Yes. Want to go up now? We've time. You'll have to turn back and take the second road to the right. After that you begin to climb."

Getting out of the car on their arrival, they stood in front of the castle and looked down at a magnificent view. On one side was the town; in front, the river widened and meandered through wooded country. A village—the village of Twinhills—began at the foot of the hill and wound its way somewhat dispiritedly for a short distance along its shoulder. Far away was the faint smoke-haze of an industrial district.

The castle's ruined walls—hardly more than stonework and window openings—stood along the north side of a courtyard. Beyond was the wing that had been occupied by the last Lord Storring and his wife.

"That part was restored in the seventeenth century," Hazel told him. "Miss Horn brings the older girls here to show them the fourteenth-century kitchen, and has to explain that *enceinte* doesn't mean what they thought it meant. Dilys brings her history pupils and tells them about the blood that was shed through the centuries. Sylvia—my godmother—had the moat drained because she said it bred mosquitoes."

"It's a pity nobody's here to enjoy those beautiful woods."

"Aren't they lovely? I used to come here after Sylvia married Edwin, and I wished he could have been her first husband instead of her third, so that I could have come when I was small. It's a child's paradise. There's a stream and a forester's hut and an old burial ground and an underground hide-out. I like to think it's a hide-out, but Edwin said it was where they put unwelcome visitors until they could dispose of them."

She pointed. "See that inn down there, the one close to the parish church? That's the Foresters' Arms. Bernie sings there every Saturday night."

"Sings what?"

"Songs his great-grandfather must have taught him. He's got a wonderful voice, right down in his boots."

"What sort of songs?"

"Oh, the sort the comedians always burlesque. His favourite —the audience's favourite, too—is the one where he asks what the trumpeter's sounding now. Then there's another:

> Hey, ho, many a year ago
> We rode along together, you and I, my old shako.

He practices every night after he's had his supper. I daresay it was that, and not passion, that drove Joby to the cottage."

"Hasn't Bernie ever married?"

"No. He says he's a loner. He gets up at dawn every Saturday and fills the trailer with fruit and vegetables and eggs and honey, and hitches it to his bicycle and pedals to market. He's back by ten, trailer empty." She turned towards the car. "We've got to go. Incidentally, the only people Miss Horn didn't impress when she came to Steeplewood were the three you're going to meet now. She made it clear that she had no intention of inheriting her uncle's staff with the Manor, and her uncle's staff made it clear that they weren't going to work for her. I don't know which side got their say in first."

The caravan was painted yellow. Its occupant was small and thin and aged, but energetic and upright. She stood on the unsteady iron doorstep and greeted them in a high and tremulous voice.

"Saw you from the winder. Saw the car stopping, and said to myself: 'Now, who's that?' Couldn't make you out at first, Miss Paget, and then as you come near I said: 'Well and all, here's a surprise.' Years, miss, since I set eyes on you and gave you that recipe you asked me for my almond cakes, remember?"

"I remember very well, Mrs. Clencher," said Hazel. "I couldn't let you know we were coming, because—"

"I know. No phone. I had one, but I made them take it away; people was always ringing up when I wanted to look at something on the telly."

"This is Mr.—"

"Wait a minute, wait a minute," protested Mrs. Clencher. "First we go inside and then we do the intros. Come on up. Mind the step; it's not all that safe if you don't know just where to put your feet. Me, I'm used to it. Wipe your feet well, if you please; the path's dry today, but people bring in a lot of dirt one way and another, and I like to keep my caravan trim."

Trim it was. It was long, divided into a small living room, an adjoining kitchen, with a bedroom and a miniature bathroom beyond. Hazel stood looking round in admiration.

"It's much bigger than I imagined," she said. "You've made it look very nice."

"Yes, I think I have. Mind you, I had to wait a bit before I got all the furniture. You didn't tell me this gentleman's name."

"Mr. Helder. He came to—"

"Don't worry why he came, not for a minute," broke in Mrs. Clencher. "I don't get visitors often, and when I do, I like to make the most of 'em. Spin 'em out, like. What was we talking about? Furniture. Yes, I waited to get some of me sister-in-law's things. She was selling up. Nearly all the stuff 'ad come from my brother, and you'd think, wouldn't you, that she'd give me something, just a small thing like a kitchen chair or something, in memory of him—but no. Prices stuck onto every single item, just like in a shop, and what's more, she didn't let you into the house if she thought you'd only gone for a look-see at what she was selling off. She opened the door and pushed a list at you and said you was to look at it and only come inside if you wanted something that was on it, and agreed with the price. She made a mint, I can tell you. Mind you, it was good furniture, most of it, and I'll say this for her, she'd looked after it. You can see the polish she put on that table, can't you?"

"Yes." Hazel made another attempt to bring her mind to William. "Mr. Helder came to—"

"What people thought," proceeded Mrs. Clencher, "was that— Sit down, sit down; what are we on our feet for? You take that chair, Mr. Helder; it's big enough to hold a big gentleman like you. You come over here, Miss Paget, and I'll move your chair into the sun. Lovely the way it comes in through these big windows, isn't it? Poky things, caravans was in the old days, but not now. Everything's for light and air now, and doesn't matter who can see in while you're dressing. What people thought, as I was telling you, was that me and the housekeeper and her sister would want to buy some of Mr. Horn's furniture, but we didn't want to. It was all grand stuff; what did we want with grand stuff? A nice plain chair with good springs, a table you can fit six people at if you're entertaining, and that's about all you need in a caravan. The bed's fixed, as you see. I could put it up every morning and let it down again at night, but I don't bother. Excuse me a minute while I make you a nice cup of tea. The kettle's on the boil; I was going to make myself a cup just as you came along."

"Please don't; we really can't stay," Hazel told her. "We just wanted to ask—"

"While you're asking, you can enjoy a nice cupper, can't you? I'm sure Mr. Helder won't say no. I never knew a gentleman refuse a nice cupper, and you've come the day after I bake, so I'll get out some of my little crackerjacks, and when you've tasted them, you'll want the recipe for those too."

She went towards the kitchen, but, as it was a mere four feet away, she could continue her monologue.

"I wasn't surprised to hear you'd come back from London, Miss Paget. When you went, I said to myself: 'You wait, she won't be able to stick it, not after the nice air she's breathed all her life.' Young people like to rush off to the big cities; only natural, I suppose, but I don't know how they put up with all them crowds and all them petrol fumes, I really don't."

William rose to take the laden tray. Hazel drew forward a small table.

"It's good tea." Mrs. Clencher poured it into large, rose-bud-decorated cups. "Comes from Kennet the grocer. I didn't deal with him in Mr. Horn's time, because he and the housekeeper was at loggerheads. She wanted to catch him for her sister Flora, but he didn't come up to scratch; he married that girl in the launderette, if you remember her. Funny name she had—Tryphena. Take another of these little cakes, Mr. Helder, they slip down a treat. Mr. Horn used to say I had the lightest hand with cakes he'd ever known. I often laugh when I think of how quick Miss Horn was to say she wouldn't be taking on any of her uncle's staff. 'Fat chance,' I told her. Take on a new post at my age? And if I'd been twenty years younger, I wouldn't 'ave gone to work for her. Looks down her nose, she does. Mr. Horn was a bit given that way, but not with us. You're not eating, my dear. You're not worrying about your weight, are you?"

"No. But Mr. Helder and I had some coffee before we came to see you, and—"

"Very bad for you, coffee. I never touch it myself. I used to try and stop Mr. Horn, but he wouldn't listen. Is that sun in your eyes, my dear?"

"No. But we have to go soon," Hazel said firmly. "Thank you very much for the tea. We came because Mr. Helder wanted to ask you about a flagon which he—"

"A what, dear?"

William took a letter from his pocket and made a swift sketch on the back of the envelope. He handed it to Mrs. Clencher and after searching for her glasses and putting them on, she studied it.

"It's a small flagon," he said, "about the same size as a wineglass; silver, with small filigree handles. Did you ever see anything like it among Mr. Horn's things?"

She handed him back the envelope and spoke in surprise. "You mean his collection, as it was called?"

"Yes."

"We never saw that," she told him. "I mean, naturally we saw the big things, the big ornaments he got hold of, the statues and things, the things he couldn't put away. But the small things went straight into the safe and stayed there. It was the housekeeper made him do that. We did all we could for him, but clean silver we would *not*. All the household things, yes, teapots and vases and such; but the odds and ends in Mr. Horn's what he called his collection, those we never 'ad nothing to do with. If you need to know about those, miss, you'd best have a word with the housekeeper, Mrs. Murray. She and her sister between them handled that sort of thing. You know where they live now?"

"Elmett Gardens, isn't it?" Hazel asked.

"That's right. No. 4. Not a bad little house," Mrs. Clencher said condescendingly, "but not as cosy, I wouldn't have said, as living in something like this, that you can keep warm in winter, and that hasn't got any stairs to brush down, and everything to your hand as I've got it here. Will you be going to see them?"

Hazel looked enquiringly at William.

"If you've time—"

"I have if you have," he replied.

"Then when you see them," Mrs. Clencher said, "you can give them my kind regards, if you remember, and tell them I'll be glad to see them anytime. They don't have to walk up the path all for nothing; if I'm out, I put a little card in this window, and that warns visitors that I'm not here."

"And informs burglars too?" Hazel asked.

"If anybody can find anything in here worth the trouble of stealing," said Mrs. Clencher, "they're welcome to it. It's all got sentimental value, mark you, and it's all well insured; I believe in insurance, the way Mr. Horn did."

In the car, Hazel spoke apologetically.

"Sorry about that. Dead waste of time. I don't think the idea's as good as I thought it was. Do you think it's worth going on to see the other two?"

"Yes."

"Then let's try and prevent them from embarking on their life histories. Turn right at the end and then right again. It's the second house from the end, on the other side."

It was a house exactly like every other house in the street, very small, unadorned, with a gravel path flanked by flower-beds. The only colour came from two rosebushes planted on either side of the steps.

"They're much more formal than Mrs. Clencher," Hazel said as they reached the front door. "Starchy."

There was at first no answer to their knock. Then a curtain in one of the lower windows stirred, and they knew that they were being inspected. A few moments later, there were foot-steps and then a prolonged rattle of chains and bolts before the door opened. When at last it did, they saw a tall, cadaverous woman in a grey dress with white collar and cuffs.

"Come in, Miss Paget." She spoke in accents of consider-able refinement. "It was a good thing you telephoned to let us know you were coming. We generally do our shopping on a Saturday morning."

"Good morning, Mrs. Murray. I'm sorry if we've—"

They were in the passage, but they had not been invited further. Mrs. Murray, hands folded over her stomach, was looking at William.

"I don't think," she said, "that I know this gentleman."

"I'm sorry. This is Mr. Helder. He—"

Mrs. Murray had given a stiff bow and was leading the way down the passage. She ushered them into a small sunless room.

"Sit down, please," she invited.

There were four overstuffed armchairs placed in exact formation round a low central table. In the fireplace was a large paper fan. An upright piano stood against one wall, a cabinet filled with stuffed birds against another. They sat down, and Mrs. Murray sat, stiff and upright, on a chair opposite.

"My sister is busy," she said, "but if I'm not able to tell you what you want to know, I'll call her in. I was Mr. Horn's housekeeper," she turned to William to explain, "and my sister was house-parlourmaid. All I know about the Manor, she knows too. Have you come to ask about the school? If so, I'm afraid you're wasting your time, for we have nothing to do with it. Nothing." Her lips set in a firm line. "Nothing, right from the beginning."

"No, it's not the school," Hazel said. "Mr. Horn wrote to . . . You tell it," she ended, turning to William.

"I'm looking for a small silver flagon," William said, "and there's a strong possibility that it was in Mr. Horn's collection. Would you or your sister—"

"Excuse me. When you say small," Mrs. Murray broke in, "what size exactly?"

William held his hands a few inches apart.

"About wineglass size," he said. "Silver, engraved, with two decorative handles. Do you remember seeing it?"

"I do not. But it will be as well to ask my sister. Then you'll feel more satisfied." She went to the door, opened it, and called. "Flora, will you come for a moment?"

Flora came, not much less formal than her sister, but with a more friendly expression.

"Good morning, Miss Paget. It must be nice for you, living in Steeplewood again after being cooped up in London."

"Yes, it is."

"We mustn't chatter," Mrs. Murray interrupted. "Miss Paget and this gentleman have come enquiring about a flagon."

"A what did you say?" Flora asked.

"A flagon. The gentleman says it's about this size, and silver, with two handles. Did you ever see anything like that among Mr. Horn's things?"

Flora shook her head and spoke without hesitation.

"I did not," she said. "But you must remember, Miss Paget, that I didn't see everything that Mr. Horn brought to the house. No, indeed. If he bought something big, as you'd say a chair or a picture or an ornament you'd have to stand on the ground, then he'd tell me where he wanted it put, and I would superintend the men when they brought it. But small things, unless of course they were anything to do with the running of the house, I never saw, because they were kept in his safe."

"He had a large safe in his study," explained Mrs. Murray. "I had to ask him to open it when he had guests to dinner, to get out a piece of silver or a dish or some old family piece he liked to keep in there; but I never saw any of his collection."

"All we knew about the smaller things," Flora said, "was when I cleared the wastepaper basket and took away the wrappings of anything he'd bought. I didn't do the cleaning of the things in the safe. I couldn't have undertaken that, with all my other work. He didn't entertain all that much, you know, but people were always coming to the door—not friends, but strangers wanting to see his collection. It would have been the work of two footmen to show them in and out, but how I used to do it, I asked them for a card, and told them to write on it what their business was. Then I'd take the card to Mr. Horn, and he'd tell me to let them in or not, as the case might be. He kept the cards in a little bowl he had, and when the bowl was full, they went into the waste-paper basket."

"The cleaning of his silver," Mrs. Murray said, "was done by Mr. Horn himself. He did it twice a month, and enjoyed doing it. I'd take him in the big twill apron he kept for the job, and hold it for him while he tied it on, and then I'd spread newspapers all over the big table under the window, and give him the cleaning things, and then I'd leave him to it."

"Gloves," Flora reminded her.

"Oh, yes. He put on gloves, of course. Then when he'd finished and the things were back in the safe, he'd ring for me and I'd clear away and put his study to rights."

"It's a pity you're only asking about the little things," Flora said. "If it was the big things, now, I could help you. I've got a good memory and I can remember a long way back, what Mr. Horn bought and what he sold. If I'd ever seen this flagon you mentioned, Miss Paget, I wouldn't have forgotten it."

There was a pause. Hazel rose. There was no point in staying. William expressed their thanks and followed her out to the car. The chains and bolts rattled behind them.

"Complete waste of your morning and mine," said Hazel. "Why did I hope one of them would say 'Yes, of course, Mr. Helder, I remember the flagon perfectly and I can tell you who bought it'?"

"It might have worked out like that. You couldn't know they didn't handle any of the objects in the collection. If you're setting out to search, you have to clear away a lot of undergrowth before you can see where you're going."

"Very kind of you to say so. Now you can relax and admit it was a washout."

He smiled. He did not think the morning had been wasted. She had come out not so much to oblige him as to take her sister-in-law's place. Her interest in the flagon had been almost nonexistent. He did not think that she cared in the least about it, even now, but if she was still uninterested in the object of the search, he sensed that the search itself meant more to her than it had done when they set out. She had suggested a course of action; it had led to nothing and they were driving back to the farm with no more information than they had had when they set out. Although she had warned him not to expect too much, he knew that she felt responsible for their lack of success. She felt committed.

He stopped at the farm gate and got out to open the door on her side. The first time he had done this, on their arrival at the caravan, she was already stepping out; arriving at Mrs. Murray's, she had waited. Now she sat where she was, a half-smile on her lips as she studied him.

"You ought to wear a peaked cap," she said. "Then you could snatch it off as the lady gets out."

"I'll buy one tomorrow."

"Do you have to do this for your stepmother?"

"Naturally."

"What—no chauffeur?"

"Now and then."

"Hers, or yours?"

"Hers. This is the office car. I use it when I need it but I usually drive myself."

She sat taking him in. "Are you frightfully rich?" she asked.

"I'm afraid so. I try not to let it show." He hesitated, and then took the plunge. "That is, when I'm not wearing a Caradon suit."

Her smile faded. She got out of the car and he closed the door and stood beside it.

"Where's Caradon today?" he asked.

"Down in Dorset, filming."

"If I were behind a camera, I'd rather film you than him."

"I don't wear Caradon suits. Did I say I was sorry I'd wasted your morning?"

She was going to dismiss him. Mentioning Caradon had been a mistake. She was going to say she must leave him because the paying guests were waiting for their lunch. There was nothing he could do now except drive away.

And then, to his infinite relief, he saw the family car approaching. In it was Dilys.

"Any luck?" she asked as she got out.

"None. Dead loss," Hazel told her.

"Why stand out here and discuss it? Can't you take William inside and give him some sherry and console him?"

"No time. I've got to get lunch on the table. Once again," she said to William, "I'm sorry to have wasted your time and your petrol, and for leaving you in such a hurry. Goodbye."

She went to the house; the door closed behind her. He looked at Dilys.

"Well . . . I must be off."

"Why? Don't you know it's almost time to eat? More to the point, it's time to drink. Come inside. There won't be enough lunch and you can't have mine, because I'm starving, but there's bread and cheese and we might hack a slice off the paying guests' joint."

He hesitated.

"Perhaps I'd better go."

She leaned against the car and looked up at him.

"Is that what you want to do?"

"No. But—"

"But what? You'd rather Hazel had tendered the invitation?"

"If it can be put that way . . ."

"While you're thinking of a better way, come in and drink and eat, in that order." She went into the house and he followed her. "I've got another teaching session at three."

Hazel, aproned, turned from the stove as they came in.

"We've got company," Dilys told her. "I've warned him that it'll only be bread and cheese."

"Mousetrap, at that," was Hazel's only comment.

"Drinks on order, but first things first," Dilys said to William. "Bathroom through there, second right. Remember to wash behind your ears."

There was no sound of music from the floor above.

"Hugo not working?" she asked.

"Yes. I heard him a few minutes ago." She waited for the sound of the bathroom door closing. "Did you have to bring him in?"

"I didn't have to." Dilys was washing her hands at the sink. "But he looked a bit lost, and if he's really interested in getting this flagon back with its fellows, the least we can do is provide a sort of launching pad. It's a bit hard to have to drive all the way down from London every time he wants to make enquiries about the Horn collection. Don't you like him?"

"What's that got to do with it?"

"Well, it has some bearing," Dilys said mildly. "Are you afraid Rupert will drop in and make another scene?"

"No. He's made the last scene."

"I like William. So does Hugo."

"So does Joby. I daresay you'd find that Bernie liked him too, if you went and asked. That ought to be enough to make him feel welcome. Don't cut any bread; I did it before I went out. You can take in the butter and the mustard; I mixed some, but Hugo likes the French kind in the bottle. If you're going to pour out sherry, get the numbers right, will you? I could use a drink."

William, on emerging from the bathroom, was directed to the sitting room. Apart from the limited view to be got through the hatch from the kitchen, it was the first time that he had seen it. It was large and, like the kitchen, had windows looking onto the fields and the cottage. The furniture was an assortment of cane-seated and upholstered chairs. The only piece at which a dealer would have paused was the table— a beautiful oak refectory table with eight wheel-back chairs placed round it.

Like the kitchen, this room did double duty: sitting room and studio. An easel stood in a corner, and unfinished canvases were stacked behind a sofa.

His eyes went to the pictures on the walls. Dilys, pouring out sherry, made no comment until he had studied them all.

"Hazel's?" he asked.

"Yes. She calls them the unfulfilled promises, but some quite good picture judges have said they're not bad."

"Only not good enough," Hazel said as she came into the room. "When I went to London, I tried to get a job with some stage designers, and discovered that anything I could paint, several thousand other people could paint better."

Hugo came downstairs and joined them.

"How was your morning?" he asked.

"Unproductive," Hazel told him. "Has anybody any idea whether Joby and Mavis are in? If they're out, they should have said so."

"How's the anthem going?" William asked Hugo.

"The anthem? Oh, finished, thank God."

"What is it?"

"A new setting to that one: 'Behold I come quickly.' I expect you know it."

"No, I don't."

"You should," Hazel said. " 'Behold, I come quickly; hold thou fast which thou hast, that no man take the crown. Him that overcometh will I make a pillar in the temple of my God.' That's all I can remember."

"It's better sung than said." Hugo ran a hand through his hair. "The choir'll like it, and it'll be a change."

The cottage door opened. Joby, in jeans and shirt sleeves, carried a table and two chairs outside, and then walked over and looked in at the window.

"Lovely day, lovely sunshine. I'd wear my *chapeau de paille* if I had one. If you'll hand out the grub, I'll come over afterwards and do all the washing up; me and Mavis is going to eat *al fresco*," he told Hazel.

William passed the dishes to him.

"If there's not enough to eat, blame me," he said. "I forgot to book a table."

"Is the pudding burnt again?"

"No. Go away and eat," Hazel said. "Does your office have a canteen?" she asked William.

"Yes. Or lunch vouchers for those who want them."

The telephone rang. Hugo rose.

"If it's Mrs. Caradon," Hazel said, "tell her I'm out."

Hugo paused before lifting the receiver.

"And if it's Mr. Caradon?"

Hazel spoke evenly.

"It won't be Mr. Caradon," she said.

"I'm sorry," Hugo said into the telephone. "My sister's out, Mrs. Caradon. Any message?"

"No message," he said, returning to his place. "Not a polite woman. In fact, a very rude woman. Next time you're passing her house, William, perhaps you'd do me a favour and knock down the rest of her fence."

4

LUNCH OVER, WILLIAM LINGERED AS LONG AS HE COULD OVER coffee. Then he rose and said goodbye. He had performed as much as he could of the business which had brought him to Steeplewood; there was no excuse for staying. Nobody, as he left—not even Dilys—asked him whether he would be returning, and with this depressing fact weighing on him, he drove back to London.

The beginning of the week was hard to bear. Monday crawled by. Tuesday came and went, and still he had been unable to think of a pretext for going back to Steeplewood. He was beginning to find it hard to concentrate on business matters, and his secretary and her assistant became puzzled by his uncharacteristic lapses of memory; they found that he now had to be reminded of staff meetings and briefed on details he had formerly had firmly fixed in his mind. As their discreet policing of his private life made them almost certain he was not pursuing any particular woman, they came to the conclusion that the trouble must be overwork. Too much had fallen on him after his father's death. He hadn't looked after himself lately. Perhaps a word with Mrs. Helder, to persuade her to say a word to him about taking it easy . . .

On Wednesday came relief of a kind. Among the personal letters waiting for him on his desk was one with a Steeplewood postmark. It was a typed letter, signed by Miss Horn.

Dear Mr. Helder,

I have been in touch with my lawyers with regard to the matter about which you came to see me. They have not, I'm afraid, been of much help, but they found, and I now enclose, the letter written by your father in reply to the one he received from my uncle. This will not, I fear, be of much use in your search for the missing flagon, but I thought that you would be glad to have the letter.

His father's letter was as brief and to the point as Miss Horn's.

Dear Mr. Horn,

I'm sorry to say that as my wife and I are on the point of leaving for a holiday, I shall be unable to avail myself at present of your kind invitation to see your collection.

I shall be back within two weeks, and shall take the first opportunity of calling on you. Many thanks for your kind offer.

There was nothing, as Miss Horn had commented, that would help him in his search, but he was glad to have his father's letter, the last he had ever written. He drove after leaving the office to see his stepmother, and showed her both letters, Miss Horn's, and then his father's. When she had read them, she sat silent for a time. Then she handed them back to him.

"Put them in the flagon file," she said. "Why can't those lawyers produce a list of the contents of the Manor? There must be one somewhere."

"I daresay they're still looking. There must be a considerable pile-up of papers; I'm told that Mr. Horn kept all his letters and bills."

She spoke despondently.

"How high do you rate the chances of getting back the flagon?"

"I don't know. But I'm inclined to be hopeful. I keep coming back to my father's impression: that Horn wouldn't have written that letter unless he had it. He seems to have been an unlovable character, sitting in his Manor looked after by three servants, polishing his own collection—the smaller items—and admitting strangers who came to look or to buy. That collection was undoubtedly his greatest, perhaps his only real, interest, and I'm certain he wasn't acting impulsively when he wrote to my father."

"If I hadn't left your father to spend that weekend alone, he wouldn't have gone to Cambridge to spend the weekend with Mr. Strickland. And if he hadn't spent the weekend with Mr. Strickland, he wouldn't have overtired himself by going with him to that regimental reunion. He'd never attended one before. He couldn't bear them; you know he couldn't. He liked to keep in touch with the survivors of his old regiment, but he didn't see any point in making an occasion of it and gathering for dinners and speeches and toasts. He preferred lunching with any of them who happened to be in London."

"He liked going up to see Mr. Strickland."

"I know. They were always good friends. But that went back to their school days."

"Has he ever been in touch with you since the funeral?"

"No. I suppose I should have made a point of talking to him when it was over. I wanted to, but somehow I couldn't. I was sorry afterwards, not only because I felt I might have hurt his feelings, but because I could have talked to him about your father's visit." She moved restlessly. "I'm not given to looking back. What's over is over. Only . . ."

"Only what?"

"I've never been able to shake myself out of the feeling that if I'd gone home with your father when we got back from Greece—if I'd driven straight home instead of deciding to go and see my sister—he would have been alive today."

"Stella, what difference could it possibly have made?"

"A great deal. Going back to an empty house couldn't have attracted him much. So he spent the weekend at Cambridge and went to that reunion dinner, and how do we know it didn't exhaust him? And to stay until Monday morning and then go straight to the office—that was a crazy thing to do. He should have come home on Sunday and had an early night. Dirk had everything ready—house warmed, a good dinner. Your father must have been feeling ill on Monday. His secretary said he didn't seem tired, but she said he got in late and left shortly afterwards. Why? Why would he leave the office in the middle of the morning? Add it all up; the journey back from Greece, then straight up to Cambridge, then all that excitement at the dinner, then back on Monday to the office—do you wonder his heart gave out, weak as it was?"

She was weeping. He went to sit beside her on the sofa.

"It's over, Stella. You've just said so. You couldn't have done anything."

"Yes, I could. I could have been with him. I could have gone to see my sister any other time. Why did I have to go then, and leave him without a car? He could at least have driven up to Cambridge. Why didn't he wait for me at the office on Monday, and drive home with me?"

"You know why. He always liked to be at home to welcome you when you'd been away. Dry your eyes and let me give you a drink."

"No, I don't want one. Are you going back to Steeplewood?"

"I was there on Saturday. I talked to Mr. Horn's staff: cook, housekeeper, housemaid."

"To ask if they'd seen the flagon?"

"Yes. They hadn't. If he had it, it was kept in his safe; he kept his smaller objects there, and apparently liked to polish the silver himself. But the things were always back in the safe before the maids went in to clear away the cleaning things. So neither of them ever saw them."

"What more is there to go back for?"

"I'm trying to get hold of that list of things that were sold."

"Through Miss Horn?"

"Either through her or through a girl who worked for the auctioneers. Her name's Paget. Incidentally, did you ever hear a work—piano concerto—by a composer named Hugo Paget?"

She answered unhesitatingly.

"Yes. They played it last year at the Edinburgh Festival. Dessin was the soloist. Ilyan conducted."

"You were there?"

"Of course I was there. Don't I go up every year? Is this composer the girl's husband?"

"No, brother. What did you think of the work?"

She paused, considering.

"Beautifully played, beautifully conducted—and a good reception. Not a bad start for an unknown composer. He lives at Steeplewood?"

"Yes."

"Has he done anything else since the concerto?"

"Nothing that's been performed. He's finished composing a symphony and he's been working on an anthem for his choir; he's the organist and choirmaster of the parish church. I think he also does new settings for some of the old hymns."

Her eyebrows were raised.

"That's one detailed list you managed to get in Steeplewood," she commented. "Did he tell you all that, or did his sister?"

"His wife. The sister now works part time for Miss Horn. Won't you change your mind about that drink?"

"Yes, I think I will." She waited until he handed it to her. "Go on about the girl."

He returned to his chair, his own glass in his hand.

"Girl?"

"That's right. G-i-r-l. Girl."

"There's no more to tell."

"What does she look like?"

"The wife?"

"No, not the wife. The girl who worked for the auctioneers and now works part time for Miss Horn. Is she plain and unattractive?"

"Miss Horn?"

"The girl."

"Oh, the girl. Well, she's got grey-green eyes and fair hair done in a vague sort of pageboy style."

"Ah."

"She's also got—or had, I'm not sure which—a fiancé."

"Oh, she's engaged?"

"Is or was. To somebody you've probably heard of. Rupert Caradon."

"Rupert Caradon? Caradon clothes?"

"That's the one."

"Then she's got pretty poor taste in men."

"Have you ever met him?"

"No. But one sees him around, making the most of his very distant but usefully titled relations. He keeps his mother in the background, but I saw her once; she was one of the bridge competition prizewinners from Steeplewood. Did you know she lived there?"

"I ran my car into her fence and it fell on her flowerbeds. She wasn't pleased. Neither was he."

"He was there?"

"Yes. You can't deny that he's made a success of his job."

"So would anybody else, pulling the strings that he's pulled. His advertisements make me feel ill. Why aren't you sure whether the engagement is on or off?"

"There was a row, and she doesn't wear her engagement ring any more. But nobody has said anything definite, and of course I haven't asked."

"There's a saying that those who don't ask don't want to know."

"There's also a saying that those who do ask very often don't get told."

"Caradon was at the opening night of the new Tatton play, and the girl with him didn't have fair hair done in a pageboy style. See what use you can make of the information."

"You think I want to use it?"

"I don't know. All I know is that in the fourteen or so years I've known you, I've never heard that note in your voice when you've uttered the word 'girl.' "

"A tremolo?"

"Stop trying to be funny, and give a straight answer to a straight question. She interests you?"

He appeared to consider the matter. Then: "Yes," he admitted. "She does."

"Are you in love with her?"

There was a long silence. She did not hurry him.

"In love? I wish to God I knew," he said at last. "There's something the matter with me, but I wouldn't have diagnosed it as being in love. I thought that was a happy state. This certainly isn't. Since I saw her, I've never been alone. She's with me at breakfast, sitting opposite, fresh as the morning. She's beside me in the car, and I have a hard fight to keep my mind on the road. She listens to music with me in the evening."

"How long have you been in this state?"

"Since I first saw her. It's odd, isn't it?"

"Odd? That's an understatement. Is she clever?"

"I don't think she ever got to the top of the class. That's part of her charm, for me. She's so—so—well, she's just herself, natural, intelligent, amusing, nice to watch, nice to listen to. She's—"

"But if you—"

"—not much of a secretary. She cooks, but not with her nose in a book of recipes from Turkey or Greece—just good plain English food, more plain than good. She kept house for her brother until he married; his wife was a history teacher in London. The wife gave up her job and took over the house, and Hazel went to London. Then the pattern changed because Hugo decided to compose. So his wife went back to teaching, and Hazel came home to run the house."

"Hazel?"

"Yes. Hazel Helder sounds rather nice, I think. She's musical, like all of them—average performer at the piano, according to her brother, but useful in copying out his manuscripts and—like his wife—listening to what he's working on and telling him how it's going. The house . . . basically, it's all right, an old stone farmhouse with outbuildings. But you can understand why the grandfather, who bought it and tried to run it as a farm, had to give up and start trimming off the edges to get money. They're blind, all of them—blind to their surroundings. The covers on the sitting room chairs are so faded that you'd hardly know there was a pattern. Broken banisters. Curtain rings off the rails. It's all clean and in its jumbled way tidy, but they'd all fall through a chair before they realized the springs were in need of mending. If they want to find out what the time is, the clocks aren't much help, so they use the telephone. It's difficult to get their full attention; behind what he's saying, Hugo gives you the impression that he's working out a musical phrase. Hazel's liable to forget what's in the oven because she wants to touch up a painting."

"She paints?"

"Yes. Not well, not badly."

"Couldn't I meet her?"

"As soon as I've found out how I stand, I'll bring her to see you."

"Does she like you?"

"I think that when she's with me, she likes me, or likes my company. But she doesn't seek it."

"How can she, if she's engaged?"

"I told you, they had a row. I don't know how things were left at the end of it. She doesn't talk about him, and she dodges leading questions."

"Surely there's only one question you have to ask: 'Is it on, or is it off?' Don't, for God's sake, tell me you're pursuing your usual policy of waiting until it works itself out. If you want her, can't you put up a fight?"

"No."

"Why not?"

"Because it's between him and her. She's got to work it out for herself. If she wants to get rid of Caradon, she'll get rid of him and there's nothing I can do to accelerate the process. She's grown up, she's not a weak character and she knows her way around. I'm pretty sure she knows I'm on the sidelines, waiting. If she doesn't want him, poor devil, she's got to make him believe it. It's like a tooth: it's got to be pulled out, and there haven't to be any pieces left behind to give trouble later."

"Such poetic images," she murmured.

"Poetic or not, it's sense."

"It isn't. I wish I could talk to her. I could tell her that what you call waiting on the sidelines is what your father, in similar circumstances, called waiting in the wings. Which is merely a verbal smokescreen to hide the fact that you're waiting for the woman to make everything easy for you. I managed to frighten your father into action, and I hope this girl does the same to you."

"Exactly what do you think I ought to do?"

"Tell her you're in love with her, for a start. Don't leave her to guess. Leave the sidelines and get onto the field and kick Caradon off it. At least tell her you love her. If you do."

"Did I say I didn't? What I said was that I didn't recognize the symptoms."

"All right, then; you love her. So make that clear."

"Clear? Stella, in this situation I'm in, nothing's clear. In fact, there isn't a situation. When I went down there, I left a well-ordered life in London and found myself tangled up in girls' schools, headmistresses, two secretaries, a composer, a wife, cooks and paying guests and hairdressers. I feel as though I'm running in circles round a building trying to find a way in. I sometimes think that if I stayed away, never went down there again, they wouldn't notice, and if they noticed, they wouldn't care."

"That's absurd. That's defeatism."

"Yes, it is, but I think it's true."

She said nothing, and after a time he made preparations to leave.

"What's the hurry?" she asked.

"A business dinner—those new people from Leyden. I hope to God I can keep my mind on it."

She did not offer her cheek for his kiss; instead, she patted his, an extremely rare mark of her approval or affection. Or, he thought as he walked out to the lift, in this case it might be sympathy.

Driving home, he found that talking to her had been a relief. She had something astringent about her that had cut through some of the fog in his mind.

A short time ago, he remembered with wonder, he had enjoyed the series of lunches, dinners, theaters and concerts that made up his leisure. Now he was beginning to find it difficult to remember his engagements and, when he was reminded, felt reluctant to fulfil them. He had a feeling that he had gone on a journey, leaving his old friends behind; but though travelling, he had no idea of his ultimate destination. His old life had fallen away and he had as yet found no place for himself elsewhere.

In love? He had not wanted to think so; he had always had a conviction, unexpressed but strong, that falling in love was a gradual process: meeting, liking, getting to know—and at last loving. There had to be, he had always thought, a base, something to build on. But in this case there had been nothing more substantial than the sound of her voice, the smoothness of her skin, the clear light in her eyes, her smile that began so slowly and then became a musical laugh. Build? He longed to build his life round her.

Could she really love, have loved a man like Caradon? That seemed to him as strange as the fact that Rupert Caradon, arch social climber, had chosen a girl from so unsophisticated a background. She was beautiful, but she was a natural and not a fashionable type; she did not look in the least like the cold-eyed, hard-faced beauties who appeared regularly on the artistically out-of-focus fringes of the Caradon advertisements.

Changing for dinner, he heard the telephone and left Dirk to answer it. A few moments later there was a knock.

"Yes?"

Dirk entered.

"A Miss Paget on the line, sir."

William crossed the room in three strides and lifted the receiver beside his bed.

"Hazel?"

"Yes. I was going to write, but it was bad news, so I thought I'd better ring you."

"You can't get that list?"

"I can. I did. There's no flagon mentioned anywhere."

"I see. Thanks for letting me know."

"You're welcome. There was one other thing—"

"Yes?"

"You remember I told you that my godmother knew Mr. Horn? She often saw his collection. Whenever she came on visits to Steeplewood, she went to see him. If your flagon was ever in his collection, she'd remember. She's going to be here on Monday, and I can go and see her because it's a school holiday; it's the anniversary of the school's opening. But you'll be working."

"I never work on Mondays."

"You don't?"

"Never. I make a point of it. If I came down, could you arrange a meeting with her?"

"Yes. But wouldn't it be easier if I asked her, and rang you to tell you what she said?"

A wave of fury engulfed him for a moment. She certainly made it as hard as she could.

"I'd very much prefer to see her, if you can arrange it," he said.

"Then will you come down in the morning, and I'll take you to see her. She doesn't stay with us—too uncomfortable. She stays at the hotel. We'll arrange to get there in time to be asked to lunch."

She rang off. He put down the receiver and stood for some time staring unseeingly at a gleam of light shining near his bed. Then he came back to the present and realized that the gleam was Dirk's bald head shining under the light.

"What is it, Dirk?"

"I was waiting, sir, to know whether you'll be driving yourself tonight, or whether you'll require Anton."

"No. I shan't want him."

"Very good, sir."

From his own quarters, Dirk transmitted the message to the chauffeur and then sat down and helped himself to one of the cheese biscuits his wife had set out for him beside his tankard of beer. Opening the evening paper, he paused to address her, and twenty years of marriage enabled her to decipher the code.

"Her name," he said, "is Hazel."

5

WILLIAM SPENT THE WEEKEND IN CAMBRIDGE. HE WAS NOT sorry that his forthcoming visit to Steeplewood was to be on a weekday; weekends could be clouded by the fear that at any moment Rupert Caradon might appear. But Monday was a working day, and unless he got wind of Hazel's appointment with another man he should be safely in London, minding his own business. In the meantime, there were old friends in Cambridge to be visited, old haunts revisited, his old college and his old rooms to remind him of the pleasant, not-so-long-ago past.

Early on Monday morning, William drove in a slight but persistent drizzle to the farm. As he stopped at the gate, he saw Bernie, with unwonted politeness, coming to open the car door for him.

"Good morning, Bernie."

"Morning, sir. Not much of a day."

"No, it isn't."

"You wouldn't want a couple of pots of nice honey, I suppose? I won't charge you as much as the shops would."

"Honey? Well . . . all right."

"I'll put 'em in your car, nicely wrapped up. If you'll settle now, it'd be more convenient. I mightn't be around when you come out."

He watched William counting out the money.

"Got some nice big eggs, sir. The hens have been laying well. Spot-fresh. I could—"

"No, thanks, Bernie. No eggs."

"Or some nice new peas. Been picking 'em nice and tender, so—"

"No, thanks."

"Some fine big hearty lettuces, like?"

"No."

"I've got some beetroots I put in vinegar, nice little ones, not much bigger'n marbles, and—"

"No, thanks, Bernie. Some other day."

It seemed likely that Bernie would have gone on working down the list, but he saw Mavis coming down the road on her bicycle and with a grunt desisted. She came up to William and dismounted.

"Good morning, Mr. Helder. You passed me, but you didn't see me. Joby and I are going to go on a picnic."

"In this weather?"

"It's not very nice, is it? But Dilys said we could take the car. Oh, Bernie, I didn't see you to ask when I went out. Lettuces are wanted. Can Joby pick them?"

"That he can't," growled Bernie. "I won't have him mucking up my plants. I'll do it myself."

"Such a pity they fight," Mavis commented as he walked away. "It frightens me, you know. If he wanted to go for Joby, then what? He'd hurt him very badly. I'm always telling Joby, 'Don't be so cheeky to him,' but he won't listen to me. You know this is a school holiday. Yes, you know, or you wouldn't have come."

"Hazel rang. I'm going to meet her godmother."

"Oh, you are? Hazel told me she was here, but she didn't tell me you were going to meet her. She's a very pretty lady. Old, but you can still see how pretty she was."

"Any decision as to when you're going to Bournemouth?" he asked.

"Soon. When Joby came he was so impatient to go back, but now he's changed a little, he's not so impatient, and that's better for me. At the end of this week, I'm going to tell Miss Horn. I won't be sorry, because since she knew Joby came here she hasn't been so nice to me."

"That's bad policy if she wants to keep you."

"Perhaps she doesn't want to any more. When she talks to me now, she's—sharp, you know? I don't feel so happy with her. But she won't be left without anybody, because Joby found a girl; she's a cousin of a man who lives in Steeplewood, and she wants to have a job here, and she's a trained secretary, so I can tell Miss Horn about her." She paused and gave a sigh. "I'll miss all of them here. I'll never find anybody so nice as Haze and Dilys and Hugo. You know what Joby's been doing? He's been repairing the inside of the cottage, so Hugo can go and work there after we go away. You can warm it nicely in the winter, and Hugo wouldn't be disturbed."

"It sounds a very good idea."

She wheeled her bicycle to the cottage. He knocked on the door of the house, and heard Dilys's voice.

"Come in. Hugo," she told him as he entered, "has been summoned to an organists' meeting in London. Hazel's just gone upstairs to change. I'm correcting exercise books, as you see. If you'll make coffee for the two of us—Haze doesn't want any—I'll get through these faster."

He made the coffee. Clearing it away later, he rather rashly asked if there was anything else he could do to help, and found himself peeling potatoes. They worked in silence until Dilys had finished correcting the last exercise book. Then she carried the pile to the hatch and put it beside the television set.

"I've taken over from Haze for the day," she said, "but there's no lunch to cook; Mavis and Joby are going off on a jaunt somewhere or other. Haze's godmother has asked you both to lunch, and with luck she'll give you dinner too."

Working, he had been summoning his courage. Now he put a question.

"As we're alone," he said, "could you give me some idea of what the Caradon situation is?"

She gazed at him in surprise.

"Why ask me? Why not ask Hazel?"

"Perhaps I'm afraid of getting an answer I won't like."

"What have you been doing—waiting for her to bring up the subject?"

"No. I thought it was better to—"

"—let matters take their course?"

"I felt it was unwise to rush things. I wanted to gain a little ground."

"You make it sound like a military operation."

"It is, in a way."

"A kind of siege?"

"You could call it that. The first time I saw her, she was wearing an engagement ring. She was going to marry Caradon. I know that there was a quarrel, but I didn't know whether the thing was still on or not. I was waiting—"

She made an impatient sound.

"That's what children do—make as little disturbance as possible in the hope of not being sent away. If you want to know what the situation is, ask her straight out and she'll tell you."

There was a brief silence, and then he heard her laugh.

"Share it," he invited.

"It isn't really a joke. I was just struck by the difference between you and Hugo. You look so much more self-confident, so much more experienced, man-of-the-worldish, but you don't appear to have his technique when it comes to wooing." She paused. "I take it you are wooing?"

"What did you think?"

"I didn't have much to go on. When I met Hugo, I was engaged to a lawyer. Hugo met him twice, decided that he wouldn't be a suitable husband for me, and from then on behaved as if he didn't exist. In time, I came to believe he didn't exist, either. I don't suppose you could employ that method with Rupert Caradon; he's not proving easy to shake off. Are you really in love with her? You've only seen her—how many times? Twice."

"What does that matter? If it's of any interest, she's the first woman I've met I've wanted to marry."

"Late developer?"

"I daresay."

"Well, the Caradon situation has folded. That's to say the engagement's off. It should never have been on. Once on, Hugo and I knew she'd have trouble getting out. Breaking off a relationship—for a man or a woman—has to be quick, and as painless as possible. Hazel's a nice girl, but there's a fatal flaw in her make-up: she feels sorry for people. She got involved with Rupert Caradon while she was in London, but when she came home four months ago, she thought it was all over. It wasn't. It's almost impossible to convince a man like Rupert that his magnetism isn't working for once. She got away from London without committing herself, but he came after her, and bought a house in Steeplewood for his mother, and installed her in it so that he could come and go as he liked. He was so persistent that Hazel began to feel she'd really hurt him—and that was fatal. Hugo tried to talk sense into her, but she got engaged, and it was a disaster, as we knew it would be. She's free now, but she doesn't believe it; she still feels he can make trouble."

"What sort of trouble?"

"Oh, just going on and on—what you call laying siege. He must feel she doesn't realize what a prize she's passing up. But she's not an easy girl to pin down. I've known her since she was twelve, and I wouldn't like to be asked to sit down and draw a character sketch of her. We went to the same school; perhaps I told you? I was four years older, but she was in my house, so I saw a lot of her. I was head of house, and I was supposed to help the younger ones, but I never got the hang of Hazel. Neither did the teachers. She was intelligent, but she didn't derive any benefit from the orthodox educational processes. Looking back, I can see that they should have given her more time to paint and to practise the piano. Nothing else interested her. She was country-bred, but when I decided to try and make a spring garden and gave her some bulbs to plant, she put them in upside down; she said she thought the pointed end was the roots beginning to sprout. I asked her if she really came from a farm, and she explained that farmers weren't gardeners. When I came to live here, I saw what she meant. If it's the actual engagement that's worrying you, it's off. I wish you luck. I hope she marries you. I'd like to see her well set up."

"Money?" he asked, and could not keep a slight bitterness out of his voice.

"Partly," she said coolly. "It's time we had some in the family. But chiefly because you're steady, and she needs someone steady. She was never what you call tough, and she's had a lot of her self-confidence knocked out of her in the past year or so. It wasn't only Rupert Caradon; she's had more than one man after her, and they got nowhere, like him. All she wants out of life, it seems to me, is what she's got here—space, freedom, and time to do the things she likes doing. I'll be interested to see if you do better than your predecessors."

There was no time for more. Hazel entered the room and

stopped in amazement at the sight of William laboriously peeling potatoes. From outside, after yodelling to announce his arrival, came Joby with a basket filled with lettuces.

"*Bonjour, mesdames, monsieur.*" He put the basket on the table. "Bernie sent this lot."

He picked up a slice of bread and was about to butter it when he realized what William was doing. The sight reduced him for some moments to silence. Then he recovered his breath.

"Cor! Look at him! Just take a look!" he exclaimed.

"He's helping me," Dilys explained.

"Helping! Call that helping? Look at the peel he's hacking off! There's more peel than potato. Here"—he abandoned the sandwich he was about to make and elbowed William aside—"lemme. I don't suppose you ever peeled a spud in your life."

"Wrong. I'm an experienced camper," William told him.

He was demoted to washing the lettuce. Joby peeled the potatoes swiftly, deftly and economically.

"My grandmum used to be the one for this job," he said. "She had a special knife she kept to herself, and there was hell-fire if we touched it. She never liked any of her things messed around."

"Does she live with you?" Hazel asked.

"Live with us?" His voice was high with astonishment. "Live with us? Not her! She's done a lot better than that. She used to have a job as an office cleaner—forty years all told—and when she said she was going to retire, her bosses said they'd give her a nice little bonus. She told them to—well, she meant they could keep it. What she wanted, she told them, was the room in the basement next to the one the cleaners kept their things in, a nice little room where they used to make themselves cups of tea when they got to work on a morning. So the bosses said: 'All right, it's yours for life.' And she's settled in it and they won't get her out till they carry her out."

"Who looks after her?" Dilys asked.

"Who? The state, Dilly-ducks. Who else? The state. England my England, and yours too, but she thinks it's all hers. The state. Aren't you on any of those committees for looking after the oldies? Don't they have 'em in Steeplewood? There's one every four hundred yards where I live. My old gran, she gets her old-age pension, and on top of that"—he spread out the fingers of one hand and counted with the forefinger of the other—"let's see: first there's her grub. Midday dinner, brought to her, all nice and hot, in those silver paper dishes she can throw away. Supper, nice and tasty, and the kind ladies stop and make her a cup of cocoa or tea, whichever she fancies. They wear their fingers out knitting, and they dole out what they've knitted; my gran's got eleven pairs of mittens put away in a drawer, as well as two shawls, two pairs of woolly drawers and five pairs of bedsocks. If she feels like a drive on a nice day, she sticks the little notice they gave her in the window, and someone comes and asks her what she wants, and she says a nice drive and they send a nice kind lady with a car to give her a whirl round Greenwich Park. Visit to the doc? Easy: ambulance at the door. If she doesn't get what she wants quick, she hobbles to the newspaper office and they put in a letter from her about the shocking neglect of old-age pensioners. It's an education to watch her. What she says is, those things are there to have, and she's going to have 'em. So you can see why she wouldn't come and live with us."

"Those tunes you're always whistling—songs your mother taught you?" Dilys enquired.

"Mum? You've got your dates mixed, sweetheart. Some of those are a lot before Mum's time. You know any of them?"

"Vaguely."

"Do I disturb Hugo, whistling?"

"Sometimes."

"I've got the habit—can't break it. Once I get out of the salon, the birds sit on the trees and listen. It was my grandmum used to sing those old tunes. She specialized in those old operas. Not operas; operettas, swing high, swing low, swing to and fro, that kind of prithee-maiden stuff. Then we'd all join in, but when we got big enough to buy our own records, that was the end of Gran's concerts." He rose, put the peeled potatoes into a saucepan and dried his hands. "Any more jobs for the unpaid slaves?"

"No. Thanks," said Dilys. "Hazel cut sandwiches for your lunch."

"They're in the fridge," Hazel told him. "Two packets—one each, in case you eat more than your share."

He took the two packets and went out, whistling shrilly. William looked at Hazel.

"Ready to ride?"

"Yes."

"Where to?" he asked, as they drove away.

"The hotel. Or rather, the annex. She always stays there when she comes to Steeplewood. The hotel was the house that she and her first husband lived in; she sold it after he died, and it was made into this hotel."

"There only seems to be one hotel in this town. Why?"

"No tourists, for one thing. And not many people who want accommodation for the night. The big crowds only come for the weekly market, and what the farmers need is a place to meet and a place to drink; that's why there's only one hotel, but about two dozen pubs: Foresters' Arms, King's Head, this inn, that inn—you can see two in every street."

"Is your godmother up here to see her trustees?"

"No. There's only one trustee now, anyway—Canon Cranshaw. This visit's one of those frustrating ones she keeps having to make when a possible buyer turns up."

"Buyer—oh, the castle?"

"Yes. If it doesn't look like coming to anything, the Canon doesn't ask her to come. It's only when things begin to look promising that he summons her. Then it all comes to nothing, and she goes home again." She hesitated. "I haven't told you much about her. Describing her rather puts people off. She's odd, in some ways."

"Which ways?"

By the time they reached the hotel, he had learned a good deal about the woman they were going to see. Lady Storring was sixty, the only child of parents who had spent more time in travel than they had in any of their widely separated homes. Her godmother's photograph albums, Hazel said, bulged with faded groups seen against backgrounds of the pyramids, the Matterhorn, Egyptian temples, Buddhist temples, Hindu temples, mosques, the Leaning Tower, the Great Wall. Ladies in topees and floating veils perched on camels; gentlemen stood on one foot with the other holding down a dead tiger. In the early groups, the small Sylvia could be seen on the fringes of the photographs in the care of a nanny or an ayah or an amah; later, she appeared in the center, dressed for riding or climbing or driving.

"I never understood what the British Empire was until I saw those albums," Hazel said wonderingly. "Some of the time they were on foreign soil, but mostly they were—"

"—standing on the spots that used to be marked red on the map. When did she give up globe-trotting?"

"Soon after she married. It took a lot of money to do it in the style her parents had done it. The point is that if you were brought up like that, you can never really adjust. She's quite certain she's completely up to date. She talks about the past as though it really is past, but she's still thinking in Empire terms. Incidentally, I rang and told her I was bringing you. She's giving us lunch."

"So Dilys said."

"Dinner, too, with any luck."

The hotel was on the outskirts of the town. They drove past the main building and stopped at the annex, a cottage that looked like a doll's house. As they walked up to it, a woman's figure appeared in the entrance—small, slim, at this distance looking like the figure of a young girl. They drew near and saw that she was under the stress of strong emotion; excitement was making the slight form quiver. She spoke breathlessly as they reached her.

"Oh, Hazel, darling! I've been looking out for you for ages! Come inside." She led them across a hall into a small sitting room. "Don't take any notice of me if I seem slightly demented, because I *am*." Her gaze, wide and excited, went to William. "Oh, you look so much nicer than that other one," she exclaimed. "I couldn't bear him!" She took William's hand in hers. "Hazel darling, I'm so glad—he looks just right for you." She released his hand and turned to Hazel. "Darling, you're not going to believe this. I don't really believe it myself. It's no use asking you to guess; I'll have to tell you. It's sold! It's *sold*!"

"Not the *castle*?" Hazel asked in bewilderment. "You don't mean—"

"The castle. I can't, I *can't* believe it. Sold, after all these years, and for a price that— Oh, why are we all standing? Sit down, please sit down anywhere and let me tell you all about it."

They sat down and her gaze went momentarily to William.

"Does he know about the castle, Hazel?"

"Yes. I told him."

"Forty-two years. Up for sale for forty-two years, Mr.—oh, I didn't give Hazel a chance to tell me—"

"He's called William. Go on, Sylvia."

"Forty-two years. I'd given up all hope, you know I had, Hazel. It had become a sort of hate thing in my mind, that awful pile which nobody would ever buy, and the farce of having to keep coming up all this way just to see buyers melting away; I'd given up *all* hope. I couldn't bear to think about it, because if I did I nearly went out of my mind with frustration. I'd got used to the idea that nobody would ever buy it. But they did! At exactly ten thirty this morning—they did!"

"Who did?" Hazel asked.

"You can't guess? No, how could you? How could anyone? It's too fantastic, the last thing people would have thought of."

"Well, who?"

"Arabs."

"*Arabs?*"

"Oil kings. Sheiks. Two splendid men in those flowing white robes and a headdress with a rope round it. I got here last night and they drove down from London early this morning to meet me. They'd had two preliminary meetings with the Canon, but he hadn't told me about them because he was afraid to raise my hopes. So this morning I knew nothing about who they were. When the Canon's car stopped at this door, I felt certain he'd come to tell me that as usual there was no deal. And then I saw another car behind his—an enormous black one with an Arab chauffeur and a sort of bodyguard sitting next to him, and the bodyguard leapt out and opened the car door, and out stepped these two figures, just like one of those old films, silent ones you wouldn't know about, so long before your time, and they came in here and stood—they wouldn't sit down, and said in English, quite good English, that they'd like to go up to the castle with me for a final look, and then they'd give a definite yes or no."

"Who fixed the price?"

"The Canon. *Astronomical!* Could you believe that saintly-looking, holy-sounding, mild-seeming prelate could ask a sum like that and go on repeating it till he got it?"

"Yes, I could. You went up to the castle with them?"

"Not the Canon. Only the other two. We went up in the black car and I sat between them and they didn't utter a word on the way up there. When we arrived, it had begun to drizzle and there was a mist which gave the place a terribly dreary look, and I thought to myself: 'Nobody, *nobody* could want this.' "

"Did they say anything?"

"Only to each other. It sounded like grunting. We went a little way into the woods and it got gloomier and gloomier and then we came to the waterfall and they stopped, still not a word, and gazed while the water splashed down onto the stones and I waited for them to say it was all off, but they exchanged more grunts and then we turned and walked back to the car."

"Where was the Canon?"

"Waiting in this room. We came in and joined him and then the taller man said: 'Yes, we have decided. We will buy.' "

She stopped, breathless. Her cheeks were flushed; from the carefully arranged curls on the top of her head, two had shaken loose and lay on her forehead. Her eyes were starry. For an instant, William saw the lovely young woman she had once been.

"Congratulations," he said.

"Sylvia darling." Hazel kissed her cheek. "I'm so glad for you."

"We must have a drink," Lady Storring said. "William, will you most kindly be barman and pour me a large whisky? This isn't the time for it, and I don't drink it as a rule, but I must have something to pull me together. Have some too— or there's sherry if you both prefer it."

William brought a double whisky and two sherries. Standing, they toasted the Canon, the castle and the oil kings.

"What do you think they want it for?" Lady Storring wanted to know. "Not to *live* in. Only people like my husband could have lived in that ghastly place, with that ruined wing looking as though it had been gutted by fire, and piles of masonry everywhere you looked. The Canon's afraid they'll make a mess of restoring it—you know his reverence for ruins? Myself, I don't care what they do. They can— Oh, dear, I'm not being very hospitable, am I? William, there are olives in that cupboard if you can find them, and nuts and things. Please bring them out. I'm afraid I've been talking rather a lot, and all about my own affairs. You said you wanted to ask me about something, Hazel—what was it?"

"We wondered," William began, placing the olives on a table beside her, "whether you could tell us—"

"You can't imagine," she burst out, "you can't *begin* to imagine what this means to me. It's going to revolutionize my life. Oh, Hazel, what happy days to look forward to! No more fights to get money out of the Canon; he'll be in charge of it, of course, that was stipulated in Edwin's will, but think how much more he'll be able to let me have! No more sacrifices or economies or beastly budgets. Oh, bliss! William, what were you saying?"

"He was explaining what we wanted to ask you," Hazel said. "Do you by any chance—"

"What I can *never* make you understand is how *extraordinary* the transaction seems to me. It's different for you two—you're young, and you're used to thinking of Arabs in oil terms. But when I was young, and travelling abroad with my parents, they were simply the natives who swarmed round the tourists in Port Said, selling those peculiar postcards. So this morning, I've had a feeling that I was suffering from double vision, seeing on the one hand the Arabs I used to pay for carrying my parcels back to the ship, and on the *other* hand, seeing those two Arabs who stood in this room and paid me, or are going to pay me, a fortune for an ancient ruin. You do see, don't you, how difficult it is for me to *adjust*? There are so many things nowadays that one didn't have to cope with in one's youth, like the Third World and so on. One really doesn't know where one is. Oh, dear, I've interrupted you again—do forgive me."

"What we wanted to know," Hazel began once more, "was—"

"What was the worst of all," her godmother broke in, "was having to listen to the Canon droning, year after year, about making money go a long way. What did I want more than to make it go a long way? I had so many places for it to go to! He would never, never give me any more than what he called my due, never advance me any, and how could I get on without money? I was too old to earn any and too stupid to learn and too spoilt, I suppose you'd call it, to adapt myself to present-day conditions. Go on with what you were saying, Hazel."

"It was something to do with Mr. Horn. Did you—"

"Mr. Horn! What a pity, what a pity he isn't alive to hear this news! How glad he would have been! Don't you remember how often I used to go and see him, Hazel, when I lived here, and I never missed having a word with him when I had to come up and see the Canon. I used to long to buy something out of the collection, but I could never afford to. How odd that you should mention him."

"When you saw his collection," William began, "did you—"

"Do you realize that if this had happened last year, I could have bought the Manor? I didn't want it, and he said he would never sell it, but he was a terrible money grubber, you know, and he wouldn't have stood out for long against a good price. But I don't want a house. I'm going to look for something that makes life easier, not more difficult. In the old days, servants were servants and they were quite happy and you didn't have to worry about them, but now you have to worry about them all the time: have you said the right thing, did your friends remember to shake hands and ask about their children, had you remembered to warn visitors never to ring the bell in their rooms, were they offended when someone forgot their names . . . oh, so very different! William, could you very kindly refill our glasses?"

"We want to know," Hazel said, "whether you ever saw, in Mr. Horn's collection, a—"

"If I found a nice little warm paradise somewhere, Hazel, would you come and share it with me?"

"Naturally. Can you remember—"

"And bring William, of course. When I saw you both coming towards me this morning, I thanked heaven you'd got rid of the Caradon man. Don't let's spoil this lovely morning by mentioning him. Do you know, for years and years the thought of going to your wedding and giving you my blessing has kept me happy. If I saw a pretty little house, I imagined you and your husband in it. If I saw a cot or prams in a shop window, I'd stop and gaze at them and imagine your children in them. I even chose a christening mug, so sweet, so unusual, just the thing for your first baby if only I'd been able to afford it. It was such a shock to learn that you'd become engaged to Rupert Caradon. But, Hazel, you haven't told me yet what you wanted to ask me about. I know I've been interrupting, but every now and then I forget what's happened just for a second or two, and then it comes rushing back and makes me too excited. Now I shall concentrate. Tell me what you want to know."

"Did you ever see a flagon in Mr. Horn's collection?"

"A flagon?"

"Yes. Did you?"

"Never."

"If there'd been one, would you have seen it?"

"Most certainly. Every time I went to see him, he'd open his safe and take out all his treasures and lay them on the table for me to gaze at. We both loved looking. What do you want a flagon for?"

"To complete a set William has."

"Does he collect flagons? Mr. Horn didn't. If only—if only I'd had some money while he was still alive, just think of the nice things I could have bought. But he would never dream of reducing anything, and he never parted with a single thing until he had the money in his hand. Cash down. He would have helped me to spend my castle money. He— Do you know, my head seems to be spinning. This excitement has been too much for me. Should I lie down for a little while, do you think?"

"A good idea." Hazel helped her gently to her feet, and with William guided her towards her bedroom. "You'll feel fine after you've had a little rest."

"But not a sleep, Hazel. I don't want to sleep. I shall wake up and find it's just been a wonderful dream."

"No, you won't." Hazel was removing the child-size shoes. "You'll find it was all quite real."

"I did sell the castle, didn't I?"

"You did. For an undisclosed but astronomical sum. Shall I draw the curtains?"

"Thank you. I'd planned to give a little cocktail party this evening to a few old friends. I made a list as soon as the Arabs went away. I was going to telephone and ask them here— not here, I mean to the main part of the hotel, for drinks at —at what time would you say?"

"Six thirty. I'll find the list and do the telephoning. Close your eyes."

They waited until she was drifting into sleep, and then left her, closing the door behind them.

"Sorry," Hazel said in the sitting room. "Another dead

end. No flagon. What's more, no lunch."

"I can afford to buy you lunch. I've still got some of my castle money left."

"Thank you. But not a restaurant. There's a little riverside pub at Twinhills; we could get beer and sandwiches."

"Is that what you'd like?"

"Yes."

They drove to Twinhills, once a peaceful village but recently discovered by town-dwellers, so that it had lost its rural aspect. Used only at weekends, the cottages were shuttered, the sun blinds rolled back on their iron supports. The single street was free of traffic. Sheltering the village was the hill on which stood the ruined castle, now the property of the Arabs.

They stopped at the Fisherman's Rest and went into a room that smelled strongly of beer, seating themselves at a table in a bow window with a view of the river. The drizzle had stopped, and the sun was making fitful appearances.

"You can tell your godmother," he said, "that it was the waterfall that clinched the deal."

"Why the waterfall?"

"Because they're desert-dried Arabs. Desiccated. To see water flowing and flowing and flowing—naturally they bought the place. Has your godmother got any family, or are you her sole heiress?"

"No family, and if I know her, there'll be nothing left for anyone to inherit. She'll wear the Canon down in time and get as much money as she wants, and it'll go where the rest of the money went."

He went to the bar and returned with two tankards of beer. He made a second journey and returned with two large plates of sandwiches.

"These be enough?" he asked.

"I think so. It depends on how much you eat."

"One plate for you, one plate for me." He sat down and

helped himself to a sandwich. "Tell me about yourself," he invited.

She raised her eyebrows.

"All about myself?"

"All. There are several blanks in your dossier that I'd like to fill in. Begin at the christening."

"Here in Steeplewood. Canon Cranshaw officiating, only that was before he was canonized. Uneventful childhood on farm, school at Malvern, passed exams without distinction, left at earliest possible moment to return home and keep house for newly orphaned brother. Brother later married, so left the house to the newlyweds and went to London to settle down as a career woman. Lack of training great stumbling block, also prices inflationary, hard to live on salary of untrained secretary. Gentlemen friends kind but not rich, dining out therefore spoilt by the thought that one was eating their month's salary. Took long course in culture—museums, monuments, exhibitions and so on. Was offered job as model, tried it, loathed it, dropped it. Yearned for life in countryside. Met well-known designer of men's clothes and was taken up and introduced to a world of smartness and success. Received letter from home saying that brother now a full-time composer and sister-in-law obliged to return to work, would I please go home and keep house? Took next train. Well-known designer took the train after that and demanded return to big city. Reproaches, pleas—and a house bought in Steeplewood for his mother, so that he could come down as frequently as he wanted to. Gave way to pressure, became engaged, found impossible, became disengaged. The end. I hope."

They sat in silence for a while. Then he spoke with an aggrieved air.

"Aren't you going to ask me to begin at my christening?"

"No need. There are no blanks in your dossier. Born, christened, indulged boyhood, Eton and Harrow, Oxford and

Cambridge. World tour. Entry into family firm at managerial level. To be continued."

"You wouldn't care for some more details, some marginal notes, some illustrations to the text, the whole thing set to music?"

"Thank you, no."

"What made you long to return to the countryside?"

She thought it over.

"They say that everybody," she said at last, "at some time in their lives—or at some time during their youth—feels the pull of a big capital. I never felt any pull. I loathed London— the rush hour, the crowds, the competition . . . I got home-sick, I suppose. I used to imagine myself back in our fields, milking the cow and feeding the hens."

"If your brother hadn't decided to give up teaching in London—"

"No problem. Miss Horn's school had started. I felt certain they'd need secretaries as well as teachers. If they didn't, I was planning to commute, as Hugo and Dilys had done; it's only an hour and a quarter by train, and the trains are frequent. Nothing would have induced me to go on living in London. I suppose you can't understand that; you live there. Where exactly?"

"In dockland. When my father remarried, I turned the top storey of our office building into a home for myself. When he died, my stepmother hoped I'd go back, but I didn't."

"Go back where?"

"The family home."

"Whereabouts?"

"Hertfordshire. About a mile out of Penston."

"But that's right in the country!"

"The very depths."

"Is it just a house?"

"And a farm."

"What's it called?"

"Helder House. Very original."

"Animals on the farm?"

"Innumerable. From horses to hamsters."

"Who looks after them?"

"The farmer and his two sons."

"How often do you go there?"

"About once a month."

"Does your stepmother live there?"

"No. She lives in London."

"With you?"

"No."

She sat lost in thought, studying him frowningly across the table.

"You mean," she said, "that you own—do you own?"

"Yes."

"You own a country house and everything that goes with it, and you prefer to live in London?"

"Yes."

"You don't look crazy, but you must be. Could you commute if you wanted to?"

"Easily. It's only twenty minutes' walk to Penston station, if you go the short way through our grounds. My father used to go to the office by car in winter, but in summer he always walked to the station and went by train. He made the walk more interesting by building a little bridge over the lake."

"There's a lake?"

"A small one. But picturesque."

"And you'd rather live in dockland?"

"Well, I'm on the top floor and I look down on the river and the view's wonderful, especially at night. I like watching the boats go by, and seeing London at my feet. I'd like to show it to you one day."

"Thank you. I'd rather see the lake and the animals."

"That's easy. We can do that now."

"Now?"

"Why not? We've got"—he glanced at his watch—"four hours. It's not more than seventy miles from here, some of it on a nice straight stretch. We could have tea there."

"At the farm?"

"At the house. There's a housekeeper. Will you come?"

She hesitated.

"We've got to telephone all the special friends on my godmother's list."

"We shall leave the list with the hotel receptionist and tell her to charge the calls to your godmother, who can now well afford it."

"Would there be time for me to go home and change before the cocktail party?"

"Yes."

He waited for objections, and while he waited, prepared to override them. He wanted to see her at the house, in the house. He wanted to show her the things, the places, the people he had seldom thought of in the past few years. He did not know why it was so important to visit the house with her; all he knew was that he had never in his life wanted anything so much.

"All right," she said.

They went out of the inn into perfect weather. In sunshine they drove to the hotel, to leave Lady Storring's guest list at the reception desk. William made a call on his own account to his housekeeper, to tell her that he was bringing a visitor to the house.

Hazel directed him for the first part of the journey, through byways that brought them by a quicker route than the main roads. Then he was on familiar ground, speeding towards Penston. He skirted the town and turned onto a wide, tree-shaded lane. At the first crossroads, he slowed down.

"From now on," he said, "you have to pay toll. You're on my land. Ahead of you is the house."

"I can't see a house."

"But it's there. Count twenty."

He turned into what looked to her an impenetrable wood. Through it had been cut a gap wide enough to allow the passage of a car. The going was rough for a short while and they were in deep shadow, the road climbing steeply. Then there was a right-angled turn and they came out into the open. Before them, below them, was the house. William brought the car to a stop.

"This is the best view of it," he said. "We don't let visitors come this way. I pioneered this path through the woods. I even helped to cut down the trees."

She was scarcely listening. Her eyes were taking in the picture before them.

"Built in 1700," William said. "We moved in 1702, losing five flagons on the way. Nothing has been added to or subtracted from the place since it was built, with the exception of the bridge over the lake. That was designed and built by my father. He was disappointed to find it looked so Japanese; it didn't look Madame Butterfly-ish on paper. My mother— it was built in her time—thought the rail too decorative."

"It's beautiful."

"But impractical, she thought. Puppies tended to get too playful, and fell through the openings."

The house was long and low, stone-faced, beautifully proportioned. They were looking at the garden front. A series of terraces led down to lawns which ended at the lake. Reflected in the still water was a small Grecian temple.

"It's beautiful," she said again. "And it looks lived in."

"It's never been closed." He began driving at walking pace along the lakeside road. "It's cheaper in the long run to keep things in good shape. Restoration costs a lot."

"Where's the farm?"

"Beyond those trees, about a mile and a half from the house. I'll take you there later."

He drove round the house to a courtyard and stopped at the foot of a flight of steps. At the top stood an elderly, black-clad woman. William took the steps in two bounds and enfolded her in his arms.

"Lovely to see you, Julie," he said. "Are you well?"

"I'm very well, Mr. William. And you?"

"Fine. Stay where you are a minute."

He went down the steps, opened the car door for Hazel and led her up to the housekeeper.

"Julie, this is Miss Hazel Paget. Hazel, this is Mrs. Julie Schenk, for nearly fifty years the prop and support of our family. Incidentally, she's Dirk's mother."

"Welcome, Miss Paget." Mrs. Schenk's voice matched her appearance—calm and composed. "Have you come a long way?"

"Not very far," Hazel said. "From Steeplewood."

"Far enough," said William, "to have given us an appetite for your hot scones. Are they in the oven?"

"They'll be ready for you when you're ready for them. I've laid tea on the terrace."

"Good. I'll take Miss Paget on a very swift tour of the house first. This way, Hazel."

He led her across the large entrance hall and down a long corridor.

"You won't see any treasures," he told her. "No Gobelins, no Aubussons, no Sheraton, no Hepplewhite. Good pictures, but apart from those, more comfort than style. There were no collectors in the family; they were all traders with their minds on profit and loss. My father's study. My mother's sitting room. My stepmother didn't use it; she preferred one upstairs. Waiting room for people who call on business. They don't, nowadays; they go to the office, but at one time they used to. That's why the room opens straight out to the courtyard. Dining room. Children's dining room. This is all the uninteresting part. Now we go upstairs. Drawing room first; it's got a balcony with a nice view."

She was reluctant to leave the balcony. It was wide and semicircular, with long chairs set out under a spreading sun blind. Leaning on the balustrade, she looked out at the lawns, the lake and, in the distance, the farm buildings.

"I like the reflection of the bridge in the lake," she said. "That's why your father made the railing so intricate."

"He died on that bridge," William said.

Her face turned slowly to his, but she said nothing, waiting for him to go on.

"He was lying in the middle. He'd walked from the station. It was just after seven when he was found."

"Who found him?"

"I did. It was a Monday. He and my stepmother had been away on a trip, and they had got back on the Friday and she had gone down to Kent to stay with her sister for the weekend. My father went up to visit an old friend of his in Cambridge. He came back on Monday morning and went to the office, but he didn't stay long. He told his secretary he'd be out to lunch and wouldn't be returning to the office that day. I'd been over to Holland. I drove straight from the airport and got here about six; my stepmother was expected at seven. I couldn't understand why my father wasn't in; it wasn't like him to let her arrive first. I thought I'd walk down towards the station to meet him; the train might have been late. If I'd come out on the garden side of the house—this side—I would have seen him. But I went down the beech avenue; you can't see the lake until you come to the end of the trees. And then I saw him lying there. One of his hands was at the edge of the bridge, as though he'd felt himself falling, reached for the railing and missed. Nobody knew how long he'd been there. The doctor said he'd been dead for less than an hour. I went down afterwards to the station to see if I could find out what train he'd come home on, but it was the rush hour and the trains getting into Penston are pretty crowded, and nobody remembered seeing him. It was a bad time for my stepmother. She still feels that she could have prevented it."

"How?"

"First, by not going on the trip. It was just after he'd got the letter from Mr. Horn, and she thinks she should have persuaded my father to go to Steeplewood because there was a chance that Mr. Horn might have had the last flagon. Then she blamed herself for not coming home with him. And she felt the reunion he went to had been too much for him."

"Reunion?"

"War. Survivors of the regiment. My father had never been to one—he disliked get-togethers of any kind—but he must have decided to go to this one as it was the last they were to have. I'm sorry to have got onto this. Let's go and look at the rooms in which generations of Helder children grew up."

They had grown up, she found, in large, sunny nurseries and bright, airy schoolrooms. They had left their mark deeply etched on desks and tables and banisters.

Although they did not linger over tea, they found that it was too late to walk down to the farm; they could visit it only if they drove there and after a brief stay, went straight back to Steeplewood. They said goodbye to Mrs. Schenk, thanked her, and left the house.

During their tour of the farm, William found Hazel responding with less enthusiasm than he had expected to the sight of baby ducklings, newly dropped calves and frisking foals. She exchanged sensible views with the farmer, admired and exclaimed and commented, but William felt that a note was missing.

"Tired?" he asked, as they left.

"No. I loved it. Thank you for bringing me."

"Anything on your mind?"

She hesitated.

"Yes," she admitted.

"Secret, not to be divulged?"

"No. It's just an idea that's got into my head and won't get out. An idiotic idea."

"Communicable?"

"Yes. But it's an idea that you should have had, not me."

"Well?"

"It's only coincidence, but have you counted the number of times the word *christening* has come up in the course of the day?"

"No. You have?"

"I haven't counted, but it's been like a—well, rather like listening to Hugo when he's found a theme or a phrase on the piano and keeps going back and back and back to it."

"Christening, christening, christening?"

"Something like that. Every time I forgot the word, there it came again."

"And this idiotic idea you have?"

"I wondered if it wasn't a kind of—of clue."

"To what?"

"To the search you're on. If I could imagine it had a connection, why didn't you? You're the one who's supposed to be the interested party. Can't you guess what I'm driving at?"

"No."

"My godmother mentioned a christening."

"She mentioned a christening mug."

"Yes." She looked at him, waiting for him to understand. "Well, don't you *see*?"

"No."

"Why are men so *slow*? Sylvia said she had seen Mr. Horn's

collection—not once, but several times. Right?"

"Yes. Do you—"

"She also spoke of having chosen a christening mug."

"Yes." He stared at her. "You think—"

"I don't think anything. I only remembered, suddenly, that she'd know what a flagon was, in a general way, but she wouldn't know what your particular flagon looked like. I didn't know, either, until you drew it in the caravan to show Mrs. Clencher. Until then, I'd pictured it as much larger, the kind of thing a medieval page would refill when standing by the king's side at table. But yours is small, a miniature flagon, so if she saw it in Mr. Horn's collection, why wouldn't she mistake it for a kind of christening mug? She said it was unusual; don't you remember?"

"Yes. You think there's a chance that—"

"It wouldn't hurt to try and find out, would it?"

"We ask her when we get back?"

"Not at once. Later. And let me do the asking. She needs a leading rein. If you asked the questions, she'd get you tangled up as she does everyone who doesn't know her. You have to make her stick to the point. It isn't easy." She saw his expression, and added a warning. "Look, don't build on this. She probably saw a silver Toby jug in a junk shop somewhere. When it first came into my mind, I almost decided not to mention it, in case you thought I was weaving fantasies."

He brought the car to a stop. For some moments he said nothing. Then:

"Is there any harm in weaving fantasies?" he asked. "Not about christening mugs. About—other things?"

Some of the colour left her cheeks.

"It depends," she answered.

"I was afraid to ask you about your engagement. So I asked Dilys. She said it was over. And when we were at the inn, you said so too. But Dilys doesn't think he's accepted the fact that it's all over."

"He took back the ring, which he'd refused to do for a long time. But he's always got what he wanted in life, and I suppose it's hard for him to believe— Do we have to talk about it?"

"Only to tie up loose ends."

"Well, I hope I won't hear from him any more."

"I heard from him. More accurately, I heard from his solicitors."

"About the fence?"

"Yes."

"Why couldn't he have left it to the insurance people to—"

"It makes more impact this way. But it doesn't make much difference to the outcome; he'll feel better for having made the gesture, and I'll pay up and his mother can buy a new fence and plant some more flowers. We were talking about fantasies."

"We're due at a party."

"No hurry. Let's clear up this fantasy business first. I've been weaving them from the first moment I saw you. Did you know?"

She hesitated.

"That would be easier to answer," she said at last, "if you put it into another form."

"I'll try. Do you think I've been coming to Steeplewood to look for a flagon?"

"That's how you began."

"Did it strike you that after that beginning, my object might have been to see you?"

"It didn't exactly strike me. The idea's been creeping up on me. Where does the fantasy come in?"

"In dreaming about a girl who's engaged to another man. Having learned that she isn't—"

"Having learned that she isn't, there should be a reasonable interval during which the girl . . ." She turned to him and he saw tears in her eyes. "William, it's been a pretty awful year. I never wanted to become engaged. I—"

"How did you get involved?" he asked.

"The first time I met him, I was trying to convince his agent that I didn't want to be groomed to be a Caradon model. Rupert came in, we talked and he asked me out to dinner. I went, and he kept asking me and usually I accepted. I didn't think he was particularly interested in me; he made a kind of joke about taking the country girl to see the bright lights. I found it interesting for a time, but my chief feeling was thankfulness that I didn't belong to that set. Rupert's main interests were keeping track of up-and-coming celebrities, finding out who was shacking up with whom, and being seen at places where he could get the most publicity. His manner towards me was a mixture of kindness and condescension, and I didn't mind the condescension because I was learning a lot. It didn't ever enter my mind that he might fall for me, let alone suggest marriage. It didn't happen in his set. Then I realized that I'd spent too much time watching his peculiar friends, and not enough time watching him. When I realized how serious he was, I panicked. I told him I'd never marry him, but he didn't believe it. Just as things were getting really complicated, I found I could go home. I got out of London as fast as I could pack and get a taxi to the station. But the worst part came after that, when he bought a house in Steeplewood for his mother, and came down and went to the farm and argued and argued and argued. I think I could have stood out against the arguments, but I realized that from his point of view I'd led him to believe that I'd marry him— once he got round to asking me. I felt that I shouldn't have let things drift on for so long, taking it for granted that he wasn't serious. So I agreed to become engaged for a trial period. And it didn't work."

"How did it end?"

"In our kitchen, when he heard I'd made a date with you. But it was his mother who really broke it up; she never liked me, and in the end she loathed me and that helped. But I can't believe it's all over. I feel there'll still be arguments, phone calls, letters, sudden visits . . . so what I'd like you to give me is—"

"—time to shake it off?"

"Yes. The only thing is—"

"Well?"

"Would you be around?"

"Naturally I'd be around. Where did you think I'd be? Wouldn't you want me to be around?"

"Yes. Very much."

"Hazel—"

"Will you try to be patient?"

"I don't have to try. I'm patient by nature. I've never told you I loved you, have I?"

"No."

"Well, take it as read. You know, and that's the main thing. Would you mind if the passers-by saw me kissing you?"

"No."

He took her into his arms.

"Do you love me?" he asked.

"Yes."

"Are you sure?"

"Quite sure. I don't know why I'm sure; we don't really know one another, do we?"

"Not yet. We'll fill in the details during our fifty years of marriage."

Some time later, they remembered the party. They drove

to the farm and Hazel poured out sherry, handed it to him and went upstairs to change. She came down at the same moment that Dilys came in from the farm with a basket of eggs. Dilys's manner seemed slightly strained.

"How did you get on with Hazel's godmother?" she asked William.

"Oh—fine."

"I suppose you heard about the sale?" Hazel asked.

"Everybody's heard. The news was round the town before the Arabs had left. The postman told me."

"Is Hugo back?"

"Yes."

"You sound—is anything the matter?"

"Well, there's news."

"Good news?"

"I think so, and you'll think so, but Hugo doesn't think so, and he's rather depressed."

"Why?"

"They're going to sing one of his anthems."

"Oh, Dilys—where?"

"Westminster Abbey. Thanksgiving Service."

"Depressed?" William said in amazement. "Doesn't he think it's good news?"

"No. He regards the anthems as a kind of sideline. What he longs for is recognition of his other work."

"But surely this is wonderful publicity?" Hazel asked.

"In church circles, yes," Dilys admitted. "But—"

"If he's known, if his name's known, he's made."

"I wish he thought so. He's been asked for permission to use his new hymn settings, and the book of anthems is being rushed out."

"I don't know what this means in money terms, but it must mean he's on the map," Hazel pointed out.

"The wrong map."

"Where is he now?"

"Upstairs. With Bernie."

"Bernie?"

"There's a big celebration at the Foresters' Arms next Saturday. The owner's seventieth birthday. Bernie wanted to work up a special item and it needed a drummer, so he borrowed a snare drum and brought it over to ask Hugo to show him how to use it. It was a godsend; it took Hugo's mind off the anthem. He—"

She stopped. From the room above had come the prolonged roll of a drum. Then Bernie's powerful voice was raised.

> "And now, small blame, I bear the name
> And drum of Darby Kelly-O
> Myself as true at rat-tat-too
> At roll call or reveillez-O"

"My!" breathed Hazel into the ensuing silence. "That's going to make the audience sit up."

"It's also going to lift the roof right off the pub," Dilys added.

William was looking dazed.

"That song," he said. "I know it. We sang it, twelve of us, all with scarlet coats and drums, at my prep school when I was ten. I had a solo bit—'When great Wolfe died, his country's pride.' For years after that, I mourned for the passing of the drummer boy. So young, so brave . . . and the glory! The entire populace turned out to cheer them when they got home, 'through laurel arch and waving banners home again.' I don't know about lifting off the pub roof; it'll lift the hearts of all the—"

He stopped. Bernie had embarked on the last verse.

"And as my sticks, the same old tricks
They play with pattering row-dow-dow,
Man, woman, child, they've all gone wild,
And the girls they gaze, you don't know how."

William moved to the door.

"Won't be a moment," he said. "I'm just going to ask him to sing that—"

"No! Dilys, stop him! We've got to go to that party."

"Back!" ordered Dilys.

"Look, I won't be more than a minute or two. I just want to ask him—"

The drum was sounding, making speech impossible. Dilys pointed to the door. He fell in beside Hazel. Together, to the rhythm of the drum beats, they marched to the car.

6

THEY FOUND LADY STORRING READY FOR HER PARTY, WEAR-
ing a long, fringe-trimmed dress of pale blue. Her curls were
in orderly rows and there were heavy bracelets on her wrists.
She greeted them with the announcement that the few hours'
rest had made her feel renewed.

"So silly of me to allow myself to get overwrought," she
said. "And to fail you over lunch was the worst of all. I'm
going to make it up to you at dinner. I've asked the Canon,
so we shall be four. He's had a dreadful day, poor old sweet,
dealing with the sale. They've all been closeted in the lawyers'
offices. He won't come to my cocktail party, of course; he
never attends frivolous functions. Hazel, my dear, how do
you think I look?"

Hazel said, with patent sincerity, that she looked lovely,
while William reflected that however difficult it had been to
get money out of the trustees, she had managed to get enough
to satisfy an extravagant taste in dress. He thought of his stepmother, quiet of manner, dry of speech, her clothes bordering
on the severe, and wondered what she would make of this ani-
mated and colourful figure.

143

"I'm worried about this party," she said. "Do you know what I've done? I've asked too many people. When I looked again at that list, I thought I must have been out of my senses to write down so many names."

"Perhaps some of them won't be able to come," Hazel suggested.

"My dear, they've all said they'll be delighted! They told me at the reception desk that the whole town's buzzing with the news of the sale. They'll all come, even if it's only out of curiosity. Is it time to go over, do you think? I must be there when the first of them arrives. Do you know many people in Steeplewood?" she asked William.

"Hazel, her brother and sister-in-law, a girl called Mavis, a man called Joby—and Miss Horn," he said.

"She's coming. I don't care for her, but she has a position in the town, and I was fond of her uncle, in a sort of way. She's not liked, you know, but she's respected. Isn't it odd how people's critical faculties get numbed when somebody's made a success of something? Dear old Mr. Horn, if the truth must be told, was an old shark. He wanted to sell antiques, but he didn't want to have the bother and expense of running a shop, what with overheads and things, so he bought and sold in his own house, and people knew he was doing it, but he did it with such style that they stopped thinking of him as a shopkeeper and regarded him as a knowledgeable and benevolent old gentleman who dabbled in antiques. It's the same with Miss Horn. Simply *coining* money up at that school, but who thinks of her as a schoolmistress? Nobody. She's turned herself into the lady of the manor. Have you got the right time, William?"

"Six twenty."

"Then we must go. Shall I drape this wrap over me, Hazel? I've got another, if you think this is too light."

"It'll get rather warm in that room, won't it?"

"Oh, I shan't wear it for long. It's only for *effect*. I think it gives a finish. I'll take it, anyhow."

They walked over to the hotel and William and Hazel left her to await her guests at the door of the reception room hired out by the hotel for festive occasions. It was not large; in it were a few chairs and a few small tables set out with cigarettes and small dishes of olives. Four waiters stood at a long table behind trays of glasses.

It was soon clear that Lady Storring's fear of having asked too many people was to be more than realized. Early arrivals were fortunate; there was no crush, conversation could be exchanged without shouting and the waiters could circulate freely with trays of drinks. Latecomers fared worse, while the stragglers could force their way in only by displacing the waiters at the other end of the room. As a result, no more drinks could be served.

William, groping round intervening bodies, found Hazel's hand and pulled her free from the group surrounding her. Keeping close to him, she followed him as he fought a way out to the lounge. Then they stopped and drew in deep breaths of air.

"Did you get a drink?" he asked.

"No."

"Neither did I. Let's get to the bar fast, before fifty others realize that the service has broken down."

The bar was filling up, but there was still space for them. The conversation was almost exclusively about the sale of the castle, and there was spirited speculation as to what differences, if any, the presence of Arabs was going to make to the town. The wags said that the streets would be full of walking tents with eyeholes. There was a sharp division between those who welcomed the new element and those who considered that there were already too many aliens in Steeplewood. The discussion was becoming heated when Miss Horn was seen approaching; it was then abandoned, for it was a subject people avoided when she was present.

She joined William and Hazel and was about to take a chair when she paused.

"Canon Cranshaw's sitting in the lounge, all alone. Let's go and talk to him," she said.

The Canon, grey-haired, red-cheeked and portly, was occupying a corner sofa. An open book was on his knee, a glass of tonic water on the table in front of him. He rose and welcomed them warmly.

"Are you coming to join me? Good, good. Sit down, sit down. It's comparatively quiet in here."

"You didn't go to the party?" Miss Horn asked him.

"Oh, dear me, no, no, no. Not in my line at all. I can't remember when I was last at an affair of that kind." He paused to acknowledge Hazel's introduction of William. "How d'you do? Were you all at the party?"

"For a time," Hazel said. "There were too many people there. Such a jam that the drinks couldn't get round."

"Ah, that's why so many people are coming out, is it?"

"It was suffocating," Miss Horn said. "I was one of the lucky ones who did manage to get something before the waiters vanished."

William signalled a passing waiter to order a round of drinks. Miss Horn and Hazel wanted sherry, but the Canon expressed himself satisfied with his tonic water.

"Thank you, but I never drink anything, except a little wine with my meals," he explained.

William raised his eyes to give the order for the drinks, and found himself looking at Joby. Hazel recognized him at the same moment, and saw to her surprise that the Canon had also done so.

"Yes, sir?"

The deferential tone was accompanied by a slight wink and

a shake of the head; they understood that he did not wish to be identified. William gave the order; Joby brought the drinks, waited for payment and bowed with exaggerated deference when William, with an expressionless face, added a peppercorn tip.

He walked away, and the Canon leaned back and sighed.

"I've had a hard day," he told them.

"But a successful day," Miss Horn pointed out. "Or are you sorry to see the castle go?"

"I'm sorry to see the end of a long, long family line," he said. "It was a splendid old place, an historic place. I feel strongly that some kind of brief history should be written about it."

"And who but you can write it?" Miss Horn asked.

"Oh, there are antiquarians in this town," he assured her. "But I do happen to have a collection of notes which I hope to put together when I find the leisure. I'm sorry that strangers are going to inhabit that beautiful old fortress. Fortress it once was, of course. Historic, historic."

"The Arabs will bring money to the town," Miss Horn pointed out.

"Oh, undoubtedly. Oh, yes, undoubtedly. That emerged very clearly in the discussions I had with them during the day. They assured me that they will use local materials and local skills, if available; and both *are* available. This is a quiet town, an old town, perhaps an old-fashioned town, but it has its professionals, its experts."

"What will Lady Storring do now?" Miss Horn asked. "Will she come and live in Steeplewood again?"

"I doubt it. I very much doubt it."

"There's a charming house for sale at the foot of the hill, just below the Manor," Miss Horn reminded him.

"Yes. The Challenger house. I'm sorry they've decided to sell it, but I suppose it's too large for old Miss Challenger to keep going. No, I don't think Lady Storring would like anything so large. Her aim, I fancy, is to settle herself in one of those service places, where there are no servant problems. She—" He broke off and glanced at his watch. "Hazel, my dear, don't you think you should try and induce her to bring this function to an end? It was unwise of her, I think, to give a party at all after the excitements of the morning, but if she can break off now, there will be time for her to get half an hour's rest before dinner."

Hazel was on her feet. Miss Horn rose.

"I'll go with you," she said. "I shall say goodbye to her and I shall add in a very loud voice that she musn't overtire herself. If people don't take the hint, I shall make the point clearer."

"And that's what I want to do, too," said a voice beside her.

It was Joby. He took a step and barred her way.

"Nice meeting you," he said politely. "The pleasure's been too long delayed, don't you agree? The name's Purley, Nathaniel Purley."

Miss Horn had had time to grasp the situation.

"Will you kindly allow me to pass?" she said, and Hazel recognized the tone; it was the one that had annihilated many presumptuous parents.

"I won't keep you," Joby said. "I just wanted to say goodbye."

"If you do not move out of my way," Miss Horn told him, "I shall summon the hotel manager."

"I'll do that for you in a minute. I just wanted to say thanks for all you've done for Mavis. We'll call our first-born after you. I suppose you won't come to the wedding?"

"Joby . . . please . . ." began Hazel.

"That's all right, Hazel my girl." Joby spoke reassuringly. "The lady's got the message. Ta-ta, Miss Horn. From me and from Mavis."

He turned on his heel and without haste went back to the bar. Miss Horn stood motionless for some moments and then turned to face Hazel. She addressed her in a voice that was low but venomous.

"You're in this too," she said. "In fact, you've been harbouring him."

"I wouldn't call it—"

"There has been far too much interference in this matter. You are the person I blame the most, since from the first you've been a subversive influence in the office. Without knowing the slightest thing about my motives, you've deliberately misconstrued them. Now you can have the satisfaction of knowing where your interference has led. That man will take Mavis away, amuse himself for a time and then leave her. She will then return to her relatives—from whom I removed her. She will revert to a life with her sluttish mother and her delinquent brothers and sisters. You have wrecked all the hopes I had for her, all the plans I made for her. I hope you are satisfied."

She walked with firm tread across the lounge and out of the hotel.

The two men had risen anxiously. William had placed himself beside Hazel.

"Unfortunate, very unfortunate," the Canon murmured. "Oh dear, oh dear." He resumed his seat. "Hazel, I must say something about this."

Somewhat shaken, Hazel seated herself beside him.

"You knew him," she said. "I saw that you recognized him when he came to take the order for drinks."

"Yes. You see, he came to see me."

"When?"

"Yesterday. Does your friend"—he looked at William—"know about Joby and why he came here?"

"Yes. What did he want to see you about?"

"He wanted to talk to me about his problem. He felt that you could do nothing, working as you did for Miss Horn. He asked me to go and see her."

"And did you?"

"I did. You wouldn't have guessed, would you, seeing her friendly manner towards me this evening, that our interview was far from cordial?"

"What did you say to her?"

"I told her that I thought he would make Mavis a good husband. I said that although I had seen so little of him, I was basing my opinion on a long experience of young people with problems."

"Didn't you tell her that he and Mavis could go back and be happy if only she'd let Mavis go?"

"I didn't put it quite in that way, but that was my purpose in going to see her. She understood quite well what I meant."

"And then?"

"She said, in more detail, what she said to you just now. She said that she was relieved to find that the matter was now in the open, so that she could state her views. She told me the circumstances in which Mavis had lived before coming to work for her—the rather dreadful home, the undesirable surroundings. She said that if Mavis left her, she would sink back into the old conditions. She told me that Mavis had picked up this young man and knew nothing whatsoever about his character. She then admitted that she was using all her weight—and we know that to be considerable, in every sense—to keep Mavis with her. So perhaps it's as well that the young man has taken matters into his own hands. I think he acted a little crudely—but wisely. And now, my dear, hadn't you better see if you can persuade your godmother to think about bringing her party to an end?"

Hazel left them, and the Canon looked after her with affection.

"A nice girl," he said. "Have you known her long?"

"No."

"I've known her and her brother since they were born. I knew their parents, not only as parents but also before they were parents. It was an extraordinary thing, you know, the way old Mr. Thane Paget—Hazel's grandfather—decided, all at once, that he would like to be a farmer. The family had never been connected with the land; they were—always had been—artists, musicians, with little knowledge of practical matters. But he bought a farm, and I met him just after he and his family went to live there. At first, things went quite well. He had a farm manager, he had a splendid cowman, he had stable lads and dairymaids. He had experts in, if I may use the expression, every field. The experts advised, the workers worked, old Mr. Paget rode round his prosperous acres. But then things changed. The trend was away from the land. The old workers left, no new workers came to replace them. And so in time the selling began—first the woods, and then the rest. What you see there now is the true Paget image, in this case a musician, a composer, living on the residue of what was once a prosperous farm. But perhaps you're not interested in this history? I forgot that you were a stranger. I'm so fond of them I get carried away and forget that other people haven't known and loved them for as long as I have. Tell me, Mr. Holford, are you staying in Steeplewood?"

"No. I'm driving back to London after dinner. The name's Helder."

"I'm afraid I didn't catch—did you say Helder?"

"Yes. William Helder."

The Canon peered at him in astonishment. His glasses slipped down his nose and he pushed them up again absently.

"That's odd," he said slowly. "That's really very odd. I know that name. A long, long way back—right back to the war. I served with a William Helder. I shared a tank with him. Your father?"

"Probably," said William.

"A Dutch connection?"

"Yes."

"Must be the one. But you don't look in the least like him."

"No. I take after my mother's side of the family. Do you know Mr. Strickland too?"

"Strickland? Of course I know him. He's another of the old crowd."

"He and my father were very old friends—school friends, to begin with."

"Then it's the same Helder. I'm not going to utter any clichés about it's being a small world. I hear he died last year."

"Yes. He was staying with Mr. Strickland the weekend before he died."

"So I heard, so I heard. I would so much have liked to see him. That reunion—you know, of course, we had an annual reunion?"

"Yes."

"This year's was the last of them. Perhaps your father told you. It was time they came to an end; the feast was beginning to look a little macabre—fewer and fewer of us left, more and more dropping off. One wondered who'd be missing the following year. There were only eight of us at the last gathering." He sighed. "Eight. But I suppose you could say that we all had a good innings. I used to make a point of meeting your father whenever I passed through London, but that wasn't often. I met your mother, but I never had the pleasure of meeting your stepmother. The last time I met your father was—let me see— two years, yes, two years ago."

"Weren't you at the reunion?" William asked.

"Of course I was. I didn't miss one, not a single one from the time we inaugurated them. But your father didn't believe in them. He dodged them all. A great pity."

"But he was at the last one."

"Your father? No, he wasn't."

"But I understand—"

"Eight of us, that's all. It was time to call a halt. Strickland made the last speech, and a good one it was. He mentioned your father, said what a good example he'd been in those old days. You get to know people pretty well when you've fought beside them."

"Mr. Strickland was at the reunion?"

"Most certainly. He wouldn't have missed one for anything. I remember his once saying that— Ah, here come our two ladies. You know," he confided in a low tone as they approached, "I don't really care for a heavy meal at night. I would have got out of this dinner if I could, but it was rather a special day for Hazel's godmother, and so I gave in. But I would so much rather go home to my bowl of soup and my little pot of yoghurt. Isn't it odd," he went on as Hazel and Lady Storring joined them, "how yoghurt has become part of our daily fare?"

"Not my daily fare," said Lady Storring. "I never touch it."

She sounded a little excited, and her cheeks were flushed, but her manner was calm and her curls were in perfect order.

"I've kept you all waiting," she said. "Forgive, forgive, forgive. But now we shall go off at once. I must go across and get a warmer wrap, and then I am going to ask William to let us use his beautiful car."

"We're not dining here?" the Canon asked.

"No, no, no! I've booked a table at the Percheron. It's a very nice new restaurant," she told William. "It specializes in seafood. Come along; let's go."

"I must give back this book I borrowed," the Canon said. "I shall follow you."

Outside the hotel, Lady Storring stopped and drew in deep gulps of air.

"Oh, lovely! A little cold, but such a relief after being *cooked* inside that room. It was a pity about the overcrowding, but good in a way, because I shan't have to ask anyone else to anything; I've got them all off in one go. I wish they'd put a light at this entrance. Coming back in the dark, I only have the hotel lights to guide me."

She handed William the door key. They followed her inside, and she sank onto the sofa and put her feet up.

"Oh, the relief! The blessed, blessed relief. Why were we only given one pair of feet?" She bent to take off her shoes. "Only for a moment or two," she said. "Then we must go out and dine. And tomorrow, I must go back to Cornwall and make my plans."

"You won't come back to live at Steeplewood?" William asked.

"I might. I might, you know. There are no service apartments here of the kind I want, but I could buy a house and convert it and keep the sunny side for myself and sell the rest. Miss Horn thought that would be a good idea. I dislike her more and more, but she's got a clear head. I wish mine felt a bit clearer."

"Is it clear enough to answer a question?" Hazel asked.

"Yes, of course, my dear. What is it?"

"Do you remember mentioning that you once saw a christening mug that you were tempted to buy?"

"For your first baby. Of course I remember. I don't know when I said it, but it's true. Only I couldn't have said I was tempted to buy it, because it was completely out of my price range. I couldn't have paid one fff—fif—fiftieth is a difficult word to say, isn't it? I couldn't have paid one fortieth of the price."

"What did it look like?"

"It was sweet. Did I say it was unusual?"

"Yes."

"Small. Silver. It was engraved, but I'm told you can have changes made to engravings. It had two delicious little ears.

Handles, if you like, but I thought of them as ears, just right for a little baby's fists to close on. How beautiful babies' limbs are, don't you think so? So soft, so rounded, so—"

"Where did you see it?"

"See what, darling?"

"The christening mug."

"Strictly speaking, I suppose it wasn't a christening mug. I don't know—"

"But where was it?"

"Oh, where? It was in the safe."

"Whose safe?"

"I told you, darling. You weren't listening. I told you all about his getting out all his treasures and showing them to me."

"Mr. Horn?"

"Yes." She gave a helpless little giggle. "You might call it a little drinking horn. Could you hand me that little cushion from over there, William? Thank you. Just tuck it under my head for a moment, Hazel dear. That's right. I feel a little heavy-headed. Or do I mean light-headed? What were we talking about?"

"The little christening mug in Mr. Horn's collection."

"Yes. Sweet, it was. He should never, never have let it go."

There was a brief silence.

"He let it go?"

"Well, of course." Lady Storring gave a prolonged yawn. "That's what it was there for, wasn't it? To go. I mean, to sell?"

"He sold it?"

"And very well. The afternoon I went to see him. I dropped in to say goodbye; I was on my way to the station, and he told me it had gone. He was very pleased with the sale—like me and the castle. Oh, what a day this has been! What a heavenly, heavenly day!"

"Did Mr. Horn tell you who'd bought it?"

"Oh, goodness me, no. He never named his buyers, and of course I never asked."

"Can you remember what date he sold it?"

"Oh, no! You know what my memory is, Hazel darling, especially now, when my head's so full of plans for the beautiful future. I was only here for two days, not to see a possible buyer but to make a desperate appeal to the Canon to advance me some money. He took no notice of my letters. It was only two weeks before my allowance was due, but he was *adamant*. How could those trustees have been so mean, so ungenerous? Oh, if only we could have foreseen this blissful end to all those years of skimping and scraping . . . skimping . . . scraping . . ."

Her eyes closed. The Canon, who for the past few minutes had been standing in the doorway, put a finger on his lips and crept in and stood looking down at her. It was clear that she was not going to move for some time. He beckoned Hazel and William out of the room.

"Don't disturb her," he advised. "Let her sleep. Let her sleep it off. She's had enough; in fact . . . Well, let her rest. Will you forgive me if I slip away and leave you two to dine together?"

Hazel merely nodded; she was not thinking of dinner. Her mind was on William. Then the Canon spoke again.

"You were asking your godmother for a date—you wanted to know, did you not, on what day Mr. Horn had sold a particular item in his collection?"

"Yes." Hazel's attention was now fully on him. "She said—"

"Yes, I heard. I can clarify the date for you. She came to Steeplewood—as so often——to ask for, indeed to demand money. We had a very painful interview, but I stuck to my guns. She went back without the money. I sent her the check when it was due—two weeks later."

"You remember the date?" William asked.

"Very well indeed. It was the Friday on which I had to go to Cambridge to attend the reunion that you and I were discussing a short while ago."

"You're sure?" Hazel asked.

"Quite sure. I remember with what relief I took the train to Cambridge, leaving your godmother to go back to Cornwall. And now, if you'll forgive me . . ."

He went out. Hazel turned to look at William.

"William, I'm so sorry. About the flagon. Are you upset?"

He looked down at her.

"No. We'll pick up the trail somewhere else."

"I wish I could feel as philosophical about it as you appear to do. Would you mind if we went home, instead of going to that restaurant?"

"Would you like me to take you home, and then go away?"

"No. There'll be dinner for four—Dilys and Hugo and Mavis and Joby. We could stretch it."

"I don't think the other four would like that."

"Let's go and see. Unless you'd rather go back to London. Would you?"

"No, I wouldn't. But I'll go just the same. I'll take you home first."

He found that the house looked very much better by night. The darkness masked its deficiencies and the lights shining out from the kitchen threw a kindly glow onto the yard.

He stopped the car but made no move to get out.

"The Canon knew my father," he said.

Her face turned to him, a pale outline in the darkness.

"How did you find that out?"

"He recognized the name. They were in the war together. The Canon went to all the reunions. My father didn't go to any of them—except the last. We thought."

"Who thought?"

"My stepmother and I. But the Canon says he wasn't there. There were only eight of them present, and my father wasn't one of them."

"Had he said he'd be going?"

"I don't know. My stepmother certainly had that impression —or did she just take it for granted that he went because he was staying with another member of the old crowd? A man named Strickland. Strickland was at the reunion. The Canon said he made a speech and mentioned my father."

"If he was staying with Mr. Strickland, and if Mr. Strickland went to the reunion, wouldn't your father have meant to go too?"

"It would be very unlike him to choose that weekend and then let Strickland go without him."

"You sound worried. Is it important?"

"No. And I'm not worried, I'm just puzzled. I can clear it up tomorrow by getting hold of my stepmother. But—"

"But what?"

"I don't know. There's something that doesn't fit."

"You *are* worried. And you're disappointed. It was beginning to look hopeful, and now—"

Her voice broke. He put a finger on her cheek, and felt tears. He gathered her into his arms and held her, letting her weep, saying nothing until she had regained her self-command. She freed herself.

"Better?" he asked.

"Yes."

"I lose the flagon, you do the crying?"

"I wanted you to find it. I wanted to be with you when you found it. I wanted to feel that I'd helped, in a small way, to find it."

"The search isn't over."

"Will you tell me what your stepmother says?"

"Of course."

"Aren't you coming inside?"

"No. I'd have to talk if I went in, and my mind's confused. I wish you lived nearer. I wish you were free to come with me. I wish . . ."

He stopped, took her face between his hands and bent to kiss her. Then he stood by the car, waiting for the door of the house to close behind her.

But before it closed, the door of the cottage opened with a loud crash. The next moment, Joby came stumbling out, propelled by an unseen but powerful hand. He staggered, lost his balance, recovered it and plunged towards the nearest tree, to which he clung. He was wearing nothing but a pair of underpants. Before William or Hazel could recover from their astonishment, the door of the cottage opened again, and Mavis hurled out several shirts, two pairs of trousers, socks and some miscellaneous toilet articles. After them she flung the canvas bag.

"You can go back where you came from," she shouted. "I don't want to see your lying face ever again. You can go and play games with every woman in this town—but you just keep away from me, you dirty cheat, you."

The door banged. Joby straightened, shrugged and began to pick up his belongings and push them into the bag. He kept out a shirt and a pair of trousers, and put them on.

"Trouble?" William enquired.

Joby nodded dejectedly.

"Any strong drink available?" he asked.

"Yes. Come inside," Hazel said.

The three went into the kitchen. Joby dropped into a chair, put his elbows on the table and stared into space. He looked pale.

"What happened?" William asked him.

Joby spoke without moving.

"That bloody Bernie. He opened his mouth. I knew he

would." He roused himself and took the drink Hazel brought him. "Whisky. Good girl. I need it. You should have heard what she's been calling me in there. I can keep up with dirty words in English, but not in that language. Have you ever heard anybody swearing in Welsh?" He shuddered. "Horrible, it was. I didn't know she could go on like that."

"What did Bernie tell her?" William asked.

"Dunno. Wish I'd been there. But I wasn't. I came home from the hotel and I gave myself a wash and brush-up in the cottage and I was going to put on a fancy shirt and my best pair of pants, all ready to tell her I'd said goodbye to the Horn. I pictured it all: the way she'd come in, and I'd tell her that it was all over and we was on our way to Bournemouth, and she'd be all happy and loving. Cor! She came in, and before I could get a word out, she'd started."

"Well, what was it about?" Hazel pulled out a chair and sat down. "What have you been doing? I can guess, but you can tell it in your own words."

"If you know, you know. I wasn't doing any harm. The way I see it, all I was doing was making a few women happy. What's wrong with that? If they'd kept their mouths shut, the way they know how to do in Bournemouth, this wouldn't have happened. But these women here, they're provincial, that's what. Peasants. Spreading the word, going round town . . . Oh, well. Bernie got hold of a few juicy details, and he met Mavis when she was coming home just now, and he stopped her and told her what he knew." He took a gulp of whisky. "So what do I do now?"

"You got your orders," William reminded him. "Back where you came from."

Joby's eyes went to Hazel.

"Is she the kind that goes on hanging onto grudges?" he enquired.

"As a rule, no. She blows up and simmers down. But that was over minor matters."

"You call this a major matter?"

"She does."

"Then she shouldn't. How do you think we got together, her and me? Where do you think I was a couple of hours after she'd shown up in the salon meeting that girl she knew? I was in her room at the hotel, that's where I was."

"You offered to do her hair—for nothing."

"Do you think she was fool enough to believe that old knock on the parlour door? Well, yes, she was. But when I explained that it was only to lead to better things, she didn't take much convincing. And look at her now: going all sour on me like a vested virgin."

"Vestal."

"What's the difference? Who cares? What am I going to do now? I'm not going back without her. I don't suppose Mum would have me back—she'd know what had happened and she'd blame me. She warned me. She said that this time I'd got hold of a girl who wouldn't be played around with. But it's not reasonable, is it? If you think about it, you can see how unfair this whole situation is—blaming me for doing something she didn't blame me for doing when I was doing it to her. Where's the sense? Where's the *justice*? And take it another way: what sort of future is there in it for me? I've got to go on doing women's hair, haven't I? That's what I am—a ladies' hairdresser. That's my job, my profession. So if she gets over this tantrum and comes round, what's going to happen? Is she going to throw me out each time she thinks I left the salon? She could have hurt me just now; that shove she gave me, you'd have thought it was a battering ram. You can see she's not safe when these moods get hold of her."

"Well, you're free—if you want to be free," Hazel said.

"We're witnesses. She told you she didn't want to set eyes on your lying face again. We heard her. If you want a lift to the station, we'll give you one."

He looked at her sourly.

"Oh, yes, very nice, very kind, very helpful. A good friend you are. Nothing about you going in there to talk her round. What's the matter? Don't you think I'm good enough for her?"

"Frankly, no. I thought you might have made her happy, but you obviously can't. You wouldn't be back in Bournemouth a week without getting into trouble. You came up here to persuade her to go back with you, and then you—"

"Look, I don't need a playback, I need help. Why can't you go in there and talk to her?"

"Two reasons: one, I don't want to interfere, and two, all I could say was that if only she'd forgive you this time, you'd never do it again until the next time."

He spoke bitterly.

"Oh, so that's your opinion of me, is it?"

"Yes. All I'd tell her, if I told her anything, would be that if she goes back to Bournemouth and marries you and then makes a pact with your mother, the two of them between them could—well, control you. Your mother could watch you during working hours, and Mavis could see that you clock in and out regularly at home."

"And you call that a life for a man, with two female policemen on his tail?"

"You'd get used to it."

"And be the laughing-stock of every chum I've got down there?"

"It depends on what your chums laugh at. If they see anything funny in a man with a good mother and a good wife and a lot of healthy and happy children, then—"

"Can I help it if I've always had women after me?"

"Mavis didn't go after you. You went after Mavis, and my

bet is that that's the way it always happens."

"Thank you. Thank you for your womanly sympathy. Do I get another drink?"

"Of course. You'll need your strength; you're going back to the cottage."

"What for?"

"To crawl."

"She won't let me in."

"If she doesn't, you can sit on the doorstep until she does."

"What—all night?"

"Yes. It'll be cold, and you'll probably get pneumonia, but that's the only way to make her feel sorry for you."

"And I get pneumonia and we get married and I never look at another woman so help me?"

"You won't if you know what's good for you."

He sipped his second drink.

"My mum said I'd got hold of a nice girl," he said thoughtfully, after a time. "But what she ought to have said—isn't there something about catching a Tartar?"

"Yes."

"Then that's what I've done. And what's more, I still don't see what she's complaining about. If she'd had any brains, she'd have seen by the way I went after her that it wasn't the first time. I didn't even pretend it was the first time I'd done a bit of hairdressing in a woman's room instead of in the salon. So why—"

"She doesn't mind what you did before you met her. That's all done with. You're allowed a run-around while you're settling on the woman you want to marry—if you want to marry, and you told her you did. Once you've made your choice, you have to stick to it, that's all. To sum up, you're free, as I said. You don't have to stay here. You've got your luggage and if you haven't got your fare, William will donate it and we'll put you on the next train. If you stay, you'll have to do your own peacemaking. You don't have to decide before you've finished your drink."

He finished it slowly and then stood up.

"I'll be found dead, frozen stiff on her doorstep tomorrow morning," he prophesied. "Then you'll be sorry."

"Not me. I'll put *He Asked for It* on your grave. I'll write to your mother and tell her you met your death with fortitude."

He was too crushed to reply. They watched him as he walked slowly to the door of the cottage. He knocked. There was no reply. William looked at Hazel.

"You won't ever do that to me, will you?" he asked.

"Never," she promised. "I'll wait till you've put on a shirt."

7

THE QUESTION THAT WILLIAM WAS ANXIOUS TO PUT TO HIS stepmother—had his father said he intended to go to the reunion, or had she merely surmised it?—could not be asked for some days. Ringing from his office on Monday morning, he learned that she was in Zurich, taking what she called her cure. This, he knew, meant that she was paying a large sum of money to an establishment in which she starved under supervision; she would come back slim but surly.

She was to return on Thursday, but he was in Belgium on business from Tuesday to Friday. Not until Friday evening was he able to reach her on the phone. His proposal to take her out to dinner was not so much refused as dismissed; her determination not to regain the lost weight would not weaken for at least two weeks.

"If you won't dine, can I come and see you?" he asked.

"No. You'll want a drink, and I shall want to join you, and I'm off alcohol."

"I'll drink plain soda."

"Couldn't you make it next week?"

"I'd rather not."

"Isn't it something you can settle over the phone?"

"No."

"Well, I'm not very—" Her voice changed. "Is it about that girl?"

"Girl?"

"I can't remember her name. I can't remember anything after one of these starvation sessions. The girl at Steeplewood."

"No. I'll be round at seven. All right?"

"I suppose so."

"Wouldn't you rather come out and—"

"Oh, heavens, no. Every time I stand up, I totter. You can come here, but you can't stay long."

He arrived punctually. He helped himself to soda water, and made the addition discreetly. He carried his glass to the window seat and sat down.

"Still feeling tottery?" he asked.

"I feel fine. At least, I shall when I've recovered."

"Why in God's name do you put yourself through these penances?"

"A lot of women I know do it. Do you want to see me billowing and bulging?"

"You're not the type that puts on weight. Have you got your memory back?"

"What do you want to know?"

"Whether my father told you definitely that he was going to that last reunion up in Cambridge."

"Of course. Did you think I'd imagined it?"

"No. But imagining is one thing; assuming is another. Could you cast your mind back and try to make this definite?"

"I've told you. He—"

"Wait a minute. When did he first mention it?"

"I don't know. I suppose it was when he got the letter from Mr. Strickland."

"Did you see the letter?"

"No. Your father read it at the breakfast table and told me about it."

"About the reunion?"

"Well, he said there was going to be one, and it was to be the last."

"And being the last, he said he'd attend?"

"He—well, I took it for granted that—"

"Think, Stella. Did he actually say he'd go?"

"I don't know. He must have said so, because he went."

"No. He didn't."

"He didn't what?"

"He didn't go to that reunion."

For a few moments she stared at him. Then she frowned.

"He must have gone. He—"

"He didn't go. I met a Canon Cranshaw, who was—"

"—another of them. Yes, I know. At least, I know the name. Your father used to see him now and then. So?"

"He was at the reunion. There were only eight of them there. My father wasn't one of them."

"If he didn't go, then Mr. Strickland must have decided not to—"

"Mr. Strickland was there. He made the last speech and in it he mentioned my father. But my father wasn't there. So I'd like to know if he said he'd go and then changed his mind, or if he said he was going to stay with Mr. Strickland but had no intention of attending the dinner."

"How could he do that? He'd either go with him, or he wouldn't go and stay with him, or— Is this important?"

"I don't know. There's something about this business that I don't seem able to work out. The flagon was in Mr. Horn's collection."

"It *was*? Oh, William! Then—"

"He sold it. And that'll upset you and it upset me too, but this odd business of the reunion came up, and I'd like to clear it up. So let's go back: my father got the letter. An invitation to go and stay?"

"I don't know. Let me think." She closed her eyes for a moment. "He read the letter, and he said he was glad that old Strickland was keeping so fit, because he'd been ill the year before and they'd all given him up. Then he said that the reunion dinner was to be held in Cambridge and it was to be the last of them, and he went on to say that it was Mr. Strickland who'd really kept the group together all these years, and sent out the reminders and got them all together for the annual reunions. Then . . ."

"Then?"

"Then he said—he was smiling, in a kind of affectionate way—he was very fond of Mr. Strickland—he said in a musing kind of way that he thought he'd look old Strickland up. I asked when the reunion was, and he said it was the weekend we got back from Greece. And then he folded the letter and asked me for another cup of coffee, and he said something about the date fitting in very well. I took that to mean that he was going to the reunion."

"He didn't mention it afterwards?"

"No."

"Not even when you got back to England and he was setting off to stay with Mr. Strickland?"

"No. Not one word about it; of that I'm quite sure. I did say one thing; I advised him to go up by car, hired car. I said that April was a treacherous month and I didn't want him hanging about on stations. I'd asked him to take our car, and let me go down to Kent by train, but he wouldn't hear of that, because he knew that my sister enjoyed going for trips and didn't often get a chance in a comfortable chauffeur-driven car. And that was all that was said about his visit." There were tears in her eyes, but they did not brim over. "So I was wrong about the meeting tiring him," she said. "I was so certain that he'd got too excited, seeing all his old group. Couldn't he have meant to go to the reunion, and not felt well, and asked Mr. Strickland to go without him?"

"That's the most likely solution."

"There's one way of finding out."

"Yes. By going there. I wanted to talk to you first."

"Have you any lead to follow in the flagon hunt?"

"No. Not one. But you'll be interested to know that I've got my teeth into it. Isn't that what you wanted?"

"Yes. Could you give me a drink?"

"But you—"

"Oh, I know, I know. I wasn't going to have one, but talking about your father has upset me."

Once more he found himself pouring out whisky for an overexcited woman. He carried the glass to her and put a question.

"Have you ever heard of a woman called Lady Storring?"

"I've heard of Lord Storring. My first husband went up to see a castle that was for sale. Decrepit, it was. He said nobody'd dream of buying it."

"The Arabs did."

"The who?"

"Oil kings."

"How do you know?"

"The castle's near Steeplewood. I arrived in time to hear the good news."

"Arrived where?"

"Storring's dead; it was sold by his widow, who'd come up from Cornwall to negotiate. She happens to be godmother to Hazel Paget."

"In that case, she might leave her goddaughter a sizable slice of the sale price."

"That thought struck me, too. I felt it would be worthwhile keeping in close touch with the heiress."

"How close have you got?"

"It's difficult to estimate."

He drained his glass and rose, seized by a longing to get home and pick up a telephone and get through to Steeplewood and hear Hazel's voice.

"I won't ask if you're going to see Mr. Strickland," his step-mother said, "because I know you are."

"Yes. This wouldn't be any good by phone. I'll let you know what he says." He bent to kiss her cheek. "I would have liked to take you out and give you a thumping big dinner."

"The less you mention thumping big dinners, the more tactful it would be. Goodbye. Keep in touch."

He drove home thoughtfully, his mind on the mystery of the reunion. This, he reflected, would have been a delicate situation if the man involved had been anybody but his father. When a man stated his intention of doing one thing and surreptitiously did another, there was very often a woman in the case. But his father's sexual urges, as far as he had been able to gauge, had been satisfied within his two marriages. He had not been a man who attracted or was attracted by women; he had been a family man, a businessman, with harmless hobbies that kept him in the open: gardening, bird-watching, hill climbing. So if he left his wife with the impression that he was going to stay with his old friend Mr. Strickland, to Mr. Strickland's he had undoubtedly gone.

There remained the possibility that he had changed his mind, changed his plans. In that case, he would have told his wife on his return. But there had been no return. For some instants the tall, loved figure lying prone on the bridge, one

arm outstretched and reflected in the water of the lake, came
to William's mind, and he forced it out and realized that he
had better concentrate on his driving.

He had ordered a light cold dinner; Dirk and his wife were
going to visit friends. Dirk took his coat and his office papers
and made a quiet announcement.

"Miss Paget telephoned, sir."

William noted the change. Not: "There was a telephone
message from a Miss Paget," as hitherto, as always outside the
circle of his intimates. Now it was "Miss Paget telephoned."
He wondered when Dirk and his wife had decided that the
change was due.

He looked at the message. She had telephoned at half past
six—from a London number.

His call was answered by the receptionist at what he learned
was the Tuscany Hotel. He was connected, and then came
Hazel's voice; and at the sound, his reactions left him in no
doubt whatsoever that hearing it, and hearing it often, had
become necessary to his happiness.

"William? I came up on Tuesday. I'm here with my godmother."

"Can I see you?"

"Not until after the weekend. She's on her way back to
Cornwall, but she's taken a suite here and she's invited all her
friends to come and see her. She asked me to come with her,
and I thought perhaps I'd better; she's still rather overexcited."

"I could take you both out to dinner."

"Thank you, but she's got four offers lined up already. I
was waiting to see which one she'd choose. I rang you because
I wanted to know if you'd found out anything about your
father's visit to Mr. Strickland."

"Not so far. My stepmother seems to have taken it for
granted that he went to the reunion dinner, but she couldn't

produce any actual proof, couldn't remember any definite statement he'd made about it. I'm going down to Cambridge to see him. Will you come with me?"

"I'd like to. But you might want to go before Tuesday."

"Is that when your godmother goes back to Cornwall?"

"Yes."

"How about staying in London and doing a tour of the museums with me?"

"I've got to get home and start looking for a job."

"Looking—"

"I got the sack."

"You—she—"

"She sacked me."

"*Sacked* you? What reason did she give?"

"It was for taking Joby's side, of course. I can't explain now; I'm in the middle of dressing."

"Did Joby freeze to death on the cottage doorstep?"

"No. She let him in at midnight. I'll give you the details when I see you."

"Tuesday?"

"Yes. What time do you leave your office?"

"I never work on Tuesdays."

"Any vacancies on your staff?"

"Only one. Want to apply?"

"I'll think it over. If you're not working, you could gain merit by coming here and taking Sylvia and her luggage— masses and masses of luggage; she's been shopping—to Waterloo."

"You too?"

"Naturally. In the state she's in, I wouldn't trust her out of my sight until I saw her in her reserved seat, with the guard tipped to keep an eye on her to see that she doesn't trans-ship half way home, and come back here."

"Has she got any of her money out of the Canon?"

"Judging by what she's spent in the last three days, plenty. Tuesday, not later than ten fifteen; and if your car hasn't a roof rack, put one on."

His first act the next morning was to send flowers to the hotel. Then he faced the weekend. To get through it, he thought, he would have to stop mooning and get moving. He played golf and tennis, he drove to the house in Hertfordshire, had a horse saddled and performed some—in his own view—spectacular show jumping. He swam in an icy outdoor pool and put himself in the hands of the club professional for a workout in the gymnasium. He was thankful to sink into his office chair on Monday morning, and apply himself to getting through two days' work in one.

He was outside the hotel at ten minutes past ten on Tuesday morning. He waited in the entrance hall and watched the lifts, and soon from one of them emerged Hazel and her godmother.

"Oh, Mr. *Helder!*" Even at this hour, he saw, Lady Storring looked radiant. He thought her overdressed, overexcitable and overindulged, but it was difficult not to be moved by the sight of so much happiness, and impossible not to admire a woman who at sixty could look, in clear morning light, no more than forty. Her purse was already in her hand; tips were distributed to the luggage loaders, the hall porters and by mistake to a passing clergyman whose sober attire misled her into thinking him one of the staff. New cases, all air-weight, all swollen to bursting, filled the luggage compartment of the car. Hand luggage, leather, crocodile, were placed on the back seat beside her. Paper carriers from expensive shops, gift-wrapped parcels, an umbrella and a pink-and-white-striped sunshade were placed on the floor. Leaning forward anxiously, the owner counted them.

"Are you sure there's everything here, Hazel, darling?"

Hazel, on the pavement beside William, said that everything was accounted for.

"You did remember to pack my beautiful new slippers? They were—"

"They're in."

"And the three bottles of French brandy?"

"In that container; keep your feet away from it." She looked at William. "Ready," she announced.

She sat beside him. They did not have to make conversation; they listened to the passenger behind them.

"It's so sweet of you, William, to do this for me! So much nicer than taxis, such a nice send-off. I don't know when I've enjoyed a week more. Hazel, it was so kind of you to come with me. What should I have done without you? I should have got into one of my muddles. Do you know, travelling isn't nearly as pleasant as it used to be. How can old ladies manage without porters? And there seem to be so many more people about than when I was young. One can't get away from them, however far or however expensively one travels. But nowadays, one doesn't seem to meet them in churches or museums or the picture galleries—only in bars and on beaches. As I don't very often go into bars and can't bear beaches, I manage to avoid crowds, but I find that I don't meet fellow travellers as congenial as those I used to meet in the old days. I often wonder what my dear father would make of these modern times. He would probably have fitted in very well; he had some very advanced ideas. For instance, wherever we travelled, he always insisted that we *must* be kind to the natives. Some of his friends couldn't understand this; but don't you see, he was absolutely right, only a little premature. Who, today, can afford to be anything but nice to the natives?"

She paused for breath, and William put a question.

"Have you decided where you're going to live?"

"Not yet. The first thing, I think, is to go on a little cruise, perhaps round the world. And then I must try to do some good works. My mother used to do a lot for Jewish charities, but I don't suppose the Arabs would be pleased to know that I'm spending their money in that way. But when you come to think of it, it's not their money I shall be spending—it's mine. Hazel, darling, I've written out a little cheque for you; you must use it to give yourself a little summer holiday, or to buy yourself something to wear. William, you must see to it that she buys something for herself; she's too prone to giving things away, and she'll probably give this money to Hugo or Dilys. You will see to it, won't you?"

"I hereby promise," he said.

Walking along the platform with their impedimenta was a slow process. Nothing, Lady Storring said firmly, nothing, not one piece should be placed in the luggage van. It was all hand luggage and it would all travel in her compartment. This created a difficult situation until she found a solution: she would pay for two extra seats and she would then be able to spread her parcels over them.

"Hazel, will you be an angel and see about it? I shall be glad to pay whatever it costs. Explain to whoever's responsible that I can't possibly put all these fragile things in with the mailbags. William will look after me while you're gone."

Hazel departed on this errand. Lady Storring stepped into the compartment and beckoned William after her.

"Sit down for a moment, William; I want to have a little talk," she said. "It's about Hazel and you." Seated opposite, she leaned forward and spoke earnestly. "You *are* in love with her?"

"Yes."

"So I thought. So I want to put your mind at rest about that other man. You may think it's all over, but I don't think you realize how persistent a person like that can be. So I have done my little bit to make it easier for you. I would have told you this before, but there has been no opportunity. We haven't much time now. Hazel knows nothing of this; I thought it best not to tell her, but to tell you. You see, although everything is supposed to be over between them, he had the impertinence to telephone to her."

"Caradon?"

"Yes. How he discovered where she was, I don't know— I think his mother must have found out from somebody in Steeplewood. He telephoned, and as Hazel was out, the call was put through to me. Now you will agree, won't you, that she was under my care?"

"Well—"

"Quite so. I was responsible for her. So I told him that she had left the hotel and returned to Steeplewood—with you. I said that I was very glad to know that you and she were going to be happy. He said a great many discourteous things, but that didn't worry me in the least; I merely told him that he must regard the matter in a sporting light and be a good loser. I knew Hazel would have trouble getting rid of him; she isn't one of those girls who can be ruthless. She could have learned from me; nobody had more experience than I did, as a girl, in the matter of putting an end to an affair. So I told Rupert Caradon that he was not to go on pestering her, and you must see to it that he doesn't. I give her into your care. And I can see her coming back, so that's all I can say. Make her a good husband."

William stepped onto the platform. Hazel said that two extra seats had been paid for. Lady Storring got out her purse and paid back the money, and spread her parcels round her. By the time the train drew out, her fellow passengers had labelled her an amiable lunatic. This would not have upset her, but she would not have been pleased to know that her behaviour was put down to an acute form of second childhood.

William watched the train out of sight, and then looked down at Hazel.

"Has she worn you out?"

"No." They were walking out of the station. "Being with her should be exhausting, but isn't."

"Stimulating?"

"Up to a point." She looked at her watch. "I've got to catch the midday train back to Steeplewood."

"Anybody meeting you?"

"No."

"Good. Then they won't worry when you're not on it."

"You have other plans?"

"Several." He waited until they were in the car, and then continued. "We begin by going to dockland, where I'll give you some nice hot coffee and some of Dirk's wife's biscuits. Then we lunch out. Then we go to the hotel for your luggage. While you attend to that, I'll telephone to Mr. Strickland and ask if we can go and see him."

"Do you know him well?"

"Not really. I used to see him sometimes when he dropped into the office to see my father; but I never went to his house, even when I was up at Cambridge and could have walked there. We'll go and see him and clear up the facts behind my father's non-appearance at that reunion. All right?"

"Sounds a nice day."

"Tell me about Joby."

"She let him in about midnight. I got the sack on the following day. I was told to collect my things and go. When I went, Mavis walked out."

"For good?"

"Forever. Odd, isn't it? All that agonizing about not leaving Miss Horn, and then walking out because I'd been given the sack. There was another reason too, of course: she'd realized that the sooner she gets Joby back to Mum and matrimony, the sooner she'll be able to keep track of what he's doing."

"When are they leaving?"

"As soon as they've said goodbye to you." She half turned to look at him. "Why do you use a car this size for driving around town?"

"An office car has to be a car like this—to impress the customers. Aren't you comfortable?"

"Yes and no. I must have some form of guilt complex. I feel comfortable in body but not in mind."

"Why? Because you're passing people on foot, and people in cheaper cars?"

"Yes."

"You feel that Helder & Son should buy a 1912 ruin, and send the difference in price to Oxfam?"

"I suppose that's it. How do you feel, sitting in a car that cost as much as this one did?"

"As I said—comfortable. In body, and in mind."

"No stirrings of conscience?"

"Not about this kind of thing, no. I suppose I've got the merchant's outlook. All my family have ever done is trade. Buying and selling. We've made large profits, not by exploitation but by honest selling. Our goods, your money. Nobody in the family has ever been what's called ennobled; they've remained plain Helders, refusing titles if and when offered, and sticking to—well, their trade. Dull lot on the whole, and not much taste; not much spent on bibelots, as I told you. If that's a bad way of life, we lead it."

"As you said, comfortable."

"You mentioned stirrings of conscience. I suppose the Helder Bequests, which are numerous and widespread and far-reaching, are the results of stirrings. Is that check of your godmother's on your conscience?"

"I don't know how much it is yet." She slit open the envelope. "Bless her. Two hundred beautiful pounds."

"Spend it; she may soon be insolvent."

They were at the Helder building. He left the car in the staff park and took her inside. The lift stopped at the top floor, and he followed her out. Dirk came into the hall. When William had performed the introduction, she stood gazing through the glass doors of the drawing room and dining room, to the roof garden beyond. After some moments, she drew a deep breath, and he waited for her comments. She made only one.

"It would have made a marvellous skating rink," she said.

Dirk beat a somewhat hasty retreat. The remark, William knew, would be repeated to his wife, and from her it would be relayed to his stepmother and would go the rounds of her friends.

"The staff could have had a skating club," Hazel continued as they went into the drawing room, "and they could have skated after office hours, and perhaps during the lunch hour too, and then you could have arranged interstaff competitions, and the winners could have taken part in national and international championships. The Helder Ice Hockey team. The Helder Company Skaters. A shield for the victors, and silver skates to individual competitors. Imagine!"

"It's a bit late to imagine. I made it into a home."

Her nose was close to one of the windows.

"Is this the view you prefer to fresh green fields?"

"I told you, I like boats."

"But you could have gone to Hertfordshire for weekends.
Do you know your Coleridge?

'Tis sweet to him who all the week
Through city crowds must push his way
To stroll alone through fields and woods.

You needn't have strolled alone. I would have joined you at
any time, once we'd met. You had only to ask me."

He saw Dirk enter, and indicated that the tray was to be
placed before Hazel.

"Couldn't I be shown round first?" she asked.

He led her through the rooms, and then she sat down to
pour out the coffee. While they drank it, he put on a recording
in which he played the cello part.

"High standard, no?" he enquired at the end.

"About the same standard as my performance on the
piano."

"Care to demonstrate?"

"Not now. One treat at a time."

He drove her to lunch at a restaurant in Soho. Their next
move was to the hotel; while she arranged to have her luggage
brought to the car, he telephoned to his office for Mr. Strickland's number, and then put through a call to Cambridge.
There was some delay while an overzealous housekeeper ex-
tracted unnecessary details about his name and business; he
said that he was driving to Cambridge with a friend, and
would like to pay a brief visit to Mr. Strickland. The answer
came at last: he would be more than welcome.

There was no hurry. When they reached Cambridge, he
drove slowly past all his old haunts—colleges, river, places
at which he had met or entertained his friends.

"The best days of your life?" she asked, when he had
stopped the car at a point overlooking the river.

"In a sense, I suppose so. A combination of hard work and freedom and companionship and new pleasures and vices. And of course the surroundings."

"How hard did you work?"

"Hard enough to keep me off the bottom; not hard enough to bring me to the top. Haven't you discovered yet that I'm a middle-of-the-road man?"

"No. I'll start discovering you when we've discovered the whereabouts of your flagon. Haven't we rather got off that track?"

"It looks like it. But when I was listening to the Canon telling me that my father wasn't at that reunion, I had a feeling—I don't know how I can describe it except by—" He paused. "I've got a pretty good bump of locality. I've always had a kind of instinct, like animals, for finding my way. I'm not talking about being in a car and reading maps, or going round a strange town with a guide book. I mean that out in open country, I don't seem to need stars or compasses. When I heard that my father didn't go to that meeting, I had a feeling that the next step wasn't in the direction of the flagon; it was in the direction of Mr. Strickland."

"You think there's a connection?"

"I've no idea. I'm just following my nose."

"Then let's go."

Mr. Strickland's house was not large. It was one of a row of unpretentious villas set in modest grounds, but every house was well kept, every garden tended, every lawn smooth and weedless. There was a certain uniformity of gables and French windows, but no two houses were alike in design.

A short drive led to Mr. Strickland's front door. William drove through the open gateway, and they got out of the car and mounted the steps and pressed the doorbell.

The door opened almost at once. A short, stout, middle-

aged woman in grey—half dress, half uniform—let them in.
"Good afternoon, Mr. Helder. My name's Beale, Mrs.
Beale."
"Good afternoon. This is Miss Paget. I hope we're not disturbing Mr. Strickland."
"Not at all. He's looking forward to seeing you. Come this
way. You said nothing about tea, but he hopes you'll stay and
have some. I've got it all ready."
"Thank you."
She was opening a door. A tall, thin man standing by the
window turned and took a few steps towards them, and William had time to make a swift adjustment. He had not seen
him for some years; time had been at work and had left deep
traces. His face looked cadaverous, his gait was slow and
hesitating. He looked a good deal more than his seventy-two
years.
"William, my dear fellow!" They shook hands warmly. "I
couldn't believe it could be you telephoning. Forgive me for
not talking to you myself. And this lovely lady?"
"Hazel Paget. Haze, Mr. Strickland was my father's oldest
friend."
"True, true. Come and sit down. We shall sit in these chairs
so as to be able to look out into the garden; the sun always
comes round at teatime and lights up the lawn. You'll stay to
tea, William? It's all prepared for you."
"Thank you."
Mr. Strickland had leaned back in his armchair and was
subjecting him to a top-to-toe survey.
"You look fit; good. I'd forgotten you were such a big
fellow. Taller than your father—and heavier, surely?"
"Yes. He never put on weight."
"Nor did I, nor did I. Miss Paget, did you ever meet him?"
"No." Hazel smiled. "I only met William recently."

"It's a pity you couldn't have met his father. A fine man. Since you telephoned, William, I've been thinking about him. There was quite a difference in your ages; perhaps you never realized what a good athlete he was."

"I saw some of his trophies."

"Oh, I wasn't thinking about trophies. I was thinking of the extraordinary ease with which he did everything when he was young: splendid swimmer, splendid horseman, wiped us all off the tennis and squash courts. I was so certain he'd outlast us all. Do you mind talking about him, or would you rather I didn't?"

"I'd rather you did."

"It was a tremendous shock, you know, hearing about his death. I felt almost ashamed at the funeral, when I looked at you and your stepmother and realized that I'd seen him, spoken to him, after you both had done. That's why I didn't go up and talk to her; I had this almost guilty feeling of having stolen a march. The papers said he was found by you. I don't know how much of the account was true."

"Most of it. They got the times wrong, but it was I who found him."

"Had he ever had any warning, any previous attacks?"

"His heart wasn't strong. My stepmother used to make him have regular check-ups; the doctors said that if he didn't overexert himself, he'd be all right."

"Your stepmother—that was a happy marriage, wasn't it?"

"Yes."

"A fortunate man to find a woman like that. Two good wives. I never found one, good or bad."

"I wanted to ask you about that last reunion," William said. "Hazel lives in Steeplewood and knows—"

"Ah! Canon Cranshaw. You know him well, Miss Paget?"

"Please call me Hazel. Yes; he christened me and he's been

a kind of uncle ever since. He's one of my godmother's trustees."

"Your—" Mr. Strickland spoke in an awed voice. "*Not* Lady Storring?"

"Yes."

"Your godmother?"

"Yes."

"Oh, dear me, dear me, dear me. I knew her husband, Edwin, very well indeed. Rather an unorthodox godmother, judging by all I've heard about her."

"Very unorthodox," Hazel agreed. "Have you heard that she sold the castle?"

"Heard? No, I saw. It was in all the Cambridge papers. Some quite apt headlines: 'The Camels Are Coming.' 'From Edwin to Bedouin.' That kind of thing. Yes, a very odd godmother. The Canon accepted her as one of life's trials, sent to test his patience. What will all that money do to her?"

"Whatever it does, it won't do it for long," Hazel answered. "She's going to get through it as fast as she's allowed to."

"*So* extravagant?"

"I'm afraid so. Once she knows there's money in the bank, she begins to dream of dresses, and luxury berths on ships."

"She's still very pretty, I hear."

"Yes."

"That's where you women have the advantage over us. Age, as a rule, deals more kindly with your sex. Here's tea. Will you pour?"

William's next two attempts to introduce the reunion into the conversation were no more successful than his first. But when the tea things had been removed, when the host had, with apologies for talking so much, told them a number of anecdotes, given his opinion of the government and lingered on the horrors of inflation, he tried again.

"There was one thing puzzling me," he said. "It was about my father's visit to you. My stepmother was with him when he got your letter. You mentioned in it that there was to be a last reunion, and she got the impression that one of the reasons my father came up to see you was to attend it."

"Oh, dear me, no!" Mr. Strickland leaned back and laughed heartily. "That was one thing I could never persuade him to do. He said he didn't believe in them. He said that old companions, old comrades could get together without making a thing of it with speeches and banquets and so on. No, he didn't go."

"But you did?"

"Me? I never missed one. Not a single one, in all those years. I enjoyed them. In fact, I inaugurated them. But I never got your father to attend one."

"Not even when he was staying with you?"

"Staying . . ." Mr. Strickland pondered. "Well, I can't remember that he was ever staying with me on what we used to call reunion day. Before and after, yes, but I think he was careful to avoid the day itself, in case he got roped in. Wily chap, your father."

"The reunion this year was on a Friday, wasn't it?"

"That's right. It went off very well. I thought it might prove a bit lugubrious, you know, being the last, but not at all; it was a great success."

"Then I've got my dates mixed. I thought my father came down to stay with you on the Friday afternoon."

"Friday? No, no, no. Saturday. Saturday morning. He telephoned to me when he got back from his trip—Greece, wasn't it?—and I said to him: 'Don't tell me that you made a point of getting back in time to attend the reunion dinner' —and he laughed; I can hear him now. How I miss those laughs we used to have! And then he said that he wasn't

coming down on Friday, but he'd look forward to seeing me
on Saturday morning. He arrived just before lunch. He said
he'd be coming by train, but I forgot to ask him which one—
just as well because, as it turned out, I didn't open my eyes
until well after eleven o'clock. The reunion didn't break up
until one in the morning and I wasn't in bed until two. It was
a good weekend—a grand weekend. The meeting on Friday
evening, your father for lunch on Saturday and the rest of
the day, and all Sunday—yes, a good weekend. A pity it had
to end so tragically. I wonder sometimes if I was wrong to
persuade him to stay on until the Monday. He had to go off
pretty early. If he'd gone home on Sunday night, he might
have—but what's the use of might-haves? He certainly didn't
overdo things while he was with me. A quiet Saturday afternoon, a walk to church on Sunday morning, a few friends
in for drinks, an early dinner—and an early night. He seemed
in splendid health, and he was certainly in excellent spirits.
I got up early—I'm always glad to remember this—and went
to the station with him on Monday morning and put him on
a train that would get him into London at nine fifteen. I never
saw him more pleased with life, even at that early hour. If I
had spoken to your stepmother at the funeral, I would have
told her how cheerful, how happy he was. It would have
pleased her. So many of us, when we grow old, tend to lose
our resilience. We— Oh now, really! Must you go so soon?"

"I'm afraid so," William said. "It was very kind of you to
let us come."

"It's been a pleasure—such a rare pleasure! Who wants
to come and see an old man and be bored?"

"We've enjoyed it very much," Hazel said. "Thank you."

"Shall I see you again?"

"Yes." Her tone was firm, and he coloured with pleasure.
"I'll make William bring me."

William put her into the car. They drove towards Steeplewood, but for the first few miles neither uttered a word. Then William spoke.

"He wasn't at the reunion. He wasn't at Mr. Strickland's. Then where the hell," he burst out, "was he?"

"He was at Steeplewood," said Hazel.

8

"HE WAS AT STEEPLEWOOD," SAID WILLIAM.

He was addressing his stepmother. She was seated on the sofa in her drawing room, her breakfast coffee by her side. It was not yet ten o'clock, but he had telephoned and told her he was coming to see her.

"It was Hazel who first guessed it," he went on. "I was getting round to it, but she got there first. After leaving Mr. Strickland's, we drove straight back to Steeplewood and went to the hotel. We got the book from the reception clerk, and it was there—his signature. William Helder."

"When?"

"The afternoon of the reunion. He had arrived, an intelligent pageboy told us, about teatime. He had gone out soon afterwards; it was raining and he asked for a taxi, but there was some delay, and when he heard that the taxi rank wasn't far away, he said he'd walk there and pick one up."

"And then?"

"There's no proof that he went to the Manor, but what else would have taken him to Steeplewood? He went there with the object of seeing Mr. Horn. He planned it before he went to Greece."

She had forgotten the coffee; she was sitting staring at the carpet, her face pale. She looked up and spoke.

"He didn't say one word about Mr. Horn, or about the flagon, all the time we were away."

"Of course he didn't. Neither did he say one word to his oldest friend, Mr. Strickland, all the time he was with him. It was going to be one of his little surprises. You know how he liked to plan them—absolutely top secret until he'd got what he was after. He couldn't be absolutely certain that the flagon was in the Horn collection, but there was a strong possibility that it was. He used the reunion as a cover, letting you assume he was going to attend it. When you drove down to Kent, to your sister's, he was on his own, free to implement his little plot. He took a train to Steeplewood, booked a room at the hotel for the night and went to see Mr. Horn. We know for a fact that the flagon was sold on that day; Canon Cranshaw's recollection was quite clear on the point. The flagon was sold on the day that my father was in Steeplewood. Can you call that mere coincidence?"

"No. But—"

"But what?"

"What did he do with it?"

"That we have yet to discover. I wanted to come and see you, to tell you what we'd found out."

"I suppose you're going back to Steeplewood?"

"Not immediately. Hazel's here."

She spoke in astonishment.

"Here?"

"I brought her back with me last night. When we'd left the hotel, we drove to the farm and had something to eat, and then she packed some things and we came to London. I'd rung up Dirk to tell him we were coming. We were met ceremoniously in the hall by his wife, and given coffee and sandwiches—it was about midnight—and then she conducted

Hazel ceremoniously to her room. I would have brought her to see you this morning, but when I looked in, she was having breakfast in bed and she said she didn't think you received strangers so early in the morning. Would you like to meet her?"

"Don't ask silly questions. Of course I'd like to meet her. Haven't I been waiting anxiously to meet her? And before I meet her, I'd like to know what the situation is. Have you decided you're in love?"

"Yes."

"Does she like you?"

"Yes."

"Does she love you?"

"Yes."

"You're going to marry her?"

"Yes. Has that cleared things up?"

"It's given me something to go on. All that worries me is that she seems to have got out of one engagement and into another in record time."

"There was never any question of her being in love with Caradon."

"Then why was she engaged to him?"

"Let her tell you. Don't judge her before you've seen her."

"Judge? Who's judging? All I'm trying to do is get my facts straight, that's all. You've moved pretty fast; I'm merely trying to catch up."

"Then I'll take you back with me when you're ready."

"Have you decided what your next move's going to be? If your father had the flagon—"

"He didn't have it on him when he died. He didn't have it in the office on Monday morning. Between his buying it and the end, we don't know anything."

When they got back to his apartment, Hazel was dressed and seated on the balcony. After William's brief introduction, she waited, standing in the hall, for Mrs. Helder to make a frank survey.

"Let's go in and talk." Mrs. Helder led the way to the drawing room. "Sit down, Hazel. I think you'd better address me as Stella. William did, from the beginning. The first thing I have to say is thank you for helping William in this search. Has he taken up a great deal of your time?"

William answered the question.

"Not at first. She had other commitments, the principal ones being a fiancé and an employer. She dismissed the fiancé and the employer dismissed her. Before you two start talking, may I outline my plans for the day?"

They said that he could.

"First, I'd like to leave you here to get acquainted. I've got a business to look after. I'll go to the office, skip lunch and work through and come back here to pick you up."

"To go where?" his stepmother asked.

"I want to drive down to the house for a couple of nights. Will you come?"

"Of course. But why do you want to go there?"

"I want to go to Penston station to see if I can learn something more definite than I did the last time I went and asked questions. If we could find out which train my father got off that Monday evening, we might be able to trace his movements in reverse. Are you free to drive down for a night or two, or are you tied up with engagements?"

"What do engagements matter? What's more important than this? I'll take Hazel to lunch, and then she can come home with me and wait till I pack a suitcase. What time will you pick us up?"

"About six. I'll come here. Dirk can get my things ready."

He left them and went down to the office. Mrs. Helder, after a glance at the clock, said that it was time for sherry, and rang for Dirk. When he had served the drinks and withdrawn, she leaned back in her chair and addressed Hazel. "I've got a reputation for plain speaking," she told her, "so I can begin by saying that until I walked in here and met you this morning, I wasn't happy about this situation. You'll admit it's all come about very swiftly?"

"Yes."

"So one can't say that you and William know one another very well. I'd like to be assured that you're not, so to speak, rebounding off Rupert Caradon. William said you were never in love with him; but if you weren't, why the engagement? I don't suppose I've any right to ask—I'm not William's mother, I'm only the woman who married his father—but let's call this family business in which I'm naturally interested. I can't picture you, somehow, in that Caradon set. How did you get in? More to the point, how did you get out?"

Hazel did not answer for some time.

"I gave in under pressure," she said at last. "Months and months attempting to convince him that I didn't want to marry him. How did I get in? I suppose it was curiosity—or vanity. Perhaps I was trying to efface my country-bumpkin image, trying to show his friends that I wasn't someone he'd picked up coming through the rye. I didn't realize for a long time that he actually wanted to marry me. I don't come out of it with much credit, but if I'm going to become your step-daughter-in-law, you'd better know the worst." She paused. "How did I get out? His mother helped to get me out. She never liked me and she knew I'd never marry him and I think she managed to make him believe it in the end."

"No loose ends?"

"I don't think so. I hope not."

"If there are, you must let William deal with them." She paused and sipped sherry. "You know," she continued, "I've always considered engagements a great mistake."

"Long engagements?"

"Any engagements. I could never see what purpose they served; they seemed such a pointless waiting period. Except, of course, in the case of women who want to go round flashing their engagement ring at unsuccessful rivals. If two grown-ups, in this day and age, decide to get married, why not go ahead and get married? I don't know many young women, but I can't imagine any of the ones I know going through the fuss and farce of being engaged. I—what's amusing you?"

"You. The little friend of all the jewellers."

"What's to prevent the diamond hoop being the bride-groom's wedding present?"

"Nothing. Go on."

"Have you and William any idea when you'll get married?"

"We haven't even discussed it yet. Somehow, there doesn't seem to be anything to discuss. What's happened to us seems so—so natural that we just accept it. Last night, driving up to London, he said he hadn't even realized, at first, that he was in love. It just—as I said—happened. In my case, I didn't have time to examine my feelings; I was too busy trying to get myself out of the situation I'd got myself into. When I was free, or almost free, there was William. He'd been there for some time, looking for a flagon. I can't say I fell in love; I only know that I realized he was there, and that there wouldn't be much joy in life if he wasn't. I haven't explained it very well. It was natural—or perhaps I mean inevitable. It's difficult to put it into words."

"It can't be put into words. Some things are made to fit, that's all. My first marriage was happy for as long as it lasted; he died young. I was a widow for nearly twenty years, by choice. William's father was a man I saw here and there, now and again—one of the crowd. Then we found ourselves side by side on a plane bound for New York. We talked about travel, and the weather, and the Middle East. But we both knew—it didn't have to be stated, it was so natural—we both knew that we were going to stay together. He was a wonderful man and he made a wonderful husband. William's very much like him. I hope you'll both be happy."

"Thank you."

"You've got humour, thank God. The Helder men—I won't call them heavy, but I had to watch William's father to see that he didn't *settle*. William's got a lighter touch, but there's still a lot of Dutch burgher—stolid Dutch burgher—under the surface." She drained her glass. "As far as I can see, trousseaux seem to have gone the way of most traditions, but I presume you'll want to buy this and that. Can you afford all you'll need?"

"I'll limit what I need to what I can afford."

"That sounds very noble and high-minded, but couldn't we look at this from a practical angle?"

Hazel laughed.

"What you call noble and high-minded," she said, "is just the way I've always lived. My brother and I grew up knowing that money was short, but I can't say it ever worried us much. We had the basic necessities and I suppose we got used to doing without the frills. We didn't notice the shabby furniture. Clothes . . . I wore some of my school things almost up to the time I went to London. I hadn't grown out of them, so why not?"

"Why not, indeed. I can see you're going to be troublesome. You'll need to do a certain amount of shopping, and I don't suppose you'll take money from William. So why not let me have some fun? Too proud?"

"Not that kind of proud. It's only that my godmother—"

"Ah. Lady Storring. You think she'll want to spend her oil gains on you?"

"She won't want to be left out."

"Then she and I will have to meet and talk about it. But you must warn her that I'm accustomed to getting my own way."

"So is she."

"Then we'll fight it out. You've already seen the Hertford-shire house, haven't you?"

"Yes. William drove me down one afternoon. How could he have lived here when he could have been living there?"

"He's been happy here. It was one of his dreams, to do this place up. But it wouldn't do for a family. The children would lean over the balcony to watch the ships go by, and disappear over the railings one by one. If he'd moved out after his father died, I would have moved in—but not now. I couldn't face staff shortages any more. I suppose he'd leave me Dirk and his wife, but they wouldn't be happy working for anybody whose name wasn't William Helder. He'll have to turn this place into a kind of hotel for clients who come over from Holland. I'll ask you, if you will, to keep a suite for me on the ground floor of the house; I know exactly how it can be arranged. Then I shall come down for all the christenings."

The telephone rang. Dirk answered it and told Hazel it was for her. She took the receiver in the expectation of hearing William's voice; instead she heard Dilys's.

"Haze?"

"Yes. Anything wrong?"

"No. Why should you think that?"

"You sound odd."

"I feel odd. Are you standing near something you can hold on to?"

"Yes. What's happened?"

"Hugo's piano concerto. Albert Hall concert, Kalstatin conducting. Soloist, Mikhail Reger. September."

"Oh, Dilys . . ."

"I had to tell someone. Hugo's out, so it had to be you."

"Give him my love and congratulations."

"I will. Are you enjoying yourself?"

"Yes."

"Is William there?"

"No. He went away and left me with his stepmother."

"Oh, my God. Goodbye."

"That," Mrs. Helder said, "was unkind. What were the congratulations?"

"Mikhail Reger's going to play my brother's piano concerto at the Albert Hall in September."

"Who's conducting?"

"Kalstatin."

"Then you can add my congratulations. Incidentally, I've met Kalstatin. I'll have to arrange a reception after the concert. Are you going to have some more sherry?"

"No, thank you."

"Then let's go out and find somewhere nice for lunch."

There was never much activity at Penston station during the day. On weekday mornings, the London-bound workers streamed in from the station road or came over the overhead bridges or by way of the disused tracks from the new housing estates. In the evenings, they disembarked from train after train and dispersed in various directions to high tea or drinks or dinner.

There was nobody about when Hazel and William got out of the car and walked on to the Up platform. They went to one of the offices and William knocked on the door. It was opened by a uniformed young man with tousled, tow-coloured hair and a cheerful manner.

"Morning, Mr. Helder. Nice surprise. Not often we see you down here."

"Good morning, Jimmy." They shook hands. "What's this I hear about your getting married?"

"Well"—the broad, beaming face grew red—"we all come to it in the end. Most of us, that is." He threw a glance at Hazel. "You'll be next on the list, I daresay. What can I do for you, Mr. Helder?"

"Can we sit down?"

"Of course. Sorry. Come on in."

He stood aside and they entered the small, damp-smelling, untidy office. He brought two chairs and then levered himself on to the high counter.

"Shoot," he invited.

"I'm trying to find out," William said, "what train my father came home on, on the evening he died."

Jimmy frowned.

"You tried that before, Mr. Helder," he said. "Don't you remember? You came here and saw me and Mr. Crouch and you asked us about it and we couldn't tell you because of the crowds that always get off those trains of an evening. I can't fetch Mr. Crouch now because he's gone off with his wife and kids—got a day off to meet his son coming back from Hong Kong. But we talked about it, him and me, when you'd gone after talking to us, and we went over it in our minds and we couldn't remember seeing Mr. Helder that evening. I'd like to help you, but you know yourself how it is: there's only two of us here, and it isn't as if everyone gets off the trains with season tickets that you've just got to let pass; some have returns that you have to tear off, and some have passes. It's a job dealing with them all. And it isn't as if I'd've made a note of Mr. Helder particularly, because he was often on the train of an evening in summer, and we got used to seeing him and we wouldn't have thought anything of it. I asked one or two people who'd been past me that evening if they remembered seeing him. No luck."

"Well, thanks, Jimmy. I was just checking."

They rose and walked to the door. Jimmy stood watching them as they walked away. Then he raised his voice in a shout.

"Hey, just a minute." He sprinted along the platform to catch them up. "I just thought of something. Mind you, it might come to nothing, but there's a chance it might help. Remember my cousin Ditty Mills?"

"Yes. She used to live with your mother and father."

"That's right. Poor little orphan child, I thought. But she wasn't an orphan really. Her mother was Miss Grayling, the teacher up at the school on Campbell Road; ever hear of her?"

"No."

"Well, Ditty was her daughter, but she didn't want it to get round, so when she brought Ditty here, my mother agreed to say she was our cousin. See?"

"Yes."

"Well, Miss Grayling couldn't make much fuss of Ditty, because of putting the old gossips onto a juicy bit of scandal, so what she used to do, she used to get her sister, a married sister, name of Loder, to come and visit my mother every so often, and she'd bring things for Ditty, presents and clothes and things, and give them to my mother. This sounds a bit off the point, but I'm explaining who Mrs. Loder is. Well, she didn't often come—about once every three months. But she's up at our house now, and you ought to talk to her. You know why? Because that evening, the evening you want to know about, Mrs. Loder came on a visit. She stayed that night with her sister and she went up to see my mum the next day. So supposing she saw Mr. Helder on that evening you're asking about?"

"Did she know my father?"

"Course she knew him, Mr. Helder. Everybody here knew him, but she knew him better than most because her husband worked in your firm once—clerk or something. So naturally she'd be interested in seeing his boss. So if you drive up there now, you'll find her with my mum, talking away sixteen to the dozen. If you can get a word in, she might help you."

"Thanks, Jimmy. We'll go straight away."

They got into the car and William spoke thoughtfully.

"They say it's impossible to keep secrets in a small town, but that's one that didn't leak out."

"Ditty?"

"Yes. Married now, and far, far away, but a scorcher in her time."

"You got scorched?"

"She practised on me. She was about the same age as I was—about fourteen."

"Cider with Rosie?"

"Yes. She liked coming up to our farm. She deserted me for a boy named Podge Parker, whose father was a brewer. I felt deeply hurt."

"It sapped your self-confidence?"

"For a time. Odd what kids get up to. When my sons get to fourteen, I'll keep wondering what's going on. Damn. I've missed the turning."

Jimmy's parents lived in a council house on a recently constructed housing estate built on the outskirts of the town. The area that was to be made into a central garden was at this stage a sea of mud. They made their way to the front door and it was opened by Jimmy's mother, not aproned as William had usually seen her, but looking spruce in honour of the visitor.

"Well—Mr. Helder! Fancy seeing you! This is a nice surprise. Come in, sir. Come in, Miss—Paget? Nice to meet you, miss. Come in. I've got a visitor here you might have heard of, Mr. Helder—Mrs. Loder. Her husband worked in Helder's once."

Mrs. Loder, small, thin and black-clad, rose and gave William a work-worn hand.

"I've often wanted to meet you, Mr. Helder. Perhaps you didn't know that my husband, my late husband, worked for your father?"

"No. It was probably before I joined the firm," William

answered. "This is Miss Paget. She lives at Steeplewood; perhaps you know it?"

"Not well. I have a cousin there who keeps a wool shop, but—"

"Opposite the church?" Hazel asked.

"That's right, miss. The name's—"

"Rennet, and I often went there," Hazel said, "to order wool for the Manor School. Mrs. Rennet doesn't serve there any more; her daughter's taken over."

"That's right; Hilda."

"Can I offer you a cup of tea?" Jimmy's mother asked. "I was just going to make some."

"I'm so sorry, we can't stay more than a moment," William said. "It was really Mrs. Loder I came to see. Jimmy thought she might be able to answer a question about my father."

"Me?" Mrs. Loder looked startled. "What is it, Mr. Helder?"

"I know what it is." Jimmy's mother spoke from the doorway of the kitchen. "You remember I was telling you, Mrs. Loder, how Mr. Helder's father was found dead on the bridge over the lake near their house? Well, they never found out what train he came home on, that evening. I know what's happened now: Jimmy's remembered that you're here today, and that on the day Mr. Helder's father died, you came to Penston. He's bright sometimes, Jimmy is. I wish I'd had the sense to think of it myself. So what we want to know now is: Did you, on that evening—I know it's a long time ago, but you don't pay so many visits to this place—did you see old Mr. Helder on the station?"

"Yes." Mrs. Loder spoke unhesitatingly, with calm certainty. "I did."

There was a pause.

"Can you remember the time?" William asked her.

"I can't tell you exactly what time it was I saw him, but I

can give you it fairly near because my own train was punctual and I caught the five eighteen from King's Cross."

"That gets in at six twenty," Jimmy's mother said. "So it was just after six twenty."

"Well, no; it was a bit after that," Mrs. Loder said. "You know how I am about crowds. I got out of the train and waited till most of them had gone through the barrier. Then I had to wait a bit longer because the other train came in and they all came over the overhead bridge and I didn't want to be caught up, so I stayed where I was for a bit longer. Then I walked out, and it was then that I saw Mr. Helder walking just in front of me."

"Was he carrying anything?" William asked her.

"Carrying . . . ? No, nothing. Well, just a newspaper, the way most gentlemen do of a morning or of an evening. That's all he had—his newspaper folded in his hand. His left hand. The other hand had his ticket. I was—"

"Ticket?" repeated William. "He had a ticket?"

"Well, yes." For a moment Mrs. Loder sounded uncertain, and then her tone became firm once more. "Yes. He certainly gave up his ticket. I was behind him, right behind him in the line. I'd been right behind him since he came down the steps and—"

"Steps?"

"He'd come over the bridge, you see," explained Mrs. Loder. "He—"

"Over the bridge? From the other platform?" William asked.

"Yes."

"Then he wasn't on the London train?"

"Oh, no, Mr. Helder, sir. I told you—there was another train had come in, and he was with the passengers coming over the bridge, and he was just in front of me when we—"

William was on his feet.

"Thank you. You've been most helpful," he told her. He looked at Jimmy's mother. "I'm sorry to hurry away, but we've got to go back to the station."

It did not take long.

"Yes, that's right," Jimmy said. "The five eighteen from King's Cross pulls in a few minutes before the other one. So Mr. Helder wasn't on the London train?"

"No. Can you tell me what other stations that train stopped at before it got to Penston, Jimmy?"

"Offhand, no. I could look it up. Come into the office. Any station in particular?" he asked.

"Steeplewood."

"Steeplewood. Let's see . . . Yes, here it is. It was a slow train. Left Steeplewood at five two, arrived Penston six twenty-four. That what you want?"

"Yes, thanks," William said. "That's exactly what I want."

He walked with Hazel to the car. They got in, but they did not drive away. They sat in silence, staring at the dusty station yard. A freight train rattled slowly by. A van drove up and parked beside them; they watched the driver get out and walk into the station. Then William spoke.

"He went to Steeplewood on the Friday to buy it. He bought it. Then why did he go back there, for God's sake?"

"He had to go back."

"Why?"

"To get the flagon."

"But—"

"What you forget—what we both forgot—was that Mr. Horn always demanded cash down. Your father didn't know that. He'd expect to be able to pay by check—wouldn't he?"

"Yes. Then—"

"That's why he took an early train to London on Monday morning. He didn't go straight to the office. Didn't his secretary say that he came in late? Why would he be late if the train he took from Cambridge arrived in London at nine fifteen?"

"I see. He went to the bank."

"Yes."

"He went to get the money to pay for the flagon. He left the office, told his secretary he wouldn't be back, and took a train to Steeplewood. He paid for the flagon, and he had it with him when he got off the train at Penston. Mrs. Loder said he wasn't carrying anything, but he had a folded newspaper. In the fold was a small parcel. The flagon. And he got as far as the bridge, and he died, and his newspaper was floating in the water—but the flagon wasn't floating. The flagon—"

"Yes," said Hazel. "So now you know where it is."

9

WILLIAM, SKILLED IN UNDERWATER DIVING, LABOURED FOR two days to find the submerged flagon. At the end of that time, unsuccessful, he enlisted the aid of professionals. But it was another three days before it was discovered and brought to the surface.

Waiting at the lakeside with Hazel and his stepmother, he took the dripping, slime-covered object from the diver's hands. Through the slime could be seen the gleam of metal. He turned to his stepmother.

"The round dozen," he said. "Happy?"

"Oh, William . . . yes. Thank you."

They drove to London, their first stop the silversmiths'.

"How long?" William asked.

"You'll have to give me two weeks."

"All right."

He went back to the car and reported.

"The question now," he went on, "is where we put Hazel. If I'm going to take time off for getting married and going on a honeymoon, I ought to put in some work first."

"Where's the problem?" his stepmother asked. "She can stay with you or she can stay with me."

"If it doesn't sound unfriendly, I'd like to stay at Steeplewood," Hazel said.

"If you do that, you'll only see me at weekends," William pointed out. "If you like the idea, I don't."

"You can take Fridays off and drive down to Steeplewood, and you can come back to London on Monday mornings," his stepmother said. "That means you'll only have to suffer on Tuesdays, Wednesdays and Thursdays. I have a suggestion."

"That I suffer during the weekends, too?"

"That you and I stay in Hertfordshire. You'll be moving back to the house when you marry, won't you?"

"So Hazel says. You'd think she would have felt unfettered enough in a place she designated a skating rink."

"She wants to walk on grass. Some people do. I prefer a London pavement, but I'm prepared to make a sacrifice. I'll stay at the house with you until you marry, and while I'm there, I'll make arrangements about that suite I'm going to ask you to give me. You can bring Hazel down at weekends to see what she wants done to the place. Do you like the idea?"

"I'll think it over," said William.

He drove Hazel back to Steeplewood on Sunday evening.

"The first time I took this turning," he remarked as they left the London road, "all I was hoping to find was a flagon."

"I could have located it a lot faster if I'd been in charge of the investigation," she said, "but I had, past tense, a great respect for your intelligence, so I left it all to you."

"I'll try to do better as a husband than as an investigator. When you were small, did you ever picture the kind of husband you'd like?"

"Not often. I didn't spend much time mooning. But I did think, when I thought about it at all, that he'd be like Hugo

—long-haired, shortsighted, steeped in music."

"I'm almost steeped. Odd how things work out. I used to imagine getting to know a girl gradually—meeting her, liking her and then learning all about her. While she learned about me. And yet you and I—there was no build-up. Here we are —in love. I don't know any of your friends, you don't know any of mine. There was no approach—we're at the center, preparing to marry, certain of each other, certain about the future. I feel like someone who went into a shop to buy a model ship and came out with a model kit; I've got what I want, but I've got to build it piece by piece. That's not quite what I mean, but it'll do."

"Don't you like it this way?"

"Yes. Life's going to be full of surprises. You're not going to regret not having married a musician, are you?"

"I'll answer that ten years from now."

"We'll have lots of music. As soon as we get back from our world tour, I'll assemble my bunch of instrumentalists."

"Why a world tour?"

"To educate you, of course. To widen your horizons. How can you claim to have lived at all if you've never seen Fuji-yama or Vladivostok or Mount Everest at sunrise or the North Cape at midnight? You haven't seen anything."

"Yes, I have. On the telly."

"I didn't know you ever watched television. I thought you kept that set on the hatch to stop people from seeing into the sitting room. Is it colour?"

"Don't be silly. Colour costs. If it had been colour, Joby would have borrowed it for the cottage. As it wasn't, he wouldn't touch it; he hired his own. For the amount of watching Hugo and Dilys and I do, colour would be a wicked waste." She paused. "In a way, I wish I were marrying someone poor. It'll be such agony, watching you squandering."

"What are you going to do—save it all up?"

"No. Hugo and I knew nothing about saving. All we learned was not to spend. There's a difference."

"There is. But knowing how to spend is an art."

"Then you'll have to teach it to your children."

"There'll be more than one, won't there?"

"What were you thinking of—another round dozen?"

"God forbid. But you at least had a brother; I didn't have anybody, and being the only one isn't much fun. My parents used to invite hordes of small cousins to keep me company and fill all those rooms built for large families."

"Has there always been a William Helder to take over the firm?"

"Always."

"What happens if I produce several Wilheminas first?"

"You won't."

"But if I did?"

"For two hundred years and more, the Wilheminas have stood aside to let their brothers come first. It's become a tradition."

"I'll try to remember."

"Don't try. Leave it to nature."

"And nature will follow the Helder pattern?"

"Assuredly. Did you tell Hugo and Dilys we were coming down tonight?"

"I rang Dilys. Hugo's away for the night, in Shaftesbury, conducting a concert."

"Any news of Joby and Mavis?"

"They're ready to leave. I'll miss them. At least, I'll miss Mavis. I like her. I liked her from the first—when I went to work at the school, and she was in the office. I was supposed to assist her; I didn't do much, but we got on well."

"You don't think Joby deserves her?"

"It'll even out. He'll get a lot, but he'll have to give up a lot."

"His freedom?"

"His bits of fun. Serves him right for saying that he was only trying to oblige sex-starved women."

"He was a good worker; pity he couldn't have stayed on the farm."

"So Hugo said. But apart from the fact that he's got his own profession and his future salon, he'd never have got on with Bernie. Bernie would have mashed him up."

Bernie was not mashing him up when they reached the farm. On the contrary, the two appeared to be working harmoniously together. Having got Hugo's piano as far as the cottage, they were struggling to get it through the door. Only when William and Hazel were within earshot was the illusion of harmony shattered.

"Not that way, you ruddy fool!" Joby was shouting. "Round a bit, round a bit."

"Can't you see the door's in the way, blast you?" yelled Bernie. "D'you expect me to bend the bloody thing?"

"Oh, do be careful!" besought Dilys. "Watch that window-pane!"

"Slowly, slowly, go more slowly," exhorted Mavis. "What is this great hurry to do it? If it won't fit in, then you must take it back upstairs, see?"

William went into action. He lifted the cottage door off its hinges and then got beside Joby to help manoeuvre the piano into the opening.

"You've got to upend it," he said.

"I told him that! I told him!" said Bernie furiously. "Thinks he knows everything, he does. Wouldn't listen to a bloody bit of advice."

"It's been bedlam for the past hour," Dilys told Hazel.

"Whose idea was it to move the thing?"

"Joby's. You know that he and Mavis have been fixing up the cottage for Hugo?"

"Yes. Did Hugo know they were doing it?"

"No. Nobody's said a word."

"Then how do you know he'll like working in the cottage?"

"You don't think it's a good idea?"

"Yes—but will he?"

"He'll have to. I'm not going through this again backwards. It got so heated at one stage I was certain Bernie was going to trap Joby between the piano and the wall and squeeze him to death. But they worked like machines—I mean Mavis and Joby did—and the cottage looks wonderful. You'll see, as soon as we can get in."

"They're in. Come on."

So strenuous had been the task, so tense the atmosphere in which it had been carried out, that it was only when the piano was in place that Joby realized that a third man had been on the job. Perspiring freely, he stood staring at William.

"How did you get in?" he asked.

"Didn't you notice that the piano suddenly got lighter?"

"No, I didn't. We've been ringing your place, trying to find out where you and Haze had got to. They said you was on your way back. You're just in time to say goodbye. If you hadn't come down, Mavis and I were going to leave our luggage at the station in London and get in a taxi and go to your place. How's that for friendship? What d'you think of this little job?"

Hazel was standing in the doorway, looking in amazement at the transformation that had been wrought. The walls of the small, three-roomed interior had been distempered, the woodwork painted, the wooden floor polished. Missing windowpanes had been replaced, intrusive ivy cut back to reveal the view of fields and farm buildings. Rugs had been freely borrowed from the house. All Hugo's papers and manuscripts had been brought down and stacked neatly on shelves.

Dilys was the first to speak.

"I can't say thank you," she said. "But every time I come in here, I'll think of you both."

"And when we come in here, Mavis and me, in let's say a year from now," said Joby, "you know what we'll see? There'll be windowpanes missing, there'll be marks on the walls where Hugo's thrown something when he couldn't find the right note; the plumbing'll be out of order and the place will be falling apart, same's the house is falling apart."

"Talking like that, that's very rude," Mavis said indignantly.

"Rude? I'm just stating plain facts. They can't help it. Artists, musicians—they're all the same. They keep their feet in one place and their heads somewhere else. I don't know what happens in their dream world; all I know is that only one in a thousand of 'em is a handyman. I'm the one in a thousand: artist *and* artisan. Every man to his job; doing the odd repair isn't on Hugo's list of talents. Take Bernie, *par exemple*. He—"

"You lay off," Bernie requested.

"I was going to pay you a nice compliment. You're the best market gardener I ever came across. Not only that, you're the only market gardener I ever knew who could keep his ground looking a picture, the way you do. In your own line, you're an artist, so I wasn't surprised when I saw the state those rooms above the stable had got into. If I'd been staying longer, I'd have had a go and fixed 'em up. And now"—he looked at Mavis—"if you'll gimme my sweater, I'll dry off and ask Dilly for a last drink. Then we push off."

"How are you getting to the station?" William asked.

"I'm glad you asked. That's one reason we was so anxious

for you to show up before we had to leave. Before you make
an offer, you'd better take a look at the collection of stuff
Mavis is taking with her."

On inspection, William found it almost as miscellaneous an
assortment as Lady Storring's had been when he drove her to
the station from her London hotel. But instead of expensive
suitcases, there were cardboard boxes tied with string, new,
cheap fiber grips and a selection of overstuffed plastic bags.
There was also a bedroll, and beside it, a bird cage containing
a budgerigar.

"What're you taking that canary along for?" Bernie asked
in astonishment.

"To remind us of you," Joby said. "When it sings, I'll say
to Mavis: 'Remember that chap at the farm, the chap who
sang about his old shako?' Go on, Bernie—give us 'The Trumpeter.' "

Bernie, reddening with embarrassment or annoyance,
grunted something that could be interpreted as farewell, and
strode away.

"Nice chap, filthy temper," Joby remarked. "Where's that
drink?"

They stood, glasses in hand, in the kitchen, but it was not as
cheerful a gathering as they had anticipated. Mavis was close
to tears.

"Will you-all come and see us?" she asked Hazel.

"Of course we will."

"They'll pop down every time they want a perm," said Joby.
He raised his glass. "To the next time. And I nearly forgot—
congratulations. I'm glad you found that mug you were looking for."

They went outside to load the car. It took some time, but
at last everything was in. Hazel sat beside William; Joby and
Mavis were at the back. Dilys stood at the gate to wave them
off.

William and Hazel returned to a house that seemed empty.

"We'll miss them," Dilys said. "Do you think it'll work out?"

"Why not?" William asked. "There's his mother there to act as referee."

"Mavis needn't have any prickings of conscience about having left Miss Horn," Dilys said. "There was a new secretary installed before Mavis had even got her things out."

"Who?" Hazel asked.

"The girl who was after the job—relations in Steeplewood. When will the flagon be back from its cleanup?"

"About a week," William said. "And when I get it back, we'll have a celebration. You and Hugo will have to come and see it restored to its fellows."

"In London?"

"No. Hertfordshire. You'll meet my stepmother, which will be nice, and my stepmother will meet Hazel's godmother, which will be interesting."

It was almost midnight before he left. He and Hazel walked slowly out to the car.

"Till Friday," she said.

"Don't stray from the phone. I'll want to hear you, even if I can't see you. Hazel—"

She was in his arms.

"You don't have to say it," she said. "I know."

"Will you marry me soon?"

"Yes."

"Without delay?"

"Yes. But—"

"But what?"

"Just you and me. And Dilys and Hugo."

"And Stella and Sylvia. Is that the way you want it?"

"Yes. I'd like to be married as I am, as you know me, just a kind of continuation of being together."

"Next week?"

"Yes."

"Hazel—"

"Yes?"

"This is going to be the last time we're apart; do you realize that?"

"Yes."

"Hazel—"

"Yes?"

"Nothing. Just . . . bless you."

TAHAR BEN JELLOUN

THE
SACRED
NIGHT

Translated by
Alan Sheridan

The Johns Hopkins University Press
Baltimore and London

Johns Hopkins Paperbacks edition, 2000
2 4 6 8 9 7 5 3 1

The Johns Hopkins University Press
2715 North Charles Street
Baltimore, Maryland 21218-4363
www.press.jhu.edu

Library of Congress Cataloging-in-Publication Data

Ben Jelloun, Tahar, 1944–
[Nuit sacrée. English]
The sacred night / Tahar Ben Jelloun ; translated by Alan Sheridan.
p.   cm.
ISBN 0-8018-6441-0 (alk. paper)
I. Sheridan, Alan. II. Title.

PQ3989.2.J4 N813 2000
843—dc21
99-088027

A catalog record for this book is available from the British Library.

Designed by Beth Tondreau Design/Gabrielle Hamberg

CONTENTS

THE
SACRED
NIGHT

PREAMBLE

T he truth is what matters.
I'm an old woman now, with all the serenity I
need. But I'm going to speak, for I feel encumbered. What weighs me down is not so much the years
as all the things I've left unsaid, all the things I've hidden.
I hadn't realized that a memory full of silence could become a sandbag that makes it hard to walk.

It took time to reach you here. Friends of the Good!
The public square is still a circle. Like madness. Nothing
has changed, neither sky nor men.

I am happy to be here at long last. You are my deliverance, the light of my eyes. Many and beautiful are my
wrinkles. The ones on my forehead are the marks and
trials of truth, the harmony of time. The ones on my hands

are lines of fate. Look how they cross, tracing the paths of fortune, drawing a star that has fallen into lake waters.

The story of my life is written there, every wrinkle a century, a road on a winter's night, a spring of clear water on a misty morning, a meeting in a forest, a broken friendship, a cemetery, a blazing sun. That furrow on the back of my left hand is a scar; death stopped one day and held out a pole to me. Perhaps to save me. But I turned away. It's all easy enough, as long as you don't try to change the river's course. There is no greatness or tragedy in my story. It is simply strange. I have conquered violence so as to earn passion, and to become an enigma. I have long walked the desert; I have paced the night and tamed my pain.

Friends of the Good! What I am going to tell you sounds like truth. I have told lies. I have loved and deceived. I have traveled countries and centuries. I have often been an exile, lonesome among the lonely. Old age came upon me one autumn day, as my face turned back to childhood, to that innocence that had been taken from me. Don't forget, I was a child whose identity was clouded, unsteady, a girl disguised as male by a willful father who felt demeaned and humiliated because he had no son. I became the son he dreamed of. Some of you know the rest; others have heard bits and pieces of it. Those who ventured to tell the story of that child of sand and wind ran into trouble. Some suffered amnesia, others nearly lost their souls. You've heard stories, but they were not really mine. Yes, I heard them, even locked up and isolated as I was. They neither surprised nor troubled me. I knew that when I disappeared, I would leave behind fuel for the most extravagant tales. But my life is not a tale, and I am determined to establish the facts, to yield the secret hidden under a black stone in a house with high walls at the end of an alleyway sealed by seven gates.

INVENTORY

After his confession, the storyteller disappeared again. No one tried to make him stay or to talk to him. He rose, gathered up his yellowed, moon-soaked manuscript, and melted into the crowd without looking back.

His listeners were struck dumb. They did not know what to make of him, illustrious and beloved storyteller that he was. He would begin a story, break off suddenly, then come back not to continue it, but to say that he ought not to tell it, for he was possessed by misfortune.

Some were no longer under his spell. They had doubts. They had had enough of those silences made of absence and anticipation. They no longer trusted this man whose words they had once devoured so eagerly. They were convinced that his memory was failing and that he was afraid to admit it. His memory might be gone, but not his imagination. He proved that when he came out of the desert, face blackened by the sun, lips cracked by thirst and heat, hands hardened by carrying stones, voice as hoarse as if a sandstorm had racked his throat. His gaze was fixed upon some high and distant line. He was talking to somebody no one could see, perhaps perched on a throne in the clouds. He spoke to him as if asking him to bear witness. The audience watched his gestures and his eyes, but they could see nothing. Some imagined an old man on a camel waving his hand so as not to hear the storyteller.

He mumbled incomprehensibly. This came as no surprise, for he often peppered his stories with words in some unknown language, doing it so well that people understood what he meant. They even laughed. But this time there was nothing else but those unfinished, mangled sentences, full of pebbles and spit. His tongue trundled along, then got tied up in knots. He blushed. He realized that he was losing not his mind—he didn't care about that—but his audience. One couple got up and left without a word. They were followed by two men grumbling their displeasure. That was a bad sign. No one had ever walked out on Boushaïb. No one ever went away unsatisfied. He looked down from the distant point he had been staring at and sadly watched the people leaving. He did not understand why they were going or why no one was listening anymore. They had stopped believing him, and that was something he could not accept. The undisputed master of the public square, honored guest of kings and princes, the man who had trained an entire generation of troubadours and had lived in Mecca for a year, would not try to bring back people who walked out on him. Boushaïb would never stoop so low, would never compromise his pride and dignity. Let them go if they want, he said to himself, my sorrow is bottomless; it is a sack of stones I will carry to my grave.

I was there, wrapped in my old jellaba. I watched him but said nothing. There was nothing I could say to tell him of my affection, no gesture I could make without revealing his secret, of which I was the embodiment. I knew too much, and my presence in the crowd was no accident. I was coming back from afar. Our eyes met, his shining with an intelligence that breeds fear. He looked terrified, as if possessed by something indefinable. He froze. He saw me as the ghost of a time of ill fortune. He spun around, hands behind his back. I waited calmly, with the patience of a sage. His eyes seemed more and more anxious when they fell upon me. Had he realized who I was, even though he had never seen me before? He had assigned me a face, features, a personality. Those were the days of legend, and I was his rebellious, elusive creature. Madness had already punched holes in his memory. Madness or hoax.

With all I had seen and done, nothing surprised or shocked me anymore. I had arrived in Marrakesh the day before, determined to find the storyteller my story had ruined. I somehow sensed where he would be and who his audience was. I waited for him the way you would for a friend who has stabbed you in the back or an unfaithful lover. I had spent the night in a room overlooking the grain market, a room that reeked of dust and mules' urine. I awoke at first light and washed at the mosque

7

fountain. Nothing had changed. The bus station was still as black as an oven's insides. Still no doors on the café. The waiter, badly shaven, his hair plastered down, his bow tie askew, wore a kind of tuxedo that had been ironed a thousand times and was shiny with grease stains. He pretended to recognize me. Calling customers by their first names was one of his affectations. As though he always knew who they were. He walked over and said, as if we had known each other for years:

"The usual, Mother Fadila, a nice hot coffee with cinnamon and a corn cake?"

He left before I had the chance to tell him that my name was not Fadila, that I hate coffee with cinnamon, and that I like barley bread better than corn cake.

I ate breakfast next to a truckdriver from the Shawia, who was eating a steamed sheep's head and drinking a whole pot of mint and shiba tea. He belched repeatedly, thanking God and Marrakesh for providing him such a good morning meal. He looked at me as if he wanted to share his satisfaction. I smiled, waving a hand to drive away the marijuana smoke he was blowing at me. He watched a girl ride by on a moped and smoothed his moustache as if to say that a nice young girl, preferably a virgin, would be the perfect dessert after such a breakfast.

He picked his teeth for a while, then gave the carcass to a group of beggar children, who took it into a corner to devour what was left. He got into his truck, turned around, and pulled up in front of the café.

"See you next week, Charlie Chaplin!" he called to the waiter.

As I was leaving, I asked the waiter who the man was.

"A vulgar character. Thinks he can get away with anything. He calls me Charlie Chaplin because my suit's too big for me. He always makes a mess of the table, and he spits on the floor. To top it off, he thinks he's great looking, a real charmer, all because he got a German tourist woman to get into his truck one day. They did their filthy stuff and he bragged about it all year long. He's been stopping here for his sheep's head ever since, on the way up and back. You know, Mother Fadila, guys like that would do better to stay in their trucks."

The square was empty. It would fill up slowly, like a stage setting. The first to arrive were the Sahraouis, selling all kinds of powders: spices, henna, wild mint, chalk, sand, and other ground and sifted magic products. Then came the booksellers, with their yellowed manuscripts and burning incense.

Then the people with nothing to sell. They sat cross-legged on the ground, waiting. The storytellers came last. Each one had a ritual of his own.

There was a tall, thin man who began by unraveling his turban; he shook it, and fine sand fell out. He was from the South. He sat down on a small plywood suitcase and started talking, all alone, with no one listening. I watched him from a distance: he talked and gestured as though an audience were hanging on his every word. I came closer, arriving within earshot in the middle of a sentence: ". . . the taste of time lapped up by a pack of dogs. I turned, and what did I see? Tell me, faithful companions; guess, friends of Kindness, whom should I see before me, proud and handsome, magnificent on his silver mare, capable of facing any trial? Time's taste is bland. The bread is stale. The meat is spoiled. The camel butter

9

is rancid—as rancid as our times, O passing friends. We tell of life, and the lonely vulture looms high." I was his only customer. He stopped, walked over to me, and said in a confidential tone:

"I can help if you're looking for someone. In fact, I may well be the person you seek. I have a beautiful story, but it is too early to tell it. I will wait. So, who are you looking for, a son or a husband? If it's a son, he's probably in India, or China. A husband is easier. He must be old, and old men hang around in mosques and cafés. But I can see that's not what you're after—your silence tells me so. Now, what does it tell me? Yes, I know. You hold in your heart a secret, and I musn't bother you. You are of the race of people of honor. No idle chatter for you. Have a good journey, my friend, and let me close my circle."

I left without a backward glance, my attention caught by the expansive, graceful gestures of a young man unpacking a trunk. He took out disparate objects, commenting on each one, reconstructing a life, a past, a time gone by.

"We have here the bits and pieces of fate. The trunk is a house, which has harbored several lives. This cane cannot bear witness to time, for it is ageless, it comes from a walnut tree that has no more memories. It must have guided the steps of the old and the blind. It is heavy, and lacks mystery. But look at this watch. The Roman numerals have faded. The hour hand is stopped at noon or midnight. The minute hand ticks on alone. The dial is yellow. Did it belong to a merchant, a conqueror, a scientist? And what about these shoes? They don't match. They're English. They carried their owner in places without mud or dust. And this faucet of silver-plated copper.

It must have come from some fine house. The trunk is mute. I alone ask it questions. Look, a photograph. Time has done its work. A family snapshot, marked 'Lazzare 1922.' The father—or perhaps the grandfather—stands in the middle, wearing a frock coat. His hands rest on a silver cane. He is looking at the photographer. His wife is self-effacing. You can't see her very well. She's wearing a long dress. A small boy, wearing a bow tie and an old shirt, sits at his mother's feet. There's a dog alongside them. He looks tired. A young woman stands slightly apart from the others. She is beautiful. She is in love, and is thinking of the man of her heart. He is away, in France or the West Indies. I like to imagine the story of the young woman and her lover. They live in Guéliz. The father is a civil inspector in the colonial administration. He hangs out with the local pasha, the famous Glawi. You can see it in his face. Something is written on the back of the photograph: 'an afternoon of good . . . April 1922.' Now look at these worry-beads; coral, amber, silver. They must have belonged to an imam. Maybe the wife wore them as a necklace . . . Coins . . . a rial with a hole in it . . . a centime . . . a Moroccan franc . . . Paper money that's worthless now . . . Some false teeth . . . A brush . . . A china bowl . . . A stamp album . . . That's enough. Anything you want to get rid of, whatever weighs you down, just put it in the trunk. I'll take anything, especially coins!''

I took a ring out of my pocket and threw it in the trunk. The storyteller examined it and gave it back to me.

"Take back your ring. It's a rare jewel, from Istanbul. And I detect something in it I would rather not know. This ring is precious, weighty, charged with memories and journeys. Why do you want to get rid of it? Was it soaked in some misfortune? No, if you want to give me something, take it from your wallet, otherwise forget it. Why don't you just go?"

I left the circle without answering, drawing worried looks. It happened that from time to time in my life I would run into people who reacted violently to my presence, to my attitude or looks. I always assumed that this meant that we were of the same type, that our feelings were woven of the same thread. I never held it against them. I would always move on in silence, convinced that we would meet again in the same spirit.

As I was pondering the fate of that family of French settlers taken from the trunk in bits and pieces, I saw a woman spinning around to unroll a huge white haïk that she used as a jellaba. There was something erotic about the way she unveiled herself, as if it was a dance. I watched the subtle, barely rhythmic movement of her hips. She raised her arms slowly, almost as if to move her breasts. A circle of curious onlookers soon formed around her. She was young, and very beautiful, with big hazel eyes, smooth brown skin, slim legs, and a hint of mischief in her smile. What was she doing in this square reserved for men and a few old beggarwomen? We were all wondering the same thing as she slipped a cassette of Berber music into a tape deck, did a few dance steps, took out a microphone and announced:

"I come from the South, from the twilight. I came down from the mountain and walked, sleeping in wells. I crossed the nights and the sands. I come from a season outside time. I am the book that is never opened and never read, the book written by the ancestors, glory to their names. The ancestors have sent me to tell you, to warn you. Don't come too close. Let the breeze read the book's first words. You hear nothing. Be still and listen. Once there was a bedouin people, caravaneers and poets, a people coarse and proud who lived on dates and camel's milk. Mired in error, they invented their own gods. For fear of dishonor and shame, some cast off their female offspring, marrying them off when they were still mere children or burying them alive. Eternal damnation awaited these men. Islam condemned them. God said: 'There are stubborn hypocrites among the bedouins around you and among the inhabitants of Medina. You do not know them, but we do. We shall chastise them twice over, and they will suffer a terrible punishment.' If I speak in verses and parables today, it is because I have long heard words that came not from the heart, words written in no book, but spawned in the darkness that kept error alive."

There were slight movements of astonishment and lack of understanding in the crowd. Some whispered, others shrugged. A voice rose up:

"We're here to listen to music and to see you dance. This is not a mosque, you know."

"I'm happy to listen to you, Madame," a good-looking young man broke in. "Pay no attention to what they say; they're cousins of bedouins themselves."

"A story is a story, not a sermon," another young man said. "And since when do women not yet old dare to flaunt themselves like this? Have you no father, brother, or husband to guard you from harm?"

She must have expected comments of that kind, for she was ready with a gentle, ironic answer:

"Are you perhaps the brother I never had, or the husband so overcome with passion that his body trembles between fat, hairy legs? Are you perhaps the man who collects forbidden pictures and takes them out in icy solitude, crumpling them under his loveless body? Or perhaps you are my long-lost father, carried off by fever and shame, by the feeling of damnation that has driven you to exile in the southern sands?"

She leaned forward, laughed, took a corner of her haïk and tied it to her waist; then she asked the young man to hold the other end. She turned slowly, barely moving her feet, until she was entirely wrapped in it.

"Thank you," she said. "May God guide you on the right path! You have beautiful eyes. Get rid of that moustache. Virility lies not in the body, but in the soul. Farewell. I have other books to open."

She looked at me, suddenly motionless, and said:

"Where are you from, you who never speak?"

She left without waiting for an answer.

I would have liked to tell her of my life. She would have made it a book to carry from village to village. I can see her opening the chapters of my story one by one, keeping the final secret to herself.

The sun had made me drowsy. Now a cold, dusty wind awakened me. I wondered if I had dreamed that young woman or had really seen and heard her. I was surrounded by a varied, attentive audience. People thought I was acting, pretending to be asleep, or that I was thinking, trying to call up the fragments of some story. It was hard to get up and leave the square. When I opened my eyes, they all fell silent and leaned forward to listen. I decided to say a few words, so as not to disappoint them completely.

"Friends! Night lingered behind my eyelids, tidying up my mind, which has lately grown so weary. Many journeys, roads and starless skies, swollen rivers and mounds of sand, fruitless encounters, cold houses, damp faces, a long march. I arrived here yesterday, driven by the wind, aware that this was the final gate, the one nobody has opened, the one reserved for sundered souls, the gate with no name, for it leads to silence, into the house in which questions fall like cement between stones. Imagine a house in which each stone is a day, lucky or lethal. And crystals have formed between the stones; every grain of sand is a thought, perhaps even a musical note. The soul that enters that house is stripped bare. It cannot lie or disguise itself, for there truth abides. Any false word, whether spoken deliberately or by mistake, is a tooth that falls. I still have all my teeth, because I stand at the threshold of that house. If I speak to you, I will be careful, for then I will be inside. You will see me as I am, a body wrapped in this jellaba that protects me. You may not see the house. At least not at first. But little by little you will be let in as the secret becomes less dim. I owe you this story, my friends. I have come just when the storyteller who was supposed to tell it fell through one of those trap doors in the stage, a victim of his own blindness. He let himself be caught in the web spun by the sleeping spider. He opened the gates in the walls and then left them. He disappeared in midstream, leaving my own life hanging. I have given my body to the river's many currents, and they swept me away. I resisted. I fought them. Now and then the water cast me onto a bank, then carried me off again at the first spate. I had no time to think or act. In the end I let myself go. My body was purified; it changed. I speak to you now of a distant time. But I remember everything with amazing accuracy. If I talk in pictures it is because we don't know each other yet. But you will see, words fall like drops of acid in my house. I know whereof I speak: my skin bears witness to that. But be patient. Gates will open, perhaps not in order, but stay with me and you will see."

NIGHT
OF
DESTINY

I t was on that sacred night—the twenty-seventh of the month of Ramadan, the night the Muslim community's Holy Book came down from above, the night when fates are sealed—that my dying father called me to his bedside to set me free. He emancipated me as slaves were freed in olden days. We were alone, the door locked. His voice was barely audible. Death lurked in the room dimly lit by a single candle. It drew nearer as the night wore on, slowly draining the brightness from his face. It was as if a hand passing across his forehead was wiping away what remained of his life. He was calm, and talked to me until the early hours. We could hear the interminable calls to prayer and to the reading of the Koran. It was the children's night. They pretended to be angels or birds of paradise free of fate; as they played in the streets, their voices mingled with the call of the muezzin screaming into the microphone the better to be heard by God. My father smiled faintly as if to say that the muezzin was just a poor man who recited the Koran without understanding a word of it.

I sat on a cushion beside the bed, my head near my father's, listening to him without interrupting.

His breath brushed my cheek. Its fetid smell did not bother me. He spoke slowly:

"You know that on this night no child must die or suffer, for 'this night is worth a thousand months.' The children must greet the angels sent by God: 'The Angels and the Spirit descend during this Night, with their Lord's permission, to settle all manner of things.' It is the Night of Innocence, but children aren't innocent. They can be horrible. If this night is theirs, let it also be ours, yours and mine. Our first and our last. The twenty-seventh night of this month is a good time for confession, perhaps for forgiveness. But since angels will be among us to set things right, I'll be cautious. I would like to work things out before they interfere, since they can be very severe, despite their appearance of immaculate leniency. We have to start by acknowledging error, the wicked illusion that has brought down a curse on the whole family. Give me some water, my throat is dry. How old are you now? I've lost count."

"Almost twenty."

"Twenty years of lies. The worst of it is that I was the one who was lying. It wasn't your fault. I'm sorry, but I want to tell you something I have never dared admit to anybody, not even your poor mother. Especially not her.

Such a vacuous, joyless woman, but so obedient, always eager to follow orders, never rebellious. Who knows, maybe she rebelled in silence and solitude. She was brought up in the pure tradition of the wife who serves her man. I found that quite natural. Perhaps she did rebel after all, taking an unspoken revenge: she got pregnant year after year and gave me one daughter after another. I was saddled with unwanted offspring. I had to put up with them. I stopped praying and I rejected anything she offered me. When I happened to go to the mosque, I would work out complicated plans to get out of this miserable situation instead of saying one of the five prayers. Sometimes I even felt like committing murder. It was exciting to have evil thoughts in a holy place, a place of virtue and peace. I thought of all the possible ways to plan a perfect crime. Yes, I was evil, but weak too. Evil, however, cannot abide weakness, since evil draws its strength from unwavering determination. But I had doubts. During the typhus epidemic I tried to draw it into the house. I didn't give your mother and sisters the vaccine or the medicine that was distributed. But I took everything. I had to stay alive, you see, to bury them and start life over again. But chance and fate kept the disease out of the house: typhus struck our next-door neighbors, skipped over us, and continued on its lethal way. I am ashamed of all this, my girl, but on this hallowed night the truth speaks through us, whether we like it or not. And you have to listen, even if it hurts.

"A kind of curse had settled over our family. My brothers spun all the intrigues they could, barely concealing their hatred for me. I couldn't stand their polite words, their hypocrisy. But I have to admit that in the mosque,

19

I began to have the same ideas, and in their place I would probably have had the same thoughts, the same desires and jealousies. But it was my wealth they were jealous of, not my daughters. Pour me some tea, it's going to be a long night. Draw the curtains: maybe that screaming idiot won't sound so loud. Religion should be a thing of silence and meditation, not that din that must displease the Angels of Destiny. Can you imagine all the things they have to do in just a few hours? All the cleaning up? Getting everything arranged? Anyway, I guess they know what they're doing. I can feel them here in this room. I'm going to help them clean up. I want to leave this world clean, free of the shame that I have carried for so much of my life.

"I had ambitions in my youth. I wanted to travel, see the world, become a musician, have a son, be his father and his friend, devote myself to him, give him every opportunity to fulfill his vocation. I fed on that crazy hope, which became an obsession. I couldn't tell anyone about it. Your mother had no desires of her own, or if she did, they had faded long ago. In fact, she was always faded. Was she ever happy, even for a single day? I wonder even now. And I was not a man who could make her happy, or make her laugh, since I was pallid myself, hemmed in by a kind of curse. I decided to do something. A son was the only thing that could give me joy and life. And the idea of conceiving that child changed my life, even if it meant challenging divine will. I acted no different toward your mother and her daughters: uncaring and severe. But I was better with myself. I stopped going to the mosque to work out destructive plots. Now I had other plans, thinking of how to get the best for you, dreaming about you. I imagined you tall and handsome. You existed in my mind at first, and then, when you left your mother's womb and came into the world, you remained in my mind. And there you stayed all your life, until very recently. Yes, I imagined you tall and handsome, but you are not tall, and your beauty is an enigma.

"What time is it? No, don't tell me, I've always known what time it was, even in my sleep; it must be a few minutes past three. The angels must be half done already. They always go in pairs, especially when they're transporting a soul. One takes the right shoulder, the other the left, and they carry the soul up to heaven slowly, smoothly, and gracefully. But tonight they're cleaning. They don't have time to worry about an old man breathing his last. I have a few hours left to talk to you, until sunrise, after the first prayer, a short one, just to greet the first glimmers of light.

"What was I talking about? Oh yes, your birth. What joy, what happiness! When the midwife called to tell me that tradition had been properly observed, I saw a boy in her arms and not a girl. I was already in the grip of madness. I never saw female features in you. I must have been completely blind. Does it matter anymore? The wonderful memory of your birth is mine forever. As far as anyone could tell, I remained what I was: a rich merchant made complete by that birth. But, deep down, in my lonely nights, I faced the monster's unspeakable image. I came and went as usual, but the evil within me gnawed at my moral and physical well-being. I felt sin, then guilt, then fear. All this I carried inside me. Too heavy a burden. I no longer prayed, I couldn't bring myself to do it. And you grew up, bathed in light, a little prince, a child spared the miseries of childhood. It was impossible to go back and reveal the truth. No one, my son, my daughter, will know the truth. It's funny how clearly we can think when death is near. It's as if what I'm telling you now comes from somewhere outside me, as though I were reading it off a white wall where angels stand. I can see them.

"I have to tell you how much I hated your mother. I never loved her. I know you must have wondered sometimes whether there was any love between your father and mother. Love! Our literature, especially poetry, sings of love and courage. Well, I felt no love, not even any tenderness. Sometimes I would forget all about her, even her name, her voice. Total oblivion was the only thing that allowed me to tolerate the rest, all the tears. I'll give her one thing, at least she had the decency to cry in silence: tears would run down the cheeks of her absolutely expressionless face. That face was always the same: blank and flat, her head covered with a scarf. Then there was that slow way she walked or ate. Never a laugh or a smile. And your sisters, they were all just like her. I'm getting angry, I can feel the fever rising. I have to stop talking about that family.

"But you! I loved you just as much as I hated the others. But it was a burdensome, impossible love. I conceived you in light, with a joy inside. For one night your mother's body was no longer a tomb, a frigid ravine. It came back to life under the warmth of my hands, it turned into a perfumed garden. It was the first time a cry of joy or pleasure came from her. It was then that I knew that an exceptional child would be born of that embrace. I believe in the power our thoughts can have when we undertake some important deed. On that night I decided I would

22

be more attentive to your mother. The pregnancy was normal. One day I found her lifting a heavy trunk. I rushed to stop her: she was risking the life of the child of light she was bearing for me. After your birth, of course, I paid no particular attention to her. Our relations of silence, sighs, and tears returned to normal. The old silent hate came back. I spent all my time with you. She grew heavy and fat, locked herself in her room, and no longer spoke to anyone. I think that worried your sisters, who were left to their own devices. As for me, I just watched the drama unfold. I acted indifferent, but in fact I wasn't pretending. I really didn't care. I felt like a stranger in that house. You were my joy, my light. I learned to take care of a child. Which is not done around here. Yet I considered you as half an orphan. After the fake 'circumcision' I started to lose my mind. Doubt infected my passion. I, too, kept to myself, sinking into silence. You were a carefree child, running from room to room, making up games, always by yourself. Sometimes you even played with dolls. You dressed up as a girl, as a nurse, as a mother. You liked dressing up. I kept having to remind you that you were a little boy. You laughed at me. You made fun of me. My image of you faded in and out, clouded by your games. It was like the wind lifting a cloth draped over a treasure chest. A strong wind would blow it off completely. You would seem distraught, frightened, but then you would calm down again. How wise was that little body that eluded every caress. Do you remember how anxious I got when you pretended to disappear? You used to hide in that painted wooden trunk to get out of God's sight. When you were taught that God was everywhere, that He knew and saw everything,

23

you did all you could to escape His presence. You were afraid of it, or maybe you were just pretending, I don't know which."

He closed his eyes. His face was resting against mine. He was asleep. I checked his breathing: his chest moved so faintly that the thick white woolen blanket hardly budged. I lay there waiting anxiously for his last breath, the final sigh that would give up the soul. I thought I ought to leave the window ajar to let it out. But he gripped my arm just as I was about to get up. Even in the depths of his sleep he held me. Once more I was a prisoner of one of his plans. An uneasy feeling of fear came over me. I was in the grip of a dying man. The candlelight was fading. Morning was slowly coming down from the sky. The stars must be dimming. I thought about what he had been telling me. What kind of forgiveness could I offer him? Pardon can come from the heart, from the mind, or from mere indifference. My heart had hardened long ago. My mind had already stopped me from leaving the bedside of this man bargaining with death. Indifference can yield nothing or everything, and I had not reached that state of lack of care for myself. I had no choice but to listen to this man's last words and to watch over him as he slept. I was afraid that I would fall asleep myself and wake up holding hands with death. Outside the chanting of the Koran had stopped. The children had gone home. The prayers were over. The Night of Destiny was about to hand the keys of the city back to the day. Light—faint, soft, and subtle—was slowly settling on the hills, terraces, and cemeteries. A canon went off at sunrise, signaling the start of the fast. My father woke up with a start. The fear had left his face, but now there was panic: his time had come. For the first time I witnessed death at work, as it moved back and forth over the outstretched body, missing nothing. Any being tries to resist. My father had a look of supplication: he wanted one more hour, or even just a few minutes. He still had something else to tell me:

"I saw my brother in my sleep. His face was half yellow, half green. He was laughing. I think he was taunting me. His wife was standing behind him egging him on. He was threatening me. I didn't want to tell you about those two monsters tonight, but I have to warn you. They are ruthless and rapacious. They feed on hatred and wickedness. They are fearsome: greedy and heartless, hypocritical and cunning, with no pride at all. They spend their lives piling up money and stashing it away. They will stoop to anything and stop at nothing. My father was ashamed of that son of his. 'Where does he get that viciousness from?' he would ask me. A disgrace to the family. He pretends to be poor and waits until the market is about to close, then buys vegetables for next to nothing. He bargains for everything, complains, cries when he has to. He always says that I'm the cause of his misfortune, that it's my fault he's poor. Once I heard him talking to a neighbor. 'My older brother stole my share of the inheritance,' he said. 'Even when he dies, I won't have the right to inherit from him, because he's just had a son. I will take my case to God, for He alone can give me justice, here or in the afterlife.' Every once in a while they would invite us over for lunch. His wife would hardly cook the meat, smothering it in a pile of vegetables. The meat was so hard it would lay on the plate untouched. The next day she would cook it properly for her own family. She wasn't fooling anyone. Neither one of them has any

25

shame at all. Be careful, stay away from them, they're evil."

He paused, then began to talk more rapidly. I didn't understand it all. He thought it was important, but his gaze wandered, drifting to the other side of the room and back. He was still squeezing my hand.

"All I ask is that you forgive me," he said. "Then let Him who owns my soul take it where He will, to His flowered gardens and placid rivers, or to a volcano's crater. But grant me this favor: forget me, for that is forgiveness. You are free now. Go away, leave this cursed house; travel, and live! Live! And don't come back to see the disaster I am leaving behind. Forget, and take the time to live. Forget this city! Tonight I have come to realize that you will have a better fate than any of the women of this country. I see that clearly now, and I speak the truth. I see your face haloed in a wondrous light. This, the twenty-seventh night of Ramadan, is the night of your birth. You are a woman. Let your beauty guide you. You have nothing to fear now. The Night of Destiny names you Zahra, flower of flowers, grace, child of eternity. You are time standing on the slope of silence, at fire's peak, among the trees, on the face of heaven descending."

He leaned forward and held me. "I can see you, my daughter, I can see your hand held out to me. You are taking me with you, but where? I don't have the strength to follow you. I love the way your hand comes close to my eyes like that. It's dark, dark and cold. Where are you, where is your face? I can't see you anymore. Is that you pulling at me? What is this white field, is it snow? But wait, it's not white anymore. I can't see anything

26

now. Are you frowning, are you angry? You're in a hurry. Does this mean you forgive me, Zah . . . ra?"

A ray of sunlight came into the room. It was all over. Laboriously, I took my hand from his. I pulled the sheet over his face and blew out the candle.

A
BEAUTIFUL
DAY

A fter that exceptional night, my friends, the days took on new colors, the walls picked up new songs, the stones released echoes long held back, and bright light flooded the terraces. The cemeteries fell silent.

Everything got quiet, and seemed changed. It was hard not to notice the coincidence: an old man finally left this life and an almost supernatural brightness flooded people and things.

Apparently the Night of Destiny, however terrible for some, could set others free. The dead and the living meet at that point where the sounds of the latter drown out the former's prayers. On such a night, my friends, who can tell the difference between ghosts and angels, between

29

those arriving and those departing, between the heirs of time and the callow guardians of virtue?

Think of those carts with bodies piled high inside, some of them still breathing but intent on making the trip anyway, for one reason or another. Walls tremble as the carts pass, drawn by sturdy mares toward unknown places. On that night it was said that paradise was promised to whoever tried to make the journey, or at least to those who would give away their fortunes and the few days or weeks they had left to live, making an offering to that night without stars, when the sky opens and the earth moves a little faster. The people who came to lay on the carts had no fortunes but a pinch of time. Everyone else clung to money and to illusion.

I watched the procession from the little window. They had to leave the city before sunrise. The morning of that twenty-seventh day of fasting was like any other. There was to be no trace of the nocturnal cleansing. I looked at my father, his body lighter now, emptied of substance. I told myself that with a little luck his soul would be in one of the last carts. Weary but relieved, I sat on the edge of the bed and wept, but with exhaustion, not sadness. I was free now, but things were not to go as I had hoped.

I was a woman again, or at least recognized as such by my father, but I still had to play the game, acting as a son until all matters of inheritance had been settled. The house was a wreck. New cracks seemed to have opened in the walls overnight. Everything had changed in just a few hours. My sisters were weeping like professional mourners. My mother, dressed in white, was acting the part of the bereaved. My uncles were busy preparing the funeral. And as for me, I simply waited, secluded in the room.

It was a sunny spring day. Spring is carefree in our country. It changes the bougainvilleas, highlights the colors in the fields, makes the sky a little bluer, fills the trees, and turns its back on sorrowful women. Which is what I was. But that year I decided to put everything that was tormenting me out of my mind. I seldom laughed and was never funny. But I did want to be a part of the spring.

It was hard, my friends, that much I admit. To be cheerful meant changing my face, changing my body. I had to learn new gestures, to walk fluidly. That day's unusual heat reinforced my conviction: spring was not in the house, but it was there outside. Scents and odors came to me from neighboring houses and gardens. The desolation in our house had a bitter, stifling smell. The incense my uncles were burning was of poor quality. What was supposed to be paradise wood was actually some mediocre stick flavored with perfume that augured ill. The three people hired to bathe the corpse were in the usual hurry. They skimped on the water and then got into an argument with my uncle, who tried to bargain over their wretched wages. Their haggling with my uncle drowned out the chanting from the Koran and was at once shameful and ridiculous. It finally got so absurd that I could not help laughing.

"You want to clean out our pockets just to wash the corpse?"

"One thing's for sure: no one will wash you the day you die; you'll leave filthy, and even if you get to paradise,

31

you'll stink so bad they won't let you through the gate. That's why happens to misers."

My uncle turned white, muttered a prayer, and paid the three men their asking price. I watched jubilantly from the window. Someone drew my uncle off into a corner: it was his wife, mistress of avarice, hatred, and intrigue. A fearsome woman. I'll tell you about her too someday, for her fate deserves a comment. She was furious with her husband for having paid the washers.

I had to be the invisible son for another day or two. Dressed in white, I presided over the funeral. I wore dark glasses and covered my head with the hood of my jellaba. I didn't say a word. People leaned over to greet me, to express their condolences. Furtively they kissed my shoulder. Everyone was intimidated, which suited me fine. At the great mosque, of course, I was expected to lead the prayer for the dead. I did so with an inner joy and barely concealed pleasure. I was a woman gradually taking her revenge on a society of spineless men. At least that's what the men in my family were. As I bent down low I couldn't help thinking of the animal desire my body, especially in that position, would have aroused in those men if they had only known that they were praying behind a woman. Not to mention the ones who start playing with themselves the moment they see any rear end thus presented, male or female.

The death rite went off without incident. What I remember best about that day was our arrival at the cemetery. A blazing sun had created an eternal springtime. The graves were covered with bright green wild grass, the poppies were enchanted by the light, and geraniums had been scattered by some anonymous hand. The modest yet immutable presence of a few hundred-year-old olive trees were meant to assure that the souls in that garden would remain at peace. A Koranic cantor had dozed off on a grave. Children played in the trees. Two lovers hid behind a gravestone high enough to let them kiss without being seen. A young student was reading *Hamlet*, walking back and forth and waving his arms. A woman in a wedding dress dismounted from a white horse. A horseman in a blue, southern-style gandoura crossed the cemetery on his mare. He seemed to be looking for someone.

The procession scattered as we arrived. Some shielded their eyes with their arms, unable to bear the intense light. The dead man was forgotten. The gravediggers began to look for the grave they had prepared. Children in the street who had followed the procession began to dance. They approached the body as if in a ballet, picked it up, and turned in a circle, humming an African chant. Then, moving slowly, they placed it in one of the graves that had been dug that morning. The gravediggers, appalled, chased the children away with spades and picks. The bride came toward me and draped her magnificent gold-embroidered burnoose around my shoulders. "He is waiting for you on a white mare with gray spots," she whispered. "Go and join him. Don't ask me why, just go. And be happy." She disappeared. What was she? An apparition, an image, a piece of a dream, a voice, a lapse of time escaped from the twenty-seventh night? I was still dazzled when a powerful arm coiled around my waist and lifted me up. The handsome horseman pulled me onto his mare. No one spoke. I was carried off, as in the tales of old. We galloped across the cemetery. I glanced back at my father's corpse, which the gravediggers were now lifting out of the ground in order to bury it according to the rules of Islam. I also saw my uncles, gripped with panic, backing out of the cemetery.

It was a beautiful day.

THE PERFUMED GARDEN

O moon of moons, star full of night and light, this gold-embroidered burnoose is your residence, the roof of your house, the wool of which your dreams are woven, the warm blanket for long winter nights when I'm away. But I will never leave you, for I have waited too long to leave you even for a single night."

We rode for an entire day. He spoke to me now and then, saying the same thing again and again, calling me "princess of the South," or "moon of moons" or "first morning light." I sat behind him, wrapped in the burnoose, my arms around his waist. The mare's motion made my crossed arms stroke his firm belly up and down.

I felt strange, and abandoned myself to the feeling, asking no questions. It was like one of those dreams that continues when you're half awake. I had never been on a horse before. Emotion rose within me in an inner freedom that warmed my body. Adventure is first of all that sense of strangeness of which pleasure is born. I rested my head against his back, shut my eyes, and hummed a childhood song. The day before I had helped a dying man's soul ascend to heaven, and now here I was holding tight to an unknown man, perhaps a prince sent by the angels of that twenty-seventh night, a prince or a tyrant, an adventurer or a bandit of stony paths, but a man—a man whose eyes I had barely seen, for he was veiled.

The slave, just free, was being carried off, perhaps to a new prison, a castle with high, thick walls guarded by armed men, a castle without gates or windows, just an entrance with a stone or two that could be moved aside to let the horseman and his prey get in.

I dozed, dreamed, forgot. A cool wind stroked my cheeks wet with tears of joy. The sky was blue, red, mauve, as the sun went down. I was neither hungry nor thirsty on that day of fasting. My horseman stopped for a moment and said, as if I knew all about his daily life:

"We're going to stop and see the children. If we're lucky, we can break the fast with them."

"What children?"

He didn't answer.

The village was in a small valley that we entered through a secret path. Obstacles had been set up and were guarded by children. There was a password for each one, made up of four sentences that formed a poem my horseman knew by heart:

We are the children, the guests of the earth.
Of earth we are made, to earth we will return.
Here on this earth, happiness lasts not,
But nights of joy erase the pain.

I did not realize it at first, but it was a poem by Abu-
l'Ala al-Ma'arri. I had read *Risalat al-Ghufran* in my adolescence, but I didn't remember those lines. That evening
one of the children asked my horseman:

"Well, Sheikh, how was hell? What did the dead tell
you, and what did the damned do to you?"

"I'll tell you all about it after supper."

It was a village of children. We were the only adults.
Simple houses made of red clay. There must have been
about a hundred children, both boys and girls. The ter-
raced gardens were remarkably well kept. It was a self-
sufficient community, far from town and roads, far from
the country itself, perfectly organized, with no hierarchy,
police, or army, and no written laws. It was a little re-
public, dreamed and lived by children. I was astonished.
My horseman sensed my impatience: I wanted to understand. We found a place to talk alone. He took off his veil
and I saw his face for the first time. I looked closely at
his features as he spoke: large brown eyes; thick, regular
eyebrows; delicate lips; a lush moustache; smooth, dark
brown skin. He spoke softly, without really looking at me.

"I have seven secrets," he said. "To earn your friendship and forgiveness for having carried you off, I will tell
you about them one by one. This will take time, for we
must get to know one another and allow friendship into
our hearts. This village is my first secret. No one knows
of it. Only those whose hearts have suffered and who

have no illusions about the human race live here. We hardly ever explain the secret, but I owe you a minimum of enlightenment to soothe your anxieties."

"But I don't feel anxious."

That was true. Not only was my mind free of fear, but I felt a deep harmony between image and reflection, between body and shadow, between a dream that had filled my lonely nights and this story I was living out in happy curiosity. I was like a child on its first trip.

That first night was the beginning of an astonishing adventure. My horseman, whom everybody called the Sheikh, had to report on his mission. He had been away from the village for a long time.

A wide-eyed boy with red hair, barely ten years old, came up to me and said:

"Welcome! I represent friendship, and possibly love."

"What are you supposed to do?" I asked.

"To really understand how things work in this village, you have to start by forgetting where you come from and how you lived back there, on the other side of the valley. Here we are ruled by principles and feelings. Forgetting is the first principle. Whether you have lived a hundred years or a hundred days, when you enter this place you have to wipe your memory clean. If you can't manage it, we have plants that can help."

"But exactly what do you do here?"

"I grow the plants that foster feelings of plenitude and harmony. What we all have in common here is that we have all suffered from injustice; here we have a chance to make time stand still and repair the damage. This village is actually a ship, a ship that sails stormy seas. We have no link at all to the past, to dry land. The village is

38

an island. Every now and then we send the Sheikh out to gather information. Often he brings back abandoned or runaway children. This is the first time he's brought us a princess. Welcome!"

The redhead kissed my hand and disappeared. A dark-skinned girl with curly hair came over to me. I must have been a real curiosity. She looked at me without a word, walked around me, ran her hand over my burnoose. Then she came closer and whispered as if we were old friends:

"Don't let the Sheikh get to you; he's too handsome and charming. In time you'll find out how to deal with men. It's not a problem here. We're all children, and we stay children. It's simple. And convenient."

She saw the Sheikh coming and ran off, saying as she left:

"I hope you'll stay with us."

I too began to call my horseman "the Sheikh." Yet he was not old, had no white beard, and looked more like an athlete in training.

He brought us dinner: rich soup, dates, and dried figs.

I was so tired that I fell asleep just after eating, wrapped in my burnoose. The night was peopled with dreams one inside the other, like Chinese boxes. Everything was all mixed up. When I woke up the next morning, I couldn't tell the difference between dreams and what I now saw before me. The grass, flowers, trees, birds, streams—everything around me—fired my imagination and troubled my senses. I decided to give up trying to distinguish the real from the imaginary or to find out where I was. From my window I saw the Sheikh carrying wood while the children worked the land, cleaned the village, and prepared food. Everyone had something to do. I went out to look around the village in daylight. Some of the children smiled at me, others stopped and greeted me with clasped hands. I was learning to walk naturally, without tension, not worrying about people looking at me. I was rediscovering a surprising innate elegance. My body was breaking free of itself. Cords and strings were unraveling, and I could feel my muscles loosening. I breathed more easily. I ran my hand over my small breasts. It felt good. I massaged them, trying to make them bigger, to make them jut out proudly and excite passersby. I remembered those days long ago when Lalla Zineb, an enormous woman who lived with some neighbors, would come over to help my mother out. She would take me in her arms, wedge my small head against her heavy breasts, and squeeze me against her, in joy or in desire. She had no children of her own, and her husband had left her for two other wives who gave him many. So she would hold me close, carry me on her back, pat my cheeks, grip me between her parted thighs. I was her toy. She sweated a lot and never realized that I found her disgusting. I never told her. Her games were a change from the comfort and attention that was showered upon me in the family. One day my father came in unexpectedly and saw me wriggling between Lalla Zineb's fat thighs. He ran over, snatched me away, and slapped the poor woman. Yes, she had huge breasts. They spilled out all over. I began to dream about those masses of flesh, Allah's bounty.

I touched my breasts. They were swelling slowly. I opened my blouse to present them to the morning wind, to the caressing breeze. I had gooseflesh and the nipples hardened. The wind blew all over my body. My blouse puffed out. I undid my hair. It was not very long, but the wind was good for it. I walked on without knowing where I was going. A wild desire came over me. I took off my saroual, then my underpants, to please the wind, to please myself, to feel the cool, light touch of the morning breeze on my belly, rousing my senses. I was in a wood. Nature was at peace. These were my first steps as a free woman. Freedom was that simple: to go for a morning walk and to cast off these binding clothes without asking permission. Freedom was giving my body to the wind, the light, the sun, in happy solitude. I took off my slippers. I tread on sharp pebbles, but felt no pain. I came to a clearing and sat down on a mound of damp earth. A coolness rose within me like a wave of pleasure. I rolled in the leaves, feeling slightly dizzy. I ran to a lake. I hadn't known that there was a lake and a spring behind the wood, but nature was infusing me with new instincts, new reflexes. My body needed water. I took off my gandoura and dived into the water. I had never learned to swim, and now I almost drowned. I clung to a branch and made my way to the spring, where I sat and turned my back to the jet of cold, clean water. I was dreaming. I was happy, delirious, all new and alert. I was life, pleasure, desire; I was the wind in the water, the water in the earth, the water purified, the earth ennobled by the spring. I trembled with joy. My heart beat wildly as I gasped for breath. I had never felt so much before. My body, which had been dull and deserted, a ruin, at the mercy of lies, was coming back to life. Before I knew it I was screaming as loud as I could, "I'm alive . . . alive! . . . My soul has come back, and it cries from my chest, I'm alive, alive!"

Naked children dove laughing into the lake. They gathered around me, repeating after me, "She's alive, alive." Other children waited on the bank holding a white bath towel. They wrapped me in it, had me sit on a wicker chair, and carried me to my room, where the Sheikh, dressed all in white, greeted me. I was still trembling with the cold, and with emotion. I was weary, happy, astonished. Things had happened fast, as though time was impatient. The Sheikh kissed my hand. I laid my head on his knee. He stroked my wet hair as he spoke to me:

"I'm glad you found the spring. That was the second secret. Now you can't go back anymore. The water of that spring does good. It works miracles. And you found it on your own. You are on the way. Whatever you do, don't turn around. It might be dangerous to look back. No, you won't be cursed, as in the legend; you won't turn into a pillar of salt or sand. But you could do harm. And to do harm is a mistake; it is to suffer a joyless fate, devoid of truth and desire. Believe me, princess, I know whereof I speak."

Suddenly the Sheikh fell silent. When I looked up, I saw tears running down his cheeks. He was weeping in silence, his eyes closed. I shivered. I got up and draped the gold-embroidered burnoose around his shoulders. He dozed off, but tears continued to run down his cheeks. Sweet tears. Tears that must have been long in coming. I was intrigued by his serenity, his placid submission to this uncontrollable outburst. I had no wish to disturb him by asking questions. On the shelf a large notebook lay open, the writing inside delicate. There were drawings, signs, questions. I was tempted to read it, but I didn't dare. That would have been worse than theft. I had a sudden, violent foreboding: misfortune lurked all around us. The dream had been too beautiful; now the nightmare was on its way. Four or five children rushed into the room and ordered me out of the valley:

"You made the Sheikh shed tears. You may be one of those beings from the past who helped tear away his soul, his breath, his life. You have to go before he wakes, before he gets violent."

I tried to absolve myself, to tell them that I had torn nothing away, that it had happened of its own, that I had no idea why he was crying. In vain. The children looked at me vindictively, their eyes filled with hate and violence. I went to the Sheikh to wake him up. One of the children jumped on me and knocked me down:

"Leave him alone. He may be dying. He can't disappear again and leave us for years!"

Thus was I driven from the so-called perfumed garden. Believe me, my friends, this was no dream, I lived it. I slept with the animals that night, in the stable on the edge of the village. Puzzled and upset, I spent the night trying to understand, but the more I thought, the darker were the shadows that settled over my mind. In the middle of the night, the red-haired boy, the one who had welcomed me so kindly, came into the stable. I wasn't surprised. I was expecting him.

"Don't try to understand," he said. "I'll help you get out of here. The Sheikh is our emblem; our fate is bound to his. If he succumbs to temptation we are lost. There is a pact, an oath, between us: never to reveal our seven secrets to a stranger. Every secret he reveals is a piece out of our skin. We lose color from our faces, and our teeth fall out, then our hair; then we lose our blood, our minds, our souls, and finally our lives. It isn't your fault. You are good. But something about you brings destruction. I don't know what it is, but I can feel it. Misfortune must dwell within you, unbeknownst to you. It feeds on others' failures and that way spreads. As you must have noticed, we are a tribe outside time. That is our strength, and our weakness. The Sheikh alone is still immersed in time. He grows, gets restless, and ages. That's why he leaves us sometimes. Usually he brings back seed to sow. This time he brought you instead. We are sheltered from the living here. That's all I can tell you. It is a secret's nature to remain buried. We are the secret, so we live under the earth. This village has no name. It does not exist. It lies within each one of us. When you leave here, think of yourself as a woman who has survived."

THE
MIRRORS
OF TIME

How do survivors walk? With their heads lowered, eyes downcast, hands behind their backs, wandering a random path until they glimpse a dimly lit house in the distance? I walked without looking back. I wanted to forget, to believe that what had happened to me was just another hallucination, a truncated dream in which everything was all mixed up: a father's burial and a freed slave's flight. I walked without speaking to anyone. Neither the children nor the men I passed bothered me. Yet I must have looked strange, badly dressed, my face haggard, wet with tears. At nightfall I curled up under a tree and wept in silence, without sadness and with no regrets. I don't think I shed a tear on the day of my father's burial.

A single sentence spoken by my mother—she who never spoke—suddenly rang in my ears. I remember I had gooseflesh when I first heard it.

It was at a time when nothing was going right. My father sensed that death was near, perhaps hastened by his persistent feeling of guilt and sin. He was bitter, irritable, impatient, and wholly without joy. Hatred, blind and violent, seethed within him. I think he hated everybody, himself first of all. Curiously, I was the only exception. I think he even loved me. I was exempt from the brutality that had become his normal mode of communication. From my bedroom window I sometimes witnessed disputes between him and the female contingent of the house. He was the only one to shout, to threaten, to laugh at his own supremacy. He had become maniacal, unable to tolerate the slightest lapse in the observation of his own rituals. Each of his daughters had an assigned role: one removed his jellaba, another washed his feet, a third dried them, and the two others made his tea. And woe betide anyone who made a mistake! Terror reigned, and he was never satisfied.

When he had an attack of bronchitis, he refused to take his medicine. When he couldn't breathe and writhed with chest pains, he accused the rest of the family of stealing his share of oxygen. He may not have even been sick, but the presence of all those useless women annoyed him so much that he was short of breath.

Rejecting sickness and death, he fought back with incredible energy. He felt a need to take his unjust violence out on his own family. He had discovered instinctively that hatred was an antidote to decay, sustaining his position as lord of the manor and warding off the progress

46

of disease. Sometimes he talked to himself, believing as he did that no one else in the house was worth speaking to. Except me. He would like to have confided in me, to have discussed his problems, but I never gave him the chance. I was hurt by the way he was acting. I understood it, but I could not excuse it or talk about it with him. In the last months of his life, I was already suffering a crisis of my own. I was fighting my own violence, determined to escape from it somehow. But as the proverb says: "It's a lot easier to enter the baths than to leave." I had to escape from that situation cleansed of the suspicions I harbored about myself, suspicions that were well justified.

My mother, who had opted for silence and resignation, out of calculation more than fatalism, said to me one day when my father's harsh words had hurt her deeply: "Pray with me, my daughter, that God or Fate let me die before you, but that I be granted just a month or two of life after your father's death! How I would love to be able to breathe for a few days or weeks in his absence. That is my sole desire, my only wish. Were I to die before him, I would go doubly battered, horribly laid waste, humiliated. I am resigned to living in silence, my voice stifled by my own hand. But may I be granted some time, however short, to utter just one scream from the depths of my soul, a scream that has lurked deep in my breast for so long, since before you were born. That scream is waiting, eating at me, ravaging me, and I want to live so that I do not die with it still inside me. Pray for me, my daughter, you who know life from both sides, you who can read both books and the hearts of saints."

I had forgotten even the sound of her voice: my mother, thrust aside by my father and by my own story. She called me "daughter" as if nothing had happened in those twenty years. I can't say that I loved her. When I wasn't feeling sorry for her—a feeling of bitter shame or mute anger—I paid no attention to her. It was as if she did not exist. I did not see her, and I forgot that she was my mother. Sometimes I mixed her up with Malika, an old servant woman, or with the ghost of a mad beggarwoman who took refuge in the entranceway of our house from time to time when children chased her, hurling stones and insults. When I came home in the evening, I would step over a body wrapped in an army blanket. I wouldn't even look to see whether it was the madwoman or my mother, thrown out of her own home. Even if I was upset, I never showed it. Just closed my eyes, so as not to see, not to hear. And most of all not to speak. What was going on inside me had to stay inside me, unseen, for there was nothing to say. Or maybe too much to say, too much to expose and denounce. I lacked the desire and the courage. Once I lost my balance on the tightrope, I felt I needed time to cast off twenty years of make-believe. If I was to be born anew, I had to wait for my father and mother to die. I considered ways to bring their deaths about, or to hasten them. I would have written that sin off to the monster I had become.

My mother sank into madness. One of her aunts took her away to live out the rest of her days in a marabout's place on the road to the South. I think she finally came to enjoy all those fake bouts of insanity, when she would tear up her husband's things. In the end she really didn't know what she was doing.

I watched her departure from my bedroom window. Her hair was tangled, her dress torn. She howled, ran around in the courtyard like a child, kissed the ground and the walls, laughed, cried, and crawled to the gate on all fours like an unwanted animal. Her daughters cried. My father wasn't there.

That night a great heaviness of silence and remorse settled over the house. We were all strangers. My sisters left to take temporary refuge with some aunts on my mother's side. I thus found myself alone with my father in his defeat.

The girls came back to get things now and then, but left without looking in on the sick man. Only old Malika remained loyal. At night she would let the mad beggar-woman in, or the coalman, who liked to chat with her. They were from the same village.

Despite the pain in his chest, my father decided to fast during Ramadan. He hardly ate anything even at sunset. He refused to take his pills, allowing himself to die in stubborn silence. I continued to go to the shop during the day. I was putting things in order. My father's brothers never came to see him. They figured that because of me, they stood to inherit nothing anyway.

I think that everything was ready on the eve of the twenty-seventh night of Ramadan.

Now it was all becoming clear. I can't say that I had decided what to do, but I knew that when my father died I would abandon everything and go away. The girls could have it all, and I would leave that house and that family forever. Once my father was gone, something else would be finished too. The monster he had created would go to the grave with him.

I lost my bearings completely after the burial. For days I did not know where I was or with whom. But I have told you of that adventure, which seemed so marvelous but ended in fear and wandering.

I went back to the house one night. I got in through a neighbor's terrace. My sisters had come back. They were well-dressed and outrageously made up; they wore my mother's jewelry. They were laughing and playing with some other neighborhood women. Burial and mourning were a liberation for them, a festival. When all is said and done, I could understand their reaction. Frustrated girls kept apart from life for so long, they were discovering freedom. All the pent-up hysteria was coming out. Every light in the house was on. They were playing records on an old phonograph. It was party time. All they needed now were men. I smiled. It was none of my business anymore: I had already become a stranger. I opened my bedroom door quietly, took a few things I had kept in a bag, and left through the same terrace.

Wearing a jellaba and a scarf I headed for the cemetery. It was a clear night. I stepped over a low wall to avoid being seen by the guard and went to my father's grave.

It was the eve of the end of Ramadan. More stars than usual. The earth covering the grave was still fresh. I dug quickly and methodically, by hand. I was careful not to disturb the dead man or to attract the guard's attention. When I saw a piece of white shroud, I slowly moved the soil away with my fingers. The body was icy, the shroud damp from the soil. I shivered, though it was not cold. I stopped for a moment and stared at the dead man's head. It looked like the white material near his nostrils was moving. Was he still breathing, or was it just a hallucination? I emptied the bag, which contained almost everything I possessed: a man's shirt, a pair of trousers, a piece

50

of a birth certificate, a photograph of the circumcision ceremony, my identity card, the marriage certificate for me and poor Fatima, the medicine I had made my father take, socks, shoes, a ring of keys, a belt, a tin of snuff, a packet of letters, an account book, a ring, a handkerchief, a broken watch, a vial, a half-burned candle.

Before filling in the grave, I squatted down to pack the objects in and felt a pain in my chest, as though something were squeezing my rib cage. My breasts were still wrapped tight to stop them from growing. In a rage I tore off the wretched disguise, several yards of white cloth. I unrolled it and wrapped it around the dead man's neck, then knotted it and pulled it tight. I was sweating. I got rid of all my life, a time of lies and deception. I tamped the objects down on the body with my hands and feet, stepping on it a little. I filled in the grave. The mound was bigger now. I covered it with heavy stones and meditated for a moment, not to pray or to ask God's mercy on that poor man's soul, but to soak up the new air I now breathed. I said, "So long." Or maybe it was "Farewell, fictive glory, and may we both live, naked and blank, the soul virginal and the body new, however old the words!"

A
DAGGER
CARESSING
MY BACK

O n that gloomy, blazing night I disappeared. I left no footsteps in the darkness. I skirted the town, choosing to skim over the countryside so as not to trouble the placid sleep of the good people in their homes. I was not one of them, for I was an uncontrollable troublemaker.

I felt happy on that September night, soaked in the fragrant whiffs of jasmine and wild roses coming from the gardens. I breathed in the scents deeply and walked down the road that lay before me. I was at peace with myself, and ready for adventure. I never looked back to see my native abyss one last time. I had entombed everything: father and possessions in the same grave, mother with a marabout at the gates of hell, sisters in a house that would someday collapse and bury them forever. My aunts and uncles had never existed for me anyway, and from that night on I did not exist for them either. I was leaving, and they would never find me.

I kept walking, avoiding the roads. When I grew tired I would stop to sleep, preferably under a tree. I slept peacefully, without fear or anxiety. My body curled up and abandoned itself to a gentle torpor. Rarely had I slept so deeply and so well. I was surprised at how easy it was, at the pleasure of feeling my body grow heavy in repose, for I had often had trouble falling asleep. I would sometimes spend most of the night bargaining for a little peace, achieving it only at first light, overcome with fatigue. But now I feared nothing. I had no bonds, no moorings. My mind was no longer encumbered with all those questions, all those things to do or undo. Completely free? No, not yet. But the very fact of having cast off everything, of having left, never to go back, of having cut myself off from all trace of the past, released my mind from fear. I was determined to dissolve my past in the coma of complete amnesia, with no regrets and no remorse. I wanted to be born anew in a fresh, clean skin.

I had no extravagant dreams or nightmares when I slept in the open air. It was a limpid sleep, smooth as the surface of a tranquil sea or a flat, continuous stretch of snow. At first I thought this was just physical tiredness, but later I realized that it was the sleep of life's first moments.

Now and then, especially during the day, I had hot waves of anxiety. They didn't last long. A lump would come to my throat, I would stop, then everything would slowly return to normal. These were the final twitches of a past that was still too close, within reach of eye and hand. That bodily discomfort was solitude's doing. I had chosen paths rarely trodden. I ate whatever I could and drank a lot of water. I asked for water whenever I passed near a hut or farmhouse. People took me for a beggar and gave me bread and fruit as well. When I tried to pay, they refused to take my money. I saw a kind of anxious pity in their eyes. I would never stay long, always leaving before the questions started. I would have liked to have stayed to talk, but I didn't know what to say. No one would have understood anyway. What's the point of having a conversation about time? But one afternoon a man followed me as I left a small village.

"But where are you going all alone, sister?" he asked, his tone somewhat ironic.

I smiled and went on my way without turning around.

"Do you realize where you're headed, sister? You are on your way to a thick wood, where wild boar wait in the dark to devour their prey. Boar with claws of bronze, with teeth of ivory and nostrils that breathe fire."

I shuddered from head to toe. I was not afraid of the man with the soft voice. I had heard talk of rapes in the forest, but had no desire to flee, or even to resist if the man turned into a boar. It was not that I didn't care. I was curious. A man whose face I did not even know was arousing physical feelings in me with words alone.

I quickened my step. We were only a few yards apart. I heard him mutter what sounded like a prayer. Nothing about wild beasts tearing at a girl's body anymore. Now the subject was God and His Prophet. This was his incantation:

"In the name of God, the Merciful, the Compassionate,

God's blessing and salvation upon the seal of the prophets, our master Mohammed, and upon his family and his companions. In the name of God Most High. Praise be to God, Who has decreed that man's greatest pleasure lies in woman's warm insides. Praise be to God, Who has placed in my path this nubile body advancing to the outer limits of my desire. It is the sign of His blessing, His bounty, His compassion. Praise be to God—and praise be to you too, sister, for walking before me that I might smell your perfume, imagine your hips and breasts, dream of your eyes and hair. O sister, walk on to the bushes where our famished bodies might dwell. Do not turn back. I am laid open to love, with you, my unknown sister, sent by fate to bear witness to God's glory for the man and woman who will be joined at nightfall. Praise be to God. I am His slave. As I am yours. The sun sinks slowly, and with it my pride crumbles. In the name of God, the Merciful . . ."

I stopped, as if gripped by some invisible force. I could not go on. I looked right and left and realized that I had gone into a copse. The man was still behind me. He had stopped praying. I could hear his breathing. Neither of us said a word. I stood sweating, rooted to the spot; there were bushes everywhere. I waited for a moment. So did he, motionless. I looked up at the sky, vivid with the colors of the setting sun. I was suddenly very warm. I took off my jellaba, unaware of what I was doing. Underneath I wore only a loose-fitting saroual. I untied my hair. I stood like a statue. In a few minutes it was dark. I felt the man coming closer to me. He was trembling, muttering prayers. He took me by the hips. I felt his tongue run over my neck, my shoulders. He knelt. I remained standing. He kissed my back, his hands still on my hips. He undid my saroual with his teeth. He pressed his face, wet with sweat or tears, against my butt. He was delirious. He pulled me to the ground with a sudden movement. I let out a little cry. He put his left hand over my mouth and held me face down with the other. I had neither the strength nor the desire to resist. I was not thinking. I was free under the weight of that feverish body. For the first time another body was mingling with mine. I didn't even try to turn around to see his face. All my limbs shook. The night was black. I felt a warm, thick liquid on my thighs. The man groaned like a dying animal. I thought I heard another invocation of God and the Prophet. I slid my right hand along my belly, feeling the liquid I was losing. It was blood.

Without trying to free myself from that unknown man's grip, I let the night carry me into a deep sleep. When the fresh morning breeze awakened me, I was naked. The man was gone. I was neither unhappy nor disappointed. Was that love? A dagger caressing my back in the darkness? A scathing violence that clasps you from the rear like a random target, punctuated by prayers and incantations?

I asked myself the question, but I was not really looking for any answers. Even now I am not sure whether that encounter from the rear had caused me pleasure or disgust. I had read books that spoke of love, but not of sex. That union of two bodies left a taste of sand in my mouth. That must have been the taste and smell of love. It was not unpleasant.

There was blood on my fingers and between my legs, but I felt neither dirty nor sullied. I got dressed and went on my way. Something echoed in my head, the sound of a hammer on stone or a piece of marble. It was the memory of the man's heartbeat.

My first man, then, was faceless. Had he asked me questions, it would have been unbearable. Had he not disappeared into the night, I would have fled.

I saw no one on the road that day. I had the feeling that all the people I would meet would come from the rear. It was an obsession. That evening I entered the town where I would become part of a disturbing story. It was a small town, and I felt a pang of anguish as I entered. A bad sign. First of all I looked for a public bath, both to wash and to find a place to sleep. It was late. The woman at the till glared at me.

"A fine time to come to get rid of male spit," she said.

I didn't answer.

"I was about to close," she went on, "but two or three women are still dawdling in there. Hurry up."

I hurried. She watched me. There were two impressively thin women in the back room, near the hot water fountain. They looked like twins of misfortune. Each one sat in a corner and mechanically poured cups of water over her head. They had staked out their territory with buckets. I could see that they did not want to be disturbed. From time to time they got up, stood back to back, rubbed their hands, then returned to their corners. I washed quickly. I had my head down when one of them appeared before me and said authoritatively:

"I'll soap you."

I did not look up. Her bony knees were in front of my face.

"No, thank you," I said.

58

"I said I'll soap you."

The other woman stood blocking the doorway with a row of buckets.

It seemed a particularly dishonest proposal, but I acquiesced to the threat. I asked if I could get some water. I filled a bucket with scalding water, hurled it at the two women, and dashed for the exit. I was lucky not to slip, and a moment later I was standing naked alongside the cashier.

"Are you crazy? You'll catch cold," she shouted at me.

"No, I'm not crazy. I barely got away. There are two of them."

"What are you talking about? There's no one here anymore. The last three left when you came in, didn't you see them go? Are you trying to fool me?"

When she saw that I was trembling—icy with fear— she hesitated for a moment, then asked me what they looked like.

"There are two of them, thin as rails and absolutely identical. They wanted to soap me!"

"You must have been dreaming. You're so tired you must have seen the devil and his wife!"

She was afraid too. She had looked mean, but now she was being very nice, though still authoritarian.

"Do you have a place to sleep?"

"I was going to ask you if I could spend the night here."

"Here? Out of the question. For one thing, it's not comfortable, and for another, the two jinn might come back late at night and scare you. A girl with such pretty skin as yours doesn't sleep just anywhere. Come to our house. It's simple, but comfortable. I live with my brother. He's younger than me."

THE
SEATED
WOMAN

T o get to the house we had to go through various intersecting alleyways that seemed laid out either at random or according to the designs of some depraved builder. One, called One-person Street, was so narrow that only one person at a time could walk through. They say lovers used to meet there. They would enter from opposite ends, and when they got to the middle, they would have an excuse to touch, since there was no room to pass. The woman, veiled and in her jellaba, would put one hand across her belly, the other across her chest. When he reached her, the man would stop for a moment and feel his beloved's breath on his face. One-person Street was the hidden rendezvous of stolen kisses and caresses, the place where bodies in love could touch, where eyes could plunge into a gaze unknown. Other eyes, hidden behind blinds, would watch these encounters.

Garbage was strewn on the ground. Every house had a pile of filth at the door. It stank, but no one seemed to care. A cat wailed like an unloved child. I followed the Seated Woman's large body.

"They really ought to call it Half-person Street," she said.

As she passed, she kicked a fat-bellied cat. It did not meow, but howled like a wounded man. She stopped at a door with iron bars and padlocks, then said:

"Behind this door misfortune has done its work. A sterile woman had children. A drought fell upon the country, then terrible flooding. This was misfortune's branch office. An otherwise normal man copulated with his children. One day the house collapsed on them. No one dug them out. The doors and windows were blocked up, sand and cement poured over everything. They're all still there, mother, father, and children, united forever by earth and hellfire. Misfortune seems to have eased off since then, causing no catastrophes, though it lurks here still."

I wondered why she was telling me these sinister stories. I was curious about what might happen to me, not about what had already happened behind the walls of those alleyways. But she went on, listing all the neighbors.

"In this house there's a family of no real interest. He's a tanner. Nobody dares to shake his hand, it stinks so much. And here there's a horse who lives by itself. And this one's empty, no one knows why. An abandoned house is like an unfinished story. Over there was the dairy. It's a Koranic school now. That's where the Consul gives his lessons. It's right near the house."

The house had two floors. Though not very big, it towered over the others. In the summer people lived on the terraces. The Seated Woman took me to a room furnished and decorated in traditional style. She told me to wait, not to move. I looked at the walls. Wrinkled human faces seemed to loom out of the stains of damp. They began to move as I stared at them. A portrait of an old man wearing a turban hung on the wall. He looked ill. It was a black-and-white photograph retouched with color, and everything had faded with age; the paper, the red of the lips, the blue of the turban, the tone of the skin. Time had done its work, restoring the weariness that had dwelled in that face when the photograph was first taken. It must have been the woman's father or grandfather, infinite sadness in his eyes. A man looking at the world for the last time.

The Seated Woman's voice tore me away from my thoughts.

"That was our father. He wasn't happy and neither are we. That photograph was taken not long before he died. Anyway. The Consul will see you tomorrow."

She hesitated, smiled slightly, and added:

"Or rather, you'll see him tomorrow. Let's eat something. I don't know why, but I feel at ease with you. Normally I tend not to trust people. But the moment I saw you I thought we might get along. I forgot to ask if you're looking for work, because if you are—"

"What did you have in mind?"

"Looking after the Consul."

"Is he ill?"

63

"He's blind. He lost his sight at the age of four, after a fever that almost killed him."

I agreed.

"You'll pick it up as you go along. I don't know anything about you, which is just as well. If you betray us, I'll come after you. I sacrificed everything for my brother . . . I am determined to have peace in this house."

I looked around as she spoke, thinking of my father. I saw him standing at the door, lecturing my mother. It was her sharp tone that reminded me of my father.

Some people shout when they feel threatened, their feelings darkened by anger. Others speak without raising their voice, and their words have greater effect. The Seated Woman was quite capable of doing what she said.

Dark and strong, with an impressive rear end—hence her name—she seemed ageless. A smooth, matt face. Her corpulence was an advantage, not a handicap, in her job. Her strategic position at the baths must have been the envy of the intelligence service. She knew everything, including all the neighborhood families; she got involved in various intrigues, helped arrange marriages, set up meetings. She was the neighborhood's registry and memory, a woman of secrets and trust, fear and tenderness. She kept an eye on everyone who came in, looked after everything, kept the fire going in the oven near the baths. She had big breasts that frightened children, but adolescents dreamed of burying their heads in all that weight. Usually unmarried, often widowed or divorced, a Seated Woman has no real family life of her own. She stands apart, and no one is interested in how—or with what jinni—she spends her nights. People make up an imaginary life for her, making her incestuous or homosexual, a fortuneteller or a caster of spells, a monster or a pervert.

There was a time when the Seated Woman, who now could barely climb a flight of stairs, had youth, a lover, maybe even a husband. She had had a dowry, a house, jewelry. She must have been slim, perhaps even beautiful. I looked at her fat, tired body and tried to discern the picture of the girl she had been before everything had been turned upside down in a matter of seconds. Everybody had perished in the earthquake, and she stood in the ruins with her traumatized little brother, his eyes unseeing forever after.

She told me the story one night when we couldn't sleep. The Consul was snoring and we lay waiting for morning, when we would go for mint for the tea and fritters. She told me nothing about her life before the catastrophe. I liked to imagine her happy, with a house, a home, a man. Perhaps she had not been there in Agadir that night, but somewhere else, with a husband who beat her and slept with other women. Perhaps he left with a niece or a cousin, going far away, leaving the country, never to be heard from again.

I said nothing. I sometimes glimpsed traces of humiliation in her eyes.

"Yes, I was abandoned, thrown into the street, and as the proverb says, 'No cat flees a house where there's a wedding.' If he left, he must have had a reason. 'Do you know how to hold on to a man?' my mother used to say. 'With this and this,' one hand on her belly, and the other on her butt. 'But who wants a body that's been used and abused like yours? No one, or everyone. Who wants a divorcée who's still married, a widow with no corpse or inheritance, a wife without a home? I bear that burden, like a mountain on my chest. What am I supposed to say to my cousins and neighbors? That my daughter didn't give her husband pleasure, so he looked elsewhere for what he couldn't find in his marriage bed? No, it's too much.' "

She must have gone away to escape such reproach, to cease to be the woman abandoned, marked for insult and contempt. Her younger brother must have followed her, clinging to her jellaba, crying and begging. Their wanderings must have been hard. Hunger, cold, and illness. The kid probably went blind from trachoma. She did laundry for rich families, sometimes cooked for weddings or baptisms, raised her brother as if he were her own son. She wanted a better life for him, fought to get him a state scholarship. He became a schoolteacher and gave neighborhood children lessons in the Koran.

She had wanted him to be a minister or ambassador, but he was only a consul in an imaginary city in a ghost country. It was she who named him to this job. He went along with it because he "didn't want to hurt her," as he told me later. She was pleased and he never crossed her. That was the deal. The unspoken conventions of their daily ritual made this brother and sister a strange and dubious couple. Reality was masked by a theatrical game.

At first I thought they were just having fun, or trying to entertain me. They were sometimes tyrannical, sometimes romantically effusive. They spoke in flowery language even when shouting at each other. The most important ritual took place in the morning. The Seated Woman would wake the Consul up by singing softly, murmuring verses as she approached his door:

My gazelle, my heart,
My beauty, my prince,
Light of my eyes,
Open your arms . . .

She took her time, always waking him up gently. She often brought him flowers and he always asked first about their color, not their scent. He would touch one and say, "The red is too bright" or "That yellow feels nice."

She would kiss his hand. If he did not pull it away, that meant that he was in a good mood and she would have his blessing for the day. Then they would shut themselves up in the bathroom together and she would shave him, perfume him, and dress him. Then they would go out, his hand resting on hers. They walked slowly, waving to an imaginary crowd.

At first I had to make an effort not to laugh. Later I learned to play the game, standing in for the huge crowd that rose early to greet the princely couple.

I was sitting on a stool at the low table where breakfast was served when I heard him say in the corridor:

"I feel there is a flower in the house. It needs water. Why didn't you tell me?"

I rose to greet the Consul when they came in. He held out his hand for me to kiss it. I shook it and sat down again.

"A flower, but a rebellious one," he said.

I smiled. The Seated Woman signaled me to get up, as if to say, "We don't eat at the same table as the Consul."

She and I had breakfast in the kitchen, in silence.

"This house is all we have," she told me. "I have to

run it and protect it from indecent, jealous eyes. I look after everything. I have to think of everything, and most of all make sure the Consul lacks for nothing. We make enough to live on. Sometimes I have to stay late at the baths, and I think of the Consul. When he gets bored, he turns on the radio. It means he's annoyed. I can't stand having to be a man at the baths and a woman at home, sometimes even both at once in both places. You're going to have to help me. The Consul needs someone to reassure him when I'm not here. He likes someone to read to him in the evenings. But I can't read, so I make up stories. If he doesn't like them he gets annoyed, thinks I'm treating him like a child. I don't know any more stories. Lately he's been getting impatient, irritable, even nasty. I can't stand it. I need help. The schedule is the same every weekday: the Koranic school in the morning, a siesta in the afternoon. In the evening he's free. You will take care of him in the evening."

THE
CONSUL

I was overcome by a strange drowsiness during the first week. It was as if I was somewhere else. I slept without dreaming. I would get up and wander around the house for hours, alone with those quaint old objects, the threadbare carpets and the father's photograph over the cupboard. I stared at that photograph until my eyes clouded over. I loved the idleness and solitude, and not having to answer to anyone. I was wide awake by the time the Consul came home in the evening. During the day time stretched into a hammock on which I could lie down and daydream. I would stare wide-eyed at the winding shapes drawn by the damp patches on the ceiling. The past swept over me, image by image. I could not resist the reckless arrival of so many memories. They were all the same sepia color. Voices, shouts, and sighs came with them in a procession in which I saw myself as a child, but not as all the others had made me.

There was a room at the back of our big house, a kind of granary where they kept supplies of wheat, oil, and olives for the winter. A windowless room, dark and cold, ruled by mice and fear. My father locked me in there once. I can't remember why. I trembled with cold and fury. Now I could not shake off the memory of that inhospitable room. From the depths of my hammock I called up my father, my mother, my seven sisters, signaling them to come into the room. I locked the door, sprinkled oil around, and set fire to it. I had to start over several times, for the damp and the draught blew out the flames. The fire blazed around my family but did not touch them. They stood together through the ordeal, waiting motionless for the joke to end.

I drove away that image with a wave of my hand and tried to think about something else. But all my visions were sinister.

A narrow, deserted street, with stones growing out of the wall like dried pomegranates. Pieces of words, obscene drawings, and graffiti were written on the whitewashed smooth parts. Parents avoided the place when they had their children with them. It was in that street, no wider than a grave, that I met my father. I stood face to face with him, not looking at the sky, but trying to decipher the words and drawings on the wall. I didn't speak to him. I read out loud what was written on the wall: "Love is a snake slithering between thighs" . . .

"Balls are tender apples" . . . "My cock rises before the sun." My father, with his back to the wall, was standing with his head between two parted thighs. I pushed him aside and saw a graphic drawing of a vagina with teeth. Above it someone had written: "The teeth of pleasure." There was a front view of a body, its sex the only clear feature; on the tip was a skull: the entire body was a penis, walking, smiling, impatient. Around the drawing were innumerable names for the female sex organ: door, blessing, slit, mercy, beggar, lodging, storm, spring, oven, tent, warmth, dome, madness, delight, joy, valley, rebel . . . I called them out one by one, yelling them in my father's ear as he stood pale, his face showing no expression. I shook him as if to wake him up. He was cold and pallid, long dead.

That narrow street, the street of shame, led to the abyss. I was curious. I wanted to follow it to the end. The street had been abandoned by its inhabitants, for rumor had it that it led to hell, that it ended at a courtyard where the heads of the dead were laid out like watermelons. No one ever went down it anymore. A street damned, where dead men from hell took refuge now and then.

I had assumed that my father, despite his prayers and his almsgiving, would spend some time in hell. Now I was sure. He must have been paying for his sins. I will probably join him one day, since I am the main source of his sins. But before that I have to live.

I was deep in these thoughts when I saw the Consul going into the kitchen. I got up. He waved at me to sit back down. I stayed put. He made some mint tea. His hands knew where everything was. They didn't hesitate or feel around, but went straight to each object. When the teapot was ready, he said:

"Could you please boil some water?"

He never touched the stove. When the water boiled, he poured it into the teapot. He turned off the gas and let the tea steep. He sat down and said:

"This tea won't be very good. I apologize. The mint is not fresh. Someone forgot to buy more. You may serve it now."

We drank in silence. The Consul seemed pleased.

"It isn't really teatime," he said, "but I felt like having some anyway. I hope I'm not disturbing you. I could have had it sent in from the café on the corner, but I wanted to make it here."

I didn't know what to say.

"Why are you blushing?" he asked.

I put my hands to my cheeks. They were warm. I was impressed by the elegance and grace of his gestures. I dared not look at him. He seemed to have a sixth sense that allowed him to know everything. I moved back a little and watched him. I'm not really sure whether he was handsome, but he had presence. No, it was something more than that. He was intimidating.

He got up when he finished his tea.

"I have to go," he said. "The kids are terrible. I try to teach them the Koran as I would a beautiful poem, but they keep asking awkward questions, like, 'Is it true that all the Christians will go to hell?' or 'Since Islam is the best religion, why did God wait so long to spread it?' I merely look up at the ceiling and repeat the question:

'Why was Islam so late in coming?' Do you have any idea what the answer is?"

"I've thought about it. But I'm like you, I like the Koran as an exquisite poem, and I detest people who exploit it like parasites and limit freedom of thought. They're hypocrites. In fact, the Koran itself mentions them."

"Yes, I see what you mean."

After a brief silence he quoted verse 2 of the sura "The Hypocrites":

" 'They have made for themselves a veil of their oaths. They have barred men from the ways of salvation. Surely their deeds are marked in the corner of iniquity.' Fanatical believers or hypocrites, what's the difference? To me they're alike. I like to stay away from both."

"I know them well. I've run into them before. They invoke religion to crush and to dominate. For myself, I invoke the right of free thought, the right to believe or not to believe. It's nobody's business but my own. I have negotiated my freedom with the night and its ghosts."

"I like it when you smile."

It was true that the hint of a smile crossed my face when I spoke of the night. He asked me to lend him a clean handkerchief. He took off his dark glasses and wiped them meticulously. On his way out, he stopped in front of the mirror, adjusted his jellaba, and combed his hair.

I straightened up the house and shut myself up in the bathroom. There was no sink or tub, just bowls placed under cold-water taps. I looked at myself in a small mirror. I had lost weight. My breasts were sticking out. I put my hands between my thighs. It still hurt. I was no longer a virgin. The encounter in the wood had been brutal and blind. There was no feeling or judgment in the memory. It was one adventure among so many others I had had. Things would cross my body without leaving wounds. I had decided all that quite calmly. I was teaching myself to forget, to not look back. I had to drive out the horde of memories that pursued me, each more shameful, execrable, and unbearable than the next. I knew that I would be plagued by that bundle of knotted rope for some time to come. The only escape was not to be there when they knocked at the door of my sleep. So I decided to look after the house and the Consul seriously, to become a woman, to be sensitive to everything, and to regain for my body the gentleness that had been taken from it.

The Consul's room was lit by two windows. It was clean, neat, and pleasant, tastefully decorated. There was a mixture of colors in the fabrics, and a Berber carpet brought brightness and warmth. A small bookcase contained books in braille. At the bedside was an alarm clock, a photograph of the Consul and his sister, an ashtray, a pitcher of water, and a glass. At the back of the room was a table with a typewriter, a half-typed page in the machine. I resisted the temptation to read even the first line, but I was curious. I moved away, then tried to make out a few words. From the page layout I decided it must have been a private journal. On the table was a red folder containing a packet of paper. I blushed. I was ashamed and annoyed at myself for having discovered the secret. The Consul was keeping a journal, probably unknown to his sister.

The first incident took place that evening. The Seated Woman arrived carrying provisions for dinner and went straight to the kitchen. On her way in she noticed the teapot, still full of mint, and the two glasses, which I had forgotten to rinse. She put down her basket and asked me whether someone had come to visit during the day. I told her no one had come.

"Who had tea, then?"

"The Consul and I."

"The Consul never drinks tea at home during the day."

"He does. He made it himself this morning. Ask him and he'll tell you."

"No. He's working in his room. He mustn't be disturbed. Was the tea good?"

"Yes, not too sweet, the way I like it."

From his room the Consul commented: "The tea was good, but the time spent with our Guest was even better."

The Seated Woman said nothing. She was in a bad mood. I offered to help her. She said no and asked me to go and wash the Consul's feet.

"It's time. Heat some water and get the towel and perfume ready."

I had never washed a man's feet before. The Consul sat in an armchair and held out his right foot, while the left soaked in the warm water. I didn't do the massage very well. With no irritation, he took my hand.

"Don't rub or squeeze. Massage is somewhere between the two, a caress that goes through the skin and circulates inside."

After the lesson, I got down on my knees again and tried to get the feel of it. His feet were not big. I massaged them slowly. He was obviously pleased. He smiled and muttered "Allah, Allah," an exclamation of pleasure.

Dinner went well. The sister was tired.

"You'll read to him tonight," she said.

"No, not tonight," the Consul said. "I want to continue the discussion I was having with our Guest this morning."

He asked me to follow him out to the terrace.

"The nights are mild and lovely out there, especially now, as summer slowly ends. And I like it when the sky's so starry. In two days the moon will be full. You'll see how beautiful it is."

There was a carpet, and two cushions lay on the ground. The town was still awake. There were people on the terraces, eating dinner or playing cards. I was watching them when he told me to look closely at the third terrace on the right.

"Are they out there?"

"Who?"

"A man and a woman, young, not married. They often meet on the terrace to make love. They kiss, put their arms around each other, and whisper sweet words back and forth. I come here when I'm lonely, and I know they'll keep me company. They can't see me. And I can't see them either. But I can feel them, and I like them. They steal a few hours of happiness, and I'm glad to be a discreet witness to that happiness. Sometimes I live by proxy, you know. That's all right, but I shouldn't let it happen too often. Anyway, I won't bore you with all my little stories. What were we talking about this morning?"

"Islam."

"Islam! Perhaps we are unworthy of the nobility of that religion?"

"Isn't every religion based on guilt? I have renounced the world, withdrawn from it in the mystical sense, rather like al-Hallaj."

76

"I don't quite understand."

"I have broken with the world, or at least with my past. Thrown it all away, deliberately cut myself loose. I am trying to be happy, to live according to my needs, with my own body. I have torn out the roots and the masks. I am a wanderer, held back by no religion. I cross from myth to myth, indifferent."

"That's what you call freedom."

"Yes, to cast off everything, to own nothing so as not to be owned. To be free of all shackles, perhaps even of time itself."

"You remind me of that Zen phrase, 'In the beginning man has nothing.' "

"Man has nothing in the beginning, that's true, and he ought to have nothing at the end either. But he is inculcated with the need to possess: a house, parents, children, stones, deeds, money, gold, people. I am learning to possess nothing."

"That thirst for possession and consumption is the expression of a great lack within us. Something essential is missing. We don't even know what it is. I once knew a great gentleman who lived with his hands in his pockets, no house, no baggage, no ties. He died as he was born, with nothing. He was a poet, and a man of his word."

"To possess, to accumulate, to save up for things— doesn't it amount to risking our dignity a little more each day, testing it?"

As we talked, the Consul methodically chopped some dried marijuana leaves on a board designed for the purpose. I paid no attention at first. His hands moved with patience and skill. He filled a pipe, lit it, inhaled deeply, then tapped out the ash. "Good," he said, as if talking to himself. He filled a second pipe and handed it to me.

"I don't know if you'll like it," he said. "I think it's good quality. I smoke a pipe or two now and then. It helps me to figure things out, to see clearly into myself. No pun intended."

In my previous existence I had sometimes smoked kif. I didn't enjoy it much, but that night everything was good, even the kif. I felt secure. I had only just come out of hell.

The man whose feet I was learning to wash every night was not my master, and I was not his slave. We were already close to each other. I forgot his blindness and talked to him like an old friend. One evening on the terrace he commented on that:

"We get along so well, we probably have a like wound hidden within us. I don't mean the same infirmity—the blind are aggressive and mean to one another—but some broken thing inside that brings us together."

Having decided to bury my past for good, I did not answer. I was already grateful that the Consul had never tried to find out anything about my previous life. How could I tell him that my life was just beginning, that a thick curtain had been drawn over a stage on which people and objects were covered with the dust of oblivion? I was struggling silently, never letting anything show, to escape from that unhealthy labyrinth once and for all. I was fighting against guilt, religion, morality, and all the things that threatened to rise again to compromise me, sully me, betray me, destroy what little I sought to preserve deep within myself.

My encounter with the Consul was a real blessing for me, despite the minor difficulties that cropped up in everyday life. The man had built a world of his own in which he lived at his own pace. He had his habits, a ritual that might seem ridiculous or demented. It was all sustained by his sister, who thereby exercised her own power. I was not sure where I stood. Hired by chance, I did not yet know what my real job would be. The Seated Woman had told me vaguely what had to be done. But he had said nothing. I was not quite at his beck and call, but I was supposed to be available at all times. In general I like to know where I stand. In this case I was in the dark, but I liked it. The three of us seemed lost in a fog.

One evening after dinner, the Consul said to his sister in an authoritative tone:

"Tomorrow you will clean up the baths. I've decided that all three of us will go for a wash."

"But that isn't possible!"

"It will be. The baths will be reserved for the family tomorrow. We will all go, you, our Guest, and I . . ."

"But—"

"There is nothing to fear. I can't very well intrude on your privacy."

I said nothing. I felt that the Seated Woman was relying on me to help her block his plan. In fact, I was intrigued and pleased at the idea of all of us washing together like a family.

"Very well, then," his sister said. "The last customers leave about nine o'clock. Come before ten."

She got up and went to her room. The Consul seemed content, though a little worried.

"I don't like to see my sister angry," he said. "She probably thinks I'm doing this to spite her. I do have strange ideas from time to time. I get that way when I'm nervous. I didn't ask your opinion. Would you mind if—"

"We'll see tomorrow!"

"I say that because you're a woman; in fact, as far as I can tell, you are very feminine. So maybe finding yourself in the steamy dark with a man . . ."

"You're right. I don't want your sister to think it was my idea, that it's a kind of plot against her."

THE
PACT

O nly the main room of the baths had any light at all; the other two were dark, with a kind of half-light in which good vision might barely tell white thread from black. If the ambiguity of the soul had light, it would be that one and none other. The naked bodies were dressed in steam. The dampness ran down the walls in gray droplets, feeding on the room's endless chatter. The baths had been emptied of customers and cleaned, and we had them to ourselves. The Seated Woman, mistress of the place, entered first, holding the Consul by the hand. I followed wordlessly. I remembered my arrival here two months before, when I barely had time to wash, hurried by the Seated Woman and tormented by two witches. I walked around slowly, examining the walls. In the back room I saw a ghost, the body of a girl hanging from the ceiling. The body grew older as I came near, until I was face to face with my toothless mother, tufts of her hair strewn over her face and neck. I recoiled in horror and rejoined the Consul and his sister in the middle room. I was convinced that my memories fed on the blood of the dead, pouring it into mine. The mixture brought on hallucinations in which dry bodies demanded their blood back. I decided not to tell anyone about it. I had been haunted by that mixed-blood story ever since my father's death. My effort to forget was making some progress, for I had managed to bury some people and things. Steambaths generally lend themselves to visions. Jinn come in at night to hold their secret conversations. Early in the morning, when the doors open, there is a smell of death, and the floor is covered with peanut shells. It is well known that ghosts eat while they talk. But what I saw when I came into the middle room was no vision: the sister, a towel around her waist, was sitting astride the Consul, who lay face down. She was giving him a massage, stretching his limbs, her movements accompanied by little cries that sounded like stifled kisses. It was strange to see them in that position and to hear the Consul saying "Allah, Allah," just as he did when I washed his feet. A little smack on the bottom and the Consul changed position. He who was so slim and tall was now entirely enveloped, intertwined in the Seated Woman's fat, heavy body. They were both clearly enjoying it. I left them to their exercises and went back to the cooler entrance room. I had wrapped a fairly large towel around my waist and had begun washing my hair when the Seated Woman, grotesque in her nakedness, appeared before me and ordered me to join them.

"You have nothing to hide. What you have, I have, and my brother can't see. So relax and come with us!"

I thought it was an order from the Consul. I rinsed my hair and joined them. They were sitting in the middle room, legs apart, eating hard-boiled eggs and red olives. Which was traditional. She offered me an egg. It wasn't hard-boiled, and the yoke trickled between my fingers. I began to feel sick. For a moment I felt as if I had become the plaything of a diabolical couple, a feeling that was intensified when the Seated Woman asked me to soap her back and buttocks. The Consul giggled. She looked ridiculous with her butt in the air. I felt like I was washing a dead mountain. She fell asleep and started snoring. The Consul put his hand on my left breast, then apologized. He had meant to touch my shoulder. He asked me to let him sleep. His body was slim. His sex was erect under the towel. I kept my distance, as he could tell from the sound of my voice. He was very good at measuring distances by people's voices. He said he was happy to be in the baths with me. I told him the egg had made me sick. I got up, rushed to a corner, and threw up. The Consul was obviously sexually aroused by the atmosphere of half-darkness, steam, and dampness, coupled with the presence of two women. It was then that I realized that the fantasies of the blind were based not on images, but on smells, on particular, staged-managed situations. The Consul had withdrawn to a dark corner, his face against the wall. I knew that if I let him touch me he would lose control. He asked me quietly to soap his back. I refused.

He didn't insist. I felt no desire. Simply looking at the Seated Woman lying in the middle of the baths made me feel sick again. I washed quickly and went out to the room to rest. I fell asleep.

Was I dreaming or was I still in the baths? I heard languorous cries, followed by groans. Then I saw—at least I think I saw—the Consul curled up in his sister's arms. He was sucking her breast like a baby. I couldn't tell which of them was moaning with pleasure. It lasted for quite a while. I watched them, but they couldn't see me. Was this possible? A man so sensitive, so intelligent, reduced to infancy in that woman's arms! She massaged his feet and legs as he sucked.

When I saw them coming out, each wrapped in a large towel, I realized that they were bound by a secret, lifelong pact. They were happy and rested. Perhaps the Consul wanted to initiate me into their secret, to have me share the complicity that bound them. He seemed vexed when his sister told him that I had left the room. I thought he would have sensed it, but all his senses were occupied in his body's diversion. I knew that the blind were very touchy. The Consul was trying to control his anger. And far from losing interest in his moods, I too was affected by what had just happened. The Consul did not sleep that night. I heard him typing. The Seated Woman snored placidly, and I waited for morning. More than once I desperately wanted to go into his room, sit in a corner, and watch him write. But I was afraid of how he would react. He was annoyed, probably because of my behavior. I was troubled. My emotions were contradictory: panic mingled with a strange joy. Something had snapped in the underlying balance of our relations, which had, of

course, been ambiguous but frank, marked by the promises of time and the courtesy of feelings yet undefined.
But flashes of sudden, unchained passion were something
else again. There may have been passion between us, but
it had been halting, still in its infancy.

The only passion I had ever known was what I felt for
my father, and I had carried that to its outermost limits,
to hatred, death, and even hatred after death. It had
destroyed everything. Unhappiness is the very essence
of any passion, its kernel, motor force, and reason. You
never realize this at first. It is only later, when the squall
has passed, that you find out that unhappiness has been
burrowing away too. That was why I was moving cau-
tiously and fearfully. I had decided to remain a passive
observer. I had to sweep out my consciousness, take the
time to slough off skin and to extinguish memories forever. I pretended to have a sore throat and stayed in my
room to sleep. I wanted to wait a few days before talking
to the Consul again. I felt that it would be difficult to face
him. He noticed everything. He was aware of the slightest
shifts in the soul of anyone he was interested in.

One day when I was still in bed, he knocked at my
door and proposed that we meet on the terrace at dusk.
He said it was a beautiful day, with a very soft light. Ideal
weather for talking. "I would love to," I said, without
opening the door.

I was telling the truth. Joy filled my heart. We hadn't
spoken for about ten days. Things were slowly getting
back to normal. The Seated Woman was sulking. She left
all the housework for me. This was her way of reminding
me that I was just a servant, a housekeeper. But the
Consul had treated me differently from the very begin-

ning. I was neither a maid nor a nurse. The Seated Woman was trying to come between the Consul and me with her wretched tricks. She put a mattress in a corner of the kitchen and told me that I should sleep there from now on. I didn't protest. It was her house. I didn't care whether I slept among cooking pots, in the open air, or in a comfortable bedroom. I had no baggage to move. I slept in the kitchen and had a wonderful dream. There was a journey in it, and a boat, and I swam in pure water.

Next morning I heard an argument between the Seated Woman and her brother. It was short, but sharp. Was it a scene in the script, or just one of the blind man's fits of anger when one of his idiosyncrasies was violated? Maybe he was chiding his sister for having exiled me to the kitchen. I did not want to know. I had no business interfering in their little scenes. I said nothing, believing as I did that the attention the Consul showed me was quite enough. I was, after all, only a stranger, a vagabond with no papers, no identity, and no baggage, coming from nothingness and heading for the unknown. I was glad that they had taken me in during those first days of my wanderings. My meeting with that complex, cultured, and intimidating man was increasingly becoming a major event in my life.

I would wash the dishes and clean up the kitchen before going to bed. Cockroaches and ants kept me company. Maids usually sleep in the kitchen, even in rich families.

But this did not last long. One evening the Consul asked me to go back to my room. I refused. He insisted.

"It's an order," he said.

"Your sister . . ."

"Yes, I know. I've spoken to her about it. She's sorry.

Her rheumatism is acting up and she's in a bad mood."

"I take my orders from her. She's the one who brought me here, and she's the one who'll have to tell me what my new position in this house is."

"You're right. But sometimes right has to be ignored. I'm asking you."

Then, after a silence during which I felt that he was searching for the words to convey something serious, he added:

"I don't like it when you're far away, in this room that smells of grease."

At that moment the Seated Woman came in, looking tired, her hair undone.

"He's right," she said. "Don't stay in this room."

Then she left.

On the terrace was a small table, a marijuana pipe, a teapot, and two glasses. He asked me to keep him company, and he talked for most of the night.

"I have seen fabulous countries where the trees leaned over give me shade, where it rained crystals, where birds of all colors flew ahead of me to show me the way, where the wind brought me perfume. Countries with transparent ground, where I spent hours and days alone. There I met lighthearted prophets, childhood friends I had lost track of, girls I was in love with when I was small. I wandered in an exotic garden with no wall or guard. I walked on waterlilies as big as carpets. I slept undisturbed on a bench. It was a good sleep, heavy, deep, and restful. I wasn't worried in the least. I was at peace with myself and with others. But the others had been expelled from those countries. That's why I found them fabulous. People passed by in a hurry, without stopping. I walked slowly, astonished at the magnificent colors of the sky at dusk. I noticed that everybody was going in the same direction. I followed them, partly out of curiosity, but also because I had nothing special to do. They all stopped at an enormous warehouse on the edge of town. There were no houses, trees, or meadows anywhere around. The warehouse, painted blue, rose in the middle of a huge, dry field. You went in one door and came out another, your arms filled with small parcels. It was strange. I joined the line with everyone else, not really knowing why. It was remarkable how well behaved people were. As you know, civic spirit is rare among us. When I got to the entrance, I saw huge signs over large shelves. Each sign bore a letter of the alphabet. The warehouse was a word depository. The town dictionary. People came to pick up words and even sentences they might need during the week. Not just mutes and stutterers; there were also others known for having nothing to say, who repeated themselves without realizing it. And there were chatterboxes fresh out of words; and others who had a word on the tip of their tongue and looked in mirrors to find that word. Some had their meanings wrong and went to the wrong shelf. Guides took them in hand. Others liked to mix up syllables, claiming to be inventing a new language. The warehouse was like a simmering pot. I wandered through the corridors. Words were piled up, covered with a layer of dust. Nobody used them. They were piled to the ceiling. I told myself that they were either words people did not need anymore or ones they had adequate supplies of at home. I left through a service exit hidden in the wall among shelves containing broken, ruined words and very old ones that nobody used anymore. I'll let you guess what those words were, just as I'll say nothing about the vulgar words stacked in a dark corner and covered with a bright red veil.

"When I opened the door, I found myself in a huge, well-lit cellar where brunettes, blondes, and redheads walked around, all young women, each representing a particular type of beauty, a particular country, a race, or sensibility. They walked back and forth but did not speak. Some sat and dozed. Others were all excited, boasting about the product they bore within them. That huge underground expanse was the town library. A superb creature came over to me and began to speak: 'At twenty-two, I have just finished my studies at Göttingen University. My father's intention was that I travel in Europe's most remarkable countries.' And after another pause: 'I am *Adolphe*. Take me, I'm a love story. Without a happy ending, but that's life.' Naturally I thought of that story about the country where all the books had been burned and rebel citizens would each learn a book by heart to preserve literature and poetry. But this was different. Here books were not forbidden or burned, but some firm had hired pretty women to learn a novel, short story, or play by heart. For a fee, they would come to your home to be read, or more precisely, to recite the book they had learned. It must have been a black market. I had to buy a ticket to get in. A woman of some years sat on a sofa. She was not beautiful, but there was something strangely attractive about her. I went over to her, and she said, 'I am *Risalat al-Ghufran*, the Epistle of Forgiveness, a most important book, which few have actually read. I was written in 1033; my creator was born in Ma'rat al-Nu'man, near Aleppo, in northern Syria. I am a difficult book, in which the dead converse, arguments are settled through poetic diatribes, and the sojourn in paradise is longer than the sojourn in hell.' It was a very lively human library. There was even a very young girl swinging on a trapeze and reciting *Ulysses*: 'Better not stick here all night like a limpet. This weather makes you dull. Must be getting on for nine by the light.' In a room decorated in the oriental style, a dozen beautiful women, all dressed as Scheherazade, each offered to tell part of the *Thousand and One Nights*. It was just like a fairy tale. It was a wonderful country, and that library was a marvel. An old man dressed in white whispered to me as he left: 'It's a sacrilege to call yourself a work of literature, to pretend to be Taha Hussein's *Days*, or Balzac's *La comédie humaine*. What nerve! Myself, I'm just a poor reader of the Koran. Can you imagine the heresy if I claimed to be the Holy Book? As well give up the keys to the world and sink into complete madness. That said, if you need someone to read a few verses over your relatives' graves, I'm your man.' A fabulous country, a country lit by the light of my sleepless nights. I get sad when I leave it. I miss it whenever I open my eyes to eternal darkness. But will and desire alone are not enough to open the gates to that country for me. I have to be in a state of grace, a particular mood. Actually, it's the country that comes to me, that visits me, with its gardens, palaces, and underground corridors teeming with life fantastic. It is my secret, my happiness. But I confess that all those mirages sometimes tire me. Their unreal beauty plagues me. But that's life. Since you've been here in the house, I feel less need to lose myself in the labyrinths of that shifting land. Are you perhaps a native of that country? I have wondered about that, because of the scent of your presence. Not the kind of scent that comes out of a bottle, but the kind that emanates from your skin, the unmistakable scent of a human being. I have a special gift for detecting that. Excuse me. I have talked too long. I must have tried your patience. Maybe you're sleepy. We didn't even drink the tea, but it is cold now. Good night!"

I fell asleep easily and dreamed of the magic country. Everything was dazzlingly bright, but I couldn't find my way to the library.

A
SOUL
DEFEATED

A t first I didn't notice—or rather did not want to see—that the Seated Woman's face was ravaged by hate. Self-hatred more than hatred of others. But it was hard to see it. Traces of more than one defeat were evident on that face, especially when she slept. The devastation was not a mask, but daily pain. Hatred alone protected that woman from physical degeneration and kept death at bay; death that would have come from immense despair.

One evening after dinner, as the Consul sat typing, the Seated Woman asked me to join her on the terrace for tea.

"Tea keeps me from sleeping," I told her.

93

"Then I'll make you a vervain, but it's what I have to tell you will keep you awake."

"What do you have to tell me?"

"Don't be afraid! I'm going to tell you who I am. That's all. And when you find out who lives behind this face you may not be able to sleep."

Then she did just what the Consul had done: prepared the kif, smoked two or three pipes, and began to talk. I drank my vervain and listened, at first by constraint, but then because it was so terrible. She spoke faster than usual, and sometimes paused for long silences.

"I was probably born by accident," she said. "I was ugly from the start and I stayed ugly. I used to hear people say, 'This kid has no business being here.' 'This kid is a child of drought.' I was always in the way, never at ease. No one wanted my misshapen body around. Wherever I went I saw desolation and disappointment on people's faces, especially the grown-ups.

"From the very beginning the other children kept me out of their games. Nobody wanted anything to do with this graceless face. I understood the people who were disturbed by my presence. My parents were unhappy. They wore defeat on their faces; and I was their own defeat. To banish the curse, they had a second child. When my brother was born, they had a big party. For them it was the end of the drought. But my poor brother got measles and went blind. Misfortune dogged the family. I felt responsible. That child had brought light and grace to a house without laughter, but in just a few days he was deprived of light forever. For the first time I let tears flow down my cheeks. My heart was broken, but not my face, which was expressionless, as always. With

94

that misfortune, which I considered greater than my own, I came to realize that I was born of loss. I had fallen like an evil, unexpected rain, the kind that arouses fear because it rots the seed.

"My face is like a watercolor smeared by a rag, all out of shape. Everything is askew, both the body and what's inside it. I am so filled with hate that it would take at least two lifetimes to spill it all out. But hatred does not really suit me, for if you want to hate, you also have to love, even if only a little. And I don't love anyone, not even myself. What I feel for the Consul is beyond love. It's the air I breathe, the beating of my heart. But that's unlivable. You show up in the house, and that's all it takes to make him smile again. Before you came, we couldn't even breathe here. He had even become aggressive, violent and unfair. That's why I asked you to come and live with us the moment I saw you, lost and unattached. I don't have to tell you that; you know it very well. Your presence has brought a little light into this house. You are innocent, but I am not.

"I let my parents die. I don't think anyone even went to their funerals. I left with my brother, took a few valuables, and left my parents with a mad old woman. I left without looking back, without a single tear. I emptied my life of everything that might resemble hope. And since then I've turned in a circle, sitting all the while. My brother grew up in my arms. I became his eyes. I worked hard so that he would lack for nothing. I'm afraid of losing him. I want you to help me not to lose him. I can feel misfortune coming, and I have no way to fight it. But I can see it in the distance. And I can see a silhouette, perhaps a man, but more like a woman disguised as a man, walking down the road alone in a garish twilight. And I sense that that shadow can keep the misfortune away. I'm not a seer, but sometimes I have premonitions so powerful that everything becomes clear. The silhouette looks like you. Fate sent you to us, though we do not know who you are, where you come from, or what's in your mind. The Consul seems happy with you, and your presence has clearly been good for him. I have to keep you here, because you have restored my brother's desire to smile and to write. It's been months since he worked at his typewriter. I don't know what he's writing, but it must be important. If he asks you to go with him to what he calls 'the perfumed meadow,' don't be shocked, and most of all don't refuse. He goes there about once a month. I used to go with him, but now he doesn't want to be seen with me. He's ashamed of his sister who spends her life sitting at the entrance to the baths. I am not the keeper of secrets anymore. I keep old clothes, that's all. Nothing to be proud of. The job I do is ill-regarded. What did you do before you came here?"

She stopped for a moment, stuffed a pipe with kif, held it out to me, and said:

"Take some and you'll speak. It helps. Frees your mind."

I smoked some. I felt sick and coughed when I inhaled. Her eyes were anxious and impatient.

"I want to know," she said. "Tell me! Who are you? What miraculous thing do you carry inside you? How have you managed to bring a dying man back to life?"

She began to sob and weep. It was a grotesque situation, and I decided to say a few words to end it.

"Before I came to this town, it was my privilege and

96

good fortune to bathe in a spring of exceptional qualities. One of them—the ability to wipe out memories—is vital to me. The waters of that spring cleansed me, body and soul, wiping my memories clean and reordering what little remains of my past, three or four memories. Everything else is gone, and in their place I see only ruins and fog. My past is wrapped in a worn woolen blanket. To gain access to that spring you have to cast off everything and renounce nostalgia forever. I destroyed my identity papers and followed the star that traced the route of my destiny. That star follows me everywhere. I can show it to you if you want. The day it flickers out will be the day of my death. I have forgotten everything: childhood, parents, my family name. When I see myself in a mirror, I realize that I am happy, because even that face is new to me: I was supposed to have another one. But there is one thing that worries me: I am threatened by indifference, by what you might call a desert of the emotions. If I don't feel anything anymore, I will wither and die. None of us are ordinary people, not the Consul, not you or me. So we might as well laugh. And just get by. Let's not let time get bored while we're here. Let's make sure we give it some satisfaction, a little fantasy, for example, a little color. The Consul adores the subtleties of colors. Hardly surprising for a blind man."

My words seemed to soothe the Seated Woman. Her eyes were wet with tears as I spoke. She had lost her usual hard look. Her face showed no sign of the hatred on which she claimed to feed. I had managed to soften her, to move her. Yet I had not said anything particularly stirring. After a brief silence, she seized my hands and covered them with kisses. I was embarrassed. I tried to pull them away, but she held on tight. Her kisses were full of tears.

"I'm sorry," she said. "Forgive me for speaking to you so harshly. You are an angel, sent by the prophets. We are your slaves."

"That's enough!" I cried, to end that painful scene. "I am not an angel, and nobody sent me. Get up!"

We could hear the droning sound of the typewriter. It was as if the Consul was stubbornly tapping out the same word over and over.

A
CONFUSION
OF FEELINGS

I had trouble getting to sleep. I could hear the Seated Woman crying in a corner as the Consul paced up and down in his room. For a moment I thought to leave that house and try my luck elsewhere. But something held me back. Partly, of course, it was my interest in the Consul, and the turmoil my presence there was arousing in me. I also had a clear premonition that I would meet only strange people and have only unsettling relations wherever I went. I was firmly convinced that this family—this couple—was my destiny. They lay on my path. I had to enter that house, where my character would inevitably arouse turmoil. For the moment, there was a confusion of feelings. Nothing was clear. Who loved whom? Who sought to perpetuate this situation? How could I leave that house without melodrama?

I found out that the Seated Woman had not allowed women in the house for a long time. She kept her brother jealously under her thumb. He would rebel, but he needed her. I think I arrived at that house when the tension was about to explode irreparably.

I who was emerging from a long absence, an illness, was becoming useful. Granted, the Seated Woman was unbalanced. She bore a hatred of humanity and reserved all the love in the world for her brother. Now and then she mentioned a truckdriver who used to meet her in strange places: the bakery next to the baths, or the potter's workshop on the edge of town. Once they met just before midnight in a mosque. Wrapped in gray jellabas, they passed unnoticed. They fell asleep in each other's arms and were awakened by the dawn prayers. They fled like thieves. The truckdriver never came back, and the Seated Woman had finally given up waiting for him. When she was delirious, she would tell this story over and over and claim that the Consul was the child of that idyll, that she told everyone that he was her brother because she could not admit that he was her illegitimate son. None of it was true. She was just raving.

The next day a new incident peaked the tension that kept us alive. The Consul came home late. He was tired; something had irritated him. The Seated Woman rushed to help him out of his jellaba. He reached out to push her away, but she ducked his hand and seconds later was holding the jellaba. She went to the kitchen to heat water to massage his feet. I stood motionless, watching the scene. He was furious.

"They're laughing at me! It's absolutely intolerable!"

He took off his dark glasses and wiped them nervously.

"The bitches! They stuck me with the one-eyed woman. The one nobody wants."

"That'll teach you to go without me," the Seated Woman called from the kitchen. "They never would have done that if I was there. Sit down, the water's hot."

The Consul sat in his armchair. She came in with the hot water, a towel over her shoulder. She knelt and took her brother's right foot. When his foot touched the water, the Consul cried out and knocked his sister over with a sudden movement. As she tumbled, her head nearly hit the corner of the table.

"The water's boiling hot," he said. "You did it on purpose, to punish me for going there. Go away! I don't want you here. The Guest will massage my feet from now on."

His tone changed as he asked if I would please do him that favor.

The Seated Woman glared at me. I felt sorry for her. She was unhappy—hurt and humiliated.

"Go ahead, you may as well," she said.

In fact I had no desire to massage that petty dictator's feet. But I couldn't refuse without triggering another outburst. I went over to him and said without raising my voice:

"Do it yourself for a change."

I left him there, his feet in the basin, and joined the Seated Woman in the kitchen. I understood why she was angry, but I wanted to know more.

"You want to know everything!"

"That's right," I said.

"It's all my fault. I have never refused him anything. I

satisfied his every whim. Since you've been here, he has wanted to do without me, wanted you to take my place. I'm not blaming you. But you should be aware that he's completely unpredictable. It's better not to love him, to keep a protective veil between him and everyone else."

She took a chair and began to talk, her voice hushed.

"At first it was once a month, then twice, then three times. He made me go with him. I would describe the women to him. It was embarrassing, of course. We would go in through a secret door. No one was supposed to see us. The madam was very understanding. She would sit us down in a room and have the girls file by. My job was to answer specific questions about each girl's skin color, eye color, chest and waist measurements, whether she had gold teeth—he hates gold teeth. I would do what he asked, then wait outside in the street. That was the worst part: waiting while the Consul did his business. It sometimes took quite a while. I would think about him, think about my life, a bitter taste in my mouth, as if my saliva held all the world's bitterness. 'As long as he is satisfied,' I would tell myself. Then remarkable peace and calm would settle over the house. He became placid, attentive, even affectionate. I would bless the woman who had soothed him. One day I thought of finding him a wife. He refused. I then realized that his pleasure was to go with me to that forbidden place. I realized that the blind need specific situations to fuel their imagination, because images do not exist for them, at least not the way as they do for us. In the end I took pleasure in going with him and helping him choose the woman. But since you've been here, he goes to the girls without telling me. I understand: he wants to be free himself, he doesn't want me to be the eye of his desire anymore. It couldn't last. In reality I was the eye of sin. And that kind of thing shouldn't exist between brother and sister. But there are so many things between us that shouldn't exist.

"When he was small, I used to wash him. I would soap him, rub him, rinse him, dry him. As if he was my doll. He obviously loved it, until the day that this pleasure—how shall I put it?—was preceded by desire. He put his head on my breast and clung to me. His face was flushed, his eyes wide open like those of a man lost and wandering in the desert. 'I want you to wash me,' he said. He was no longer a child. He stayed alone in the washroom for a long time. Then I went to clean the floor. I don't know whether he had urinated or done something else, but there was filth everywhere, a little like at the baths in late morning after the men have gone. He said nothing. I said nothing. I'd have done anything to make him happy. Even now I'd stoop to anything to keep him. Then you came along. You're our savior, an angel who knows everything. You will damn us or save us. The exterminating angel will clean up this spiderweb. Or perhaps become our accomplice.

"Now you know a lot. It will not be easy for you to extract yourself from this hell. Hell or paradise—that's for you to decide. We are people of the night: the Consul carries it in his eyes forever, while I seek it obsessively. And you, you must have been born on a night of uncertain moon, a night when the stars were within reach of all hopes, perhaps on that terrible night when fates are sealed, when every Muslim feels the shudder of death. When I saw you come into the baths, gripped by cold and panic, I could see in your eyes that you had been sent by the last Night of Destiny. I knew at once that you were alone in the world: without parents, family, or friends. You must be one of those exceptional creatures born of absolute solitude. I was waiting for you. On the twenty-seventh night of Ramadan I had a clear vision that stopped my heart. I too, though I am not a good Muslim, felt the slight shudder of death run through my body. I saw a silhouette lean over the Consul's bed and kiss him on the forehead. I thought it was death. I rushed into his room and found him crying like a child. He wept, but he did not know why. He spoke of our mother for the first time. He was convinced that she was alive and was going to visit us. I held him in my arms and rocked him like a baby; I gave him my breast. He fell back asleep with his lips still on my breast."

THE
CONSUL'S
ROOM

S o my destiny was sealed. I had become essential to that unusual couple.

The night before some holiday—I forget which one—the Consul brought two live chickens home. Taking advantage of his sister's absence, he decided to kill them himself. Anything that might call attention to the Consul's infirmity was scrupulously avoided, but when I saw him standing on the terrace with a chicken in one hand and a straight razor in the other, I was afraid. The blade gleamed in the sunlight. The Consul was excited at the thought of cutting the chickens' heads off. I offered to help. He said no. He crouched on the ground, stepping on the wings to hold the chicken down, grabbed the bird with his left hand, and slit its throat with his right. The chicken flapped around, spattering walls and clothes with blood. It lay twitching in a corner as the Consul, pleased with himself, began the same operation with the other chicken. He was sweating, almost jubilant. But this time he was careless and cut his left index finger. There was blood everywhere. The Consul wrapped his finger in a handkerchief. It must have hurt, but he didn't show it. He didn't laugh as much. It had been a half success. As I cleaned up the blood on the terrace, I smelled paradise incense, small pieces of black wood burned on holidays. The smell brought with it memories of a holiday with a lot of music. I must have been three or four. I was in my father's arms as he handed me, legs slightly apart, to a barber who did circumcisions. I saw the blood again, my father's sudden but deft gesture, his hand splattered with blood. There was blood on my thighs too, and on my white saroual.

It was a scented memory tinged with blood. I laughed to myself, then thought of the madness of my pigheaded father, trapped in the vortex of misfortune. I put my hand on my belly unconsciously, as if to reassure myself, then went back to washing the terrace.

The Consul bandaged his finger. He was proud of himself despite everything. I laughed at the ridiculous situation my father had put himself in. The Consul suffered in silence, believing that he had risen to the challenge of his blindness.

An atmosphere now of suspicion, now of complicity had settled over the house. I was drawn deeper and deeper into a drama that had long been underway. I was the missing character who arrived just as the conflicts had been winding down, the drama hovering on the brink of a burlesque tragedy mingling blood and laughter. I was even beginning to wonder whether the Seated Woman and the Consul—supposedly brother and sister, ghosts come out of some age-old night blackened by the vomiting of a ruined soul—were even related. Maybe it was all just a game in which life itself was a mere accoutrement, a piece of folklore. Perhaps the Seated Woman was a professional stage director, the Consul a pervert pretending to be blind, and I the prey in some imagined hunt along a clifftop. I told myself that I had lived too long in lies and pretense not to realize that this was a strange, even sordid affair. I decided to redouble my vigilance, to be ready for an honorable exit or a sudden flight.

I began to examine things as I tidied up the Consul's room, discreetly looking through the things in the cupboard, which I had never opened before. Clothes were carefully folded on one side; on the other were drawers filled with all kinds of things. In the top drawer were several bunches of keys, most of them rusty; old keys, broken keys, locks blackened by layers of dust, nails of every shape and size.

I gently shut that drawer and opened another at random. There I found something like twenty watches, all of them working but each showing a different time. Some were of gold, others of silver.

Another drawer held all kinds of glasses and monocles: sunglasses, prescription glasses, glasses with a lens missing or with both missing. In the back was a packet of papers tied with string. They were ophthalmologists' prescriptions, opticians' bills, advertising brochures for vision products. The dates were all very old.

I continued my search, trying to establish some link

between the contents of the various drawers. I opened another. It was lined with embroidered cloth. Several barbers' razors were laid out carefully, open, their blades gleaming. A sheep's eye in a bottle swam in a yellowish liquid. It looked at me. You would have thought it was alive and was watching over the razors. I felt sick and shut the drawer.

What I found next sent a shiver down my spine. The bottom drawer seemed to be empty, but as I was about to close it, I noticed that it was not as deep as the others. I pulled it all the way open, pushed a partition, and saw a well-polished revolver, in perfect working order. It was unloaded. Three magazines of bullets were piled beside it.

Why did he keep this weapon? I was intrigued, but not disturbed, by his collections. Yet that revolver—brand new—frightened me. Was it for murder or suicide? I sat on the edge of the bed and tried to puzzle out the meaning of all those accumulated objects. Across from me I saw the typewriter, a packet of white paper, a folder of typed pages. I got up and carefully opened the file. I leafed through it, reading at random. It was a journal, but also a story, with pasted bits of paper and chaotic drawings.

On one page this reflection was underlined in red: "How can one go beyond death? There are those who have erected statues for the purpose. Some are very beautiful. Others are awful. I know them better than those who look at them. I touch them. Caress them. Measure their thickness and immobility. That is not the answer. I shall leave behind neither a statue nor a street name, but a gesture, one that some will consider absurd, others sublime; good Muslims will think it heretical, while those who know death and who set cemeteries ablaze will find it heroic. This gesture will take death by surprise, will anticipate it, make it bend, and lay it in a pile of straw that will be set on fire by innocent hands, by the hands of children stilled by the unbearable light this gesture will leave."

I heard footsteps in the alleyway. It was the Consul coming home. I quickly put things in order and went back to the cleaning. The Consul arrived with a big bouquet of flowers and handed them to me.

"These are for you," he said. "I picked them out myself, one by one. We rarely give people flowers. But your patience and presence deserve them."

He sat in the armchair. As I was about to heat the water for his feet, he said:

"Where are you going? I don't want you to take care of me like a maid anymore. No more washbasins, no more foot massages. That's over with. You deserve much better. On the other hand, I am eager for you to be a partner in my thoughts. I like having you near me when I read or write. I have to confess that I started writing again when you came into this house. You know that I am not a simple man. I try to make blindness an advantage and refuse to consider it an infirmity. That sometimes makes me unfair. I do things that involve taking risks. You must have wondered what it is I'm writing. One of these days I'll have you read certain pages. My world is largely inside me. I furnish it with my own creations: I am forced to resort to what inhabits my dark room. You would be astonished, even embarrassed, if I told you all it contains. It is my secret. No one has access to it, not even my sister.

"I am surrounded by objects. There are some I can

master, but others are indomitable. Try to master a razor, for instance, or a pair of scissors that cut everything in their path. So I'm suspicious. I must admit I'm terrified of anything with a cutting edge. Maybe that's why I insisted on slaughtering the chickens myself the other day. I cut myself, but it isn't serious. Imagine if the razor had slipped from my hand: surely it would have cut off my nose or all five fingers. I'm not trying to scare you. I envy you. I wish I was in your place. You are an observer, a witness, sometimes an actor. You are lucky to have been invited to share in the life of a house without having to know or accept the past that has shaped us. That is why I have made no attempt to pry into your past either. I rely only on my intuition and my emotions. Now put those flowers in a vase."

I thanked him and left him rubbing his forehead, trying to banish a headache. He became fragile and disoriented when his head hurt. It made him aware of his infirmity. He cried for help as I was looking around for somewhere to put the vase. I rushed in and found him waving his arms, in a panic because he could not find his painkillers, which were right behind him, well within reach.

"I can't breathe with this pain," he said. "It's like a hammer smashing a block of marble. Every blow is a jolt."

I gave him the pills with a glass of water and put my cold hand on his forehead. At first, he could not bear my touch, but he felt better when I massaged him.

"Go on," he said, "this is good for me. Your hands are full of kindness. I was born with migraine, and it has pursued me all my life. That is my main infirmity."

I made him coffee and helped him to bed, not to sleep but to rest from the effects of the attack. He took my hand

and would not let me leave. I found it quite natural to rest my hand in his. I felt his warm body. We spent much of the afternoon like that. When I heard the key in the lock, I got up and went to open the door. I had closed the safety catch. The Seated Woman looked surprised. She asked me why I had locked myself in. "It was an accident," I said. She let it drop. I told her about her brother's migraine. She was upset. I stopped her from going to wake him up. Later in the evening, she asked me:

"Do you remember that time the Consul came home furious? It must have been at least a month ago."

"Maybe more. But what does that have to do with today's attack?"

"Yes, of course, you have no way of knowing. But I see a connection between abstinence and headaches. When a man keeps that cloudy water inside him too long, it rises to the head and causes pain, because it's not the head that needs it. Do you understand?"

"Vaguely. Do you mean that a man who doesn't let his semen out regularly gets headaches? What about women?"

"They get irritable. They shout about nothing. But I'm used to it. I don't even shout anymore."

I laughed softly to myself. The Seated Woman gave a little smile, then burst out in loud laughter. She put a hand over her mouth and tried to stop.

A
LAKE
OF
HEAVY
WATER

I spent the night fighting currents of heavy, sticky water in a deep lake peopled by all kinds of plants and animals. A stifling smell, thick and undefinable, rose from those waters, dead but roiled from within by the scurryings of rats playing with an injured cat.

I could see everything in the stagnant yet somehow moving water. I was in a glass cage, and a hand pushed me to the bottom and brought me up again at will. I felt smothered, but my shouts could not escape the cage. I recognized the body of Fatima, my poor epileptic cousin to whom I had been married to keep up appearances and whom I loved because she was a gaping wound deprived of all affection. Her face was serene, her body intact. She lay at the bottom of the lake like some old object nobody wanted. Oddly, the rats left her alone. When I saw her I shouted so loudly that I woke up terrified, dripping with sweat.

It was not the first time I had had that kind of nightmare. In each one I saw a face from my past. To forget completely was impossible. What could I do to stop feeling guilty, to stop being hounded by rats and spiders?

I thought of the theory of cloudy water rising to the head and began to laugh. I would have to pay tribute one way or another, here or elsewhere. That much was clear. If it would speed the process of forgetting, I would not quarrel with destiny's rules and regulations.

So it was that I emerged from a heavy nightmare as the Consul cast off the pain racking his head. We were both emerging from the same ordeal, which reminded us that we were both cursed. That freed us. We felt freer just because we knew that the ghosts of our past would catch up to us in the end.

That morning, my body still weary, I decided to take another step closer to the Consul. As he was leaving the house for school, I asked him not to be late coming home. He looked surprised.

"You sound like my sister. I'll be home early, just to make you happy. I won't go to the cafe, and I won't stop to see my friend the barber."

I wanted to go with him to the women. The Seated Woman would never find out. He would show me the way. I liked this preposterous idea, whose audacity appealed to me. I was curious. My body felt lighter, forever relieved of the weight of the night's dead water. The feeling of cheer gave me gooseflesh. I leaped about like a madwoman as I did the housework. I spent a long time in the bathroom, washing and scenting myself as if I were going to a wedding.

The Consul came home about five. He brought a sheaf of mint and some pastries. I told him that both would have to wait and that the Seated Woman had told me to take him to the women. He stood stock-still in surprise, then swallowed. He drank a glass of water, then he asked me if his sister had really assigned me such a mission. He was incredulous.

"This is very embarrassing. It's between my sister and me. It's not possible."

As he spoke, I saw that his face lit up at the idea of going to the women.

"Would you really take me there? You wouldn't be embarrassed?"

"Not at all. I'm curious. It would be a chance to go someplace I'd never see. With you I have an excuse."

"Well, if that's how you see it, what can I do but follow?"

After a short pause, he added:

"Or rather, you will follow me."

"I'll take your arm, and you tell me where to turn."

It was the first time I had walked in the street holding a man's arm. We looked like a normal couple. Nothing at all unusual about us. If some ill-intentioned eye had followed us and found out where we were going, perhaps it would have put an evil spell on us and cursed us to the end of time. That eye was there, behind a door left ajar.

A woman watched unseen. As I passed close by her, I felt struck by an arrow and shuddered. A wave of misfortune had been set in motion. My body sensed it like a sign, an apprehension. I preferred to make light of it and continued on my way. We passed the celebrated building, easily recognizable. The Consul told me not to stop. I followed him. He led me into a dark alleyway and we went in through a low door in an unlit corridor. For once we were even, surrounded by the same darkness.

"Don't be afraid. There's a step."

I held his arm so tight it hurt him. We went up the stairs and came to a closed door. The Consul knocked twice, then a third time. A woman, the madam, let us in and greeted the Consul:

"Long time no see. You have a new companion?"

"Make us some tea, please, not too sweet."

She took us into a sordid room with a none-too-clean sink. The faucet dripped. In the back was an old cupboard smelling of mothballs. I sat in a chair. The Consul stretched out comfortably on the bed. He took out a pipe already filled with kif and lit it. He smoked alone. We waited in silence for the tea. I looked around, my eyes wide, taking in everything. I was impatient. A little girl, barely ten years old, brought us a tray with a teapot and glasses, then disappeared without a word. We were drinking the tea—too sweet—when the madam came in, followed by two women in their early twenties. They were neither ugly nor beautiful, but clearly had no desire to stay with the Consul. The Consul asked me to describe them.

"One is dark, and has tattoos on her forehead and chin. Her hair is oiled and gathered in a brightly colored scarf. She has big but sagging breasts. She has a belly. Her butt is fat, her legs are hairy, and she's chewing gum. She's looking at you, and making a face. She's not beautiful, not ugly either. Takes no pleasure in her work. The other one is thin. She has beautiful breasts and a trim waist, but a huge butt. Her hair is black, her eyes light. She isn't chewing gum, but she has a twitch; she spits all the time. It's up to you."

The madam, who had gone out, came back.

"Which one is staying?" she asked.

"Neither one," the Consul answered from his bed.

When the three of them had left the room, the Consul handed me some money.

"I forgot to give you the money to pay."

It was a not inconsiderable sum. We waited for a while and a beautiful young woman came in, frightened, as though the madam had pushed her in from the other side of the door. She looked at us, bewildered, not knowing what this man and this woman wanted from her. I noticed she was trembling; she must have been new to the business. The madam reappeared, apparently pleased with her choice. She held out her hand and I gave her the money. She was about to leave when I began my description of the young woman, who was almost blonde and had large, firm breasts:

"She is very thin, dark, with little breasts, a narrow waist, short hair, a well-balanced butt, plump lips. She isn't chewing gum. She wants you."

I motioned to the madam and the young woman. They left, and I waited for the Consul's answer.

"You say she has small breasts and a well-balanced butt? All right, I'll take her."

I had already taken off my jellaba and my dress. I went quietly to the bed and undid the Consul's saroual. I left the dim room light on, climbed up, and straddled him.

Slowly I let him penetrate me, holding his shoulders to stop him from changing position. He came very quickly. I stayed on top of him, motionless, waiting for him to recover his energy. Not long afterwards, he had an enormous erection again. Complete lack of modesty or embarrassment made up for my inexperience. Desire directed my body by instinct, dictating the appropriate movements. I had gone mad. In a brothel with a blind man I was discovering pleasure for the first time in my life! He was insatiable. Neither of us said a word. I stifled my moans. I could not let him realize the deception. When he finally dozed off, I dressed quickly and knocked at the door.

"Don't come in yet. I'm dressing."

He got up, taking his time. I crouched in a corner. I knew he had not been fooled, but I wanted the afternoon's events to be shrouded in doubt. Our bodies were bound in a complicity of silence and secrecy. Most of all we could not speak, could not put into words an apparent lie that was in fact a truth that could not be spoken.

When I closed my eyes that night, I found myself back in the lake of heavy water. But the cage was gone. I dived in and easily swam back to the surface by myself. The land around looked much as it had the night before. There was an abandoned park, with red grass and bare trees. A swing—broken and untouched, like an old piece of junk—hung from a branch of an enormous fig tree. Unconsciously, I touched my forehead, looking for a scar. It was hidden under my hair. I used to go to that park with my father. Dressed as a boy, I would tease the little girls, until one day the brother of one of them knocked me out of the swing. My face was covered with blood, and I cried. The brother, who was older than me, said before running off, "If you were a girl, I'd have done something else to you." My father, panic-stricken, rushed me to the hospital. I had completely forgotten the incident.

My dream ended with a violent gust of wind that lifted the dead leaves weighed down by lichen and carried off the unused swing, whose desolate presence recalled distant memories.

In the morning I did not have the heart to face the Consul. I had retained his scent and sweat. But he knocked at my door, bringing me a glass of orange juice he had prepared himself, testimony to his tender affection. I blushed, a warm flush rising within me that made me clumsy. He sat on the edge of the bed, took out an embroidered handkerchief, and held it out to me. Our fingers touched. I thanked him. He said nothing. I felt, deep down, as an evident, natural truth, that this man had a remarkable quality, a kind of grace that had been suppressed by the Seated Woman's brutal possession of him, which he accepted so as to avoid tragedy.

He had no need to talk. His gaze, which rested nowhere, disturbed me. There was sometimes an uneasy gentleness about him, probably the product of pure animality. A silent intimacy had filled that room so used to solitude. We could hear people passing in the street outside, yet we dared not speak. I slowly moved my hand close to his, then pulled it back. I was afraid of breaking something fragile, something that I could neither name nor forget. I felt as if we had been deliberately sealed up in a tomb, as if we ourselves were a secret to be closely guarded. There are intense moments when just one presence is enough, and something powerful, perhaps even

119

decisive, occurs. You cannot say what it is, but for some obscure reason emotion alone reveals it, and you are ignited by it, as happy as a child transported by joy to a world of wonders. I had never dreamed that one day I would reach that state in which body and feelings seemed to float, bearing me to summits of pure air. A high mountain wind blew through my thoughts. Confusion had vanished. I was at peace with myself.

The Consul got up. I wanted to stop him, to keep him near me, to touch him, to run my lips over his neck, to remain in his arms. But I didn't move, for fear of ruining everything. He left the room without a word. My mind had been blank during those moments of silence in his presence. I did not want to think about the Seated Woman's reaction or about the new atmosphere that would now prevail in the house. It was too soon.

The Seated Woman was still asleep. The Consul had gone out. I didn't know what to do that morning. I decided to stay in my room.

THE
BROTHEL
CHARADE

W e played out the brothel charade for some time, out of desire for silence and secrecy more than out of fear of arousing the Seated Woman's suspicions. Her role and status in the house had shrunk in just a few days. Though she did not react, I did not think she would allow herself to be ousted from the stage entirely. She had a lot of work to do at the time. Apart from the baths, she was arranging marriages.

One evening she came home late and spoke to me as though I had asked her for a favor or for some piece of information:

"That's it, I've got what you need."

"What do you mean?"

"Don't play dumb with me. You know what it is. It's

what you think about all the time, what keeps you up at night."

"A lot of things keep me up at night."

"Yes, but this is like an itch, like a worm under the skin that you can't pin down and scratch once and for all."

Of course I knew very well what she was talking about, but I was trying to provoke her vulgarity, which would make her lose her temper. Especially since the Consul would never have suspected that his sister had become a rather dubious marriage-broker.

"All right," she said, "let's not beat around the bush. I've found a man for you. A widower, but still in good shape. Impressive resources. He was looking for an orphan girl, an unattached woman, someone alone in the world. You fit the bill, don't you?"

The Consul listened to this exchange without comment.

"I don't want to get married. I never asked you for any such thing."

"That's true, you didn't. But in this house I'm the one who decides who gets married and who stays single."

She had raised her voice, suddenly becoming authoritarian and inflexible. Her brother frowned. She grabbed me, dragged me to the kitchen and locked me in. She was absolutely furious and was now trying to turn the Consul against me. I was afraid, because she seemed to know things about my past. Someone must have talked to her. She lowered her voice when she spoke to her brother, but I put my ear against the door and heard some of it.

"She's a usurper and a liar. She's dangerous. She lied to us, and I have proof. She is stronger than you think.

122

That woman has led a life of betrayal. It seems that she killed her parents. Her mother died mad and her father was never even sick before he died. We're sheltering a thief and a murderess in this house. Did you know she ran off with the family inheritance? You must believe me, my brother, my life, light of my eyes."

"Enough! I don't believe you. You're jealous, and crazy too. You made this story up to cast me back into loneliness and servitude. It won't work."

Rejected by the Consul, who locked himself in his room, she screamed at the top of her lungs:

"That woman is a man! I have proof, photographs, papers. She's tricked us."

The Consul burst out laughing. The Seated Woman went on shouting, then I heard her begging:

"No, brother, no. Come on, you're frightening me. Put the razor down, you'll hurt yourself. Please! All right, it's not true, I made the whole thing up. You know how much I love you and how unhappy I am. I take it all back."

"Then open the kitchen door."

She did.

The Consul was standing there furious and determined, a straight razor at his throat. I took his hand and led him to his room. He was trembling and drenched with sweat. I took the razor away and sat down beside him.

"My eyes are dry," he said, "but I am weeping inside. I weep because my sister is mad, and because I might lose you. I won't be able to stand it if you leave. I don't even know your name. From the very first day I've called you 'the Guest.' I could have given you a name, but names and family ties don't matter. You have brought a bit of life and feeling, warmth and grace, to this madhouse."

The Seated Woman had gone out again. I took the opportunity of this crisis to confess everything to the Consul. I told him the whole story, from my birth to my flight, including my wanderings, the rape, my encounter with the Seated Woman. I told him of my regrets, my sadness, and the hope I had rediscovered thanks to his quiet, tender friendship. I told him that I knew they would find me and punish me someday, that I was waiting with resignation for that day, but that I too could not bear being separated from him.

He smiled at my story. He considered it a tale I had concocted to account for the first twenty years of my life, the imaginary story of a bored child who dealt with serious matters through laughter.

"Laughter is important," he said. "It breaks the wall of fear, intolerance, and fanaticism."

We were still recovering from the Seated Woman's outburst. He was very good at talking his way through an unpleasant situation.

"I don't have to close my eyes," he said. "I can sit right here and my mind drifts to the other room or out onto the terrace. I like to laugh when nothing goes right, because nothing is ever completely clear or completely obscure. The way I see it, everything is complex, and the truth is closer to the shadow than to the tree that casts the shadow. If what you have told me really happened, then you must have had a lot of fun. But I wouldn't say the same for your parents and the people around you. You were lucky to be able to play two roles so subtly. As I told you once, blindness is not an infirmity. Or at least not for someone who knows how to use it. Using it does not mean deceit; it means revealing the virtues of the obscure. It's like intelligence, which someone once defined as the failure to comprehend the world. Which recalls our mystical poets, for whom appearance was the most perverse mask of truth. You know from your own experience that clarity is a delusion. How can anything be clear and definable in the relations between two people? It sounds to me as though there was a moment of inattention in your life, a moment that lasted until you came to like it, took pleasure in it, and decided to use it to cover your tracks and to escape prying eyes."

He paused for a moment and felt for my hand. I made no effort to move closer to him. I was still thinking about what he had just said. "A moment of inattention." That was my life all right, or my semblance of one. I was convinced that had I met this man when I was disguised as a boy, I would have either loved or hated him, for he would have unmasked me at once. I was careful of appearances, but underneath I was the same, and this man without sight saw with all his other senses. It would have been impossible to lie to him. You can't lie to a blind man. You can tell him stories, but he trusts the voice more than the words spoken.

Though he pretended not to believe my story, his smile told me that he had suspected something. He took my hand, brought it to his lips, and kissed it, nibbling at it slightly. I gave a little cry.

"Our sin," he said with a dreamy air, "the thing that saps and spoils the soul, that gradually robs it of its purity, is our rejection of loneliness. But what can we do? We are all so vulnerable. Perhaps you and I, with our unique destinies, have learned to go beyond that fragility. That is what I felt the moment you came into this house. We owe nothing to anyone—that is our strength. We could leave this world at a moment's notice, with no fuss and no regrets. I have spent my whole life thinking about just such a voluntary departure. I carry my own death with me; I wear it on my sleeve. All the rest is just aimless thrashing to avoid disappointing time. We must not let time get bored with us. That would be stupid, unworthy of our intelligence. I say 'our' because we are alike, joined by a pact sealed in secrecy."

I thought about the Consul threatening to cut his throat if the Seated Woman did not let me out of the kitchen. I couldn't resist asking whether he had been serious. He claimed not to know and remarked that in any case seriousness is just a sharpened form of play. He may have been sincere. He admitted that he was sometimes afraid of his sister, and he described her in the most unflattering terms:

"She's a little crazy, because she's unhappy. She was very brave when we found ourselves destitute overnight, with no family, no home, no shelter. We were in ruins. The town had quaked, had slid toward a red horizon. Ever since then my sister has carried an inner fury that nothing has soothed or extinguished. She has grown bitter. She can be mean and unfair, and is capable of destroying everything, for no apparent reason. The only thing that makes her back off is an even greater violence. Which is why I sometimes get violent. Not against her, but against myself. That touches her inmost being. And she knows that I am capable of acting on my threats. What I blame her for most of all is her lack of generosity, her rather too obvious inclination to hatred and nastiness. I am her prisoner, I know that. It grieves me, and I hope to break free someday. Just think of it! I have been able to free myself of the shackles of blindness, but not of the affection my sister lavishes upon me."

I had moved closer to him as he spoke and was now in his arms, feeling his warm body.

We made love in the house for the first time. Then we lay in silence. I thought of the Seated Woman's threats and schemes again. She was quite capable of destroying us, or me at least. There had been spittle in the corner of her mouth as she screamed that morning. An outward sign of hatred. Her eyes were not red anymore, but yellow. She was like a furious wounded animal that refuses to die alone. She must have found out some bits of information about my past. Though I had nothing to apologize for about that part of my life, I wanted to avoid being confronted with the masquerade. When I buried my father, I had been careful to inter all the objects I had used during that time. There was no evidence. The uncles, sisters, cousins, and neighbors were still around, of course. But I had wiped out all traces and fled to the other end of the country. My wanderings, as it happened, did not last long. Fate led me to the baths. It was the rape in the forest that drove me there. I knew that for a while I would be able to live only with strange people. I was pleased that the first man to love my body was blind, a man with eyes in his fingertips and whose soft and slow caresses had reshaped my image. That was my victory; I owed it to the Consul, whose grace was expressed through touch. He had restored vitality to each of my slumbering, fettered senses. When we made love he spent long moments staring at my body with his hands. He had not only awakened my desire, but also gave a rare intensity that he satisfied magnificently, in silence and soft light. He was very concerned about the light. Sometimes he would be clumsy and get irritated. Then he would ask me to light another lamp or candle. "I need a little light to see your body," he would say, "to breathe its scent, to let my lips trace the lines of its harmony." His experience with women was probably limited; he would concentrate like an artist about to begin a new work. He compared himself to a sculptor. "I have to sculpt patiently and carefully," he would say, "so that your body becomes familiar to me and ceases to rebel."

I had spent my adolescence rejecting desire with all my strength, until finally I no longer even thought about it. I had no right to it. I got by with my delirious dreams peopled by phalluses, ephebi, and vulgar orgies. Often I would ease my body myself, and then feel ashamed. All that seemed very remote now. I did not want to think about it anymore. The miracle had the Consul's face and eyes. He had carved me into a statue of flesh, eager and desired. I was no longer a creature of sand and dust, of uncertain identity, crumbling at the slightest gust of wind. I felt each of my limbs growing firm, solidifying. No longer was I a creature whose skin was but a mask, an illusion designed to deceive a shameless society based on hypocrisy and the myths of a twisted religion, an illusion devoid of spirit, a delusion fabricated by a father obsessed with shame. To be reborn and to live I needed to forget, to roam, to find grace distilled by love. But the happiness, the fulfillment, the self-discovery I had found in a blind man's sublime gaze were not to last. I knew that, felt it. My brief but intense happiness would be violently inter-rupted.

THE MURDER

I t all happened very fast. The Seated Woman had been gone for more than a week. The Consul thought she was busy with her marriages. I was convinced that she had gone on a journey in search of something. Before leaving she had sent a servant woman from the baths to tell us that she had a lot to do and that we should not worry.

She came back early one morning. I was fast asleep in the Consul's arms. She opened the door and dragged me out of bed by the hair. The Consul woke up with a terrified jolt, thinking he was having a nightmare. She was screaming, foaming at the mouth:

"Come here, you bitch! Thief! Whore, come and look

who's waiting for you downstairs! You killed them both and ran off with the inheritance."

She pushed and kicked me. I grabbed at anything I could reach. The Consul got dressed as she pushed me down the stairs. I fell, and when I picked myself up at the bottom, I found myself staring at my uncle, Fatima's father, the miser my father had told me to be careful of. He was cold with rage, his face drained by a pallor that boded ill. I knew he was a cruel man, and that his wickedness had made his daughter a neglected epileptic. My father used to call him "my brother rancor." He was the one who taunted my mother—coldly and cynically—for not giving birth to a boy. The snot that hung from his nose was poison. I had always hated him, but I was stronger because I never let him get close to me or have the slightest contact with me. I knew he harbored boundless hatred. I went along with the fake marriage to Fatima mainly to get her away from her family, who left her all alone during her seizures. My uncle had spent his whole life envying his brother and trying to hurt people. He loved to set traps, to trick people, and to take advantage of their weakness or misfortune. He was a son of a bitch. The moment I laid eyes on him, I knew he had trapped me. He stood in silence, savoring his victory. I could have denied everything and pretended not to recognize him, but the image of the lake with the heavy, sticky water swept over me, and I got nauseous and lost my self-control. We stared at each other. In his eyes I saw hatred and lust for revenge. In mine there was pity and an immense desire to get it over with. I asked him to wait while I got my things. I went up to the Consul's room: he looked shattered, helpless, and numb. I went straight to the bottom drawer, loaded the pistol, and went slowly downstairs. When I was a yard away from my uncle, I emptied the pistol into his body.

In a split second I knew that this was the end of the episode. It was my duty to finish it, to put my signature on it with that murder. I sank into a morass of thoughts and images. I was swept up in their flow and knew that my hand had been moved by Fatima's energy, by my father's and mother's, and by everyone who had ever fallen victim of that man's wickedness.

I was relieved when I saw the greenish-yellow blood flowing from the body as it lay on the ground. The Seated Woman howled and clawed her cheeks. The Consul, prisoner of his own silence, seemed distracted. I was cold. I wrapped a scarf around my shoulders and waited for things to take their course. I stared at the ground, no longer hearing anything. I was already far away, running through a meadow pursued by a pack of children throwing stones at me. I was at a happy age now, barely a year old. I no longer had any notion of loss. I had lived with such passion for these few months that it could nourish me to the end of my days.

I was tried and sentenced to fifteen years in prison. I did not want a lawyer. The court appointed one for me, a young woman who delivered a superb summation about the condition of women in Muslim countries. The Seated Woman and the Consul appeared as witnesses. I can't remember what she said. As for the Consul, if it was an ordeal for him, he did not show it. He made a prepared statement to the court:

"He who seeks to shame a man is unworthy of our esteem. He who spares no one shame is not a man. One who has grace and whose soul is endowed with greatness may sometimes become cruel, and may thus dispense justice. The woman on trial here today is one of those exceptional beings who survive all the shame hatred can inflict. She went out to meet her greatest pain, an act dictated by the greatness of her soul. I am bound to that woman by a pact, by our own secret. That is our love. It is unusual to hear talk of love in this place. But be advised that the love that binds us lifts the darkness from me. I will wait for her."

IN
THE
DARKNESS

My life in prison soon fell into a routine. I did not consider imprisonment a punishment. Finding myself behind bars made me realize how much my life as a man had been like a prison. I had been confined to a single role, and in that sense deprived of freedom. Beyond the limits of that role lay catastrophe. At the time I had not been aware of how much I had suffered. My destiny had been twisted, my instincts suppressed, my body transfigured, my sexuality denied, my hopes destroyed. And I had had no choice.

Prison is a place where life is simulated. It has the color of absence, of a long day without light. It is a sheet, a narrow shroud, a parched face abandoned by life.

My cell was small and I was glad of it. It seemed to

foreshadow my grave; my stay there was like preparation for the great leavetaking. I was not bothered by the dampness of the walls. I was content to have a territory proportionate to my body. I had as little as possible to do with the other prisoners. I refused to go out for exercise walks. I asked for paper and a pencil. I wanted to write. Words seemed to beckon me from all sides, coming to me in packs, in large numbers, knocking at the wall of my cold cage. Words, smells, images, and sounds lurked around my captivity. At first I took no notice of them; I was learning how to wait. I did not want to measure time, so I blocked out the faint light that came in through an opening at the top of one wall. What was the point of simulating the brightness of day when everything was plunged into black night, long and deep? I wanted darkness, and in the end I got it. I preferred to live in a stretch of unvarying color, to get used to the flat terrain on which I walked. Little by little I entered the universe of those deprived of sight as I was deprived of freedom. I lived with my eyes shut. I blindfolded myself. Not only was there nothing to see in that sordid place, but it was my way of being close to the Consul. I tried to enter his darkness, hoping to meet him, touch him, and speak to him.

He came to visit every Friday, in the early afternoon. My life was punctuated by those weekly visits. At first this amused a few idiots who made sarcastic cracks about "the blind man who comes to see her—get it?—to see her." I never answered them. In the early days, before I closed my eyes, we would look at each other without speaking, holding hands for the whole visit. He brought me books, paper, pens. When I blindfolded myself, I had

136

to give up writing. At the same time, my desire to write became ever more urgent. The lights were on in the cells from seven to nine at night. I decided to open my eyes and write during those two hours. I scribbled and scrawled. I had so many things to put down, but couldn't decide where to start. Then I would put the blindfold back on and bury my head in the pillow. It was reassuring to return to the darkness, where I was in communion with the Consul. He did not know what I was doing, and I didn't want him to know. My love for him was taking its own shortcuts, and that was the only way I could be with him.

Since I was unable to write properly, I used the two hours of light to read. I could not help interfering with all the characters in the stories I read. I would blindfold them and send them to prison for premeditated murder. My reading was never innocent. Sometimes I even transfered a character from one story to another. That was fun, and it gave me some scope for action. It all got mixed up in my head and came out at night, as dreams and nightmares to mingle and harass me. Little by little I myself became a character in those restless, fantastic nights, and I could not wait to get to sleep, where I had those uncommon adventures.

I was caught up in a cruel love story in which I was both Sasuke, the disciple in love with his teacher, a music master, and Shunkin, the woman blinded by a kettle of boiling water poured on her face. I was both the man and the woman, now an angel possessed of grace and love, now a vengeful, pitiless storm. I was both musical note and instrument, passion and suffering. I lived through so many stories that I happily mixed them all together, curious to see how I would be garbed by each new night.

I read the *Thousand and One Nights*, of course, bit by bit. I leaped from night to night, well imagining the consequences of the disorder I was causing.

My nights were rich. I fed them with reading. I had annulled the days, immersing them in darkness, tying them all in the same sack. I had decided not to see anything of the prison, or at least as little as possible. That was my right and I insisted on it, despite occasional comments from the guards. The first year went by in that regular rhythm: darkness during the day, eyes open for reading or writing between seven and nine, darkness again with the night and its processions, the Consul's visit on Friday. It all became a ritual.

One Friday morning, I had a foreboding that he would not come. My heart was heavy, my mood bad. I couldn't say why, but I knew something was wrong.

At five o'clock the guard brought me a letter. The envelope had been opened. I took off my blindfold. It was too dark to make out the letter, so I climbed up on the bed and took down the piece of black cloth I had hung over the window. This gave me a trickle of light, and I began to read. My legs trembled and it was hard to open my eyes all the way. I waited for a moment.

Friend,

My sister died of a cerebral hemorrhage on Wednesday morning. I buried her all by myself that same day. She went quickly, thank goodness. Life in the house was unbearable. We were arguing constantly. I couldn't stand anything about her anymore: her habits, her food, her snoring, her smell, her voice. It was as though I was allergic to her very presence. I lost patience and snapped at her. I realize now

how someone who is constantly and systematically frustrated
can turn violent. My violence was physical at first; later,
when things kept happening again, it became internal: I cul-
tivated my hatred for that poor woman. Her whole life was a
series of failed and unacknowledged ambitions and yearn-
ings; she was determined to isolate me, to keep me for herself alone. She wanted to devour me. But I kept my head. I
was watchful. After the tragedy and your departure, she
said she felt guilty, but when she spoke of you, she said, "In
any case, you could not expect anything true from someone
whose life was built on lies." I let her talk. I never answered. She wept and hoped for death. Silently, I wished it
on her. Her jealousy ruined us; she destroyed everything;
nothing remains alive in our house.

    She was the one who went to ask about you in your home
village. She said she wanted to expose you. She managed to
find that miserable uncle of yours, that usurer who used his
shoe shop as a lending counter. Did you know that his death
made many people happy? People had only contempt for
him. He was involved in many suspicious dealings, but
none of any real consequence. I'm telling you all this so
you'll see that what you did was right.

    I think about you. My eyes, closed on thoughts of you,
wish to find you again. I have to settle the problems caused
by my sister's death. I am not afraid of solitude. I don't
know how long it will take to work everything out. I need
someone to take care of the house and to light the stove in
the kitchen for me. A young man, the son of some neighbors, is keeping me company for the moment. He reads to
me and calls himself my disciple. I find that funny. His parents send me three meals a day. They are very kind. Their
children go to my school. The day before yesterday I stopped
receiving people; they come to offer help more than condolences. My sister was not well-liked. I think that must be the
worst of it. To die alone and not be missed by anyone is so
unbearably sad. I have always known that the iniquitous end

their days in horrible loneliness. My sister did not have the time to experience that suffering, but she was unloved, and that made her suffer constantly. I was all she had in the world. Sometimes I did love her, and yielded to her requests. She insisted on taking care of everything, even washing me. I never loved her as a sister, but as a beggar who gives all she has in exchange for a little warmth. That is what pity is. I am being harsh, for I owe my survival to her. But must we carry with us all our lives those who condemn us to live? Now that she sleeps a soundless slumber free of images, a slumber beyond all nights, let us not awaken her with merciless judgment.

The suffering that dwells within me speaks not of her, but of you, day and night. My thoughts are rooted in the twilight forest where you are now held captive. My heart is a stone bench covered with leaves, placed on the roadside to offer rest to the weary. Chance or the wind will bring you back. I await you. Till we meet again.

I was moved by the death of the Seated Woman. I thought about her unhappiness, her barren body, her failures and the marks they had left on her face. I tried to understand why she could not resist doing evil. She wanted everyone else to pay for the wretchedness of her body, soon confused with the anguish of her soul. Some people draw their energy from hatred. You often see them at dusk, roaming around a lake of dead water, rats going before them to spill all their venom. However much they claim to be purifying themselves by secreting misfortune, the truth is that they bear negative charges which they must pass on to others before they cause their own paralysis and death. The Seated Woman had to die, a victim of her own determination to hurt others. Disturbed by the tragedy she herself had caused, she must have lost her mind, finding nowhere to discharge all her rancor.

I put my blindfold back on and sought the night again. There was nothing for me to do but wait out the placid hours that love alone would trouble. With all my being I sought calm, that state of slowed rhythms that brings relief and happy lassitude. All I wanted now was to sleep, to meet those characters who still lived within me, as if I were their storehouse, the hearth and crypt in which they lurked during daylight hours. But the moment I closed my eyes they rushed out from all over, chiding me for my long absence. I laughed, and with them I continued adventures begun in days gone by. What bothered me was that there was no trace of the Consul in that world so full of excitement, laughter, and fury. I had to find the secret door through which to bring him into those spectacles. True, there was a blind man, watchman at the gates of the Andalusian garden, but it was not the Consul. This man had a stick and stopped children from going in. Sometimes he even hit them. He was nasty, not because he could not see, but because he was a watchman and was poor.

THE
LETTER

W ith the black blindfold I entered the world of the blind, little by little. I relearned the motions of daily life, reduced to a minimum in prison. I took off the blindfold only to read, write, and wash. The layer of darkness I drew over me thickened day by day. It helped me to separate from my body, the final caresses of the man I loved a burning memory now. Time was abolished of its own accord. Now I feigned nothing. I adapted, learning to tame loneliness and waiting. I was perhaps the only prisoner who never complained of loneliness. I imposed silence, even oblivion, around my cell. I paid to be left in peace. Most of all I did not want to have to justify my acts, or my inner isolation. A curious thing happened when I was imprisoned: I ceased to be obsessed with my past as a woman disguised as a man. I forgot all about it. With my uncle's death I had liquidated the past (or so I thought). Besides, as I saw it, I was not in prison to pay for that crime; I was there almost voluntarily, to await the Consul's return from some distant continent. While I waited, I was learning to live in darkness. That seemed necessary to me if I were to deserve his love. I adapted to my new life, cultivating patience.

The Consul's visits were more and more infrequent. He preferred to write to me, and almost every letter repeated that he suffered to see me in this state of reclusion and submission. I clarified this misunderstanding in a letter that took me a long time to write and an even longer time to decide to send. I could not get used to the idea that he would not read this letter directly but would hear it from a third person. I had hoped to read it to him myself in the visiting room, but they listened to our every word there. I wished I knew how to write in braille. Today I would have used one of those small tape recorders, but this was before the days of cassettes. It was my first love letter, and I must have rewritten it several times.

Friend,
   I leave it to humble words to tell you of the wavering shadow of memory, which is all that remains of our poem. It has now been several months, perhaps a century, that I have been walking toward you, arms outstretched like the legendary statue that goes to the sea. I am not following you, but have instead taken the opposite path to meet you, that our faces might be lit by the same light. I walk forward, and beneath my feet I feel a part of me taking root in the earth. The thick layer of shadow I am building around me is my sanctuary. It covers and protects me, now a mane, now a

veil drawn against the light. You and I are of the same
dream, just as others are of the same country. Like an echo
of a morning song, your voice leans over me and comes with
me as I walk. A bare voice, without words or sentences, just
a murmur's warmth. The seasons pass here without touch-
ing us; they come and go behind the mountains. I say no
prayer for our friendship, which you call love. It is beyond
words. It is a plant with broad leaves anchored in my mind
and in my heart. It prevents me from falling apart and from
failing to wait. Sometimes sadness comes over me; a stupid,
heavy sadness shrouds me like a cloak of dead stars. Then I
do nothing. I let these moments that separate me from you
pass. You draw away, your gaze averted. I know it, but can
do nothing. I am nourished by the emotion I feel at the mere
thought of you. I walk in time that is a desert, the sand
sometimes cold, sometimes searing. I wear thick, woolen
socks and nomad's sandals. I take care of my feet because the
road is long. I feel time as a deep and fast-running river. I
follow it. It is the direction that points to the place of our
next encounter.

Friend, I hope this letter finds you in good health. Here,
as you know, all I lack is the sight of your face. Between my
wait and your return lies an expanse of blue sea. I kiss your
hands.

I sent this letter telling myself that he would surely
find a discreet and faithful reader. My body was cold. I
ate a piece of bread and some olives and curled up in a
corner, so weary that it was as if I had finally lost all
sense of myself. I slept soundly, and the night passed
with no encounters with the characters of the stories I
was reading.

ASHES
AND
BLOOD

J ust when I thought that I was so free of my past
that I no longer even remembered people's faces,
my five remaining sisters—one of the seven was
seriously ill, perhaps even dead, and another lived
abroad—paraded by in a procession even more grotesque
than it was ridiculous. Whether this was a vision, a nightmare, a hallucination, or a reality I cannot say. I remember
the details clearly, but I cannot seem to locate the time
or place.

They were all dressed the same: white shirts, black ties
and jellabas, hoods over their heads. They had mous-
taches drawn in black pencil, and they wore sunglasses.
They introduced themselves, one at a time. They each
carried plastic bags. Everything seemed identical and

carefully rehearsed. The tallest came first, staring at me with bulging eyes. She put the bag on the table and ordered me to open it: inside was a dead rat. I screamed, but my voice made no sound. She held a straight razor in the other hand, ready to slash a face or a throat. I stood pressed against the cold wall, submissive, unable to escape their torture.

The next one, a butcher's knife in her right hand, put the bag down in front of me and gestured to me to open it. Inside was a small box containing a reddish scorpion, live and ready to sting.

The third waved a pair of scissors and held out the bag. It was empty. The moment I opened it she pressed my head against the wall and started to cut my hair. She held her knee against my belly. It hurt. The others laughed and said: "That'll teach you, liar, thief. You took everything from us, you bitch, you murderous bitch."

The fourth—very small, perhaps a dwarf—jumped on me and bit my neck. Blood flowed. I tried to fight back, but the others held me. The dwarf collected the blood in a jar and put it in the plastic bag. "That and the hair will do the trick," she said.

The last one—apparently the youngest—put down her sack between my legs, came toward me with a desolate look, leaned into my arms, and whispered in my ear: "I love you. I don't want them to hurt you. And look, I'm empty-handed. I'm not bad." Then she hit me in the forehead and left with a laugh. So hard was the blow that I almost fainted, but then I felt something brush my legs. This last sister turned out to be the worst. There was a viper in the bag she had left so casually at my feet. I jumped onto the table and howled. By the time I realized where I was, they were all gone. On the ground were a few tufts of hair, drops of blood, and small piles of ash.

I was in tears, deeply shaken. Evil had swooped down on me like the wings of a bird of prey. That story happened to me, though I don't know where or when. Was it in prison, or while my father lay dying? I lived it and relived it in a kind of relentless plague of murky images risen from the darkness. They all had to do with mourning, with a widow despoiled, and with vengeance.

Perhaps it was a nightmare that preceded or followed the punitive expedition of which I was the victim.

One day, as I was deep in darkness in search of the Consul's silhouette, a strong and ugly guard came and took me from my cell. She tore the blindfold from my eyes and made me follow her.

"You have a visitor, and it's not the one you think."

Instead of taking me to the visiting room, she brought me to a cellar, probably a place used for interrogation and torture. She took me to a gray, damp room with a table, a stool, and a lamp.

She left me alone for a few minutes in that room without the tiniest opening for air. Several coats of dark gray paint hid traces of blood on the wall. The door opened and five women filed in, as if in a play, all dressed identically: gray jellabas, white scarves concealing hair and foreheads, gloves, pale faces devoid of all makeup. They were all ugly, and exuded unease. I realized who they were: a sect of Muslim sisters, brutal and fanatical. They gathered around me. I opened my eyes wide and recognized my own sisters. The guard was standing there. They had paid for her complicity and silence. They had come to execute a definite plan, to hurt me, perhaps disfigure me, or

simply to threaten and frighten me. The oldest soon explained the intentions of this demented group.

"We have come, five fingers of one hand, to put an
end to a situation of usurpation and theft. You were never
our brother and you will never be our sister. We have
expelled you from the family in the presence of men of
religion and witnesses of good faith and high virtue. Now
listen to me: you made us believe that you were a statue,
a monument radiating light, bringing honor and pride to
the house, whereas in fact you were only a hole wrapped
in a scrawny body, a hole just like mine and your six ex-
sisters'. But you plugged up your hole with wax; you
tricked and humiliated us. Just like Father, you held us
in contempt. Haughty and arrogant, you ignored us. We
would have taken care of you if we could, you last little
sister. We would have simply slaughtered you. But God
provides. Whoever departs from His path is brought to
kneel on a sheet of iron reddened by fire. Now order
must be restored. You will not escape. You will pay. There
will be no mercy, no respite. Our father lost his reason;
our mother, poor woman, fell into the wells of silence;
and you took advantage of the calamity, packed your bags
and took everything. You left us penniless, in dire pov-
erty, in that ruined old house all moldy, with no more
room for life. You ransacked the house and carried off
the inheritance. You are in prison now because you deserve it. You ruined the whole family. Now you have to
pay. Remember, you are nothing but a hole between two
scrawny legs. We are going to plug up that hole forever.
You're going to have a circumcision. Not fake this time,
but real. Not a cut finger. No, we're going to cut off that

little thing that sticks out, and muzzle that hole with a needle and thread. We're going to get rid of that sex you hid. Life will be simpler. No more desire. No more pleasure. You'll become a thing, a vegetable that will drool until you die. You can start praying. You can shout. No one will hear. Since your betrayal we have discovered the virtues of our beloved religion. Justice has become our passion, truth our ideal and obsession, Islam our guide. We render to life that which belongs to it. And we prefer to act in love and family discretion. Now, in the name of God, the Merciful, the Compassionate, Just and All-Powerful, we open our little case."

As she spoke, two of her companions tied my hands to the icy table. They tore off my saraoul and lifted my legs. The guard, who knew the place well, showed them two hooks in the ceiling and brought them some rope. My legs were held apart, tied on each side. The oldest stuffed a damp rag into my mouth. She put a hand on my belly and crushed the lips of my vagina with her fingers until what they called "the little thing" came out. They sprinkled it with something, took a razor blade from the metal box, soaked it in alcohol, and cut off my clitoris. I fainted, screaming inside.

Excruciating pain woke me in the middle of the night. I was in my cell, my saroual soaked with blood. My sex was sewn up. I knocked on the door to call for help. No one came. I waited until morning and begged one of the guards to take me to the infirmary. I gave her money. The nurse, probably in collusion with the guard-torturer, gave me some ointment and had me sign a paper acknowledging that I had mutilated myself. The signature

was the price for the ointment. I realized then that everyone had been corrupted by my sisters. The medicine eased
the pain.

I was lost and bewildered for more than a month, mad,
delirious at night, feverish, on the brink of the abyss. The
Consul had come to see me twice, but I could not bring
myself to speak to him. I hadn't the strength to tell him
what had happened. Yet I was haunted by the idea of
revenge. I thought of several plans, but shame for myself
and disgust with that family brought me back to my crippled and ruined state.

After his second visit, I was able to write a few words
and send them to him through a prisoner who had shown
me some sympathy. This is what I wrote:

> Lost track of you. Am in darkness and no longer see you.
> Sick. Sick. My body wounded. You are my only light.
> Thank you.

THE
FORGOTTEN

W ounded and stricken, I continued my nocturnal wanderings to escape pain more than to seek new encounters. I cleared myself a path between skeletal bodies hanging in a huge warehouse. They dangled naked and transparent, the skin stretched over their bones. It was an army of bodies emptied of all substance. I saw a door at the other end of the warehouse. I went to it. There was an exit sign in several languages, with green arrows. I followed the arrows. But I never reached the exit. I wandered in that vast barracks of bodies, amid icy silence and the smell of fear. I never knew that fear could have a smell. There was a slight draught, which made the bodies sway ever so slightly. Sometimes bones clacked together, the sound amplified by the echo. I heard a voice behind me:

"Come closer, I have just enough time to reveal the secret of life and to tell you of the face of death. Don't be afraid. They thought I was dead. I was only wounded, but I can already see the landscape of the afterlife. Are you wounded too? I have nothing to fear anymore. I want you to know, I want everyone to know. Wait, don't go!"

I turned and saw a man with blood on his knees; his face had a greenish cast. He was not a jinni, but a dying man. He was straining to tell me some secret. I moved closer:

"All the people you see here were poor; beggars and tramps, diseased. One day an order was given to clean up the town for an important visitor, a foreigner who was to take a short walk in the streets. We were the dirty, unacceptable face of the country, whose image had to be polished. So we had to be sent away, at least temporarily, during the few days of the foreigner's visit. The order was carried out. There were raids. They stuck us all here and completely forgot us. We fought among ourselves. I am the last survivor, the one who has to disappear because his testimony is so horrible. Tell everybody what you have seen here. This is no nightmare. We are not ghosts. We are human castoffs, forever forgotten. No one came to claim us. You are the first human being to enter this warehouse."

I had no doubt stumbled into that place, drawn there by my sharp pain. I was awake, and this was a vision. It was all true. It had happened in winter. The townspeople still talk about it. All those bodies were discovered on the day the fairgrounds were opened for a new show. There was more fear than pain. Fear and disgust. I felt my body. The flesh and bones were bruised. I tried not to urinate, because I knew it would hurt. My belly was swollen. When I finally urinated I held my breath. I was sweating. The dying man's voice entered me and merged with mine until it became my own voice. I could no longer hear the dying man, but I spoke inside myself, endlessly repeating what he had told me. Strangely, this eased the intensity of my pain.

I spent two nights mired in fever, pain, and fear.

My mutilation was a form of vengeance. But how had my sisters come by such a barbarous idea? I later discovered that the torture inflicted on me is a commonly practiced operation in Black Africa and in parts of Egypt and the Sudan. Its effect is to deprive young girls just awakening to life of any possibility of desire and pleasure. I also learned that neither Islam nor any other religion has ever permitted this kind of slaughter.

The dying man's voice that dwelled within me became clear and precise:

"The guard is a slave brought long ago from the Sudan. She is a witch, an expert in torture."

It must have been she who suggested to my sisters that they make me an invalid and expel me definitively from life.

The persistent fever was due to infection. Rage flowed in my blood. My visions became more and more sinister. My voice changed. I felt possessed by death. To rid myself of it I had to report what I had seen in the warehouse. I looked for someone to talk to. Not a guard or a nurse. I was lucky, for as I was dragging myself up to go to the sick bay, I collapsed in the corridor just as a doctor was passing. I was half-conscious. He was furious. He shouted that they were all savages and barbarians. Someone from the prison administration showed him the declaration in which I acknowledged that I had mutilated myself. He became even more violently angry. I was taken straight to the hospital, where he treated me for the infection and waited several days before removing, under anesthetic, the stitches that had sewn up the lips of my vagina. When I told him how it had happened, he found it hard to believe. He wanted to call the police, but a moment later he raised his arms in a gesture of impotence.

"Everyone here is corrupt," he said. "No one will believe your story. The police won't challenge what the guards say. Besides which, there is the paper you signed. But why? What did you do to those women?"

He reassured me that my general health was sound and promised to do all he could to keep me in the hospital as long as possible.

"At least it's better than prison," he said.

Despite the medicines, I was still in pain. I was convinced that I would continue to suffer until I revealed what I had seen in the warehouse—seen or imagined. Those images and the words of the dying man weighed heavily on me mentally and physically. Every word was like a sharp glass needle piercing my body's every sensitive point.

I asked the doctor if he could spare me a moment after work. At first he hesitated, but finally agreed. I began by warning him of the extraordinary nature of my visions, explaining that even if they did not really exist, they were still affecting me.

"I am not insane," I said, "but I live in a world without

156

much logic. Believe me, all I ask is that you hear me out."

I told him in detail of my nocturnal wanderings. He did not seem surprised. He nodded as if there was nothing unusual about my tale. When I finished, he got up and said:

"You may not really have seen all this, but it is true. The police did lock up beggars and then forget about them. The press never mentioned it. But here rumor is a sure source of information. Everybody knew, but no one went to check, so it became an incredible story. What I find astonishing is the connection between your suffering and this incident."

"Great pain affords me a lucidity that borders on clairvoyance. Let's put it that way."

I felt much better after that session. I did not think of the Consul during those days. I had not forgotten him, but I was determined not to involve him in these stories of blood and death. He did not know of my hospitalization. When he came to the prison, he was told that I did not want to see him. He suspected something. He thought I was sick or depressed, that I dared not let him see my gloomy, joyless face. He clung tightly to that version of things. When he came to the hospital, this was the first thing he said to me:

"Are you ready to show me your face now?"

He was far from suspecting the bloody ordeal I had just suffered.

His first act was to look at my face. He sat on the edge of the bed and gently caressed my forehead, cheeks, nose, mouth, and chin.

"You have cried a lot and you've lost weight. You mustn't neglect yourself! It's not good."

The doctor took him aside and told him why I was in the hospital. He didn't say anything to me about it. He held my hand and squeezed it hard. When he left, I ran my fingers over my cheeks; they felt gritty. My face looked terrible. I had not washed in several days. That evening I locked myself in the bathroom and did something about my appearance.

The Consul came to see me often. He brought flowers, fruit, perfume. He never came empty-handed. He never mentioned what had happened. I appreciated his discretion, yet it also disturbed me. How was I to interpret his silence? Was it an expression of sympathy, of solidarity, or was it a sign of embarrassment slowly digging a furrow between us? It was hard for me to broach the subject. When he came, he would ask me whether I was sleeping well and then move on to something else. Sometimes he talked to the doctor, but not in my presence. I later found out that one of the things he was obsessed with was whether I could still have children. That tormented him, though he did not show it. I thought about it too. Earlier I had rejected any idea of pregnancy, birth, and bringing up children. I never had time to consider the notion of being a mother. I admit that the thought had never even crossed my mind on the few occasions I had had sexual relations with the Consul. Which gives some idea of how new to me it all was and how much I still considered my body a sandbag. I saw myself as a straw scarecrow who attracted crows instead of scaring them away, some happily nesting on my shoulders, others even pecking holes where the eyes were. I was losing any sense of my presence in the world. I felt as if I was crumbling into ruins, and endlessly putting myself together again. Everything was confused. I was looking for some way to ease the pain, not only the pain that coursed through my veins like poison, but also the pain I was beginning to feel after the Consul's visits. He would come and sit in silence. His presence weighed tons. He seemed overwhelmed, unhappiness dwelling within him. I was increasingly disoriented, disturbed, sinking into confusion and nightmarish visions. I was alone again, without anesthetic, facing the final reverses of fortune, disaster, sadness, and violence showing me no mercy. I decided to go back to the prison. Partial freedom in the midst of all that whiteness was too cruel for my eyes to bear. I had to beg the doctor to send me back to my cell.

I was getting ready to leave when the Consul came in. He looked a little less sad than usual. He had a sprig of mint with him.

"Let's make some tea, as we used to," he said.

I had a powerful feeling, leaving no room for doubt, that something had finally broken between us. I couldn't say why, but I felt it, and was not surprised.

We didn't make the tea. I told him I was going back to prison. He said nothing. He sat in a chair. I was on the edge of the bed. I noticed he was blushing.

"Please stop moving," he said.

"I'm not moving."

"I know, but there's such a lot of traffic in your head. I can hear your thoughts rattling around." Then he said, in a tone more calm:

"My hands don't have the strength to look at you today. They're tired. They feel useless and guilty. I feel remorse that I have never measured up to your enthusiasm and courage. I am condemned never to feel enthusiasm. Ever since childhood I have been mired in tragedy, and my orders from heaven or from life itself forced me to persevere, not to cut the thread of life, to consolidate my being, making it normal. I can't seem to tell you everything I think and believe with any real coherence. I accepted the Seated Woman's death, but not your departure and imprisonment. Ever since then I have been relentlessly seeking some shelter, some place of peace for my thoughts and for my weary body. I try to open the sealed lips of my mother underground. To hear her voice just once, to hear her bless me or even curse me, but just to hear her. I know I have to travel in darkness, in the distant desert, in the Far South. I am writing now, and you are dictating to me. What I write scares me, possesses me. Where do you get that power to go through life, disrupting it with such arrogance, such courage? When I used to write for myself, I did it at night. But now your fraught voice comes to me in the morning. Your thoughts cross the night and arrive in the early hours. It is my task to organize and transcribe them. I add very little. Your story is terrifying. You yourself are the secret that possesses me. I can free myself of it only by pressing on to the story's very end. But what will I find then? You are not the type to end a story. You're more the type to leave it open, in order to make it an endless tale. Your story is a series of doors opening onto white spaces and spinning labyrinths. Sometimes you come upon a meadow, sometimes a ruined old house closed in on its occupants, all long dead. The place of your birth perhaps, a cursed place struck by the law of absence and oblivion. My friend! Since I have become your voice, borne by it to silk-wrapped, bloodstained nights, my world has been strange. I am sure I'm not imagining all this. I am verging on your gift of clairvoyance. How can I tell you that to reach you I must pass through a narrow door? I hear you, my hands seek you out. But I know you are far away, on another continent, closer to the full moon than to my gaze. Yet I see you, now a man, now a woman, superb creature of childhood, eluding love and friendship. You are out of reach, a being of darkness, shadow in the night of my sufferings. Sometimes I cry out unconsciously, 'Who are you?' Sometimes I feel that since the tragedy I have been trapped in a spell cast by your family, woven by wicked hands. I would like to ask you, even to beg you, to remain what you are, to press on, for neither prison nor others' tears will stop you. I waited so long for you. You came into my life with the strange grace of a lost animal. With you my heart became a home. Since you left, I have ceased to live there. My loneliness is stark, no longer protected by your care. Your voice alone animates my body, and I write. However terrified, I transcribe what you tell me. I have come to say goodbye and to ask forgiveness. Our story has become impossible. I will continue to live it elsewhere, in some other way. I am going away, going where my blindness will become a mere infirmity again, a gloomy fate I could not escape despite your visit. But I want you to know that I have learned your beauty with my hands, and that this has moved me like a child who first looks upon the sea. I will take care of my hands, I will cover them with fine cloth, for they bear the imprint of your beauty like a secret. I am telling you this because I have also learned that the peculiar quality of this emotion is that it is unique. I close my eyes and hands around it and keep it forever. Farewell, my friend!"

MY STORY, MY PRISON

T he Consul's confession left me perplexed, though I was sure of one thing: my story, which had made me a child of sand and wind, would pursue me all my life, leaving no room for anything else. Everything that would ever happen to me would be an extension of it, a direct or disguised manifestation of it in one form or another.

My story was my prison; that I was locked in a gray cell for killing a man was secondary. I carried my prison like a shell on my back wherever I went. Perhaps the isolation might help me sever the threads woven around me by that twisted destiny. I was a closed box kept in some tight, sealed shed. A stifling torpor pressed down on me from so far off that I felt I had suffered the ordeal for centuries.

The Consul had left me a sheet of paper folded in four. I opened it. On it was a drawing, or rather a road map. An arrow pointed clumsily to the south, another to the north. In the middle was a palm tree, and not far away some waves drawn like birds with outstretched wings. On the back of the sheet of paper he had written this:

> *Friendship alone, total gift of the soul, absolute light, light on light, the body barely visible. Friendship is grace; it is my religion, our territory; friendship alone will give your body back its mistreated soul. Follow your heart, follow the emotion that runs in your blood. Farewell, my friend!*

After that I abandoned my blindfold and my wanderings in the darkness. I began to be obsessed with the idea of a great light from the sky, a light so strong it would make my body transparent, cleanse it, restore to it the pleasure of astonishment, the innocence of knowing the beginning of things. The idea excited me. I devoted myself entirely to developing it, until the Consul's image was lost, becoming hazy and elusive. I had lost track of him.

I found life in prison natural. I forgot the need for freedom. Being shut in did not oppress me. I now felt receptive. Women came to see me, brought me letters to write for them. I was happy to do favors, to be useful. I was given a small desk, paper and pens. I had become confidant and counselor. My only recompense was an inner satisfaction, something to do that took me away from my own prison. Meanwhile, my nights increasingly resembled a house people were moving out of. Little by little they were emptied of their dubious, often monstrous tenants, as all the characters I had accumulated during my life were asked to leave. I evicted them without hesitation. The moment I closed my eyes I saw them leaving like so many ghosts getting off a train in a thick fog. Some protested, others threatened to come back for revenge. They were taken by surprise by my sudden lack of hospitality. I noticed that they all seemed crippled, half-awake, nonplussed. They dragged their feet. There was even a legless man moving very fast and punching the laggards as he passed. They should have been happy to leave that rotting carcass. My nights were becoming more and more like an unused railway platform. The characters were lost in the darkness as they fell from my nights. I heard their footsteps fading, then there was silence, with the occasional sound of someone falling.

My days were filled with my work as public scribe. I spent the night cleaning up, for they left behind piles of old things that stuck in my memory and gave me no peace.

It had taken a long time—months—to clean out the inside of my head. Among the images I lost was the Consul's. Yet I never saw him leave. I only knew that he was no longer inside me. Only the memory of our entwined bodies cropped up vividly from time to time. You can forget a face, but can never really wipe out the memory of the warmth of an emotion, the sweetness of a gesture, the sound of a tender voice.

My phase of activity won me official recognition by the prison administration as "public scribe and secretary." I also had to draft letters for the warden. As a prison functionary, albeit an inmate, I had to wear regulation dress:

gray jacket and trousers, blue shirt, black tie, navy blue cap, black shoes.

At first these accoutrements bothered me. But I had no choice. It was a request, but it sounded like an order. The work, especially in uniform, helped me to take some distance from myself. The Consul's image continued to fade until it became a shifting point in the center of a flame. My memories were falling away; I was losing them gradually the way others lose their hair. My head gleamed, no memory sticking to it.

When I put on my uniform in the morning, I would look at myself in the mirror and smile. I was wearing men's clothes again. But it was no longer a disguise. These were work clothes. The women dressed like the men so as to look harsh and to bolster their authority. I didn't give anyone orders, yet the prisoners greeted me as though I were their superior. It was ridiculous. Some called me "sir," perhaps not on purpose. I did not correct them. I let that doubt stand, but my conscience was clear. I wasn't fooling anyone. I took care of my face. I used more makeup than before. I had become coquettish. People in prison continue to play on appearances despite everything, but I no longer had the heart to play.

Little by little my conditions improved. I was granted some privileges. I was considered neither fully a prisoner, nor a prison employee like the others. I was envied by some, feared by others. I came and went between the two camps as though I was written in two languages.

When there were few letters to write, I gathered together those prisoners who were still interested in life outside and I read to them from several-day-old newspapers. Earth-shaking events—wars, coups d'état—did not affect them. They wanted the crime and human-interest stories. "Blood! Love!" they would shout. Crimes of passion were their favorites. The reading sessions turned into storytelling evenings. I would make them up as I went along. The basic plot was always the same: an impossible love ending in bloodshed. I took pleasure in creating characters and situations. Sometimes I wandered so far afield that the audience protested, making fun of my commentaries. What they wanted were the bare facts. When the audience got too noisy, I would stop the story. But my storytelling talent soon ran dry. I began to tell the same tale again and again. It was about two secret lovers facing risk and danger. Then came tragedy: discovery, punishment, and vengeance.

Some women came to me privately and told me the story of their lives. They made a lot of it up. They thought their lives were novels, that they suffered the fate of misunderstood heroines. In prison words were all they had left, and they used them and misused them. They invented stories full of adventure. I listened patiently. I had not had much experience of life. I learned a lot through those stories about the mores of my society, about the meanness of men, and about the greatness and weakness of the soul. I realized how sheltered I had been during childhood and youth, how far I had been from the wind, cold, and hunger. It was as if my father had kept me under a glass, protected from dust and people's touch. It was hard to breathe, because I wore a mask of steel and was trapped in a family that was itself trapped in sickness, fear, and madness. Had I been a girl among girls, my fate might have been violent, but not wretched, not tainted with shame, theft, and lies.

Between the gray walls I could not stop pondering these tales of woe. My gaze lost its balance and wandered at random. Sometimes I felt useless, and that made me deeply angry. I was back in the cursed place where my father was buried. I turned into an evil shadow. I dug him up and stepped on him. I was insane. When I thought about being released, I felt sick, broke out in sweats.

With time and the habits of everyday life, things died away inside me: my fits of rage disappeared, my feelings were blank with the whiteness that leads to nothingness and slow death. My emotions had been dissolved in a lake of stagnant water. My body had stopped developing; it no longer changed. It was fading, no longer able to move or feel. It was neither a woman's body full and eager, nor a man's serene and strong. I was now somewhere between the two; in other words, in hell.

HELL

They had been walking for a long time. Since sunrise. In silence. You could see them in the distance, women coming forward in small groups. They came from afar, some from the north, others from the east. Their desire to reach that dune, to enter that mythical place, source of all light, concealed the hunger, thirst, and exhaustion on their faces. Their lips were cracked by the heat and wind; some were bleeding from the nose; they all accepted these annoyances, with no weariness, no regrets. They walked in the sand until they merged with its movements, bearing their shadows like a standard to hail the final dune, to forget the dry wind and the morning chill, to arrive just at the moment when the light turns soft and ambiguous, when it drifts away from the sun and joins the sky on the threshold of night. They had to arrive at exactly that instant of indeterminate duration. I, in my solitude, had decided that eternity would begin here. Any walk would have to end and melt into that light. The desert had its laws, and grace its secrets.

The women making that journey asked no questions. They knew they had to arrive just at the moment when light makes the passage from day to night. That was one of the conditions for acceptance of their request to the Holy Woman.

I was holy and merciless. Now a statue, now a mummy, I ruled. My memory was gone, and I came from nowhere. My blood must be white. My eyes changed color with the sun.

Most of them were young. Accompanied by their mothers or aunts, they dared not look into the sun. They had to look down, staring at the sand silently marked by their feet in their thick, woolen socks.

They had heard talk of the Holy Woman of the sands, daughter of light, whose hands had grace and the power to halt the irremediable, to ward off misfortune, and perhaps even to prevent sterility in young women. They came here after all else had failed. I was their last resort.

It all had to happen in silence. The silence in that place had the color of dry ice, something like blue. It spread like a light slithering between stones. Only a distant echo, a child's cry, dwelled permanently in their minds.

I sat on a throne, wearing white gloves, my face veiled. One by one the women crossed the room on their knees, heads lowered, until they were half a yard from me. They kissed my hand and raised their dresses. I had to stroke their flat bellies softly and brush their pubes.

I took off the glove and passed on the warmth that was supposed to assure them fertility. Sometimes my fingers ploughed their bellies as if they were soft, damp soil. The women were happy; some gripped my hand and slid it toward their vaginas. They thought that caresses were not enough. To make doubly sure they forced my fingers to bruise their skin, even to wound it. I was tireless. The women filed in all night. The Law of this place and of an omnipotent but invisible master was that they had to leave at dawn, at first light. I was perplexed by the very young women who were brought to me. They were sometimes so young that I dared not touch them. I simply dipped my fingers in a bowl of argan oil and barely touched their lips. Some licked my fingers, others turned away, perhaps finding the oil's strong smell unpleasant. Often their mothers would slap them on the back of the neck, forcing them to rub their faces in my hand.

Later I came to know hell. It was one of those clear nights when everything is larger than life: sounds were louder, objects moved, faces changed, and I felt lost and brutalized.

I was seated as usual, my hand ready for the ritual. I went through the motions mechanically. Everything seemed unsettled, false, immoral, and grotesque. Suddenly silence fell over the dune. The women were lined up to receive the key of their deliverance from my hand.

Hell was inside me, with its disorder, its hallucinations, and its madness.

The naked belly before me was hairy. I lowered my

hand slightly and found an erect penis. I took my hand away and looked at the face that was trying to hide from me. In a low voice he said:

"You went away long ago. Why did you leave us so suddenly? You left us only your shadow. I could not sleep anymore. I looked for you everywhere. Give yourself back! Give me back my breath, my life, the strength to be a man. Your power is immense. The whole country knows it. You went away long ago. Put your hand on my belly again. You can even tear it with your nails. If I have to suffer, let it be at your hands. You are beautiful and inaccessible. Why have you turned away from life, why do you sit in death's shadow?"

The hood of his jellaba was pulled down over his head. I was afraid of what I might find. Perhaps that voice was known to me. I did not have to raise the hood. He did it himself. The face changed color and shape. Images were piled one atop the other, forming now a picture of my father, now that of the uncle I had killed. Suddenly the image of the Consul appeared to me in those ancient faces, his eyes open, shining and laughing, eyes bright, perhaps even blue. The man was no longer talking to me. He stared at me. I had to lower my eyes. I leaned forward and kissed his hands. I had no wish to speak. I felt all the warmth of his body rising within me, a warmth that came from his open gaze, from his eyes freed of darkness. That gust of heat tore my eyebrows away tuft by tuft, then my eyelashes, then pieces of the skin of my forehead.

I felt a pain in my belly, then an emptiness, rising persistently within me. I was bare-headed, my shoulders scorched, my hands immobilized. And I suffered time and its misfortunes, unknown to the rest of the world, as if

172

that man and I were locked in a glass cage. I was a failure and I walked alone on a road paved with marble where I might fall at any moment. I realized that I was coming out of myself, that the entire scene would have to lead to this departure in a ravaged body. I was filled with old rags, delivered to that light that was supposed to be beautiful. But I had no strength and no feeling; I was burned from inside, hurled into the whirlpool of emptiness. It was white all around me. "So this is death," I said to myself, somewhat hesitant. "A barefoot journey on cold marble, wrapped in a sheet of mist or white clouds. It is not unpleasant. But where is the end? Will I spend eternity in this burning light that leaves me no shade? This is not death, then, but hell!"

A voice, unknown but clear, spoke to me: "One day you will give birth to a bird of prey, who will perch on your shoulder and show you the path. One day the sun will sink a little closer to you. You will not escape it. It will leave your body intact, but will burn everything in it. One day the mountain will open and will carry you off. If you are a man, it will keep you; if you are a woman, it will grant you a robe of stars and will send you to the land of endless love . . . One day . . . One day . . ."

The voice was gone. Perhaps it was my own voice, taken from me by another. They must have taken my voice and left it to wander in the clouds. Then it spoke to itself all alone. I was unable to say a single word. My voice was gone, but I heard it in the distance, coming from somewhere else, crossing other mountains. My voice was free. But I was still a prisoner.

———

My sleepless nights were peopled by images of those women in white walking laboriously in the sand. They headed toward a white point on the horizon. Would they someday reach that place that exists only in my madness? And even if, by some miracle, the hand of fortune led them to a holy woman's tomb, they would then stand facing a hoax. I know this now, but cannot tell them. They would not believe me anyway. I am only a criminal who must serve her sentence, using this imagery to outwit ennui. But suffering—the kind that bores holes in head and heart—cannot be spoken or displayed. It lies within, locked away and invisible.

I had no need of these new visions born of burns and fever to batter down fate's heavy door. I would get out, I sensed that, but I did not want to leave prison burdened with all those tormenting images. How could I get rid of them? How could I consign them to the gray stones of my cell?

I put the black blindfold on my eyes again, undressed, and lay flat on the ground. I was completely naked. The cement was icy. My body warmed it.

I was shivering. I had sworn that I would resist the cold. I had to endure that ordeal to cast off the images. I had to remind my body of the site of my confinement, to recall that there could be no escape through dreams become nightmares.

If the soul were flayed, the body could tell no more lies. I fell asleep despite the damp and cold that gnawed at my skin. My night was long and beautiful. And free of all images. In the morning I was coughing, but I felt better.

THE
SAINT

I wept as I left prison, my sentence commuted. I was glad that my eyes were wet with tears, for it had been so long since that had happened. They were happy tears, because they came from a body being reborn, a body once again capable of feelings, of emotion. I wept because I was leaving a world where I had succeeded in finding a place. I wept because no one was waiting for me. I was free. And alone. I thought of the Consul, but I knew he had left town, that he had gone far away, to a place where he might free himself of our story.

I yearned to see the sea, to smell its scent, see its color, touch its foam. I took a bus headed south. We drove all night. People smoked and drank lemonade. My eyes stayed open, waiting for the sea. Early in the morning I saw a light mist rising from the earth like a vast sheet stretched over the ground, a sheet or an expanse of snow. Then I glimpsed ships and sailboats. They seemed almost suspended, hanging over a patch of fog. The bottom of the air was white and soft. Everything had a kind of innocence, a magic that made them seem near and inoffensive. Objects were vague, undefined. Perhaps my sight had not adjusted yet. Dreams must take their images from that whitish layer crossed by rays of blue.

It was autumn. I was wearing a man's jellaba of thick, rough wool. My hair was covered by a pretty, brightly colored scarf. I put on lipstick, and black kohl around my eyes. I looked at myself in a little mirror. My face was slowly coming back to life, lighting up from inside. I was happy and carefree. I looked funny in my truckdriver's jellaba. The drowsing passengers looked uneasily at me. I smiled at them, and they looked away. Men cannot stand being looked at by a woman in this country. They like to stare, of course, but always obliquely.

The bus station was opposite the sea. Step over a low wall and you were on sand. I walked slowly along the deserted beach, moving through the mist. I could see only a few yards ahead. I looked back and felt hemmed in by the belt of mist; a white veil separated me from the rest of the world. I was alone, cloistered in the happy solitude that comes before a great event. I took off my slippers. The sand was damp. A slight, fresh wind from afar pushed me along. I let myself be carried like a leaf. Suddenly a powerful, almost unbearable light came down from the sky, so violent that I thought I glimpsed a floating balloon, the source of that light. It drove the fog away. I felt naked. Now there was nothing to protect me. Opposite me, on the now miraculously close horizon, I saw a white house perched on a rock. I scaled the stones and reached the top. The sea was before me, the sand behind me. The house was open. There was no door. It had only one, very large room. No furniture. Old, worn mats covered the floor. Hanging oil lamps would have provided faint light at night. In one corner were some men. Some were asleep, others prayed silently. There were women and children on the other side. Only one old lady was praying. I went across and stared at her. Absorbed in her prayers, she did not see me. I sat down beside her and pretended to pray. But I made a wrong gesture, and that drew her attention. She was strangely like the Seated Woman. Less fat, but with the same movements, the same way of sitting. I stopped praying and looked at her anxiously. She was telling her beads, her lips barely moving. Our eyes met, and a moment later she leaned toward me and said, her beads still clicking:

"Here you are at last!"

It was she! The Seated Woman! Her voice had not changed. Her face had a few more wrinkles, but it was calmer now, more human.

I recoiled for an instant, then said without thinking:

"Yes, here I am!"

I was in the grip of some spell. I was about to say something when she took me by the arm.

"Speak softly," she said, "or you'll wake the Saint."

Now everything was becoming clear. Between life and death, I thought, there was but a thin layer of mist or darkness; the threads of lies were woven between reality and appearance, while time was but an illusion born of our own anguish.

The Saint rose later than everyone else. He came out of a door at the back. Dressed all in white, he wore a veil and dark glasses. Men and women alike rushed to kiss his hand. Sometimes a man lingered near him, apparently to whisper some secret. The Saint would nod, then reassure him as if to bless him.

I too got up and joined the line of women. But then, in a playful mood, I crossed to the line of men. In my jellaba I could pass for a man. When I reached the Saint, I knelt, took his outstretched hand, and instead of kissing it, licked it, sucking each of his fingers. The Saint tried to pull his hand away, but I held it in both of mine. He seemed troubled. I rose and whispered in his ear:

"It has been so long since a man caressed my face. Go ahead, look softly at me with your fingers, with the palm of your hand."

He leaned toward me and said:

"You're here at last!"